LETHAL SECRETS

BOOKS BY PETE EARLEY

FICTION FROM FORGE BOOKS
   The Big Secret
   Lethal Secrets

NONFICTION
   Family of Spies
   Prophet of Death
   The Hot House
   Circumstantial Evidence
   Confessions of a Spy
   Super Casino
   WITSEC

LETHAL SECRETS

PETE EARLEY

A TOM DOHERTY ASSOCIATES BOOK
NEW YORK

LETHAL SECRETS

Copyright © 2005 by Pete Earley

This book is printed on acid-free paper.

Book design by Mary A. Wirth

A Forge Book
Published by Tom Doherty Associates, LLC
175 Fifth Avenue
New York, NY 10010

www.tor.com

Forge® is a registered trademark of Tom Doherty Associates, LLC.

Library of Congress Cataloging-in-Publication Data

Earley, Pete.
    Lethal secrets / Pete Earley.—1st ed.
        p. cm.
    "A Tom Doherty Associates book."
    ISBN 0-765-30784-7
    EAN 978-0-765-30784-2
    1. Terrorism—Prevention—Fiction. 2. United States marshals—Fiction. 3. Washington (D.C.)—Fiction. 4. Nuclear weapons—Fiction. 5. Chechens—Fiction. I. Title.
    PS3605.A76L48 2005
    813'.6—dc22

                                                                        2005045064

First Edition: June 2005

Printed in the United States of America

0 9 8 7 6 5 4 3 2 1

Dedicated to my son,
Kyle Steven Luzi

After the attack on September 11, 2001,
everyone knew it was only a matter of time
before America would become a target once again.
What we didn't know was that the weapon of mass destruction
the terrorists would use was already in our midst,
sleeping peacefully, much like a
princess awaiting a kiss.

CAST OF MAJOR CHARACTERS

Rodney P. Ames, FBI Counterterrorism Expert

Wyatt Henry Conway, U.S. Deputy Marshal

Igor Aleksandrovich Fedorov, Russian Criminal

Movladi "the Viper" Islamov, Chechen Rebel Leader

Vladimir Mikhailovich Khrenkov, GRU Colonel

Kimberly Lodge, CIA Counterterrorism Expert

Sergey Pudin, Protected Witness

Ivan Sitov, Russian Mafia Kingpin

LETHAL SECRETS

Prologue

"There's no vodka!"

"But the delegation from Moscow— It will be here any moment!"

"I can get us some," Andrei Bobkov volunteered.

"Where? There's no place open this late."

"My friend Nikolai has enough bottles for a toast and he lives close by."

"Hurry then! You must return before the delegation arrives!"

Slipping on his heavy wool coat and black cap, Bobkov tugged open the thick wooden door and stepped into the evening darkness. A blast of wind slapped his freshly shaven cheeks. As he carefully inched down the ice-encrusted, badly worn stone steps, he thought about the monks who had built this ancient compound where he and his fellow scientists now worked. How had they endured bleak winters and the bitter cold?

Because Bobkov was a physicist, he didn't believe in God. Still, he was familiar with the religious fairy tales that surrounded the old monastery. The last Russian czar had made the three-hundred-mile pilgrimage from Moscow to the sanctuary here when this town was still called Sarov. The czar had prayed for a male heir, and a few months later his son had been born. To the faithful, this was evidence of the bond between the Russian monarchy and the Almighty. But Bobkov saw only ignorance in such tales. If there were a God, why had He allowed His beloved czar to be murdered? Why had this monastery been seized by Stalin? And why had God permitted the Kremlin to transform it into a scientific hideout created for a single deadly purpose: to create the ulti- mate instrument of destruction? No, it was obvious to Bobkov. There was no God hovering over this monastery, just as there was no vodka to be found inside it!

As he trudged through the snow, his thoughts turned to a happier topic: tonight's festivities. Had those arrogant Americans truly believed they could keep the design of their atomic bomb secret? Had they thought the rest of the world would sit by idly after Hiroshima and Na- gasaki and allow President Eisenhower to clutch their throats? Not Mother Russia. Not when geniuses such as Andrei Sakharov were still alive.

Bobkov hadn't been part of Sakharov's original scientific team at the monastery, which was being used while new laboratories for the Russian Scientific-Research Institute of Experimental Physics were being built. But he'd been given copies of every classified report written about the design, development, and testing of Russia's first atomic bomb and later thermonuclear devices. Sakharov's team had detonated a nuclear bomb August 12, 1953.

In Bobkov's mind, if someone wished to find evidence of a genuine miracle here, then they needed to look no further than what Bobkov and his comrades had accomplished since Sakharov's successful bomb test. They had performed the impossible. That was why tonight was so impor- tant. It was why there would be many toasts given!

Bobkov tried to walk faster, but the snow on the frozen terrain was simply too deep for him. He'd made a mistake when he'd first left the monastery compound. Rather than proceeding down the paved road, he'd chosen to cut across a large park, thinking this shortcut would save him time. Instead, his boots had sunk deeper with each step until the snow now reached his knees and forced him to gasp for breath as he huffed toward the communal house where his pal Nikolai lived.

Bobkov thought about how as a child he had dreamed of escaping from Russia's winter. But even then, he'd known the chances of him be- ing allowed to travel outside the U.S.S.R. were remote. There was even less of a chance after he'd become an accomplished scientist. And then, ten months ago, the unthinkable had happened. Bobkov and a handful of other scientists had been dispatched on an extraordinary mission. They had been smuggled into the United States, disguised as Soviet diplomats, protected by protocol and watched over by a stern team of KGB watchdogs. Together, the scientists had successfully completed a secret assignment that Bobkov proudly believed was as momentous as Sakharov's design of a fusion bomb. Their work, however, had been cloaked in complete secrecy and would remain that way. It had to be. In his pocket, Bobkov was carrying orders that he'd received only hours before. He was being sent far away from here to a new assignment. The entire scientific team was being disbanded. Every member was being reassigned. They'd been warned never to tell anyone about what they had done in America. After tonight, they were never supposed to communicate with each other again. This gathering was to be their final session together. This is why the special delegation from Moscow was coming to the monastery. Rumors were that Igor Kurchatov, himself, the leader of Russia's infant nuclear development program, was personally traveling here to honor them!

Vodka!

As soon as he reached the park's edge, Bobkov ran precariously down the slick roadway to the entrance of the two-story house that Nikolai Aleksandrovsky shared with sixteen other scientists and laboratory coworkers. He burst in without knocking. There was no privacy in a commune.

Bobkov felt sorry for Nikolai. Initially, he had been selected to serve on the same secret team as Bobkov, but a week before they left for America, Nikolai had been injured during a radiation experiment. Another scientist had replaced him. Out of respect to his friend, Bobkov would stay long enough for the two of them to share a drink. It would be the least he could do, especially since it would be Nikolai's vodka that the team would be using tonight!

No one was in the front room, which is where the residents ate and socialized. Removing his boots, as was the custom in Russia, Bobkov put on slippers kept by the door for visitors, and made his way up the nearby stairwell. Nikolai and his wife shared a room with another couple on the second floor. Theirs was the first door that Bobkov reached and it was cracked open.

"Kolya?" Bobkov called, referring to his friend by the traditional nickname for Nikolai.

No one answered.

"Kolya?"

In the past, whenever Bobkov had visited the commune and Nikolai was gone, one of the other residents would tell him. But no one stepped from the adjoining rooms into the hallway, even though Bobkov could hear muffled sounds behind the doors. He gently pushed open the door to Nikolai's room.

Four bodies were sprawled on the floor. All looked dead. It appeared as if the couples had been forced to kneel and then had been shot in the backs of their heads. Nikolai Aleksandrovsky was splayed next to his wife.

Bobkov's entire body began to shake. He'd never seen such carnage. His first impulse was to flee, but his eyes refused to let his body turn away. Instead, he examined the bodies from the doorway with a scientist's detailed eye, noting the display of contorted limbs, the pierced skulls, the ink blot–like splotches of gray, black, and dark red splattered across the old wood-plank floorboards. Once he had recorded these sights in his mind, his hand instinctively reached out and quietly pulled the door shut. Only then did his mind allow his body to flee.

Bobkov burst downstairs, where he quickly shed the slippers and snatched up his boots. Within moments, he was outside, still trying to make sense of what he had just observed.

How had this happened? Who had done it?

The entire town of Arzamas-16 was encircled by a barbed-wire fence and was patrolled round the clock by soldiers. No one entered or left without permission. It had been like this ever since Stalin had chosen this community to become Russia's secret atomic bomb research center. The town of Sarov had vanished instantly from all maps.

Bobkov thought of Viktor Yakir. He was the team leader and would know what to do. He was older, politically well-connected, and would know which authorities to telephone about the murders.

He was almost at the monastery compound's outer gate when he spotted several military trucks parked in front of the main building.

The delegation from Moscow had arrived! How would it react to the murders!

Several soldiers were guarding the doorway about a hundred meters ahead and Bobkov decided to call out to them, but he stopped when two soldiers emerged from the building carrying a body. One was holding the dead man's arms, the other his legs. The corpse's head bobbled sideways with each of their steps. It was Viktor Yakir.

The men stepped to the rear of a flatbed truck and swung Yakir's corpse back and forth three times before heaving it upward. It landed with a dull thud. Pausing, one pulled a pack of cigarettes from his jacket and offered it to his cohort. They leaned against the truck, smoking and talking to the other guards as Yakir's face stared out blankly from behind them.

In that instant, Bobkov understood. He turned and ducked for cover beside a nearby building and pressed his back against the wall. The murders of Nikolai, his wife, and the other couple at the commune had not been some random act of violence. They'd been executed, just as Viktor

Yakir had been shot, just as the other members of the scientific team were now, no doubt, being executed. This then was the reward sent from Moscow! This was their prize for going to America! There was only one way for the Kremlin to guarantee that they never revealed their mission. They were being silenced permanently. It was in keeping with the Stalinist tradition.

Bobkov was alive only because he had volunteered to fetch vodka. The military death squad had missed seeing him on the road because he had taken his shortcut across the park.

Bobkov peered around the corner. The two soldiers he'd seen earlier were gone, but another pair had come outside. They were carrying a new corpse: Georgi Shchelokov.

Bobkov had to hide. It would be only a matter of time before they realized he was missing. A search would be undertaken. But where could he go inside Arzamas-16? And if he did somehow avoid the soldiers and escape from town, where would he go?

Bobkov didn't know. For now, he focused only on getting out of the cold and away from the soldiers. He started to run. Hurry. Escape. Or die. From this second forward, Andrei Bobkov understood that his life, as he had lived it, was finished. He would no longer be a scientist. He would no longer be able to contact his parents, siblings, or friends. Communicating with them would be too risky. He had to vanish. Behind him, he could hear automatic weapons being fired.

The secret.

Again, he understood. His government had caught the smug Americans napping. Bobkov and his fellow scientists had managed to slip into America and build a nuclear bomb right there on U.S. soil. *Yes! A bomb more powerful than the ones that the Americans had exploded in Japan.* This bomb was hidden in a prime location in a major U.S. city and was fully armed. It was waiting. All that was necessary to explode it would be an order from Moscow.

Armageddon!

Andrei Bobkov knew too much. He had helped build the bomb with his own hands. He knew its hidden location, how to disarm its built-in defenses, how to dismantle it, or, if he chose, how to detonate it. This is why he had to run, had to hide, had to escape, and somehow, had to disappear.

Forever.

PART I

"Er, uh, would you like to go for coffee?" he asked, lingering near the door of their college economics classroom.

"Not today," she said. "But maybe some other morning."

She stepped by him into the crowded hallway. He was an American, and although she had lived in Brooklyn for five years, she still felt uncomfortable whenever she socialized with non-Russians. Still, he was handsome and seemed polite. He sat behind her every Tuesday and Thursday morning in the lecture hall. It was an easy class for her. She'd always been good with numbers.

It had taken him several days to screw up his courage. There'd been clumsy attempts. Once, he'd rushed to open the lecture hall door but was too timid to speak. Another time, he'd borrowed a pencil. It was innocent. She was nineteen. He appeared to be about the same.

Perhaps she was making a mistake. What harm would there be in going for coffee? He wasn't a stranger. But her stepfather expected her earlier than usual today. Their restaurant hadn't been open for very long. Her parents and uncle had invested everything in it.

She left the building. The sun felt warm. There were no clouds. Blue sky. It was mid-October and the trees in the park across from the NYU library were dropping their leaves. Despite the sunshine, the air was crisp. She thought about Moscow. She missed her friends there. She missed her older brother. But she didn't miss the city. It reeked of decay, stagnation, the past. New York was electric. It was her future.

Because she was preoccupied, she didn't notice the U-Haul truck edging up the street behind her as she walked to the subway. But even if she had, it wouldn't have mattered. There was nothing odd about rental trucks in Manhattan. The driver hid behind sunglasses and a navy blue baseball cap with white stitching. New York Yankees.

"That her?" the driver asked.

"*Da, da, da,*" snapped Victor Manakov, the passenger sitting beside him.

The truck eased by the girl and slipped into a no parking zone four car lengths ahead. The driver kept the engine running.

Speaking into his cell phone, Manakov said, "She's the skinny one wearing a white blouse, black pants, carrying textbooks." The description was hardly necessary. The only other people on the sidewalk were a black youngster riding a skateboard and an elderly Hispanic woman walking with the aid of a cane.

Manakov climbed out of the truck's cab. It's rear cargo door jerked upward. Three men crawled out. Each was wearing blue overalls. They appeared to be moving men about to deliver furniture.

"Olga! Can that be you?" Manakov exclaimed in Russian.

She stopped, examined his face, but didn't recognize him.

Stepping closer, he said, "I'm a friend of your brother, Vladimir! We were fighters together in Afghanistan!"

The other men quietly encircled her, yet she didn't sense any danger. She was trying to match his face to a memory. He opened his arms, as if he were about to embrace her. That's when the others sprang into action.

One grabbed her left arm, the other her right, while the third reached around her waist and easily lifted her from the sidewalk. Manakov snatched her legs. Caught completely by surprise, she dropped her books and tried to struggle. But her reaction came too late. They tossed her into the truck. The door slammed down. The vehicle lurched from the curb.

"Shut up! Bitch!" Manakov yelled. He slapped her hard across the cheek. Olga was shoved onto her chest. Her hands and feet were pushed together and bound with gray duct tape. A torn strip was slapped across her lips. It all happened in a matter of seconds. One moment she had been recalling Moscow and daydreaming about the friendly American boy in her class. Now she was being abducted in the darkened rear of a rental truck.

Why?

Her body began to tremble. She couldn't control the shaking. Her face burned.

How had they known her brother's name? What did they want?

Most of all: *Why me?*

2

WASHINGTON, D.C.

"This is stupid," I said.

William Jackson sighed. He'd come from the U.S. Army's Criminal Investigation Division and missed those days when all he had to do was issue a command.

"I knew you'd find something to bitch about," he grunted.

"The White House is doing this to help Parrish Farthington get re-elected."

"Yeah, so? You got a point?"

"Someone could get killed."

"Not if you do your job. Stop being naive. Everything in Washington is about politics. If Farthington is defeated, the Republicans lose their majority in the Senate, and the White House doesn't want that to happen. Neither does our director, who, may I remind you, is a political appointee."

I pictured myself flinging my shield onto Jackson's desk just like in an old *Dirty Harry* movie. Telling him to take this job and shove it. Lately, I've been having that fantasy a lot. But if I did, Jackson would put one of my younger team members in charge. Then I'd feel guilty, especially if something bad happened. Besides, I'd already developed a warm working relationship with Sergey Pudin. Okay, that's an exaggeration. I don't especially like the fat Russian fuck. But that doesn't mean I wanted to see him bleeding on a sidewalk somewhere.

"I'll do it," I declared, as if I'd really had any choice. "But, Bill, you tell the suits upstairs, they should care more about their own people than kissing ass at the White House."

Jackson smirked. "I'll be sure to do exactly that!"

Six hours later, my United Airlines flight began its descent into Denver International Airport. I hate this airport. The terminal is supposed to be a gigantic sculpture. That's why the roof isn't covered with traditional materials. Instead, it's made of fifteen acres of Teflon-coated, woven fiberglass that looks a lot like shiny white plastic. The building cost taxpayers a whopping $37 million. What really bugs me is the building is butt ugly. The architects divided the roof into thirty-four individual tepees. All of them are different sizes. Each is propped up on a pole and joined to another tent by steel cables. This is supposed to create the illusion of snow-capped, floating mountains. Except the white cones don't look like any ranges anyone has ever seen.

Thankfully, I got through the gates quickly. I hadn't bothered to bring luggage. Just a bottle of pills. There was a Chevy Blazer waiting for me in an Avis preferred customer spot. I drove west, following a bypass around the Mile High City, and entered the Rockies via State Highway 160. I was heading to Central City, which is about a forty-minute ride away.

I'm a bit of a history buff, mainly because I like to learn how people before me screwed things up. Central City is a former gold-mining town founded in 1859 after a prospector named John Gregory literally stumbled upon several nuggets in a gulch. I think about money sometimes. And blind luck. And how both influence our lives. I've never expected to stub my toe on a rock and discover gold. But I wouldn't mind claiming one of those $200 million lottery jackpots. Who wouldn't? It's like my uncle used to say: "If you didn't like me poor, you're really going to hate me rich."

Back to Central City. For a while, it was "the richest square mile on earth." But the ore didn't last and neither did much of the town. Those who got stuck behind lived off tourists who'd come to go horseback riding, tour the closed mines, or to see the Teller Hotel, where a drawing on the floor inspired the Western poem "The Face on the Barroom Floor." Central City was on the verge of becoming Ghost City when the Colorado legislature decided in 1991 to allow casino gambling there. Now the streets are paved with dreams once again—only this time it's fool's gold.

I'd hidden Sergey Pudin in Central City a couple of weeks earlier, and he loved it. He reveled in the chilly weather, and I liked the fact that strangers came and went without attracting much attention. The odds of Pudin bumping into someone from his past were slim. He had a better chance of meeting a retired couple from Wichita, Kansas, who'd driven out in their RV to bet five bucks at blackjack, than to encounter one of his former high-rolling, organized-crime pals. I also liked the fact that Denver was close by. That way, Pudin could slip down and buy some female companionship whenever he got the itch. The suits in Washington, D.C., don't like to talk about sex. But getting laid has been a priority of every federal witness I've ever hidden. And I've protected a lot. Crime and sex seem to go together.

From the beginning, Sergey Pudin proved to be a demanding man of much excess. He weighed four hundred pounds, oftentimes drank a half bottle of vodka per day, and once bragged that he'd satisfied four women before his pocket rocket had spent its fuel. In Brooklyn, he'd been used to carrying wads of Ben Franklins in his pocket and banging a different broad each night. I thought he might object to Central City, because it was small potatoes, but when he learned he'd be able to gamble and occasionally see a hooker, his interest peaked. He got genuinely giddy when I told him the alternative was Salt Lake City.

I'd stashed Pudin in Harvey's Wagon Wheel Hotel and Casino under the alias Sasha Petrovich. He'd immediately complained that Petrovich was a Serbian name. Then he told me that he wanted to use his name: Pudin. "It's a derivative from the word *pud*, which is an ancient Russian measure of weight and is usually used only when describing really heavy stuff. We have a proverb in my country," he explained. "We say, 'We've eaten a *pud* of salt together,' which means that we've been through some really hard times together but have still remained close friends."

I'd politely thanked him for his little linguistic lesson, and then told him that I didn't really give a damn whether or not he liked Petrovich as a last name. All I cared about was keeping him alive.

There are different threat levels when it comes to protecting federal witnesses. Obviously, Pudin was in the most danger before he was scheduled to testify. Once witnesses spill their guts on the stand and the bad guys have been shipped up the river, the peril to them decreases. But in this case I had a hunch the Russian mob wasn't going to be so forgiving. Sergey Pudin was classified by the Justice Department as a "hot" target, which is bureaucratic shorthand for "in imminent danger." Put simply, the mob wanted him dead. Right now. No matter the cost.

My bosses at first had suggested hiding Pudin inside a federal prison. We've got an isolated cell in the pen in LaTuna, Texas, that's called the Valachi Suite because it was built specifically to house Joe Valachi, one of the most famous Mafia stool pigeons of all time. But even though it's been used to protect scores of other witnesses, things have been known to happen to snitches even in special cells. I'd rejected that solution.

The suits then had come up with the idea of holding Pudin in a hotel with round-the-clock bodyguards. That was an even dumber idea. Too many people would've known where he was being hidden.

At that point I'd announced that I was personally going to make Pudin vanish. I added that I'd be the only person who'd know his whereabouts. Of course, the suits had objected, but then they realized that if something unfortunate happened to him, they'd have me to blame. My neck was again on the chopping block. Suddenly, everyone jumped on board my idea.

Pudin had always preferred dealing only with me. Before we'd met, he'd developed a weird respect for what I do. At one point, he'd plotted to execute a former gang member who'd agreed to testify for the government. I'd kept that witness healthy and safe despite repeated attempts by Pudin and others to kill him. So I hadn't been that surprised when I learned that Pudin had switched sides and specifically asked for me.

I wasn't worried about leaving him unsupervised in Central City. Where was he going to run? He already had the Russian Cosa Nostra hunting for him. And I knew he didn't want the U.S. government searching for him, too. Besides, Pudin had plenty of reasons to behave. His high-priced criminal attorneys had struck a helluva plea bargain. Like the perpetrators behind the Denver cone-headed airport, Pudin had pulled off a nifty scam. All of his past crimes were being forgiven. Plus, American taxpayers were going to be paying him a hefty reward for years to come. In exchange, Pudin had promised to testify against his oldest, dearest, and most trusted pal—a fellow compatriot even higher up on the Organized Crime most-wanted list.

All Pudin had to do was stay alive long enough to collect his little personalized lottery jackpot. Unfortunately, I was now on my way to Central City to inform him that Washington politics were about to complicate both his life and mine.

Vladimir Mikhailovich Khrenkov ignored the withered woman whose dirt-caked hand was thrusting fresh-cut red roses into his face. He wove through the crowd of commuters at the Alexeevskaya subway station and slipped outside into the evening dusk. A drunk was peeing on a pile of discarded newspapers and broken glass in the back of the station. Khrenkov hurried past him and made his way along a worn footpath that led through a patch of trees and down a slight embankment into a parking lot. There were two apartment buildings here, one on either side of the lot, and like much of the housing in Moscow built during the Khrushchev era of the 1950s and 1960s, they had no exterior ornamentation. The drab brown-brick buildings were designed for function, not vanity. It had been the Communist way.

Khrenkov dodged the potholes in the corroded asphalt that was wide enough only for one row of parked cars. Every space was claimed, but it was obvious from the flat tires and rear axles supported by wooden blocks that many of these vehicles had not been driven in a long while. Russian automobiles during the Soviet era were identified by the initials of the nation's four car manufacturers. ZAZ (Zaporozhskii Avtomobilnyi Zavod—Ukraine) made the smallest and least expensive cars, commonly called Zaporozhets; AZLK (Avtomobilnyi Zavod Imeni Leninskogo

Komsomola—Lenin Youth Communist League Auto Works) built the Moskvich, which was better than the Zaporozhets, but not by much; VAZ (Volzhskii Avtomobilnyi Zavod—Volzhskii Auto Works) made the most popular car models—the Lada, Niva, or Zhiguli—and finally GAZ (Gorkovskii Avto Zavod—Gorkovskii Auto Works), which made the most expensive car, the Volga, which was primarily used by party officials.

Khrenkov moved briskly down the line of Zaporozhets, Moskvich, and Lada models. Most of his neighbors had been able to afford them before the breakup of the Soviet Union in 1991, but now they were hard pressed to keep them running or even pay for a liter of petrol. The few cars that were drivable had been patched together with makeshift parts lifted from junked vehicles. Khrenkov's own Lada had a driver's door that once was salvage.

As he approached the apartment building on his left, Khrenkov spotted Zina Kovtun perched inside her wooden guard station and quickly glanced down at the ground to avoid making eye contact with the old sentinel. Her booth had been built decades ago directly in front of the metal door that served as the only entrance and exit to his apartment house. He had known Babushka Kovtun—which is what she insisted on being called—all of his life. She had always seemed ancient to him, a rotund, smelly hag who wore unchanged layers of sweaters and kept her legs wrapped with wool strips even in the summer. She had a Russian peasant's round face and was missing most of her teeth. The few that remained were dingy yellow. Her breath reeked of raw onions. Every morning at exactly nine o'clock, Babushka Kovtun arrived at her post. She stayed there without bathroom breaks until six o'clock.

When the Communists were in power, Babushka Kovtun used to scribble in a green ledger book the date and time that the apartment house residents came and went. It was a mind-numbing job, but she had been diligent because she knew her records might be needed by the KGB. In addition to tracking each tenant's comings and goings, Kovtun added notes about anything she thought might be useful to the secret police or to the Communist Party. This included the names of children who were rude or rowdy, anyone who drank too much, suspected adulterers, and, most important of all, people who had been overheard uttering antiparty comments or complaints about the government. While such snooping might have outraged U.S. citizens, none of the inhabitants of Khrenkov's building had held a grudge against Babushka Kovtun after the "new Russia" formed. There were two reasons for this. First, every apartment house in Moscow had a Babushka posted outside its front entrance. And second, in one way or another, every Muscovite was accustomed to providing personal information about coworkers, friends, and even their own family to the old Soviet machine. Simply put, Babushka Kovtun had not done anything they had not done.

Though no one came from the KGB to collect them, Babushka Kovtun still kept copious notes in her daily ledgers. As a teenager, Khrenkov had wondered where those records were taken. He'd imagined that her scribblings, along with thousands of other official green log books, had been sent to a cavernous warehouse close to the Kremlin, where General Secretary Leonid Ilych Brezhnev occasionally had thumbed through them, himself, pausing periodically to examine a clause.

YOUNG VLADIMIR KHRENKOV BROKE THE WINDOW IN YURI SUSLOV'S CAR TODAY WHEN HE THREW A BALL OF SNOW AT EVA BLUM.

YOUNG VLADIMIR KHRENKOV WAS CAUGHT HAVING SEXUAL INTERCOURSE WITH EVA BLUM IN THE TREES BETWEEN THE AUTO-MOBILE PARKING LOT AND THE ALEXEEVSKAYA STATION.

The ancient watchdog survived now on her miserly state pension— when it was actually paid—and the kindness of the tenants, on whom she still spied. She never missed a chance to remind them that their cars and apartments were safe from thieves because of her vigilance, although Khrenkov could not recall the last time the old busybody had notified the police of an intruder. There was no phone in her booth.

"Hello, Tovarish Polkovnik," she called out, referring to him respectfully as comrade colonel.

He nodded and reached quickly for the five-button combination lock on the building's door. He punched in the three-number code. He'd already given her a fifty-ruble note this week. That was enough.

A blast of hot air hit his face as he entered the foyer. Moscow was enjoying an unusually warm October. Regardless, the apartment's steam pipes had been turned on weeks earlier per the rigid annual schedule in anticipation of much harsher temperatures. The sticky air was suffocating.

There was no lobby in the building. Rather, Khrenkov walked directly into an enclosed folded stairway. An elevator shaft rose through the center of this staircase. It could carry a maximum of four passengers. The heat of this tiny cubicle exacerbated the foul smells of human sweat, vodka, and urine. Once this area had been kept clean by two women, but when the state stopped paying them, they stopped cleaning, and now it was littered with cigarette butts, rainbow specks of discarded chewing gum, spit, and stains best left unidentified. In Khrenkov's mind, the piss on the floor was the result of too much freedom too quickly gained. In the old Soviet Union, no one would have dared to shit in the elevator.

Khrenkov rode to the sixth level, where he unlocked door 68. In Moscow, the units were numbered serially. Since there were twelve on each floor, the range ran from 61 to 72. He'd been told by a neighbor that the Americans did things differently. Apartments that began with the number 2 were located on the second floor. Those that started with 3 were on the third floor. His neighbor had argued that the American system was easier to follow, but her listeners suspected that she was simply showing off because she had actually visited New York City. Few of them had ever traveled outside Russia.

As soon as Khrenkov entered his apartment, he replaced his shoes with slippers. Despite constant sweeping, the sidewalks and streets of Moscow were perpetually dirty. His mother had trained him well.

Khrenkov had been born in this apartment, and by Russian standards it was spacious. Its door opened directly into a narrow hallway. There were three rooms to his left. The first was a twelve-by-eleven-foot study furnished with bookcases, a dresser, a sofa, and a wooden desk and chair. This had been his parents' room. The sofa was pulled out into a place to sleep each night. In the morning, the bedding was stored. The second room was smaller. It had been used by Khrenkov and his younger brothers, Yuri and Boris. There were two wooden dressers inside it, a student's desk, and shelves filled with games and childhood knickknacks. The boys had slept on featherbeds on the floor. The final door opened into a cramped kitchen. This is where his mother, Irina, had taught his younger sister, Olga, to cook. At the end of the hallway were two more doors. A narrow one led into their only bathroom, with the most basic toilet, sink, and tub. The other exposed a deep storage closet. There was only one room on the opposite side of the hallway—directly across from the kitchen. It was the family's living room and contained a dining table, love seat, one chair, a television, a stereo, and a dozen plants. Olga had slept on the settee when she was younger and then had moved to a pad on the floor as a teenager. The plants had been lovingly tended to by his mother, and Khrenkov had promised her that he'd take care of them after she and the rest of his family emigrated to the United States. But Khrenkov had neither the time nor the patience. All were now dead or dying, shriveled and brown in their enamel pots.

Khrenkov filled a kettle with water and set it on the kitchen stove's gas burner. The dials were broken so the jet remained permanently lit. It didn't matter, the monthly usage fee had been set ridiculously low. The politicians knew that most Muscovites couldn't afford to pay much. For this reason, it was one of the utilities that hadn't been privatized.

The extra heat from the burner made Khrenkov even more uncomfortable, so he edged closer to the kitchen's cracked-open window. He kept this window ajar, even in the winter, because a friend of his had died from carbon monoxide poisoning when he fell asleep in a tightly closed room with the gas turned on during a particularly harsh winter.

Khrenkov's building faced the apartment house across the parking lot. He watched a woman in her midthirties preparing dinner in the unit directly opposite his. This was Eva Blum, the Jewish girl for whom he'd had an infatuation as a youngster and the first woman to grant him sex. He'd been fifteen. She'd been fourteen. They always smoked cigarettes afterward in imitation of those much older. Later, she would abort two of his children. When she had been accepted by Moscow University, her interest in him waned. He'd been drafted into the army, and although the Communist Party had preached that it had created a classless society, women intelligent enough to go to college did not fraternize with men being sent to fight in Afghanistan. He'd also been pressured by his parents to avoid her because she was Jewish.

Khrenkov lit a cigarette.

Eva Blum had three boys now. She was married to an older college professor. Although Khrenkov hadn't spoken to her in seventeen years, he knew that they were poorer than he. In the new Russia, professors barely got by. Only the importers and criminals were becoming rich, not members of the old intelligentsia.

The kettle whistled. Khrenkov had leftover bread from the day before, and he trimmed mold off some cheese to eat with it. He was frugal. His father, Mikhail Ivanovich, had worked for the railroad as a locomotive engineer and had earned four hundred rubles per month when Khrenkov was young. That had been an excellent salary, and his family had enjoyed a rich life—as privileged as any non-Communist official had dared live under the old regime. There were vacations at the Black Sea and weekends spent at the family dacha six miles outside the city. But in 1985 his father was killed in a car crash caused by a drunk driver, and soon the family fell on difficult times.

Khrenkov's mother eventually remarried, and five years ago, his stepfather, Stanislav Polov, moved his new family to America. Everyone—his mother, two brothers, and sister—now lived in Brooklyn. But Khrenkov had remained behind. His family understood why. His mother was secretly glad. She had not wanted to sell their Moscow apartment or their dacha. It was good to have him stay.

However, finances had little to do with Khrenkov's choice. He felt a continuing loyalty to *rodina*, the motherland. Despite the hardships in the new Russia, he had no interest in abandoning his country. Besides, even if he had tried to leave, it was unlikely the government would have permitted it. He was a colonel in the Glavnoye Razvedyvalelnoye Upravlenie, the intelligence arm of the Russian military, commonly called GRU. He'd risen quickly through its ranks and now worked at the KP GRU (Komandnyi Punkt GRU—Command and Control Center of the GRU), where he was assigned to a special task force created to monitor the war in Chechnya. In the Soviet days, he would have been fired instantly from the GRU if his family had run away to live in his nation's chief adversary. Even now, such a move could damage an officer's future. But Khrenkov had been lucky. As required, he had reported his stepfather's decision to emigrate. He'd told his commanding officer—a general who liked him. The general had quietly suggested that Khrenkov's family adopt his stepfather's name to distance themselves from Khrenkov. His mother and siblings obliged, changing their names to Polov. His mother had even made a joke of it. Khrenkov, she said, comes from the root word *khren,* which stands for "horseradish." She didn't mind leaving it behind.

As he chewed his cheese and bread, Khrenkov felt uneasy. He wasn't a religious man, but he believed in the supernatural and paid attention to intuition and omens. His mother had called him the day before with troubling news. Something horrible had happened to Olga. No, she wasn't sick. Nor had she been in an automobile accident. Irina had refused to say exactly what, but it was bad.

"You'll find out soon," she'd said cryptically. And then his mother, who had weathered many hardships during her life and who rarely showed emotion, had begun to weep.

He assumed that she was intentionally being vague because she feared their call was being tapped in Russia. But as he ate his meager meal, he decided she'd been afraid because there was a listener on *her* end of the call, someone in Brooklyn who frightened her.

4

Kimberly Lodge stepped from her shower and wrapped a mustard-colored terry-cloth towel around her black hair. She plucked another one, a faded turquoise, from its hook, draped it over the closed commode lid, and sat down. Kimberly had intended to buy a matched set of towels after she returned from her four-year stint in Georgia, a former republic in the old Soviet Union. That was two years ago. She'd never gotten around to it.

Lifting a pale green bottle of moisturizing lotion from a nearby shelf, she squirted white cream onto her right leg. She'd just finished shaving her legs in the shower, a daily chore that she abhorred. Applying the cream was one of the few beauty treatments in which she indulged herself. She raised her leg from the cool gray tile floor as she massaged the balm into her bronze thigh. She was vain about the way her muscles tightened under her fingertips. Now that she was stuck at a desk job inside CIA headquarters, she had become fanatical about exercising. She usually was inside the gym by five a.m. On Mondays, Wednesdays, and Fridays, she worked on toning her lower body. On Tuesdays, Thursdays, and Saturdays, she focused on her upper body muscles. She ran three miles every day, either on a treadmill or the paved pathway that ran alongside the Potomac River near her apartment. On Sunday mornings, she did ten miles. If she didn't exercise, she became irritable, restless, like an animal pacing back and forth in a cage.

Kimberly had volunteered for the overseas assignment. It had been listed as "hazardous duty"—an agency euphemism that meant you could end up dead if you accepted it. Shortly after the Republic of Georgia had declared its independence from Russia, a CIA officer named Freddie Woodruff had been sent there to help train state security forces. The new country's leader, Eduard Shevardnadze, was popular in Washington, D.C., and had asked for U.S. help. Woodruff had been murdered by an unidentified gunman who attacked his car.

Kimberly had thrived in Georgia despite the danger. The hardships gave her a sense of purpose.

Now finished with her legs, she moved to the bathroom sink and began to blow-dry her hair. It didn't take long. She wore it cut short in the once popular Dorothy Hamill–style. Her no-nonsense haircut was intended to send a subliminal message to her testosterone-driven male coworkers at the Counterterrorism Center where she now worked. Kimberly Lodge was a professional, not some fluff with an IQ only a little larger than her bra size.

She caught a glimpse of her nude silhouette. What she hid under her intentionally nonsexual black business suits each day was more than enough to excite any man. Her most recent lover was Spencer Harper, a promising careerist in the State Department's foreign service. They'd met in Georgia when the assistant secretary of state for international narcotics and law enforcement affairs was presiding over a summit being held to examine drug trafficking in the Black Sea region. Kimberly had been working under cover as a cultural attaché assigned to the U.S. embassy in Tbilisi. The sex between them had been hot, but by the end of the six-day summit, Kimberly was ready to say goodbye. Harper was urbane and intelligent and could be devilishly witty at a dinner party. But he had been cast in the same mold as other careerists. His ultimate goal was to become the deputy chief of mission, the number two official, at a foreign embassy, and that required living a cautious life.

Kimberly checked the time. Her boss had warned her not to be late for today's nine o'clock meeting with the chief assistant to the DCCIs—the deputy director of Central Intelligence. In this case, Gregory Stephenson. He was scheduled to testify before the Senate Intelligence Committee on Friday morning, and his top aides were holding this morning's meeting to prepare answers for him. Kimberly's boss, the head of the Counterterrorism Center, Henry Clarke, had described the session as being informal.

"We'll sit around a table with the agency's congressional liaison offi-cer who'll tell us what sort of questions the senators are likely to ask the DCCI," Clarke had explained. "Our job is to think of something clever but not too forthcoming for the DCCI to tell them. You know, good sound bites."

Clarke, who'd intentionally developed a slight British accent while serving overseas, added, "Apparently, one of the senators is interested in Chechnya."

The fighting between the Chechens and the Russians was Kimberly's speciality.

It was already eight thirty, which gave her only thirty minutes to get to work. Her apartment was in Crystal City, a sprawling complex of glass-enshrouded high-rise buildings on the Virginia side of the Po-tomac. It was under ten minutes from the Pentagon, only a few subway stops from Capitol Hill, and, on a good day with little traffic, only a twenty-minute commute north along the George Washington Parkway to CIA headquarters.

Unfortunately, this wasn't one of those days.

Kimberly honked and swore at the crawling traffic. There are three gates into the 258-acre agency complex. She decided to use its main en-trance located off Chain Bridge Road. She only had ten minutes to get there when she took her exit.

Fate was against her.

The traffic light at the intersection leading to the CIA entrance turned yellow just as she reached it. The blue minivan directly in front of her stopped. Kimberly smashed down on her car's brakes and horn. *Who stops for a yellow light?*

The van bore an Ohio license plate. That explained it all. Like many in Washington, Kimberly felt superior to Americans who didn't live ei-ther on the West or East Coasts. She drummed her fingers on the steer-ing wheel and then let loose with a string of expletives when the Ohio driver flipped on his left-turn signal, indicating that he had just now real-ized that he was in the wrong lane.

"Butthead!"

She looked through the windshield beyond the minivan and noticed that someone had placed a fresh bouquet in the median under two wooden crosses erected there. Every agency employee was familiar with this makeshift memorial. It was at this intersection on a bitterly cold day on January 26, 1993, that an Islamic fundamentalist from Pakistan named Mir Aimal Kasi had stepped from his Isuzu pickup truck, lifted an AK-47 semiautomatic rifle to his shoulder, and began killing motorists.

The thirty-eight-year-old terrorist had walked methodically along the line of cars waiting to enter the complex and had shot nearly every man inside them. He'd spared the women because he considered killing them a cowardly act. Two employees had been murdered and three others had been wounded before Kasi casually returned to his truck, disappointed that there were so few targets. The FBI later declared that he'd not been part of any terrorist organization. He'd simply acted on his own because he'd wanted to "teach a lesson" to the U.S. government.

The CTC had helped track down Kasi. It had taken four-and-half years to locate him. FBI agents had slipped into Pakistan and surprised him while he was sleeping in a three-dollar-a-night rented room. He was returned to the United States, given a trial, and executed. The mood inside the CTC had been understandably somber when Kasi was strapped to a gurney at the Greensville Correctional Center and given a fatal cocktail of drugs. He had died peacefully, confident that he was going to paradise. Kimberly would have preferred a more violent justice: lashing Kasi to a pole at the intersection and letting CIA workers dispatch him with the same AK-47 that he'd wielded.

She checked her watch again. It was now 8:52 a.m. The stoplight finally turned green, and Kimberly hit her car horn. But the Ohio driver didn't budge. He couldn't. He had to wait for the long string of cars in the left lane to slowly pass through the intersection. There was not enough room for Kimberly to squeeze by. She was stuck. When the minivan finally edged over, Kimberly blasted by, turned right, and drove immediately into the far left lane of the CIA's entrance. The right lane split off and was used by visitors. They were required to stop at a speaker and give their names before moving forward to a two-story concrete guardhouse. CIA employees stayed to the left and drove directly to a security checkpoint. A maze of concrete pillars forced them to slow and weave carefully toward the gate.

Before September 11, the agency's internal security force often waved cars through without making them wait. Not now. Kimberly had her ID badge ready as her car nudged forward.

"Late for a nine o'clock meeting!" she called from her window.

The guard recognized her.

"You're saying exactly the wrong thing, Ms. Lodge," he replied. "We're supposed to be suspicious of anyone trying to hurry through at the last minute."

"Hey, who do you think sent you that memo?"

The officer waved her by. She maneuvered through more concrete obstacles and then shot up a short hill that led to the main administration building. She was five minutes late when she entered the lobby and strode briskly across the CIA emblem embedded in the gray marble floor. To her left was a white stone wall inscribed with a quote from John, chapter 8, verse 32: "And ye shall know the truth, and the truth shall make you free." The wall on her right was decorated with five rows of stars carved into it. Each represented a CIA officer killed in the line of duty.

There was a bank of stainless-steel turnstiles directly in front of her. Two security officers were stationed at a desk there.

"Late again, huh, Ms. Lodge?" one asked.

She swiped her ID through the slot, heard a loud *kerchunk,* and shoved the bar at her waist so she could pass through to the other side. The device automatically logged her name and time of arrival into a computer that compared it to a list of employees authorized to enter. Her heels clanked as she dashed up a short flight of stairs, turned right, and hustled down a wide hallway to a row of elevators. By the time she reached the floor where the DCCI's office was located, it was 9:15 a.m. One of the DCCI's three secretaries pointed at the conference room that was being used for the briefing and added the obvious: "You're really late!"

When she reached the door, Kimberly paused, took a deep breath, and walked inside. Everyone stared. Lansing Schaeffer, one of the DCCI's assistants, was standing near the center of the longest oblong wooden conference table that Kimberly had ever seen. There were at least twenty-five men and women seated around it. Henry Clarke, her boss, had saved her a chair next to him.

"As I was saying," Schaeffer continued, "Andrew Crossman, our liaison with the Senate Intelligence Committee, will now share with you the senators' chief concerns."

Kimberly slipped into her seat. She should never have wasted time shaving her legs, she thought. Better yet, all tourists from Ohio should be banned from driving during rush hour. Then she would have been on time.

"He was captured at the Kavkaz border checkpoint," Oleg Kotlyar, the commandant of Chernokozovo prison, explained. "There were negotiable bonds worth fifty thousand U.S. dollars hidden in his bag."

If the Russian border guards reported confiscating $50,000 in bonds, Mikhail Artyukhov thought to himself, *then the prisoner was probably carrying at least three times that amount. The missing bonds would have been pocketed by the soldiers who arrested him.* Artyukhov studied the black-and-white photograph attached to the prison file. The bearded face of a gaunt, thirty-something man glared back at him. Artyukhov could see the hatred pouring from the inmate's eyes though they were puffy from a recent beating,

"How long did you torture him before he told you his real name?" Artyukhov asked.

"Tortured?" Commandant Kotlyar replied, as if this accusation insulted him.

Artyukhov had no time for such nonsense. Even though the prison commandant outranked him militarily, Artyukhov was an attaché assigned to the staff of General Lev Stepanovich Rodin, and only the president of the Russian Federation wielded more power.

"Commandant," Artyukhov replied sternly, "you're not speaking to a

United Nations delegation or investigators from Amnesty International. If this Chechen rebel has exaggerated his importance because he was being tortured and the general is embarrassed, then you will share this man's fate."

Artyukhov let the file with the prisoner's photograph slip from his hand to the commandant's desk. "Now, tell me why you believe this prisoner is, in fact, K. Salman —?"

Commandant Kotlyar began recounting everything he knew about Salman, one of the most trusted lieutenants of the rebel leader Movladi Islamov. Like all new inmates, Salman had been greeted at the prison by a throng of guards yelling, "Welcome to hell! You'll never leave here alive." As a matter of routine, each "detainee" was forced to run a gauntlet of baton-swinging officers as he entered the "filtration" camp, so-called because this is where the Russian military attempted to separate rebel Chechen freedom fighters from ordinary citizens. The beating was supposed to teach inmates to "respect" and "instantly obey" their captors. Artyukhov, who had read classified reports about the camp before arriving from Moscow, knew this initial thrashing was only the start of a ghastly cycle of abuse. Every inmate, whether man, woman, or child, would be tortured, usually by having iron bars smacked against their feet. It didn't matter if the prisoner had no ties to the resistance. They were beaten just the same. Of course, those detainees who were actually suspected of being rebels were treated even more harshly. The most common torture was jolts of electricity shot into the genitals. Females, even those as young as eleven, were gang-raped by guards. There were only two ways for a prisoner to leave the camp. He could bribe the guards or die.

Because Salman had been attempting to cross the border while carrying a huge sum of negotiable bonds, it was assumed that he was trafficking in illegal drugs or in stolen military arms. Knowing how rampant corruption was in the Russian military, Artyukhov suspected that Commandant Kotlyar himself had probably set a high price for a bribe in order to arrange Salman's release. When no one came forward to pay the ransom, Kotlyar had ordered more torture. It was while Salman's front teeth were being rasped into nubs with a metal file that he'd finally admitted being a member of the Chechen resistence. Kotlyar hadn't believed him at first, because Chechen rebels traditionally didn't have access to huge sums of money. But a comparison of the prisoner's footprints with those on birth records at a Grozny hospital had confirmed his identity.

"As soon as we realized he was one of Movladi Islamov's top officers, we stopped our interrogation, except for sleep deprivation and some light beatings, and notified the proper officials," Kotlyar concluded. "We didn't want him to die before you could personally interrogate him."

For several moments, Artyukhov said nothing. He was considering how he wanted to proceed. He was also enjoying his position of superiority over the pompous prison commandant.

"Obtaining information from a leader such as Salman is going to require more subtle interviewing techniques than the crude ones you employ here," Artyukhov declared in a smug voice. "We must take into account that Salman is a devout believer in Islam. He is convinced he will enter paradise as soon as he dies. This is part of the reason why he told you his name. He realizes his religious beliefs will not protect him from the physical torture we can inflict, so he wants credit for resisting. There is honor now in his refusal to divulge information and there is glory in his ultimate death. He has given the torture that you inflict a religious purpose. Through it, he will achieve martyrdom."

Kotlyar sneered, "I mean no disrespect for your psychoanalytic theories, but I have seen many men tortured here. Whether Salman believes in Allah or in the devil doesn't matter. Every human being will squeal like a pig if you inflict enough pain. He will talk or he will die, just like every other detainee here."

"And what good is he to us dead?"

"Death is always a risk when you torture someone."

Artyukhov considered the commandant's statement a personal challenge. "I will teach you how we can torture Salman without killing him. Take me to him now."

Kotlyar led Artyukhov outside the administration building. They walked across the compound to a nearby stockade. Within minutes, Artyukhov was standing in front of a naked man kneeling on a wet concrete floor. The prisoner's hands were tied behind his back with a thin white plastic strip that bit into his wrists. Three guards surrounded him. Each held a narrow silver baton. Salman's bony white flesh was badly bruised, and his head hung down, resting against his chest. As Artyukhov watched, one of the guards picked up a pail of cold water and doused Salman.

Artyukhov said, "I want the prisoner to stand up."

The guards glanced at their commandant, who nodded his approval. They immediately pounced on Salman, jerking him to his feet. He continued to stare at the floor and didn't look at the commandant or Artyukhov.

Artyukhov said, "If he attempts to sit down, your guards can strike him with their clubs. But they are not to hit him unless he refuses to stand. Is that clear?"

Kotlyar repeated the instructions to his guards.

Continuing, Artyukhov said, "Now, Commandant, I want a table with food and drink brought into this cell. Place it directly in front of this prisoner and tell your guards that if he chooses to eat the food or take a drink, they are to let him."

"What?" a clearly surprised Kotlyar replied.

In a deliberate voice, Artyukhov said, "You are to offer this prisoner food and drink, but you are to only give him items that devout Muslims are forbidden by the Koran to consume."

"Like pork?"

"Any meat is fine if you first tell him that it came from a strangled animal. Eating garroted meat is against Muslim dietary laws. Also offer him only alcoholic drinks."

"Tell me, comrade," Kotlyar asked in a tone that was as incredulous as he dared, "do you actually believe that threatening a man with pork and whiskey is torture?"

"Just do as I have ordered."

Once again, Kotlyar parroted Artyukhov's instructions to his chief guard, who was clearly as stunned by the instructions as his commandant had been.

"In an hour, I will return here to begin questioning the prisoner," Artyukhov said. "Be certain that your men force him to stay standing on his feet the whole time I am gone. When I return, I'll expect to find my other orders have been carried out, too. Now, take me back to your office so I can telephone Moscow."

As soon as they left the stockade, Artyukhov said, "From your attitude, Commandant, it's clear you don't believe my techniques will work. Do you?"

"Giving a prisoner food will only make him stronger," Kotlyar answered, "and liquor will only dull his pain."

"Then you will find my next command ever more outrageous. I want you to bring a prostitute into the stockade. I want her to seduce Salman. Have her strip naked in front of him. If needed, she can masturbate herself. Your guards are to urge him to have sex with this woman, and they should not interfere if he decides to fuck her. However, if he turns his head away from watching her or closes his eyes, they are to beat him."

"What do you think this will accomplish?" Kotlyar asked, with a hint of anger in his voice.

"Do you know what the most effective torture was during the Stalin purges?" Without waiting for a reply, Artyukhov continued. "Everything was tried, of course. Beatings, rape, castration, mutilation, every cruelty known to man. But what worked best turned out to be rather simple.

Prisoners were ordered to remain standing. They were not allowed to sit or even squat to relieve themselves."

Kotlyar seemed unconvinced.

Artyukhov said, "Imagine the throbbing in your legs as you try to lock them in place after several hours of standing still. Imagine the embarrassment of being forced to urinate and defecate on yourself in front of your captors. Did you know that after fourteen hours of standing up without moving most people will collapse?"

"What do you do when they fall over and can no longer stand?"

"You tie them to a wall with a rope wrapped around their chest, under their arms. You force them to continue standing. Apparently, the pain becomes excruciating. The rope twists into their flesh as they sag onto it. They have trouble breathing and gasp for air. Their legs bloat in size, and after several days their hearts can no longer pump blood to the brain. Gravity wins. They die. Incredible, isn't it? But the real beauty of it is the psychological damage it inflicts."

"What damage?"

"If we beat a prisoner, then *we* are inflicting the pain. He will fight us for as long as he can. His silence makes him feel heroic. But it will be *his* body that will ultimately fail him if he is forced to simply stand up for hours in his cell. He will be in intense pain because *he* is weak. And because he is weak, *he* will not feel heroic or brave and he will lose his determination. He will think of himself as a failure."

"If standing up is such a successful torture, then why offer Salman food and a whore?"

"These are additional psychological torments. Call them an experiment. Besides, I will only allow him to eat, drink, and have sex one time. Then I will take these pleasures away from him."

"Most prisoners would not think of food, liquor, and sex as tortures."

"To us, they aren't. But if Salman eats contaminated meat, *he* will be sinning. If he drinks liquor, *he* will be sinning. If he screws a prostitute, *he* will be sinning. In each case, *he* will be violating his own religious beliefs. Trust me, Commandant, for a devout Muslim such as Salman, my offers of food, drink, and a woman are worse tortures than having you gouge out an eye or burn his testicles. And the reason should be obvious. The sins that his own body will soon be begging him to commit can stop him from entering paradise, prevent him from becoming a martyr, and cause him to suffer in hell for all of eternity."

Having finished his lecture, Artyukhov said, "I believe you're going to be surprised at how much Salman is going to tell us about the legendary rebel commander known as 'the Viper.' Watch and learn."

6

CENTRAL CITY, COLORADO

It was starting to snow. The flakes melted as soon as they touched the rented Blazer's windshield. I thought about Petey McGraw, a bank robber turned protected witness.

"Can you tell me an easier way to make money than robbing banks?" Petey once asked me. "You walk in, hand them a note, and they give you their money."

Of course, he was serving serious time in Leavenworth Penitentiary. I often think about Petey during cold weather because of another pearl of wisdom he'd told me. Like now, white flakes had begun falling. I was thinking about how serene and beautiful the snow made it. Petey said, "What a great day to rob a bank! The cops would have a damn hard time responding to an alarm."

You see, criminals do think differently from the rest of us.

I'm a United States deputy marshal. You could say I never had much choice except to become one. To begin with, there's my name: Wyatt. That's right, Wyatt, as in Wyatt Earp, the Wild West lawman from the shoot-out at the O.K. Corral. My father insisted on naming me Wyatt despite my mother's strong objections. She preferred Henry, which was her father's name. She thought it was a better match for our last name—

Conway. But my father dug in his heels, so I ended up being named Wyatt Henry Conway.

My father was a deputy marshal. One of my uncles was a state highway patrol trooper in Virginia; another was a sheriff in Lyon County, Kansas; and my grandfather was a Pinkerton detective. Cut an artery, law enforcement bleeds out.

I'm currently assigned to the U.S. Marshals Service headquarters in Arlington, Virginia. On the organizational chart, I'm identified as a "floater." That's a polite way of saying that none of the supervisors really wants me grouped with them because—now, how shall I put this?—I have a reputation for not being a team player. Consequently, I report directly to William Jackson, who's higher up than a department head. His official title is assistant to the assistant deputy director. Or the AADD. The suits in Washington, D.C., love titles, especially those that can be converted into long acronyms. I think it makes them feel special, as if they had earned the letters Ph.D. after their names.

My boss is sort of like a sergeant major in the army. You've met the type. He worked his way up through the ranks. He's street-smart and hates bullshit. This seems to have automatically disqualified him for senior management, which is reserved for the suits who rarely come from the streets and seem to wallow in bureaucratic red tape. Still, the suits need a guy like Jackson. Otherwise, they couldn't control the few old-timers like me whom they haven't yet driven away. The truth is, they'd like to get rid of all of us politically incorrect dinosaurs. But they need us when things get really dirty, which is what always happens when they worry more about pleasing federal judges, Congress, and the White House than staying out of the way and letting us do our jobs.

It was the brass at the Justice Department, which has jurisdiction over the Marshals Service, who first ordered our director to give me a free hand with Sergey Pudin. Why? Because Pudin is their star-of-the-day. Besides, he didn't give them a choice after Pudin insisted on having me guard him. I was thrilled. Not because I gave a damn about Pudin, but because I enjoyed sticking it to the FBI. If it were up to J. Edgar Hoover's boys, the bureau would've had its own agents protecting Pudin. But that's not how things are done nowadays. More than thirty years ago, the Justice Department decided it didn't make much sense for each federal law enforcement agency to protect its own witnesses. Like nearly everything in Washington, D.C., this decision was prompted by money. In the late 1960s, a couple of smart-ass wiseguys had tried to see how many concessions they could squeeze out of Uncle Sam. If the FBI was willing to offer them a new identity and a ten-thousand-dollar reward in exchange for their testimony, what was the IRS willing to cough up? The suits hadn't liked being blackmailed.

There was another reason why the Justice Department chose to put the Marshals Service in charge of protecting *all* government witnesses. Defense attorneys had started pointing out to judges that it's against the law for prosecutors to pay witnesses for their testimony. So the Justice Department had come up with a ruse.

The suits proclaimed that the U.S. Marshals Service didn't really investigate crimes. We were created by the First Congress to maintain order in federal courthouses and to protect judges. We weren't founded to catch bad guys. Federal prosecutors say this makes us a "disinterested third party." What that means is that we really don't care if a defendant is convicted or walks out of the courthouse flipping prosecutors the finger. After all, we hadn't arrested him. Our only concern is making certain the U.S. attorney's witnesses aren't intimidated, harassed, or murdered before they can testify.

It was that small distinction between us and the bureau that earned us an edge. It may not sound like much, but in a courtroom nuances matter. If the FBI offers a witness a new identity, new house, new car, and monthly stipend in return for his testimony, defense attorneys will squawk and accuse the government of bribing its witnesses. But if the U.S. Marshals Service gives a witness all of those goodies and more, we can insist that those payoffs are essential to protect the witness from harm. They're also needed to help him reenter society as a rehabilitated citizen. It's crap, of course. And the defense attorneys see right through it. But the federal judges buy it, and that's all that matters.

That's why Sergey Pudin was turned over to me. Let's just say that hiding him in Central City, Colorado, with a couple of thousand dollars of taxpayers' cash to fritter away gambling was all part of my "rehabilitation" plan.

What's funny about all this is that a few months ago the Justice Department considered Pudin to be one of America's most-wanted. The FBI had formed a special task force in Brooklyn specifically to arrest him. He was the underboss of the *capo di tutti capis,* the "boss of all bosses," in the Russian Mafia—American style.

I don't really like the term "Russian Mafia" because it was coined by the media and really isn't accurate. The only similarity between La Cosa Nostra and the Russian Mafia is that both can be equally ruthless. But that's it. To begin with, Russian criminals don't belong to traditional crime families, like the Italians, and they sure as hell don't adhere to any blood oath or written code of conduct. There are more than a dozen Russian kingpins operating today in Brighton Beach, the oldest and most prominent Russian community in Brooklyn. But unlike their Sicilian counterparts, it's opportunity that brings these goombahs together, not the whispered commands of an aging Marlon Brando figure. If a Russian gangster decides to extort money from the owner of a thriving Brooklyn bagel shop, he recruits other Russians who don't mind swinging baseball bats. Together, they form an ad hoc crew specifically created for a single-minded purpose—bleeding the bagel shop owner dry. Now that doesn't mean the Russian thugs won't continue working together in the future. But if they do, they'll still operate as free agents. Their only loyalty is to their own greed.

In spite of this inbred independence, a Russian gangster named Ivan Sitov had risen up from the garbage heap and seized control of nearly all drug smuggling in Brooklyn. His skill: importing heroin from several republics of the former Soviet Union that served as duty-free zones for his couriers. They got most of their junk from the Middle East. It was the sheer size of Sitov's operations that led the *New York Post* to dub him the "Godfather of Little Russia."

The tabloids were quick to compare Sitov to the late, legendary John Gotti, but the Russian godfather had neither the Dapper Don's class nor his media savvy. Sitov came across as ill-tempered and repulsive, and that was something even his $500 Stefano Ricci shirts and his $5,300 cashmere Ermenegildo Zegna suits couldn't conceal.

My witness, Sergey Pudin, and Ivan Sitov had been best friends since childhood. Sitov had always provided the brains, Pudin, the muscle. The FBI had shown me photographs of their victims, mostly other Russian criminals who had dared to irk Sitov.

To appreciate just how sadistic Pudin could be as an enforcer, you needed to put his criminal tactics into context. Over the years, the five Italian families that ruled New York have developed genuine creativity when it comes to terrorizing their own. I once found a snitch's belly sliced open and his entrails piled onto his chest—a not so subtle reference to "You spill your guts to the cops, we'll spill your guts literally." And there have been plenty of incidents where tongues have been ripped out or a man's sexual member has been chopped off and stuck in his mouth. Thanks to Hollywood, everyone knows the persuasive power of waking up in silk sheets with the severed head of a thoroughbred warming your toes with blood.

But Pudin's brand of brutality pushed beyond those limits. He'd begin by jamming an ice pick into his victim's ears so he couldn't hear his own screams later. Then he'd gouge out one eye. During the next several hours, he'd fillet his victims with such precision that he'd earned the nickname "the Butcher of Brighton Beach."

You might ask: How did this sadistic son of a bitch end up on the FBI's side? The answer: He got caught. The FBI task force trailing him collected enough evidence to indict Pudin for three separate murders. He was facing life in prison without any chance of parole. That's when the U.S. attorney for the Southern District of New York had offered him an out. If he testified against Ivan Sitov, the Feds would drop the murder charges and give him a juicy payoff. It was a repeat of how the government had nailed John Gotti after getting his second in command, "Sammy the Bull" Gravano, to betray him. And just as in that case, the Feds had offered to put Pudin in the federal witness security program. Same story, different snitch.

Ivan Sitov hadn't taken kindly to Pudin's betrayal. Word in Brighton Beach was that the Russian thug was offering as much as a million dollars for Pudin's head. Without his testimony, the Feds didn't have a case.

By the time I reached Harvey's Wagon Wheel in Central City, it was dark. There weren't as many tourists at the four-story brick resort as I'd expected. But it was a Monday in October and a cold front had swept in to the mountains. I could hear Pudin's raspy voice above the action the moment I entered the casino. But I didn't walk directly to the blackjack table where he was playing. I meandered through the rows of electronic Monopoly and Wheel of Fortune slots—adult equivalents of Nintendo and Game Cube. The crowd was mostly grayhairs, some lanky cowboys, and a handful of preppie, college-age students wearing Denver University sweatshirts. When I felt it was safe, I made my way to the blackjack table where Pudin was playing four hands at a time.

There was a chubby, middle-aged redhead perched on the stool to his left and a younger, gaunt bleached-blonde on his right. Both were wearing too much makeup, but in this setting it seemed normal. I'm not particularly good at guessing women's ages, but the plump one looked as if she were in her late forties, although she might have been younger and had simply lived a rough life. Her black jeans were way too snug. She was also wearing rattlesnake-skin cowboy boots and a buckskin vest without anything underneath it but a set of sagging breasts. The blonde was outfitted in a black leather miniskirt, black spike heels, and a sheer cream-colored blouse with a high Victorian buttoned-up collar. You could see her black lace bra under the fabric, but she was only about nineteen and flat-chested.

"I told you not to take another card!" Pudin declared. "But you didn't listen to your new Ukrainian daddy, did you?" He leaned toward the redhead and whispered in a voice loud enough for anyone within earshot to hear, "You'll be punished later!"

"Mr. Sasha," the older woman answered, in a surprisingly deep voice, "I'm being a bad girl." She said these words without any real hint of sorrow or genuine emotion. In fact, she seemed bored by the fantasy.

"How 'bout me, Mr. Sasha?" the blonde squeaked. "I'm winnin'. That mean I don't get punished?"

"Oh, no!" he replied. "Daddy's going to give both of his naughty little girls a good hard spanking!" The blonde crinkled her nose. The pit boss looked disgusted. The redhead drank her vodka and tonic.

I scanned the room and cautiously reached out and tapped Pudin's left shoulder. "We need to talk," I said.

He spun around, but he looked neither startled nor fearful. I saw in his eyes the same hollowness that I'd seen when interviewing hardened convicts in prison who'd long ago given up all hope of being on the outside again. There was no emotion there. His pupils were like shark's eyes. They betrayed nothing.

"Ah," he said, "my good friend!"

For some reason, Russian criminals seem to enjoy using the phrase "my good friend." Maybe it's because they don't really have any. He grasped my right hand with his beefy paw and shook it vigorously.

I bent forward and whispered, "Time to leave. Now!"

His eyes darted around the casino, but he didn't see anything suspicious. "You work much too hard, my good friend, and worry much too much," he said. "Sit down. Join me." Without warning, he abruptly shoved the redhead from her stool. She frantically grabbed the blackjack table so she didn't fall to the floor. I seized her arm to help hold her up.

"Thanks," she mumbled.

"Clumsy cow." Pudin laughed.

"We don't have time for this," I said. "My car is outside."

Pudin raised his hands from the table in an exaggerated gesture, as if to say, "What can I do?"

"Ladies, I must leave now with my good friend here." He reached for his stack of five-dollar chips and tossed one to the dealer. Then he slid his immense girth from the seat, and I was again struck by his intimidating size. Pudin stood six feet, six inches tall, some five inches taller than I. He also outweighed me by a good two hundred pounds.

"Do I need my suitcase?" he asked.

"Only necessities and a business suit. I'll have my people get your belongings tomorrow and take care of the hotel bill."

"Okay, then pay these women while I go to the cashier." He started to step around me, but I reached out and firmly put my flat hand on his chest.

"I'm not your pimp," I said. "You pay 'em."

This was the second time Pudin had tried to manipulate me. Tough guys always want to see how far they can push you. There are several ways to deal with it. If you're quick, you get things straight on the very first day. Right away, you remind the witness of the tremendous favor you're doing him by keeping him alive. If he wants to continue breathing, he needs to do exactly what you tell him. The U.S. Marshals Service has never lost a witness who's followed its rules. *Never!* You then warn him that you've got the entire federal government backing you up. If a witness steps out of line, you can call in a hundred marshals to beat his ass. You also hint that he can be tossed out of the witness protection program. He can kiss his new identity, new house, new car, his monthly stipend, and his sorry ass *adios* if he doesn't listen to you.

Those are the tactics that the suits tell you to use. But there's another way to deal with a predator such as Sergey Pudin. The moment the two of you are alone, you whip out your 9-millimeter Glock, jam it under his throat, put your nose an inch away from his, and tell him that you're going to shoot a hollow point into his fucking forehead if he gives you any shit.

Personally, I prefer the second approach. There's no ambiguity.

Pudin knew better than to argue about who was paying for his pair of red and blond "dates." He turned and dropped a handful of chips onto the blackjack felt. Then he fished another two hundred dollars from his pocket and pitched the bills there, too. "Unfortunately, pretty ladies, I am not going to be able to complete our evening of entertainment." He shrugged.

The redhead looked ready to complain about the cash, but the blonde one-handedly scooped up the bills and plastic chips and strutted for the cashier's cage. The redhead followed behind in her stilettos.

"A mother-daughter team," Pudin explained. "Money-hungry whores. Like all American women!"

I was about to defend American womanhood, but knew my words would be wasted. We rode an elevator up to the third floor of the hotel, and when we were alone in his room, he asked, "Is there a security problem?"

"No. But there's been a change in plans. You're going to testify in Washington."

He didn't ask any questions. He simply went into the bathroom and began stuffing the hotel's soap and shampoo into his overnight case.

"Hey, don't forget to take towels," I yelled sarcastically.

"Already have!"

He wasn't joking.

He fell asleep during the drive to Denver, where I'd chartered a private flight. After our jet took off, Pudin found a bottle of Smirnoff and a glass. He never used ice.

"I was informed earlier it would be at least two more months before I would have to testify," he said. "Why is this being changed?"

"Ever heard of Parrish Farthington?"

Pudin emptied the glass in one long swallow. "The New York senator?"

"That's right. He's running for reelection and he's behind in the polls, so he's decided to pull a rabbit out of his hat. You're the rabbit."

"I don't understand."

"There's a long tradition on Capitol Hill in which United States Senators haul mobsters before various congressional investigative committees. It makes for great television and reassures voters that their elected leaders are doing something about rising crime rates."

Pudin poured himself another vodka.

I continued: "I'm fairly confident that some wunderkind on Farthington's reelection campaign staff conducted a private poll and discovered that Brighton Beach voters are—"

Pudin interrupted. "This senator wants me to tell Congress about crime in Brighton Beach?"

"Not the entire Congress, just his subcommittee. Like I was saying, Farthington's pollsters have probably told him that he needs to carry Brighton Beach if he wants to win reelection in three weeks. So he's using you to get publicity."

"It would be much simpler if he bought the votes."

"Maybe in Moscow, but votes aren't as easy to buy in Brooklyn."

A sneer lifted his lips, but he didn't reply. Instead, he reached for the bottle of vodka and said, "There something you're not telling me, my good friend. Something about this bothers you."

I was surprised that he had sensed my edginess. "I don't like publicity stunts," I admitted. "Especially ones that put my people in danger."

Pudin took a gulp, finishing off his second shot. "I know Ivan Sitov better than any man alive. He'll send someone to kill me, and his hit men will now know the time and the exact location of where I will be—since I will be appearing before a committee."

"That's right. You'll be vulnerable."

He refilled his tumbler for the third time.

"So tell me, how will you deliver me safely into the arms of Senator Farthington under the very nose of Ivan Ivanovich Sitov's hired killers?"

I reached for the bottle of Jack Daniels that was in the aircraft's liquor cabinet and got myself a drink. As I raised it to my lips, I gently shook it and listened to the ice clink against the crystal.

"Ever play the game Post Office when you were a kid?" I asked.

Pudin didn't understand.

"Don't worry," I replied. "I'll get you to that hearing and out of it safely."

He stared at me with his dead, seen-everything eyes and I wondered at that moment if he truly believed me. Without warning, he burst out laughing and raised his glass of vodka. "A toast," he proclaimed. "To you—protecting us both!"

MOSCOW, RUSSIA

Babushka Kovtun knocked on Vladimir Khrenkov's apartment door. As soon as he opened it, she thrust a package at him. "For you." There was no name or address on it.

"Who gave this to you?" he asked.

"A Russian," she replied nervously, "driving an American vehicle."

Khrenkov suddenly understood why the old woman was frightened. The only Russians who could afford American cars in Moscow were members of the Mafia. It was one of the ironies of the new Russia. On every corner, you could find a state auto inspection officer directing traffic with his white baton. In the old days, these men's jobs were to keep traffic flowing and investigate accidents. But now most had become petty extortionists. They would wave a driver over and fine him for a traffic violation. One of Khrenkov's friends had been accused of "timid" driving. These fines had to be paid in cash on the spot and usually were a few hundred rubles—small enough that it was not worth protesting. The only drivers not harassed were Russians in American vehicles. The police weren't about to confront a real criminal.

Babushka Kovtun had never allowed any outsider to make a delivery into "her" apartment building. She always intercepted every parcel, and she was not above snooping through them and stealing whatever she wanted. Later she would insist a package had arrived already opened, and, to add insult to injury, she would demand a tip for personally carrying up the ransacked goods. But Khrenkov noticed this one had not been touched. The old woman had not dared risk rifling a delivery that she suspected was mob related.

Khrenkov handed Kovtun a hundred rubles and closed the door. In the kitchen, he used a knife point to gingerly pry open one side. In the new Russia, murder came cheap. There was always a chance that one of the Chechen terrorists he monitored had paid to have him killed. He peeked inside the box and, seeing nothing suspicious, carefully slid its bubble-wrapped contents onto the table. A leather pouch, a videotape, and five hundred U.S. dollars lay before him.

Khrenkov opened the pouch first. Inside was a passport issued to Vadim Tolomasin, but the photograph was of him. This was not a counterfeit. It was imprinted with all of the proper seals and contained the necessary signatures. There was also an airline ticket and a visa that authorized Vadim Tolomasin to visit the United States for two weeks starting the next day. Someone had spent thousands of dollars in bribes getting these documents.

Khrenkov carried the cassette into the living room and plunged it into the player. An image appeared on the screen, but it was too murky and dark for him to make it out. He could hear cars honking, men talking, a truck engine.

"There's the place," a voice said. The camera had been aimed at the floor, but now the lens lifted up and shot through a windshield. There were people walking on a sidewalk. The lens zoomed in on a box-shaped structure. The eye adjusted automatically. Khrenkov could read and speak English, but he recognized only one of the words displayed on the building: Library.

Elmer Holmes Bobst Library.

The video went out of focus as the cameraman lowered his equipment toward the floor. Just as quickly, he raised it again. Now he was filming people coming out of the library entrance. He centered on a young woman. It was Olga, Khrenkov's younger sister.

The cameraman stayed on Olga as she walked in the same direction as the vehicle was now traveling.

"That her?" a voice on the tape asked.

"*Da, da, da.*"

The vehicle accelerated and pulled into an opening several car lengths ahead of Olga. The image went dark. A few seconds later, it came back on, only this time Olga was tied to a chair in front of a white wall. A bright light shone onto her face, but her eyes and mouth were covered with gray duct tape. The torso of a man's body entered the screen. He was standing beside Olga, but the camera was intentionally being trained downward so the man's face couldn't be seen. He wore a black jogging suit and a black polo shirt. A gold chain dangled from his neck. He spoke fluent Russian. There was something familiar about his voice, but Khrenkov couldn't immediately place it.

"We've got a job for you," the man said. "Come to New York and your little sister will be freed unharmed."

The man turned and faced Olga. His legs were now blocking the camera's view. Khrenkov could hear the sound of fabric being ripped.

"Don't come to New York," the man declared, moving clear of the chair, "and your sister will pay." The man had torn open Olga's blouse and pulled down her bra, exposing both of her breasts. He reached over with his right hand and pinched Olga's left nipple. Though bound, Olga's head jerked in pain. He raised his free hand and Khrenkov saw a flash of metal. A knife!

"We'll have fun with your sister before we kill her!"

The video went blank.

8

Andrew Crossman was a portly, distinguished-looking man wearing a dark gray wool suit that looked amazingly like the one that the CIA's public liaison officer, Lansing Schaeffer, wore. Kimberly Lodge eyeballed the others sitting in the conference room and noticed that nearly all of the men, including her boss, Henry Clarke, were dressed the same. There was one exception. A man sitting across from her. She didn't recognize him, but his double-breasted, olive-drab jacket, which had clearly been tailored for him and was probably Italian, made Kimberly suspect he was an outsider. She guessed he worked for the U.S. State Department.

Crossman said, "Because of September 11th, we've been taking a real tongue-lashing on Capitol Hill, especially you people in the CTC." He nodded toward Clarke and then continued. "Congress is looking for someone to blame for intelligence failures. And the CTC is taking the brunt of the criticism."

No one seated at the conference table was smiling, although Kimberly noticed the guy in the imported suit had a smirk on his face that seemed to say, "You folks are getting exactly what you deserve."

Crossman continued. "Several senators are pushing for the creation of a new intergovernment agency—a Department of Terrorism—that would answer directly to the Homeland Security Office. It would swallow up the government's current counterterrorism operations, including our own CTC center, the FBI's counterterrorism task force, the State Department's operations, etcetera, etcetera, etcetera. The DCCI is opposed to this consolidation, and when he testifies Friday, he'll come out swinging in defense of the CTC."

Several eyes glanced at Clarke, but he remained stone-faced.

"Our task this morning," Crossman concluded, "is to develop ammunition for the DCCI."

During the next thirty minutes, Kimberly listened quietly as her colleagues offered suggestions. Much of what was said was already well known. The CTC had been formed in 1985 after the hijacking of TWA Flight 847. A navy diver had been murdered during that terrorist attack. The idea behind the CTC was to put the best and brightest of the CIA's operatives—analysts from its Directorate of Intelligence, case officers from its Directorate of Operations, and gadget makers from its Directorate of Science and Technology—together on one team with a single mission: "To preempt, disrupt, and defeat terrorists."

The center had been quick to impress. It had destroyed the terrorist organization of Abu Nidal—a pre–Osama Bin Laden madman. It had linked the 1988 bombing of Pan American Flight 103 to Libyan agents, uncovered Saddam Hussein's plot to assassinate George H. W. Bush in 1993, and successfully tracked down a series of terrorists, including Ramzi Ahmed Yousef, the mastermind of the first World Trade Center bombing and Wali Khan Amin Shah, who attempted to blow up twelve U.S. airliners and wanted to kill the pope.

"I think you should remind the senators," Henry Clarke declared, "that the CTC was the first government agency to identify Osama Bin Laden as an emerging Islamic extremist who was establishing a worldwide terror network. That was in 1996, and no one listened to us."

"Thanks, Henry," Crossman replied. "That's an excellent point."

Kimberly hadn't heard any new ideas, but Crossman appeared ready to end the session. "Oh," he said, after he glanced down at a yellow legal pad of notes, "one of the senators on the intelligence committee is interested in Chechnya."

Crossman glanced around the table, but rather than stopping on Kimberly, his eyes settled on the outsider in the olive suit.

"It seems," Crossman explained, "that the senator was watching CNN and saw a reporter interview a Chechen rebel who goes by the nickname 'the Viper.' His men compared him to George Washington, and swore they'd rather die fighting Russians than live under Moscow's iron fist. We've been warned that this senator will ask the DCCI about the Viper."

Crossman looked at the odd man out and said, "I invited Randolph Fletcher, director of the State Department's counterterrorism office, to join us this morning to discuss the Viper and the current Chechen situation."

Kimberly felt her face growing red. Why had Crossman felt it necessary to invite a State Department official to speak about her area of expertise?

Fletcher said, "First, let me thank you for having me here with you this morning. I've enjoyed your stimulating discussion."

Patronizing phony! Kimberly thought.

He continued. "The problem in Chechnya is actually very simple. Russia doesn't want it to become an independent country. As in many of these uprisings, it first appeared that the rebels, although badly outnumbered, would win. But the Russians, especially under the leadership of President Vladimir Putin, sent in so many troops that nearly all of the rebels have been defeated."

Fletcher paused for a moment as if he were collecting his thoughts. Then he said, "We estimate that more than eighty thousand rebels have been neutralized and another thirty-five thousand Chechens have disappeared since the Russians seized control of the capital city, Grozny. The few remaining rebels have abandoned traditional military tactics and have started to depend on terror tactics. This has given rise to the so-called Viper."

Fletcher paused again. He was clearly enjoying being in the spotlight. "We believe he was behind the bombing of Moscow apartment buildings that killed three hundred, and that he helped mastermind the surprise takeover of a Moscow theater that resulted in seven hundred hostages being threatened and ninety persons being killed. I'm certain you remember that incident and how Russian security forces pumped sleeping gas into the theater and then stormed inside, killing all fifty terrorists, including ten women."

Pleased with his explanation, Fletcher now summarized: "The White House is supporting Russia's stance in Chechnya, and, because of this, the State Department views the Viper not as some romantic or sympathetic George Washington figure, but as a terrorist, just as dangerous as Osama Bin Laden. We would suggest that the DCCI use his testimony to remind the Senate that the Russians have supported our country's ongoing war against terrorism. It would be foolhardy and inconsistent, therefore, for us to criticize the Russians efforts to stabilize Chechnya or to glamorize a terrorist who has killed innocent men, women, and children."

"Excuse me," Kimberly said, interrupting, "but, with all due respect, I think your analysis is a bit one-sided."

"And who might you be?" he asked.

From the corner of her eye, Kimberly could see a pained expression on Henry Clarke's face.

"My name is Kimberly Lodge. I'm the CTC officer monitoring Chechnya." Before anyone could interrupt, she said, "Our information suggests the Viper may have more in common with George Washington than you want to acknowledge. He was a twenty-nine-year-old, political comer in 1991, when Chechnya first declared its independence from Russia. He played a key role in helping draft the Chechen constitution. Because he was educated in the United States, he incorporated significant elements of our constitution in his."

Kimberly didn't want to give Fletcher a chance to disagree, so she briskly continued talking. "At first, the Russians didn't object to Chechnya becoming independent. But then Russian President Boris Yeltsin realized that a very lucrative oil deal with the neighboring country of Azerbaijan required that a pipeline be built directly across Chechnya, linking Novorossisk, Russia, with Baku. Yeltsin reacted by sending six hundred troops into the former republic. But his own legislature voted to withdraw them a few days later and it appeared that Chechnya was, indeed, going to win its freedom. Three years later, however, Yeltsin sent in forty thousand troops and the first war began. In 1997, Yeltsin and the Chechen leader at the time signed a peace treaty that gave Chechnya special rights, but two years later, when Islamic militants tried to unite Chechnya with the neighboring republic of Dagestan, Russian again invaded and the current, second war began."

Kimberly took a deep breath. She hadn't realized how fast she'd been speaking.

"While this history lesson is entertaining," Andrew Crossman announced, "I don't see what it has to do with the DCCI's upcoming testimony."

"The DCCI needs to be careful," Kimberly volunteered, "when it comes to the Viper. If we were still in the cold war, the CIA would be arming Chechen troops right now and describing them as freedom fighters. The White House would be demanding in the United Nations that Russia withdraw its troops. But we're not doing that because of some rather questionable political reasons."

"What reasons might those be?" Crossman asked.

"We don't want to embarrass the Russian president. We, ourselves, invaded Iraq without getting U.N. approval, and Chechnya is predominantly an Islamic fundamentalist country. That's why we're letting Russian troops engage in genocide against the Chechen people."

"Genocide?" the State Department's Fletcher asked. "I'm sorry, but what did you say your name is?"

"Lodge, Kimberly Lodge," she replied. She assumed he'd heard her name the first time and was simply reminding everyone there that she wasn't someone important enough for them to already know.

"What proof do you have that the Russians are committing genocide?" he asked.

"The Russian army has executed or driven underground every civilian and top military leader in Chechnya. It has destroyed the country's administration and installed a pro-Kremlin puppet government in its place. Last year alone, it conducted thirty-three sweeps through Chechen villages supposedly to look for rebels. According to the Russian human rights group, Memorial, some two thousand Chechens disappeared during those sweeps. At least twelve thousand men, women, and children were killed outright, and thousands more have been arrested, tortured, robbed, and raped."

"You're citing statistics from a human rights group that has produced questionable data in the past," Fletcher said scornfully. "But even if what you claim is true, in the cold, harsh world of realpolitik, it's still in our country's best interests to continue supporting Russia and to distance ourselves from the rebels."

"Can you tell me, please, when the State Department decided that democratic revolutions against tyrannical regimes were no longer worth supporting?" Kimberly retorted.

"Let's not be naive, Ms. Lodge," Fletcher replied, his voice edged with unhidden contempt. "Chechnya is a predominantly Islamic country. If it were to combine with other Islamic countries in the region, the fundamentalist movement would gain more power. The Viper is not our friend, no matter how hard he tries to wrap himself in George Washington's clothing. You may not like it, but there's a power struggle going on in the world right now. It's not between democracy and communism. It's between the Western world and the radical Islamic world. And it's a battle we can't afford to lose!"

"I think we've heard enough," Crossman declared. "Mr. Fletcher, please rest assured that the DCCI will testify in full support of the White House's point of view."

Kimberly knew better than to say another word. She'd lost the debate, and embarrassed her boss. But she couldn't stop herself. "Excuse me, but I'm not naive or unaware of what is happening in the Islamic world," she blurted out. "But I would still warn the DCCI not to underestimate the Chechen freedom fighters. Our most recent analysis suggests that Moscow will eventually *lose* this war with the rebels."

"Lose? Russia? How?" Fletcher replied, clearly astonished.

"The history of colonial wars in the twentieth century shows that when a war drags on for a long time, the intervening party will not win for several reasons. The invading army will grow weary of fighting and become demoralized. As the war continues, support for it in Russia also will dwindle because of the human toll and economic costs. But most important of all, the rebels will stop being afraid of an army that for a long time has failed to achieve victory. The DCCI should be aware that, in five to ten years, the Viper may be president of an independent country called Chechnya."

"It's comforting to know," Fletcher said with complete sarcasm, "that Ms. Lodge is not only an expert on Chechen history and its rebels, but also is a military tactician who can predict the outcome of the Chechen conflict—something our very own generals haven't been able to do."

Kimberly heard a few hushed chuckles. And with that Crossman announced that the meeting was finished.

Kimberly knew she had stepped out-of-bounds. She owed her boss an apology. He'd always said not to speak at meetings unless he'd specifically asked her to. But when she turned in her chair to make amends to Henry Clarke, he angrily whispered, "Don't say another goddamn word!"

He stood to leave and she fell in behind him. But before they reached the exit, Andrew Crossman intercepted them.

"A word with you, Mr. Clarke," he said.

Kimberly suddenly felt like a Catholic schoolgirl about to be disciplined by mother superior.

The two men spoke in whispers. Five minutes later, Clarke returned and Kimberly followed him in silence back to his office at the CTC. He shut the door behind them.

"What the hell were you doing?" Clarke roared. "You weren't supposed to say a goddamn word."

"I'm sorry, but I couldn't let that State Department blowhard say those things without challenging him."

"Why not? That State Department 'blowhard' happens to oversee their counterterrorism operations, and that means he's got access to a hell of a lot more classified information than you!"

Kimberly didn't argue. She was in enough trouble.

"And," Clarke continued, "what in God's name made you think that Andrew Crossman even wanted to hear your point of view? Didn't it dawn on you that today's session could have simply been window dressing? Did you consider that maybe Crossman was holding this meeting simply as a matter of bureaucratic protocol?"

"No," she stammered. "I didn't think that. I thought he wanted to hear our opinions."

"That's your problem, Lodge!" he snapped. "You speak before you think!"

Kimberly was worried. "Am I going to be transferred out of the CTC because of my statements this morning?"

"Much to my total shock and utter amazement, you're not being relocated to some foreign post in an African backwater. Incredibly, the DCCI wants us to attend Friday's Senate hearing—just in case he's asked a question about the Viper and Chechnya. But you listen to me, Kimberly, and you listen *good*."

Clarke was now standing directly in front of Kimberly and jabbing his index finger in her face.

"I've not spent thirty-two years at this job," he continued, "to have you ruin my reputation as a manager. We *will* attend Friday's hearing as ordered. You *will* be at the Senate hearing on time. We *will* be sitting in seats directly behind the DCCI. And we *will* not utter a single syllable— not a single one—unless and until we are specifically asked by one of the DCCI's assistants. Even then, you will express your opinions only to me and only in a whisper. I will decide what is worth passing along. Is that perfectly clear?"

"Yes, sir."

Clarke loosened his tie and undid the top button on his shirt as he walked behind his desk. "Jesus Christ, Kimberly, what you did today— interrupting and challenging a State Department official such as Fletcher—that could have easily ruined your career. Now, get out of here."

Having been completely dressed down, Kimberly suddenly remembered the quote downstairs that she had passed when she had run through the CIA lobby.

"And ye shall know the truth, and the truth shall make you free."

Apparently that didn't apply when it came to the White House, the Viper, and Chechen politics.

9

Khrenkov buckled the airline seat belt and removed the plastic card from the seat back that described the Boeing 767 jet now lumbering down the Sheremetyevo International Airport runway. He'd only flown on Soviet military airplanes and was curious about the American-manufactured 767. The card noted that the plane was first introduced into service in September 1982 and had flown more than 7.5 million flights and carried some two billion passengers. But this was not the sort of information that he was after. He wanted to know the aircraft's wingspan, weight, cruising speed, maximum range, and fuel capacity. Instead, the card contained "fun facts," such as: "If the aircraft's jet engines were attached to a standard American automobile, the car would travel from zero to sixty m.p.h. in less than a half second." Khrenkov considered this trivia useless. *Who would attach a 767 engine to a car?*

Searching for technical details was a habit that he'd been taught during his GRU training. In the old Soviet days, GRU personnel were expected to soak up as much as they could about western technology the few times they were allowed to travel abroad.

Khrenkov replaced the card and thought about how easily he had passed through airport security earlier that morning. The computers at Sheremetyevo were linked to data banks maintained by the Sluzhba vneshney razvedki (SVR) that contained the names, fingerprints, and photographs of Russians prohibited from exiting the country. Because of his GRU rank, he knew that his personal information and photograph were stored in those computers. Yet no one had questioned him when he'd presented his "doctored" passport.

Khrenkov closed his eyes and let his mind wander. He found himself thinking about a specific date: August 22, 1991. He had reluctantly joined several of his friends that day in Dzerzhinsky Square outside Lubyanka, the dreaded headquarters of the much-hated KGB. How many men, women, and children had been snatched from their beds at night and imprisoned inside Lubyanka? How many had been tortured in its basement cells before they faced *vyshaya mera* (the highest measure of punishment), where the condemned was ordered to kneel and then shot in the back of the head. The blast made it difficult for relatives to identify the body—if they were lucky enough to find it buried outside the city in an unmarked grave.

As a youngster, Khrenkov had been taught in school about the glorious Russian revolution when the Bolsheviks had overthrown the czar in 1917. Lenin, himself, had created the first national security service, which he called the All-Russian Extraordinary Commission for Combating Counterrevolution and Sabotage, or Vserossiyskaya Chrezvychaynaya Komissiya po Borbe Kontrrevolyuisiyey i Sabotazhem (VCHK), simply known as Cheka. Lenin's handpicked secret police were patriots—or, at least, that is what Khrenkov had been taught. They were fearless men who had spent their careers ferreting out traitors and Western spies. But as Khrenkov had grown older, his parents and relatives had whispered a different truth to him. During Josef Stalin's reign, between 1924 and 1953, the Cheka had arrested, abducted, tortured, and murdered not thousands, but millions of Soviets. Most had done nothing illegal. When Nikita Khrushchev had taken control, he'd given the secret police a different name: the KGB (Komitet Gosudarstvennoy Bezopasnosti), which means Committee for State Security. But that facelift hadn't helped. The hated Cheka still operated under its new mask. When General Secretary Mikhail Gorbachev introduced *glasnost* (openness) and *perestroika* (restructuring) in an effort to modernize communism, the KGB had tried to undermine him. But this time, its Cheka generals had miscalculated. With the backing of President Boris Yeltsin, Moscow's citizenry had risen up.

On the August afternoon in 1991 when Khrenkov had joined his friends outside Lubyanka, no one in the crowd had known what was about to happen, only that it was something momentous. As Khrenkov had watched, a young man had scaled the towering black statue of Felix Dzerzhinsky standing guard in the center of the square. Dzerzhinsky had been the first director of the Cheka. The climber looped a rope around the figure and tossed the other end to the ground. Surely, Khrenkov thought, the great doors of Lubyanka would burst open and KGB storm troopers would burst into the crowd with their black clubs swinging and pistols firing. But none appeared.

Buoyed by the man's bravery, the crowd began pulling the rope, trying to topple the granite sculpture. But try as they might, the weight was simply too much. "Iron Felix" refused to fall.

And then something incredible took place.

The Moscow police, who had been called by the KGB to disperse the crowd, actually joined the protest. They brought a huge crane into the square. Its operator quickly steadied a steel noose around the neck, and within minutes Dzerzhinsky was brought down—the huge piece slamming into the pavement amid a chorus of hoots and hollers that rose in spontaneous jubilation.

That day had marked a turning point. In the preceding days, Gorbachev and Yeltsin had appointed a reformer as the head of the KGB, and he'd begun dismantling the Cheka, splintering it into parts, so that it could never again become the powerful snake that it had been. With much ceremony, the dreaded KGB had been officially dissolved on December 20, 1991. That date was symbolic because it was the anniversary of the creation of the Cheka.

Like so many Muscovites, Khrenkov had felt confident the old days of Cheka terror were finally over. No longer would any Russian be forced to hide in fear or be threatened, extorted, and preyed upon.

But as time passed, Khrenkov's hopes were dashed. The idealistic reformers who had sought change inside the Kremlin had been replaced by pragmatists who were neither romantics nor visionaries. The SVR, the biggest slice of the old KGB, had taken advantage of this opening by quietly reassembling its old adherents. By the year 2000, the SVR had become the Cheka once again. The snake had shed its skin and was alive!

But by then the SVR was not the only Russian institution terrorizing its own people. A new band of predators had risen up: the Russian Mafia. Painfully, Khrenkov understood why. The former Communist system had opened the door. Lies and bribery had been the norm in the old Soviet system—only then it had been party officials who'd reaped the benefits of widespread corruption. After the old guard was finally deposed, a vacuum had been created. There had been uncertainty, chaos. Everyday life had nearly ground to a halt.

And that is when the Russian mob had jumped in.

Now it seemed that every problem in Moscow was being settled through *rasborka,* which had come to mean "the Mafia way." Eight brotherhoods—known as *bratvas*—currently controlled the city and no one escaped from their tentacles. Business owners were forced to pay a "security tax" to whatever Mafia brotherhood ran their street. The normal rate was thirty percent of all profits. Those who refused were beaten, their stores burned. The brotherhoods owned the kiosks where vodka, chocolate, and fruit were sold at a huge profit. They ran the money exchanges where rubles were converted into dollars, often counterfeit. Newspaper and television reporters, who dared expose them, were harassed and, if necessary, murdered. The brotherhoods preyed on the elderly by cheating them out of their apartments, which they sold quickly for immense profits. They caused car accidents and then threatened innocent drivers if they refused to pay damages. They bribed government officials and, in return, got access to valuable natural resources, which they sold to the West at ridiculously low prices.

Dishonesty was now the norm. Several of Khrenkov's friends had deposited their meager savings in a downtown bank named the EI Nabejan Investment Bank. Khrenkov had cautioned them against it. When spelled backward, *Najeban IE* means "fuck you" in Russian. But its clever owner was offering a one thousand percent interest rate on all deposits. Six weeks after the bank opened, its owner vanished with his customers' cash. The police added his name to a long list of Ponzi scheme artists but made absolutely no effort to hunt for him. Why should they? It wasn't their money. The only investors who recovered a fraction of their funds were the customers who turned to the Russian mob for help. The gangsters tracked down the swindler and threatened to kill him. He gave up what money he had left, most of which the mob had kept.

Khrenkov had now come to accept a sad truth about his nation. After fighting capitalism for seventy years, the new Russia was poorly prepared for a free market economy and democracy. The only rule in Russia today came by way of the dollar and the fist.

As the Boeing 767 reached the end of the runway, turned, and revved its motors for takeoff, Khrenkov peered through the window next to him. At least a dozen abandoned Aeroflot passenger aircraft had been ditched there. Like so much in his beloved country, the rusting, picked-over airplanes—many with shattered windows and aluminum skeletons stripped clean—reminded him of how far his once great motherland had fallen, not only in the eyes of the entire world, but in his own countrymen's as well.

As the jet shot down the tarmac and lifted off the ground, Khrenkov realized he had just committed an act of treason by using a doctored passport to escape from Russia. But he told himself that he didn't really have a choice. In the moral cesspool that he called home, there was but one redeeming goodness. Family. He loved his mother, brothers, and especially Olga.

Aeroflot Russian Airlines Flight 317 flew directly from Moscow to Dulles International Airport, twenty-six miles outside Washington, D.C. Although Khrenkov had never been to the United States, he felt as if he already knew the capital city. When he'd been twelve, Khrenkov's teachers had assigned every student a foreign city to study. The District of Columbia was given to him. He was expected to know the names of the main avenues, the locations of its monuments, and the history behind them. His teachers had asked him what streets he would use if he needed to walk from the Capitol to the White House, and he'd been asked specific details about the city's demographics. *What is the average citizen's age, income, life expectancy?* At the end of the school year, he presented his class a detailed report.

Like most other Russian children, Khrenkov had thought the project useless. At the time, the Soviet Union did not allow its citizens to travel abroad. Only later would the importance of that childhood assignment come to light. After his stint fighting in Afghanistan had ended, Khrenkov had entered the GRU, where testing had revealed that he possessed an exceptional knowledge of Washington, D.C., and American history. This had led to his being assigned to work with GRU operatives stationed at Russian consulates throughout the United States. Although he had remained stuck behind a desk in Moscow, as a GRU intel officer, Khrenkov had to study maps of the capital city block by block. He had memorized a dozen tourist guidebooks. He knew where every political and military and known CIA employee lived. He provided information to station chiefs and case officers. By the time he was promoted, he was familiar with every nook and cranny of the city, even though he had never laid eyes on any of it.

As the jet engines thrust the aircraft forward, Khrenkov thought about old scraps of information from his childhood lessons that had lingered in his mind. He remembered that the original thirteen states had not trusted one another. At least that is what his Russian text had reported. These new states had been afraid that if a national capital was built inside one of their rival's borders, then it would dominate the others. To solve this problem, the country's leaders had decided to create an independent area named after the explorer Christopher Columbus. They'd called it the District of Columbia.

Khrenkov had been confused during his studies when he'd examined a map of the city's boundaries. According to his textbook, Virginia and Maryland had each surrendered acreage near the Potomac River. This property was chosen because it was midway between the northern and southern states. The land was a ten-mile-by-ten-mile square, and it eventually became known as Washington, because George Washington lived nearby and the locals referred to it as "Washington's town."

What puzzled Khrenkov was that this federal district had been divided into quadrants: Northwest, Northeast, Southwest, and Southeast. Yet the maps did not show the District of Columbia as a ten-by-ten-mile square. Rather it was shaped like a diamond with one jagged edge.

Khrenkov had asked his teacher about this, and she'd explained that the U.S. government had decided it would never use all of the property inside the original federal district. Because of this belief, all of the land on the western side of the Potomac River had been deeded back to Virginia. The cities of Arlington and Alexandria came to occupy this space. If Khrenkov added the borders of these two towns to the jagged diamond, he would see the original ten-mile-square district.

This slice of history was one of the odd tidbits that had always stuck with him.

Khrenkov tried to sleep, but couldn't. Thoughts of his sister bound in the chair, her blouse ripped open, ate at him.

Because he was traveling west across the earth, Khrenkov's flight was scheduled to arrive at Dulles on the very same Wednesday that it had left Moscow. The flight departed at 10:00 a.m. and was due to arrive at 3:40 p.m., though actually the trip could take as long as fifteen hours, depending on air currents and the aircraft's speed. He shut his eyes and tried to remember more about Washington, D.C. He had a feeling that during this trip he was going to need every scrap of knowledge that he had ever learned.

10

"Are you trying to embarrass me?" Sergey Pudin asked.

I looked at the Butcher of Brighton Beach. He was wearing a bright yellow jumpsuit with luminous red, blue, and green dots sewn on it. White gloves hid his hands, and his face was covered with white theatrical makeup. Orange yarn poked from underneath a cone-shaped pink-and-white hat. A bright crimson ball ringed his already bulbous nose.

His costume was the only clown outfit in the Halloween shop large enough to accommodate his large frame. Even then, I'd had to pay a seamstress to alter it. She'd attached ruffles to each pant leg to make them longer. The costume had come with giant bright blue shoes, but I didn't want Pudin wearing any foot gear that might slow us down. His Salvatore Ferragamo loafers were out of place, so I'd bought him a cheap pair of black high-top sneakers.

"You don't look any more ridiculous than I do," I said.

I was wearing a medieval jester's costume—maroon tights with a crimson and orange tunic. The hat resembled ram's horns with bells dangling from each curved tip. My face was painted red and orange.

While Pudin continued to stare at himself in a full-length mirror, I stabbed the blade of my Swiss Army knife through a cardboard box that had been covered with birthday wrapping paper. I made a hole big enough

for my hand to slip through the bottom while holding my Glock semiautomatic. I ruined about seven nicely decorated boxes before I finally got
an opening shaped exactly the way I wanted. I tested it to make certain
my hand and gun could slip in and out quickly.

"This plan of yours," Pudin announced. "It makes me uncomfortable."

I assumed he had a frown on his face, but I couldn't tell because of
the clown makeup. I'd had a lipstick-red grin painted around his lips.

"The men Ivan Sitov has hired to kill you aren't going to pay any attention to a couple of clowns."

"But this clothing— It's demeaning!"

I handed him ribbons attached to twenty-five helium balloons and
replied, "Better humiliated than dead."

I was ready to smuggle him into the Hart Senate Office Building on
Capitol Hill even though it was Tuesday morning and he wasn't scheduled to testify before the subcommittee until Friday afternoon. It was
safer. No one would be expecting us.

I led Pudin into a hallway. We were inside the U.S. Marshals Service's Safesite and Orientation Center, which is located in a Washington,
D.C., suburb. We keep its actual address a secret for obvious reasons.
This is where all protected witnesses are brought before they are given
new identities and relocated. Built in 1988, it was designed to blend in
with other office buildings, but the place actually is a fortified bunker. Its
exterior wall is made of reinforced concrete. Then there's a second wall
made of thick concrete just a few inches behind the first. This double-
layer design is supposed to prevent suicide bombers from crashing
through into the safesite even if they somehow learn its location. Witnesses are brought here in vans with blacked-out windows to keep them
from retracing their steps. Inside, their movements are restricted. All of
the doors are electronically bolted and can only be opened by deputies
inside a control room. We can house up to six families of five, as well as
six prisoners, without any of them knowing the others are staying there.

We walked together into an enclosed garage.

"Climb in," I said, pointing toward a commercial cargo van parked
there. It had the words THOMAS ELECTRICAL SUPPLIES painted on its
side. Two members of my witness protection squad were already in the
rear waiting for us. Another team member, Charles Henrick, was wearing a gray jumpsuit with a Thomas Electrical Supplies patch sewn on it.
He was our driver. I followed Pudin into the truck, blindfolded him, and
nodded an okay to Henrick.

A couple of unmarked federal Marshal Service cars joined us after
we'd driven about a half mile. We kept riding around for nearly an hour,

frequently doubling back to make certain no one was tailing us. Eventually the two chase cars dropped off and I removed Pudin's blindfold.

"Let's head into the city," I suggested.

When we reached American University, I gave Henrick more specific instructions. I was taking him to a nearby public park called Battery Kemble. It looks much like a finger that stretches from the C&O Canal near the Potomac River several miles northeast until it reaches the university. The park's main entrance is near the canal, but there's a narrow road near the campus that also leads into the park. The road is unpaved and drops to the bottom of a sharp incline into a gravel lot. A friend of mine found it when he was a student looking for secluded spots to be alone with dates. Its narrow entrance made it impossible for anyone to follow us without being seen.

We rode through a neighborhood of expensive homes until we came to the unpaved road. As our truck bumped down the path, another cargo van came into view. It was waiting for us in the park. Bozo-like clown faces were painted on the sides with the words: MAKE U LAUGH: CLOWNS FOR HIRE FOR EVERY OCCASION!

Henrick stopped near the clown vehicle and we waited to see if anyone had followed either truck. No one had. After several minutes, two men wearing costumes—identical to the outfits that Pudin and I were wearing—exited from the harlequin truck and entered ours. A few moments later, Pudin and I left the electrical truck and got into the entertainment one. This was a tactical move guaranteed to confuse anyone who might be watching.

Having switched places with our decoys, Henrick spit dust going back up the hill and turned left toward Maryland. After ten minutes, I drove south toward Georgetown. Pudin stayed out of sight in the rear. For about thirty minutes, I meandered through several neighborhoods before eventually driving onto Constitution Avenue. I headed toward Capitol Hill.

Our nation's one hundred senators are housed in three different grandiose structures, and each is named after a former senator. Politicians love naming places after one another, although I doubt that most of the current senators could tell you much about Richard Brevard Russell Jr., Everett McKinley Dirksen, or Philip A. Hart, whose names adorn the pediments. All three Senate office buildings (which are called SOBs) look out onto Constitution Avenue, a frantic thoroughfare located on the north end of the Capitol if you are driving east toward it. The north side of the Capitol is known as the Senate side by employees because the Senate Chamber is located there. The 435 members of the House of

Representatives meet on the southern end, dubbed the House side. Their offices are across the street in three massive edifices on Independence Avenue. They're also named for politicians—in this case former House Speakers Joseph Gurney Cannon, Nicholas Longworth, and Sam Rayburn.

The Russell Building is the first SOB that a motorist reaches. It's followed by the Dirksen SOB and then the Hart SOB. Because all three are open to the general public and attract throngs of tourists, I knew it would be easy for Russian thugs to familiarize themselves with the floor plans. But it would take a bit more digging to learn that all of the SOBs and the HOBs (House office buildings) are linked to the Capitol by several underground tunnels. There's even an electric subway that whisks elected leaders back and forth between them. This tunnel system worked to my advantage. Once I got Pudin safely onto Capitol Hill, I could use *any* entrance to *any* of the various locations to get him down into the tunnel system. Then I could move him undetected through the labyrinth. And that's exactly what I planned to do. I was going to smuggle him into the Dirksen SOB, although he would later be testifying in the Hart SOB.

I'd walked through each of the three office buildings earlier that morning to acquaint myself with them and the security that is provided at each by the U.S. Capitol Police. The Russell SOB is the oldest. It was built in 1903, according to a plaque inside it, and was a classic example of Beaux Arts architecture, although I'm not certain what the hell that means since I never even paid any attention to the differences between Doric and Corinthian columns. What I did know was that the Russell SOB was made of tons of marble, and, more important, it had four main entrances.

The Dirksen SOB was not nearly as decorative. It was first occupied in 1958, and the politicians who approved of its construction had done something truly extraordinary for Washington. They'd actually voted to eliminate an entire wing of the original blueprints to save taxpayers' money.

The final SOB—the Hart—is not actually a separate building. It's a much-enlarged version of the original Dirksen wing that got cut in 1958. By 1975 Congress had decided that it really did need more space. When this addition was finished, it had grown into such a monstrosity that the Senate declared it to be a separate building even though the two were joined at the hip.

The backs of the three SOBs face C Street, which runs east to west. Because the U.S. Capitol is the starting point for all of Washington's north-south numbered streets, First Street separates the eastern end of the Russell SOB from the western end of the Dirksen SOB. That was my delivery point. There's an imposing guardhouse at the intersection of First and C Streets, and it's manned round the clock. I'd already spoken with the U.S. Capitol Police's commandant and he'd promised that his officers would cooperate. Because I wanted to keep the details of our arrival secret, he swore he wouldn't tell anyone about my arrival plans until 12:45 p.m. That was fifteen minutes before Sergey Pudin and I were scheduled to show up dressed as entertainers.

At exactly one p.m., I stopped our happy clown truck at the curb. Neither of the Capitol Police officers inside the guardhouse stirred, so I assumed they'd been briefed. Either that, or they weren't very alert. No vehicles—especially vans and trucks—are supposed to park outside a federal office without first being inspected. That was a lesson learned April 1995 after homegrown terrorist Timothy McVeigh left a rented truck stuffed with explosives next to a federal building in Oklahoma City and killed 168 persons.

I checked the intersection's crosswalks, but didn't see anything suspicious. Only a handful of people were hurrying by, which seems the normal pace for Capitol Hill workers. Most were white men wearing dark suits, white shirts, and yellow or red ties. The few women were dressed mostly in those godawful business suits that Washington women seem to favor. The fact that nearly all of them had congressionally issued, photo-ID badges dangling on cords from their necks suggested they worked in the Senate offices.

It was less than fifteen yards from our vehicle to the Dirksen Building's corner entrance. I telephoned Paul Chestnut, one of my deputies, on my cell phone. I wanted to learn if he was in position just inside the entrance. His job was to alert the two Capitol Police officers stationed at a metal detector there that we were coming inside dressed as clowns. Chestnut was also responsible for clearing about a hundred feet of the hallway—from the doorway to a stairwell that led down into the tunnel system.

"Speak," Chestnut said as soon as he answered his phone.

"The package is here," I announced.

"We're good to go," he replied.

I like to use cellular phones rather than police radios. You never know who might be listening to radio traffic. I dialed a different number and a phone attached to the belt of a slender man paused at the corner of the intersection began to ring. He was an undercover deputy. He'd timed his pace so that he'd arrive at the crosswalk at one p.m. Taking a map from his pocket, he'd pretended to be lost, which gave him an excuse to linger at the curb and look up and down the street.

"Hello?" he answered.

"We're ready!"

"I'm still lost," he replied, which meant, "You can proceed. I don't see anything suspicious."

If it hadn't been safe, he would have said, "I'm running late, but should be there soon," which meant, "Get the hell out of here!"

I snapped shut my phone and glanced at Pudin, whose makeup had gotten smudged from the blindfolding. He looked like a sad sack suffering from facial palsy.

"It's showtime!" I announced.

I slipped my Glock inside the dummy birthday present that I was carrying.

"Listen, Sergey," I said, "you grab the balloons. Hold them low to hide your face. Stay close to me. We don't want to look rushed. Walk at a normal pace. Remember, we're simply two entertainers hired to surprise some schmuck at work. If something does happen, I've got my people at key points. We'll have you safely out of here in seconds."

There were two deputies in a car parked down the street. I also had an ambulance circling the area—a detail I didn't mention to Pudin.

He looked unenthusiastic.

In training classes, the Marshals Service teaches recruits to take a cleansing breath before they do anything life threatening. I didn't bother. I jerked open the cargo van's side door and stepped outside toting my birthday package. I fought the urge to glance around, which would have been a tip-off to any hit men watching. Twenty-five balloons floated outside, followed by Pudin, who looked even bigger to me than he was. There was a chance that onlookers would assume he was wearing clown padding much like a department store Santa. I mean, there aren't a lot of other clever ways to disguise a four-hundred-pound goombah!

If we were going to be targets, this is when it would happen. I strained, listening for some tip-off—squealing tires, the heavy breathing of a jogger running toward us—anything that might give me a much-needed extra split second in which to react. Time seems to slow down when you're afraid. But it doesn't really. Instead, your mind simply gets hyperfocused. There isn't anything else spinning in your head.

We strolled toward the Dirksen Building. I reached the door first, opened it, and Pudin sauntered inside. Like clockwork, we "cleared" the security check. Five minutes later, we entered the basement, where I led him to a storage room off the main tunnel. At least, it had been a storage room up until a few hours ago. It had been emptied by my protection team. They'd reinforced the door with a heavy blast plate and moved in several creature comforts, including three cots, a color television, DVD player, table, chairs, chessboard, snacks, minirefrigerator, portable shower, and toilet. It wasn't the Ritz-Carlton or even Harvey's Wagon Wheel, but Pudin and his two bodyguards were only going to be stuck there for three nights.

Once our Russian stool pigeon was safely locked inside, he began bitching and stripping off his clown costume. That's what all witnesses do as soon as they feel safe. They complain and start making demands.

"Listen, Sergey," I said, "there's a couple different restaurants in this building. My deputies will get you whatever you want to eat for lunch. Then you can relax and watch a movie."

"You got *Goodfellas*?"

It was one of the films that nearly every federal protected witness wanted to see.

"Of course."

"Then maybe your guys can arrange some female companionship for me."

"Forget it."

"What, not even an intern?"

He laughed.

11

Vladimir Khrenkov got his first glimpse of the United States as the jet dropped through the clouds on its final approach to Dulles International Airport. He was shocked by the paved roads that he saw. There was no such infrastructure in Russia. Next came the suburbs. In his eyes, they were mansions. His family's dacha, which was expensive by Moscow standards, didn't even have indoor plumbing. A sense of resentment bubbled up inside him. His schoolteachers and political leaders had preached that the living standard in Russia was superior to any other place in the world. Lies!

The plane landed, and fifteen minutes later Khrenkov followed his fellow passengers into the International Arrivals Building, where they divided themselves into two color-coded lines. U.S. citizens went through a fast-moving line under a sign marked with a big blue dot. Everyone else waited in the yellow-dot line. They were called one at a time to stand in front of an enclosed security booth where a uniformed U.S. Immigration and Naturalization Service officer inspected their passports and visas.

"What's the purpose of your visit? Business or pleasure?" the officer asked Khrenkov.

"Business."

"What sort of business?"

"Fur hats," he replied. "I sell them. Very good quality. Very inexpensive."

"Those square ones?" the officer asked cheerfully.

"I'm certain I can get you one," Khrenkov volunteered, not certain whether or not the officer was hinting for a bribe.

"That won't be necessary." He stamped Khrenkov's passport and handed it back to him. "Have a nice visit."

Khrenkov was next directed into a cavernous room where several circular baggage carousels were located. He found the one with his flight number displayed above it on a television monitor and waited for his suitcase to be belched out by a conveyor belt that disappeared deep into the floor. As passengers claimed their luggage, a woman police officer led a German shepherd on a leash though the claim area. The dog ran eagerly from bag to bag sniffing for illegal drugs and other contraband.

Khrenkov retrieved his brand-new suitcase and stepped to another checkpoint, this one manned by the United States Customs Service. Here he was asked if he had any fruits, vegetables, or plants in his possession.

"No, only my personal clothing and toilet articles. Nothing else."

"How about liquor?"

Do all Americans believe Russians are alcoholics? he wondered.

"No," Khrenkov replied. He was permitted to pass without having his bag inspected.

Khrenkov made his way along another hallway under surveillance cameras. It led into the main airport terminal. Through a doorway, he could see friends and family members waiting to welcome passengers. He passed through the hordes, stepping by a man and woman embracing and a grandfather twirling a tiny girl in the air. The crowd formed an inverted funnel. Near its end, Khrenkov saw limousine drivers holding placards with names written on them. This is how chauffeurs at Sheremetyevo also located their arriving guests. He stopped in front of a sign that read *TOLOMASIN* in Cyrillic letters.

"I'm Tolomasin," he said in Russian.

The chauffeur, who had a weightlifter's thick neck, grunted. "Follow me." He didn't offer to carry Khrenkov's bag. As they passed through the terminal, Khrenkov felt the presence of a second man stepping in behind him. The trio walked down a slight incline and through the building's self-opening glass doors. They crossed a two-lane pavement reserved specifically for taxis. There was a concrete median on the far side of the blacktop. Passengers were huddled there under signs waiting for buses that would carry them to the airport's satellite parking lots, rental car agencies, and area hotels. The three men crossed another road and entered a vast parking lot. There were Mercedes-Benz, Cadillac, and Lincoln limousines here. They were parked in straight rows divided by white lines that sectioned the blacktop into individual spaces. At Sheremetyevo, vehicles were parked anywhere their owners could squeeze them—on the dirt, gravel, mud, and crumbling chunks of concrete that passed for a paved lot.

A black Lincoln limousine was sitting far away from the others, and when the three men reached it, Khrenkov's escort grunted, "Give me your bag." The driver carried it to the trunk and tossed it inside. "Now get into the backseat." Khrenkov looked behind him at the man who'd followed them. He was even larger than the driver.

Khrenkov opened the rear door and glanced in. There was a man sitting there.

"Private Khrenkov!" he exclaimed. "Welcome to America!"

Khrenkov suddenly knew why the figure in the videotape—the man who had ripped open Olga's bra and pinched her nipple—had seemed strangely familiar. He was now looking at him. It was Major Igor Aleksandrovich Fedorov.

Khrenkov thought about attacking him, but assumed the bodyguard now behind him had been warned to expect such a move. There was also a good chance that Fedorov was armed, and the chauffeur now perched behind the steering wheel, too.

Be patient, Khrenkov told himself. *Olga's life is at stake.*

Khrenkov sat in the limo and the bodyguard followed him inside.

"Life is filled with unexpected twists and turns, is it not?" Fedorov asked. "I'm certain you never expected to see me again. Now tell me, how are things in the Aquarium?"

The Aquarium was the Western nickname for the GRU's main building in Moscow. But Khrenkov and other GRU officers rarely used the term. They called it *Steklyashka,* which means "piece of glass," because the walls of the nine-story structure are made entirely of glass.

Khrenkov didn't reply. He had no interest in making polite chitchat with his sister's abductor.

The limo approached a tollbooth at the lot's exit. Khrenkov noticed there was a monitor mounted on the wall in the booth that was positioned so that it faced the toll taker and the motorist paying for parking. Because the booth was built on the same level as the driver's window, the monitor could be seen by Khrenkov even though he was seated in the rear seat. There was a quick flash of light outside the tollbooth and the image on the monitor froze for a second, indicating that a camera had snapped a photograph of the limo's license plate. The tag number had then been displayed on the screen. Khrenkov noted the limo's New York license: 6750-LD.

Fedorov continued shooting the breeze as if he and Khrenkov were long-lost pals. "When I learned you had gone to work for General Valery Yablokov—the commander overseeing the war in Chechnya—I nearly collapsed from laughter. Did you not learn anything from our days of hell in Afghanistan?"

Khrenkov ignored him.

"Perhaps a cigar will put you at ease," Fedorov volunteered. He carefully removed a dark brown stogie from his jacket pocket and was clearly surprised when Khrenkov didn't reach out his hand to accept it. Fedorov said, "You don't realize how generous an offer I'm making here. These are handmade from Cuban tobacco. They're called El Presidente and are the very finest in the entire world. I buy them through a maker in Mexico City and they cost me a fortune. There are only fifty Americans on his supply list who can afford to buy them. One of them is Donald Trump!"

Fedorov lit the cigar for himself. He took a long puff once it was glowing and a sticky sweet aroma quickly engulfed the rear of the car.

"Obviously you don't give a damn about being polite," Fedorov said, "so I will be direct. It is happenstance that has brought us together— once again. To be entirely truthful, I haven't thought of you for years and I didn't have any reason to remember you until last week when I visited a restaurant in Brighton Beach. I believe you are familiar with the Pushkin Café."

Khrenkov's parents and uncle had just opened it. It was their dream business. Khrenkov's stepfather had named the business after Aleksandr Sergeyevich Pushkin, the poet whom many Russians consider to be the father of modern Russian literature. His mother had spoken excitedly about it during their regular weekly telephone calls.

"You ate at my parents' restaurant?" Khrenkov asked.

"Yes!" Fedorov answered enthusiastically. "And the food— It was delicious! Your mother, she is an excellent Russian cook."

The thought of Fedorov being served by his family made Khrenkov cringe.

Fedorov continued. "It was when I saw the photograph that your stepfather has on display behind the cash register—that is when I recognized your face. I introduced myself and explained how we had fought together as comrades during the ten-year war in that Islamic hellhole."

Khrenkov had been sent to Afghanistan in 1981 for two years and was assigned to the platoon that Fedorov had commanded.

"I told your stepfather about the incredible shots you made there. You remember, don't you?"

Khrenkov remained quiet. He was trying to figure out what this conversation had to do with Olga's kidnapping. He glanced outside. The limo was now cruising down a two-lane divided highway edged by office buildings. Most appeared to be computer companies.

"I saw many snipers in Afghanistan and most could hit a target at six hundred to eight hundred meters," Fedorov continued. "I'd even seen a few lucky shots made at a thousand meters. But what you did one evening was not some trick of fate. No, I saw you kill an Afghan soldier who was standing more than twelve hundred meters away and had no clue he was about to die! That's the equivalent of thirteen of these Americans' much-beloved football fields! Then you fired a second round and hit the soldier who was next to him!"

Fedorov waited for Khrenkov to react, but he didn't, so Fedorov bent forward, and when his suit jacket gaped open, Khrenkov spotted the butt of a handgun in a holster. Fedorov removed a manila envelope from a briefcase and handed it to him. A black-and-white, eight-inch-by-ten-inch photograph was inside. Taken with a telephoto lens, it showed an enormous man surrounded by four physically fit younger men all wearing sunglasses, coats, and ties. Although none of the four men wore an insignia or a badge, Khrenkov deduced from the barrier they'd formed around the fat man that they were protecting him.

Fedorov stabbed his index finger on the glossy, striking the huge man's head. "We have brought you to the United States to shoot and kill this man," he explained.

Now Khrenkov understood.

Fedorov's visit to the Pushkin Café had reminded him of Private Vladimir Khrenkov's sniper skills in Afghanistan. Knowing that Private Khrenkov—now Colonel Khrenkov—would never help him voluntarily, Fedorov had kidnapped Olga. It was a simple case of extortion, only this time the Russian Mafia wanted a killing instead of cash.

"I'm now a GRU bureaucrat," Khrenkov protested.

"But you are a superior hunter. You haven't lost your skills," Fedorov coldly replied. He slipped another envelope from his briefcase. "Here are several maps of Washington, D.C., and the address of your hotel, as well as directions to where your target is going to be in two days. There's also a cell phone inside this envelope with two numbers already programmed into it. One will be answered by my driver, and the other will be answered by Mr. Pankov here." Fedorov nodded in the direction of the behemoth sitting across from them.

"Mr. Pankov will be accompanying you during your American vacation," Fedorov explained. "We'll be calling him every hour to make certain you are on good behavior. If you get separated from him for any reason, you will need to telephone my driver. Otherwise, we'll assume that you do not care about the fate of your sister."

Khrenkov thought about this for a moment and then asked, "How do you know where the man in the picture will be on Friday?"

"He is testifying before a United States government committee. It would be better if you killed him before Friday, but the men protecting him have already managed to sneak him into the building. They disguised him as a circus clown."

"Why kill him—if it's already too late?"

"What he tells these politicians is of no real consequence. It's only what he says in the courtroom that matters. This is why you must kill him now. You'll have only one opportunity. When he exits the building."

Fedorov continued. "This man's name is Sergey Pudin and he's a professional criminal. He has murdered many men and tortured even more. He enjoys cutting men into little pieces with a knife while they are still alive. This should make it easier for you to shoot him. He's not an innocent person."

"And what happens after I kill him?"

"You'll use the cell phone to notify my driver. I'll call Mr. Pankov to verify that you have completed your assignment. Mr. Pankov will then deliver you to Dulles Airport where you'll board an Aeroflot flight back to Moscow. It will be as if you were never here."

"And my sister—my family?"

"They will be released, of course, completely unharmed!"

Khrenkov didn't believe him. Fedorov wouldn't want any witnesses left behind.

"How do I know my sister is still alive?"

Fedorov dialed a number on his cell phone and spoke in Russian to the person who answered. "Put on the girl." He then handed it to Khrenkov.

"Olga?"

"*Da.* Is that you, Vladimir?"

"Have they hurt you?"

"They don't hurt me much. But I'm very afraid. Afraid for mama and papa and our brothers, and me, and for you. These are very bad men."

Khrenkov heard someone tell Olga in Russian that she'd talked enough and the line went dead. He fumbled with the instrument, pretending that he didn't understand how it worked. He poked several buttons and said, "Hello! Hello!" into the mouthpiece. He was acting as if the call had been accidentally disconnected. Fedorov snatched it from him.

Khrenkov watched Fedorov's face for a signal that he was suspicious, but there was none. *Good,* Khrenkov thought. Fedorov hadn't noticed that Khrenkov had pushed the "last number dialed" feature on the cell phone while handling it. The number had popped up on the display. It was the same prefix as Khrenkov's parents' telephone number in Brighton Beach. This meant Olga was being held somewhere in Brooklyn.

"And my parents?" Khrenkov asked.

Fedorov dialed another number and once again handed the cell phone to Khrenkov.

"Mother, is that you?"

"*Da.* I'm here. They got two men watching us."

Someone swore in Russian and his mother screamed. She'd been slapped. He heard a stranger's voice say, "I told you not to tell him anything about us."

Khrenkov's mother was crying when she was able to speak again. "Do what they tell you," she whispered. The connection ended. Khrenkov handed the phone back to Fedorov.

Think! Think! What choices do I have?

He stared out the limo window. He wanted to make certain that he could retrace his steps to Dulles. Alone. The highway had merged with another road. The limo now slowed as the blacktop banked sharply to the left and melted into yet another road. A sign identified this route as Interstate 66. A silver subway train was running parallel to the blacktop. Eventually it disappeared underground.

Khrenkov read an overhead green sign with the word "Rossalyn" and from his schoolboy studies, he knew they were approaching the Potomac River and soon would reach the Theodore Roosevelt Bridge. He looked for other markers to confirm his memory. When the car crossed the bridge, he could see the gold-columned rectangular John F. Kennedy Center for the Performing Arts and the serpentine Watergate complex to his left. To his right was the Lincoln Memorial—a monument he had seen hundreds of times, but only in textbooks.

The car was traveling east along Constitution Avenue and Khrenkov peered outside as if he were a visiting tourist. He spotted the Washington Monument and remembered that the White House was in a direct line to its left. When the limo slowed for traffic, he saw the top of the presidential residence through the trees. He easily recalled the order of the Greek-inspired federal buildings that were now materializing on his left—the Department of Commerce was first, next came the Environmental Protection Building, followed by the Justice Department, the National Archives, the Federal Trade Commission. On the right side of the grand boulevard were museums of the Smithsonian Institution.

Khrenkov gawked at the mixture of tourists and office workers on the sidewalks. He noted a vagrant wrapped in a dirty brown blanket asleep on the grass on the Mall. The man's possessions were stuffed into a dark green plastic trash bag. Because of his childhood studies and GRU intel experience, it was as if Khrenkov were returning to a familiar city, yet he'd never traveled along this street.

As the car neared the Capitol, the driver took an oblique left turn onto Louisiana Avenue and then another onto New Jersey Avenue. Khrenkov recalled that many of the streets in Washington had been named after different states. The car stopped under a light brown canopy at the Hyatt Regency Hotel.

"This is a very fine hotel," Fedorov volunteered, as if he were a tour guide and not a kidnapper. He handed Mr. Pankov a plastic room key. "The number is 587." Then he turned to address Khrenkov. "Today is Wednesday. This gives you tomorrow to survey the area and to find a suitable location for what you must do. A Dragunov sniper rifle is in your room. Mr. Pankov will give you three rounds of ammunition."

"Three?"

"That is enough. Your rifle is inside a hard plastic case made to carry golf clubs, a game that fascinates Americans. Do you have any questions?"

"No, but there is something I wish to tell you." Khrenkov shifted his body so he was now directly facing Fedorov on the rear seat. "I'm going to kill you when this is over. If you molest my sister or harm my family, I will use my connections in Moscow to locate all of your family members—your father, your mother, your uncles, your aunts, your brothers, your sisters—and I will kill them, too. From our days together in Afghanistan, you should know I am a man who keeps his word."

Fedorov's mouth gapped open, revealing a row of newly capped teeth. "I would expect nothing less. And you should know this: the men whom you are dealing with also have connections. They, too, can reach out. If you want to see your sister and your family again, do as you are told. Kill Sergey Pudin. And then go back to Moscow and forget about me and what has happened. To do otherwise is foolish and deadly. You are not in charge of your own life now. We are."

12

"Did they kill Salman?" Movladi Islamov asked.

"Yes," Aslan Akhman answered. "A guard at Chernokozovo says our brother freedom fighter died two nights ago while being tortured. Moscow sent a special military attaché specifically to interrogate him."

"Then we must presume that Salman told them everything he knew."

"You mean about Vienna?"

"Yes, but it doesn't matter."

As in any well-planned military operation, Salman had only been told enough to complete his part of the mission. His assignment had been to smuggle $150,000 worth of negotiable bearer bonds from Chechnya to the Austrian capital. Once there, he was to check into the Intercontinental Hotel and wait for a telephone call with further instructions. Only Islamov and Akhman knew the complete mission. Akhman was Islamov's second in command. He had been married to one of Islamov's sisters before she and her children were taken prisoner and executed by the Russians because they were rebel sympathizers.

"Do the sellers know the bonds that Salman was carrying are worthless?" Akhman asked.

"I don't think so," Islamov replied. "They are good counterfeits. But we must act quickly before the Russians discover they are fakes and release that information to the news media. If that happens, the arms dealers will turn against us and back out. As of this morning, they have agreed to rush their delivery, but they are insisting that I personally bring the remainder of the bonds to them."

Akhman replied, "No! That's much too dangerous. I'll go."

Islamov smiled appreciatively. "My loyal brother, we each risk our lives every day. This purchase is too important. You and I both know it could change the course of our war with the Russians."

Akhman asked, "When will you leave? Where will the exchange take place?"

"Iceland. Reykjavik. Four of us will go tomorrow morning. That will give us time to enter the country undetected and prepare for delivery. I want you to remain here and oversee our operations."

Akhman changed the subject. "The man who says he is Salman's father is waiting to see you. I had three of our fighters bring him here after I was satisfied that this wasn't a Russian trick to find us. Do you want me to tell him that Salman has been murdered?"

"No," Islamov replied. "That is my job."

Akhman left the room but returned moments later with an older man. Islamov noted that his visitor had weathered skin, calloused hands, and walnut-shaped knuckles. There was a pained look in the man's eyes as he nodded respectfully.

"Thank you for seeing me," he said.

"You've been persistent," Islamov replied. "You're lucky that the Russians didn't arrest you."

"I went to every possible location where I thought rebel supporters might gather—mosques, markets, restaurants—I was trying to find anyone who could arrange this meeting."

"You succeeded. Now that you are here, how can I help you?"

"Help me free my son from Chernokozovo. The Russians came to our house after he was arrested at the border. They warned me that he will be killed unless I pay them a bribe. But I'm a farmer and have no money."

"I'm sorry, but there is nothing I can do," Islamov said. He was about to explain that Salman was already dead, but before he could get his words out, the man interrupted him.

"No, you're wrong! You can offer the Russians someone in exchange for my son who Moscow wants even more than him, even more than you—the much-feared Viper!"

Curious, Islamov asked, "Who would you have us exchange for your son?"

"Me," the old man said softly. "Give them me."

Akhman, who was in the room, scoffed: "Why would they want to exchange Salman for an old farmer?"

"You believe I am a nobody, but you really have no idea of *who* I actually am," the man replied. "For fifty years, I've been living here under a false name. Not even my own family knew about my past life."

"Who are you?" Islamov asked.

"I will tell you, but only after you agree to help me free my son. I want you to arrange the prisoner transfer."

"I'm sorry, but I must tell you a sad truth," Islamov said. "Although I would have gladly helped you arrange an exchange, you're too late. Your son, Salman, already is dead."

A look of sadness swept across the old man's face. Yet he seemed neither surprised nor angry. Islamov had seen this gaze before. Like so many in his war-ravaged homeland, the killing of a loved one had become so commonplace that even torture and execution had lost its shock value.

"How certain are you that he has been killed?"

"We pay bribes to a guard at the camp," Akhman volunteered. "This guard has never given us faulty information in the past."

"Then I have no reason to continue living. My wife died last year. My daughters are dead now, too. Innocent victims of this horrible war. And now Moscow has finally succeeded in robbing me of my will to live by taking away my son."

Akhman felt compelled to say something. "Your son died a martyr. The Russians forced him to stand up for days on end. They tried to tempt him with unclean meat, liquor, even a common prostitute, but he took their beatings rather than sacrifice his soul. He died in agony, but he died a devout Muslim."

"Thank you," the man said, "but I already knew my son was brave and honorable. That is how I raised him. And although he followed Islam, I am not a Muslim."

For several moments, no one spoke. Then the old man said, "There is a way for me to take my revenge, but I will need your help. I will tell you my secret in exchange. I have no reason to keep it any longer."

"I can't make a promise," Islamov said, "until I know more."

"Fair enough. Does the Russian village known as Arzamas-16 mean anything to either of you?"

He could tell from their blank expressions that neither Islamov nor

Akhman recognized the town. He continued. "How strange. I've not ut-tered that name in such a long time that I was beginning to believe that maybe it existed only in my own head. It was as if my past was a bad dream, a nightmare that was imagined. But now that I have said its name, everything has come back to me, every pain-filled memory." He seemed lost in his own thoughts.

Islamov said, "Who are you? And what happened in your past that would make you assume a new identity?"

"I was still a young man when I first escaped into Chechnya. I met Salman's mother when she was only nineteen, and even though I was much older, I married her. From that day forward, I lived as a farmer and pretended to be Chechen. We had two daughters and then my son was born. He was a miracle, and now he has been killed by my own people. I'm Russian."

"Did you flee during the Stalin purges?" Akhman asked.

"No, no, I came later, during the winter of nineteen hundred and fifty-four, only days after I managed to escape from Arzamas-16."

He paused to collect his thoughts. Then he said, "In the first days of the cold war between the United States and what then was the U.S.S.R., the very best of the brightest Soviet scientists were brought together in Arzamas-16. I was among them. Our job was to build and perfect a nu-clear bomb."

The words "nuclear bomb" caused Islamov and Akhman to listen even more intently. The old man said, "My real name is Andrei Bobkov. I was a physicist, and I was chosen for a secret mission." He paused and mumbled, "So many murdered. Viktor Yakir was our team leader. Georgi Shchelokov. Nikolai. All executed. All betrayed. Names I've been afraid to speak for decades! Ghosts haunting me."

"You worked on the first Russian nuclear bomb?" Akhman asked impatiently.

"Not the first. But almost. We were made to look like diplomats and were sent to the United States. Our assignment was to make a bomb there and hide it where it could do the most damage to our enemies."

"Wait!" Akhman interrupted. "Are you telling us that you built a nu-clear bomb in America?"

"Yes, that's exactly what we did. We put the pieces together right un-der the American's noses."

"And it's still hidden there? It still works?"

"I'm sure of it. The KGB called it a 'sleeper' bomb. It was con-structed, concealed, and covered up, like a sleeping bear waiting in a cave to awake from hibernation."

"How is it possible no one knows about this?" Akhman demanded.

"Because the KGB murdered everyone involved in our secret mission—everyone but me. That's how we were repaid for our loyalty. With murder! With treachery! We had assembled together to celebrate our success. We foolishly believed we were going to be awarded medals for what we'd done. Instead, the soldiers came with their guns."

"But you escaped?" Akhman asked.

"It was a chance of fate. Blind luck. Before the delegation from Moscow arrived, we noticed there was no vodka for toasts in our meeting room so I went out to collect some from my friend, Nikolai. By the time I got back, troops were lifting out bodies. I could still hear the gunshots. I ran away. That night, I sneaked into the laboratory where we conducted radiation experiments. I crawled into a narrow opening between two large cages filled with rats. The next morning I hid in a disposal bin where animal carcasses were discarded. I covered myself with decaying rats and monkeys and other vermin and waited for the garbage truck to take me outside the town to a large radiation pit. From there, I made my escape."

"This bomb that you constructed," Islamov said, "will you tell us where it is hidden in the United States?"

"Yes," Bobkov replied. "I will give you the location. I can remember everything about this bomb as if my colleagues and I had just built it. There are a series of complicated fail-safe locks that we installed to prevent tampering and accidental detonation. I can tell you how to open them. There is nothing about this bomb that I don't know and I'm willing to share all of my knowledge with you—in return for a promise."

"What?" Islamov asked.

"Swear that you will use this bomb to avenge my son's death. Swear this to me and I will tell you how to wake up this slumbering bear."

"I will do what you've asked," Islamov declared.

"Then get me a pen and some paper," Bobkov replied, "so I can begin drawing you a map and sketches of the bomb."

By daybreak, Bobkov was exhausted. Akhman led him to a bedroom to sleep and stationed a guard outside the door to protect him. When Akhman returned, he asked Islamov, "Do you think this is some sort of Russian trick? Could the old man be setting us up for a trap?"

"No. I believe him."

"Then this truly is a great day!"

For a moment, both of them savored the events of the night. Then Islamov said, "*Alhamdo lillah,*" which means, All praise belongs to Allah.

"*Subhaan Allah, Alhamdo lillah, Allahu akbar,*" Akhman replied.

"Glory to Allah, all praise belongs to Allah, Allah is the Greatest." Then he added, "This is incredible! We now know of two bombs, and both of them are about to be delivered into our hands."

"I will leave in a few hours for Reykjavik where I will complete the purchase of the first bomb that we are buying from the arms dealer," Islamov said.

"Yes, with bogus bonds!" Akhman interjected, smiling broadly.

"While I am gone, you will learn as much as you can from Salman's father about this sleeper bomb hidden in the United States. When I return, we will decide how we can sneak into America and take control of it."

"*Inshallah*," Akhman said.

"Once we have these nuclear weapons, everything will change," Islamov replied.

"*Fee amaan Allah*," Akhman shouted. "Go in the protection of Allah."

"*Allahu akbar*," the Viper replied. "Allah is the Greatest."

13

"We've got a problem," William Jackson announced. "Come to my office."

It was Wednesday afternoon, and when I got to my boss's office, two men were waiting inside with him.

"Meet Charles Anderson and Fred Beacon," Jackson said. "Detectives from the D.C. Police Department's street-gang unit."

Anderson got right to the point. "The O Street Crew has been hired to kill your witness."

I could tell these two had worked as partners for a long time because Beacon finished the thought: "Some Russian called 'Sir Guy.'"

"What can you tell me about this gang?" I asked.

"It's composed of neighborhood thugs," Beacon replied.

"Homies," I volunteered, but neither Anderson nor Beacon appeared impressed by my attempt at ghetto speak.

"The gang gets its name from O Street in Southeast Washington, a few blocks from the Washington Navy Yard and the Anacostia River," Beacon continued. "They're tough, they're violent, and they're heavy into drug distribution. Heroin."

"Which is why we think they got this contract," Anderson explained. "The DEA has done a good job shutting down the regular supply routes from the South and L.A. The O Street Crew has been reaching out to other sources."

"They apparently hooked up with a Russian heroin dealer from Brooklyn," said Beacon.

"The 'Godfather of Brighton Beach,'" Anderson continued.

Beacon said, "This Russian is laying out some heavy green to smack your 'Sir Guy' witness."

"It's Sergey," I said.

Usually, the U.S. Marshals Service doesn't refer to anyone by their actual names after they enter witness protection. But since Senator Parrish Farthington had already announced in the *Washington Post* that Sergey Pudin was going to finger Ivan Sitov this coming Friday during testimony in the Hart Building, I figured I wasn't revealing any secrets.

"We've been told the O Street Crew was planning on hitting your witness sometime Friday morning, but then they learned you'd already snuck him inside," Anderson volunteered.

I tried not to react, but I was surprised. *How had a D.C. street gang found out that Pudin was already hiding on Capitol Hill?*

"Our informant says you dressed this Sergey witness like a Barnum and Bailey clown," Beacon continued. "Pretty clever."

That tidbit made me even more nervous.

Anderson noticed. "Gangs pay for information, just like cops do. I'm guessing a janitor or someone else happened to be there when you brought him in. They tipped off the gang."

It then dawned on me that I was the only white person in Jackson's office, and while that was something that I normally didn't notice, I needed to ask a question about race. That's always a sensitive topic in Washington, D.C. Not long ago, a white member of the predominantly black mayor's staff was forced to resign after he used the word "niggardly" to refer to the city's tight budget. The *Washington Post* noted in an editorial the next day that "niggardly" means "miserly" and doesn't have any racial connotation. But several blacks still remained offended by the use of the word and had interpreted it as a slur. The aide's firing quickly set off another political controversy. It turned out the white aide was a homosexual and he accused the mayor of picking on him because of his sexual orientation. The embarrassed mayor rehired him.

Like I said, race is dicey territory.

I tried to think of a politically correct way to put my question, but finally I just asked it: "Are all members of the O Street Crew black?"

Both detectives gave me a puzzled look. "Of course, they're black," Anderson said. "No whites or Latinos live in that neighborhood."

But my boss understood why I'd asked. "Wyatt," he said, "there will be no racial profiling, even in a case like this one."

"Bill," I replied, intentionally calling him by his first name, "I'm not planning on violating any departmental regulations here, but if the entire gang is black, then I think we should probably focus our attention Friday on watching young black men who might be congregating on Capitol Hill."

"And I'm telling you right now," Jackson replied. "You'll not single out any racial group."

Beacon and Anderson didn't seem at all offended. But I decided to let the issue drop. I figured all of us were smart enough to swear that we weren't going to single out young black men. Just the same, if a white guy wearing a suit and tie and a black kid parading around in a gang bandana both were seen loitering, I was pretty certain which one was going to be rousted.

"What else can you tell me about this gang?" I asked.

"They intimidate everyone," Beacon replied.

"We've got more than two dozen homicides in Southeast we know were done by the gang," Anderson explained. "Some in broad daylight in clear view of onlookers, but nobody is willing to testify."

"Gangbangers who didn't take part in the shootings are always the first at the crime scene," Beacon said. "Hell, they'll stand around drinking sodas and chomping on chips just waiting to see who's talking to the cops. You talk, you're dead."

"We've got cases," Anderson added, "where the gang hired private detectives to follow us around to see who we're interviewing."

"What age group are we talking here?" I asked.

"Some as young as ten or twelve," said Anderson. "The oldest are in their twenties, if they live that long."

An image of several black youngsters being gunned down on Capitol Hill by a squad of predominantly white federal marshals suddenly flashed through my head.

"What sort of weapons can we expect?"

"Anything money can buy, usually from Virginia gun shops," Anderson replied. "They've got money and these punks get hopped-up over maximum firepower. We're talking military-grade weapons."

That mental image suddenly became even worse. Now I saw federal marshals keeling over from rapid-fire machine guns.

We spent another hour discussing the options and deciding what other law enforcement agencies needed to be brought into the loop. There are more than 114 different ones operating in this city. Everyone knows about the big bureaucracies—the FBI, DEA, Secret Service, Bureau of Alcohol, Tobacco, and Firearms—but that's just the tip. We've also got the Metropolitan Police Department, the U.S. Capitol Police, the U.S. Park Police, Metro Transit Authority Police, and nearly every federal agency has some sort of departmental police force of its own. Add in the various military cops and you've got a multijurisdictional, interagency law enforcement quagmire.

We agreed that we'd need to notify the U.S. Capitol Police, the Secret Service, and the FBI. Jackson said he'd cover those bases. Beacon and Anderson promised to coordinate our operational plans with the Metro cops. That left me with only one real job: trying to figure out how to get Sergey Pudin out of the Senate building alive after he'd testified.

By the time I returned to my office, it was well after six o'clock, but my secretary, Marcella Penbrook, was still at her desk even though she normally left at five.

"I wanted to make certain you got these messages," she said, handing me several pink "While You Were Out" slips. The name Kimberly Lodge was scribbled on the first one, along with a telephone number. She'd called at 9:45 a.m. The second slip also identified Ms. Lodge as the caller. She'd tried this time at 3:40 p.m. Under comments, there was the notation: *State Department— CTC Center— Urgent*. Ms. Lodge had left a final message at 5:10 p.m. and, according to the last pink slip, she'd been hostile. The note said she needed to talk to me *IMMEDIATELY! Subject: Movladi Islamov, a.k.a. the Viper.*

"I'm afraid Ms. Lodge and I got off on the wrong foot," Penbrook said sheepishly. "I thought she was one of your girlfriends, and she didn't like that."

I hadn't had a serious love interest for several weeks. "What made you assume that?" I asked.

"You know, she has one of those throaty voices, like she smokes too many cigarettes or drinks too much coffee. She sounds a lot like Janis Joplin singing 'Bobby McGee.' She sounded angry at you, too!"

Her analogy dated us both, but I let that pass. Instead, I wondered why Penbrook equated angry, raspy-voiced women with my girlfriends. While I was still pondering this, Penbrook said, "The second time Ms. Lodge called, she told me she worked at the CTC center. She got incensed when I asked her what CTC stood for, but I didn't know what it meant."

"Forget about it," I said. "Go on home."

I didn't hang around long either after she'd gone. Still, there was no reason for me to hurry back to my empty apartment, so I strolled across the street to a bar and ordered a shot of Jack. After I'd finished it and started another, I thought about Ms. Kimberly Lodge's telephone calls and her interest in the Viper.

I usually don't mind providing information to other law enforcement officers. Hadn't I just left a long afternoon meeting where I'd cooperated with detectives Beacon and Anderson? But the truth is that I hate to help two specific agencies. The FBI is notorious for gobbling up every scrap of intel you can give it. Meanwhile, its agents won't offer you squat. Even worse, if there's an arrest, they're always the first to run in front of the television cameras claiming credit. But as much as I dislike the FBI, I loathe the CIA even more. Why? Because its operatives not only take everything you bust your ass getting, they always act superior. They act as if they know something you don't. Besides, you can't really trust CIA officers, because you never know if they're fabricating facts and manipulating you as part of some "wilderness of mirrors" bullshit. Detectives Beacon and Anderson had been street cops who had shot straight from the hip with me. Consequently, I'd felt immediately comfortable. But I didn't envision Ms. Kimberly Lodge, throaty, angry voice or not, as being someone who'd paid her dues working in the streets. I had no reason to believe that she'd be truthful with me either.

There was another reason why I wasn't eager to return Ms. Lodge's nasty telephone messages. Movladi Islamov, a.k.a. the Viper, was more than just a name to me. I'd never referred to him as the Viper. To me, he was Moe, which is what we called him when he was a student at George Mason University in Fairfax, a Virginia suburb. A buddy of mine had convinced me years ago that I would make a great professor. I'd let him wrangle me into teaching night classes about the so-called criminal mind. Moe had been older and more serious than the fresh-eyed innocents who'd come into my class directly from mommy and daddy's house. I'd invited him to join me one night at a nearby pub to discuss a particularly insightful paper that he'd written about terrorism. Because he's a Muslim and doesn't drink alcohol, I had to do double duty. During our talk, at least what I can still remember about it, I discovered that his father had been a cop in Chechnya. There was only a five-year difference in our ages, and we'd become good friends. I especially enjoyed drinking his share of the booze.

I'd heard from him off and on during the past six years. I'm not much of a letter writer and neither is he. I assumed Ms. Kimberly Lodge was contacting me now about Moe because he'd recently surfaced on CNN as the leader of Chechen freedom fighters. I'd not been surprised. He was a really dedicated guy. A true believer.

I decided to wait to return Ms. Lodge's call—if I ever did. I had plenty to do before Friday's hearing, and multitasking is not something I can handle well—just ask my ex-wife. But then, she could tell you lots about my faults, some real and some imagined.

I took another drink and told myself that I had to remain focused on keeping Sergey Pudin alive, especially if the O Street Crew had an inside source. I'd deal with Ms. Lodge later.

14

Olga was being sexually assaulted. Men were raping her.

Khrenkov willed his eyelids to open. His face was drenched with sweat. It was a nightmare. But it had happened just the same. He knew it. A vision.

His knuckle-dragging watchdog, whom he knew only by the name Pankov, was mesmerized by a mind-numbing television rerun and polishing off a second plate of medium-rare steak and scrambled eggs delivered by the hotel's room service. Khrenkov checked the time. Nine thirty a.m. He'd overslept. Jet lag. He stumbled into the bathroom, retrieving his suitcase as he went.

Pankov was still sunk stupidly into the sofa, gnawing on the T-bone like a hyena feasting on a chewed carcass when Khrenkov reappeared moments later. He spread out the maps that Fedorov had given him the day before. One was an overview of the Washington, D.C., metropolitan area. The second displayed just the U.S. Capitol grounds. He found the Russell, Dirksen, and Hart Senate Office Buildings. A red circle had been drawn around the Hart location and in the margin was written: *10 a.m., 211 Senate Intelligence Committee Hearing Room.*

"I need to check the area," he announced. "But not with you. People will notice if we're seen walking together."

Pankov pondered this for a moment and then said: "I'll follow. But disappear for more than one half of an hour . . ." He didn't complete the sentence. Instead he swept his right hand under his chin as if he were cutting someone's throat.

They rode the hotel elevator together into the lobby and then Pankov paused at the newsstand to buy cigarettes while Khrenkov exited out the front revolving door. Most of the passersby were wearing light jackets, but not Khrenkov. He welcomed the cool October air. He walked briskly south on New Jersey Avenue toward the immense Capitol that loomed before him. After he'd gone two blocks, he reached the intersection of New Jersey and C Streets. There was a guardhouse next to an entrance to an underground garage. Directly across the street was a tall stone monument. Curious, he went to inspect the memorial, pausing, as if he were a tourist, in front of a life-size bronze statue—identified as Robert A. Taft—at its base. Taft was not a name Khrenkov recalled from his history studies. An inscription read:

This memorial to Robert A. Taft,
presented by the people to the Congress of the United States,
stands as a tribute to the honesty, indomitable courage,
and high principles of free government
symbolized by his life.

There was a dry moat encircling the figure. Khrenkov estimated the tribute rose a hundred feet from the ground. It was at least eleven feet thick and thirty feet wide. There were no obvious doorways. Despite its height, Khrenkov decided it wouldn't suit his needs. It was too far from the Hart building for an accurate rifle shot, and the tower itself was edged by trees. They would obscure his vision. He noticed Pankov lingering about a hundred yards away. *Stupid man*, Khrenkov thought. Pankov was staring directly at him. Any observer could easily have guessed Pankov was tailing him.

Brrrrrraaaaannngggg! Bells were suddenly clanging. The sounds came from the top of the Taft monument. It was a bell tower. It was also ten o'clock. Khrenkov timed the tune. Exactly two minutes. Such a noise could help mask the sound of a gunshot.

Khrenkov crossed the street and hurried up a flight of stairs, two steps at a time. He was now going through a much larger park that had been installed atop the underground parking. Khrenkov counted his one-yard strides. In the center was a stone fountain decorated with lion heads. Water was supposed to spew from their mouths, but the pool had been drained for the winter. The nearby trees each had postcard-sized signs nailed on them. "Northern Red Oak," read one. Khrenkov feigned interest, while he surveyed the western end of the Russell Building, now directly in front of him. The structure was one block wide. There was a guardhouse at its southwest corner but no one was inside it.

Continuing to count his steps, Khrenkov exited the park at the corner of Delaware Avenue and C. He paused there to study a poster-sized map on display under a thick clear pane. All of the three senate offices were now on his right. He was standing on a sidewalk that ran east-west. He strode along the back side of the Russell to the next corner—where C now met First. As he crossed it, an odd sensation came over him. He realized this was where Sergey Pudin had been taken into the Dirksen Building. He could sense it, like a hunter tracking a wounded deer.

C Street was closed to traffic from this point east. The conscripted asphalt was now being used as a parking area. Two barricades—both poles were painted red and white—had to be lifted before vehicles could enter the blocked-off lot. As Khrenkov watched, a car approached and two uniformed officers came out of a booth to inspect it. While one questioned the driver, the other waved a mirror attached to a long pole beneath the vehicle to search for explosives.

A white truck with *UNITED STATES POSTAL SERVICE* painted on it pulled over to the curb where Khrenkov was now standing. A mail carrier got out, unlocked a bright blue letter box on the sidewalk, and removed its contents.

All of this activity was being recorded by a video camera hidden behind a black glass dome hanging from the northwest corner of the Dirksen building. The lens was positioned so it could see the length of C or be adjusted to watch First Street.

Khrenkov continued east along the sidewalk. Halfway up the next block, the Dirksen Building's exterior changed. This marked the beginning of the new addition. It was the start of the Hart Building, where Sergey Pudin was scheduled to testify. Although the two buildings had different names, they were mortared together in an awkward alliance.

A tall building on his immediate left caught his attention because it was the only structure to run parallel to the three Senate buildings. About four hundred yards away, it was surrounded by parking spaces. Eight stories tall, it was perfect "high ground" for a sniper. He walked over to read its entrance name: Headquarters—United States Capitol Police. A nearby plaque said:

CREATED BY CONGRESS IN 1828, THE ORIGINAL DUTY OF THE UNITED STATES CAPITOL POLICE WAS TO PROVIDE SECURITY FOR THE UNITED STATES CAPITOL BUILDING. TODAY, OUR MISSION HAS EXPANDED TO PROVIDE THE CONGRESSIONAL COMMU-

NITY AND ITS VISITORS WITH THE HIGHEST QUALITY OF A FULL
RANGE OF POLICE SERVICES.

It wasn't worth the risk to try to see the roof. He retraced his path
and quickly recognized another promising site. The Saint Joseph's
Catholic Church at the corner of Second and C streets had a bell tower.
The date October 25, 1868, was chiseled into white stone near the
church's front door. Khrenkov entered the vestibule and was greeted by
a sign that read ROBERT F. KENNEDY WORSHIPED HERE. No one was in
sight. He began to climb a narrow staircase but was stopped by a priest
descending from the second floor.

"May I help you?" the father asked.

"I'm visiting from Ukraine," Khrenkov said, improvising. "My grandfather was a maker of church bells and I'm curious to learn where your
bell came from."

"I don't know," the cleric answered. "But after September 11th, the
Capitol Police sealed our tower. We can only let someone up there if one
of the police officers is with them."

"There's no need to disturb them."

Khrenkov backed out and walked toward the Capitol Building via
Second Street, until he was directly in front of the Hart's main entrance.
There was a half-moon driveway here and a portico, but the drive was
blocked by steel gates that rose from slits in the pavement to prevent motorists from simply pulling up to the building's doors. A uniformed police
officer, who was stationed behind bullet-resistant glass, controlled the hy-
draulic gates. A waist-high wall made of thick gray granite had been laid
the length of the sidewalk to stop anyone from trying to circumvent the
barriers. Khrenkov correctly realized that this was the Hart's most secure
access. It would be the most logical place for the police to bring Sergey
Pudin after he had finished testifying and was leaving the building.

Still, there was something about this scene that ate at Khrenkov. His
gut instincts told him that Pudin had been sneaked into the building via
the entrance at the corner of First and C Streets. If that were the case,
wouldn't the police use that same doorway when it was time for him to
escape?

He decided to go inside the Hart Building, but first he needed to
make certain that Pankov could still see what he was doing. He didn't
want his babysitting goon to panic and think he'd disappeared. Khrenkov
cooled his heels until Pankov saw him and then he entered the Hart
through a door on Constitution Avenue. Stepping inside, he found himself face-to-face with two Capitol Police posted at the entry. One was
reading the *Washington Post* and didn't even bother to glance up.

"Place any metal object, such as keys or coins, in one of the plastic containers on your left," the other said. "This includes cellular telephones. Then proceed through the metal detector directly in front of you."

Khrenkov did as instructed and walked through the magnetometer without setting off the alarm. Neither guard asked why he was there, nor did anyone demand to see his identification papers—two questions that would have been routine in Moscow when entering a government building.

He ambled across the polished marble into the building's atrium. Eight floors of offices ringed it, much like ribs. A modern art sculpture, entitled *Mountain and Clouds,* by Alexander Calder, rose up from the floor. Khrenkov pretended to study the towering metal piece as he assessed the building's security.

Once he had memorized that interior, he rode an elevator to the second level to look for the Senate Intelligence Committee hearing room. He was surprised when he located it because no one was standing guard. He continued walking and realized midway down the corridor that he had actually exited the Hart Building and he was now inside the adjoining Dirksen Building. At the end of the passage, he rounded a corner and nearly bumped into an oncoming police officer.

"Excuse me," Khrenkov said.

"No problem," the startled cop replied.

There were at least a dozen more officers milling about the entrance of the Senate Finance Committee hearing room.

"After the dogs finish, lock it up tight," one of them said. "We don't want any screwups tomorrow."

The double doors to the conference room were open, and as Khrenkov walked by, he saw two black Labrador retrievers sniffing under the rows of chairs inside. Once again, Khrenkov had a strange feeling. *This* is where Sergey Pudin will be testifying, *not* the Senate Intelligence Committee hearing room, as advertised. He felt sure of it. The extra police and bomb dogs were obvious clues, but it was his gut instinct again that convinced him.

Khrenkov checked the time. He'd been inside nearly twenty minutes. He could only be out of sight for ten more before Pankov would report him missing. He ducked inside a pay phone booth.

"This is an emergency," he told the operator. "Please connect me with the FBI in New York City."

"You need to call 911 for local emergencies," the operator replied.

"No! New York. FBI. Now!"

After a momentary pause, a woman's voice said: "New York Field Office, how may I direct your call?"

"I want to report a kidnapping in Brighton Beach."

"Have you called the police there?"

"No, I will deal only with the FBI."

"Just a minute," the woman said. A few seconds later, a man's voice came on the line. "This is Special Agent Bunker. How may I help you?"

"A woman has been kidnapped and her family is being held hostage in Brighton Beach by the Russian Mafia."

"Who are you, sir?"

"I'm of no consequence."

Khrenkov gave his parents', brothers', and sister's name to the FBI agent. He then explained how Olga was being held hostage in a different location from the others. "I can give you the phone number of the man guarding her," he said. He recited the digits that he had memorized while fumbling with Fordorov's cell phone during the limousine ride.

"How do I know this is legit?" Bunker asked.

"One of the kidnappers is named Igor Fedorov. He rides in a black Lincoln Town Car with a New York license tag number—6750-LD. I'm certain he has a criminal record."

"What about you? You in the Russia Mafia?"

"I will call you again. You need to have men standing by to rescue the Polov family. But first, you must find where Olga Polov is being held hostage. Wait until you hear from me before you do anything. Is that understood?"

"I'm not going to do anything unless you tell me your name and what role you have in all this. Let's start with you telling me why this family was kidnapped."

Khrenkov hung up. He had only three minutes to get outside and flag down Pankov. He dashed down a stairway. There was an exit to his right. When he stepped outside, he realized that he was now at the corner of First and C streets.

Khrenkov guessed Pankov was still waiting on Constitution Avenue. He didn't have time to run around the massive building so he tried the cell phone that Fedorov had given him. He hit the key for a preprogrammed number.

"*Da*," the huge Russian said when he answered.

"I'm on the other side of the Dirksen building. I'll wait for you in the park by the fountain with lions heads."

"What took you so long?"

Khrenkov closed the phone. When a puffing Pankov reached him several minutes later, Khrenkov said, "I need some items. We'll ask at the hotel for directions to a store."

"What items?"

Khrenkov had no intention of disclosing his plans to Pankov. "Things I need to do my job," he replied. Then he began walking toward the Hyatt Hotel. When they reached it, Khrenkov went directly to the concierge.

"I'd like to visit a costume shop and a store where I can buy black fabric."

"Let me give you some addresses," the young woman replied. "Is this for a Halloween party? The big night is only a few days away, isn't it?"

Khrenkov nodded, even though he didn't have the slightest idea what she was talking about. Halloween was not a holiday that he recognized.

15

"I'm changing our plans," Movladi "the Viper" Islamov declared.

"What? Why?" the startled voice on the telephone line replied. "What the hell are you trying to pull here?"

"Circumstances require it."

The arms dealer, whom Islamov knew only by the name Rafe, clearly disagreed.

"There's no need for any last minute screwing around. Everything is arranged."

"Then rearrange it."

Islamov had always planned on switching the location of their meeting. Even if he had liked the setup that Rafe had made. He had never met this arms dealer and knew almost nothing about his past or his operation.

Rafe had suggested earlier that they finalize their deal at midnight inside a warehouse located along the outskirts of Reykjavik. But Islamov was not willing to walk blindly into unfamiliar turf, especially at night, especially after the Russians had interrogated Salman. Islamov had learned long ago that his soldiers often gossiped behind his back about his war plans. It was possible that Salman had overheard more about the impending arms deal than anyone suspected, information he could have leaked to his torturers.

"If you want to sell your merchandise," Islamov said forcefully, "then we will make the exchange under my new terms. Otherwise, the deal is off."

"Bullshit!" Rafe snapped. "You want what I'm selling. You *need* what I'm selling. You aren't going to walk away from here without it."

"You shouldn't be so confident," Islamov coolly replied. "Perhaps I have found another source besides you."

His comment took Rafe by surprise, and the telephone line went silent. "What do you have in mind?" Rafe asked finally.

"Put your merchandise in the hull of a powerboat and sail it into Reykjavik Bay at noon," Islamov said. "Once you are anchored there, two of my associates will board your craft and inspect your product. Please have only two of your people on the boat. This way we will have an equal match."

"This is ridiculous!"

"As soon as my associates call me and confirm that what you have for sale is authentic, I will tell you where you can pick up the first half of the payment."

"What do you mean the 'first half'?"

"The rest will be paid after my associates sail out of the bay."

"What do you expect my guys on the boat to do? Swim back to shore?"

"There are hundreds of fjords along the Icelandic shore. I will have a second boat waiting. As soon as the merchandise is moved off your powerboat and onto mine, your men will be paid the remainder of the funds and they may return to Reykjavik in your boat."

"Whoa! What's to keep you from simply taking off with the merchandise and dumping my men at sea?"

"Common sense. If I betray you, then you could notify the Icelandic Coast Guard and tip them off about our cargo."

"I wouldn't need to do that," Rafe replied, "because if you try to cheat me, I'll hunt you down personally, rip a hole in your chest, and shit in it."

"Then I'll be certain that your money is delivered to you," Islamov calmly answered.

Once again, there was a long pause, and then Rafe said, "I don't like it, but okay, we'll do it your way."

Islamov was about to hang up when Rafe added, "Just remember, I want you to deliver that first payment personally to me. I always insist on looking eyeball-to-eyeball with my buyers."

Islamov felt uneasy as soon as they finished speaking. Rafe had not quibbled enough. At the last minute, Islamov was demanding that Rafe hire a powerboat, move the atomic bomb from its hiding spot onto this ship, and sail it into a busy harbor. If Rafe were a cold-blooded arms mercenary, then why hadn't he demanded more money for the additional risks?

That was not the only oddity.

Salman had been on his way to Vienna to deliver a down payment of $150,000 to one of Rafe's partners. The negotiable bonds were supposed to be a sign of good faith. But after Salman had been nabbed at the border, Rafe had dropped his demand for any prepayment. This had initially delighted Islamov because it meant Rafe would not have time to thoroughly examine the counterfeit bonds or attempt to cash them. But, once again, it was a shoddy business practice.

Rafe seemed too eager to make this sale, and his blustering on the telephone about how he would hunt down Islamov and "rip a hole" in his chest sounded as if he were reading from a script written for an American tough-guy movie. Islamov knew several deadly killers and none of them ever made a threat. They didn't need to. If they wanted to kill you, you wouldn't know it until they jabbed a blade into your ribs.

Mansur Mukayev, whom Islamov had brought with him to Iceland to inspect the bomb, could tell from Islamov's somber mood that the conversation with Rafe had made him apprehensive. Mukayev had driven Islamov to a pay phone and now the two of them were returning to their hotel.

"Forcing him to meet us in the bay is a good idea," Mukayev volunteered. "You'll be able to see from the shore if anyone is following us after I inspect the cargo and pilot the powerboat out to sea. I will sail far enough into the ocean to guarantee that we aren't being shadowed. Then I'll slip back to the coast and duck into the fjord. There is no way that the seller will know our destination in advance."

Islamov wasn't so sure about the plan. Why had Rafe agreed without a fight? Why had he not demanded a partial payment up front? Even more troubling, why was Rafe so insistent that he and Islamov meet "eyeball-to-eyeball."

The Viper had always been willing to gloss over his earlier doubts because of his need to buy the bomb that Rafe was selling. But now that Islamov knew there was a second one hidden in America and ripe for the picking, he was becoming more skeptical and nervous about his dealings with the mysterious Rafe.

16

CAPITOL HILL,
WASHINGTON, D.C.

Kimberly Lodge was late—again. The Blue Line train she'd boarded in Crystal City had been delayed after one of the cars traveling on the same track broke down. Her boss, Counterterrorism Center Director Henry Clarke, had warned her not to be tardy. They had a plan to meet at 1:30 p.m. at the Court of Neptune Fountain outside the Library of Congress on Capitol Hill. That would give them plenty of time to walk the short distance to the Hart Senate Office Building for the two o'clock congressional hearing with the DCCI. But by the time Kimberly's train reached the Capitol South station, it was already 1:57.

"Damn!" she muttered as she jogged up the moving escalator steps from the subway line. As soon as she was outside, she slipped off her high heels and began running. Within minutes, she'd spotted Clarke. He was pacing in front of the fountain just where he'd said he'd be.

"I'm sooooo sorrrrry," she stammered when she got within earshot.

Much to her surprise, he broke into a big grin. "Our hearing doesn't actually start until two thirty," he explained. "I figured changing the time was the only guaranteed way to get you here early."

Kimberly felt her face flush. She'd torn heel and toe holes in her nylons in her sidewalk sprint.

"Let's head over to the Hart Building and get a cup of coffee," he suggested. "We can talk a bit more there about Chechnya and what's going to happen at the hearing."

"Cute," Kimberly said sarcastically. "Very cute."

"It worked, didn't it?"

They strolled north and passed in front of the U.S. Supreme Court. As they turned the corner onto Constitution, Kimberly heard police sirens. Two D.C. officers riding on motorcycles roared by them. They were followed by a Chevrolet Suburban with blacked-out windows, a Lincoln Town Car, and a second Suburban, all with flashing emergency lights.

"Who do you think that is?" Kimberly asked.

"The only other important witness, other than the DCCI, listed on today's schedule is some Russian Mafia thug. And the only reason why I know about him is because there was an apparent misprint in the newspaper. It said the Russian witness was testifying in the Senate Intelligence Committee hearing room. And since that room was already reserved for the DCCI's testimony, I knew someone had screwed up."

As they watched, the noisy motorcade turned left onto Second Street, en route to the Hart's main entrance. Two Capitol Police officers immediately dashed into the street after the entourage had gone by and blocked it off with sawhorses.

"Let's go see if we can get a peek at him," Kimberly said.

Clarke hesitated, glanced at his watch, but then relented. "Okay, we've got the time." Rather than entering the Hart Building at its Constitutional Avenue entrance, they continued walking east on the sidewalk. When they reached the corner at Second Street, an officer stopped them.

"Sorry," he said. "Access to the Hart's main entrance is temporarily closed."

"The vice president visiting?" Kimberly asked.

"Naw," the cop replied. "We're moving a witness out. He just finished testifying."

"It's that Russian mobster I read about," Clarke said.

Just then, a Cadillac Escalade that had been traveling down Constitution Avenue accelerated, swerved to its right, and rammed through the barricades blocking Second Street. A shattered piece of wood nearly hit Kimberly as it sailed by. She and Clarke fell instinctively to the ground.

This happened at about the moment deputies were leading a portly man through the Hart's doors. He was being escorted to the motorcade of SUVs and motorcycle cops now waiting under the portico. The man was surrounded by deputies who were holding a black raincoat over his face, apparently to shield him from photographers.

A police detective would later theorize that the O Street Crew had stationed one of its members inside the Hart's atrium and he had used his cell phone to alert the driver of the Cadillac Escalade when the witness was about to walk outside.

The SUV roared forward and screeched to a stop directly in front of the entrance. Its rear tires fishtailed, causing the Cadillac to spin in a half circle in the middle of the street. The passenger side of the SUV was now positioned so it was facing the building's glass doors. Two gunmen in ski masks leaped from the vehicle and began firing Russian-made Kalashnikov AK-47 modified assault rifles at the witness and the horde of deputies around him. The federal protection detail lunged forward. It was as if all of the bodyguards had the same synchronized step. In one swift motion, their huge witness was practically pitched into the rear seat of the armored Lincoln Town Car.

Because the two gang members were wearing army surplus body armor, they mistakenly thought they had protection form the deputy marshals' return fire. But both would-be assassins were instantaneously knocked dead where they stood. A sharpshooter from the Secret Service's special response team was the first to draw blood. Hiding in the bell tower at Saint Joseph's Church, his rifle shot ripped through the skull of one attacker. The second assailant was dropped by a barrage of armor-piercing rounds shot by the deputies hovering behind the motorcade. A third gunman bolted from the SUV, but he, too, was killed, even before he was able to pull a trigger. It was the Secret Service marksman who drilled him.

Having just seen three of his buddies slaughtered, the Cadillac's driver jammed down on the gas pedal and the SUV burst forward in the same direction from which it'd just come.

The gun battle had happened so quickly that Kimberly and Clarke were still both lying on the sidewalk near the corner when they saw the SUV racing toward them. Several Capitol Police officers began shooting at the driver with their handguns and the Cadillac's windshield became a shattered web of cracked glass holes surrounded by white streaks. A single round punched into the driver's head, snapping it back. His hands released their grip on the steering wheel, but his foot remained firmly planted on the accelerator. Incredibly, the SUV sped up.

The Cadillac veered to the right, hit the curb, and the impact lifted the vehicle airborne. It landed on its side on the concrete. Its wheels continued spinning uselessly as the SUV now slid forward. It had been traveling so fast that not even the steel scraping against the walkway slowed it. Sparks flew. It was aimed directly at Kimberly and Clarke. She rolled to her left, but Clarke was frozen in fear as the nearly six-thousand-pound monster bore down on him.

"Roll! Roll!" Kimberly screamed, but Clarke seemed catatonic. Kimberly leaned forward, grasped his arm with both hands, and jerked it hard. She was not strong enough to pull him to safety, but her sudden tug snapped him from his paralysis. He rolled away seconds before the Cadillac skidded over where he'd been lying.

It was over.

Or so it seemed.

As the caravan sped out the curved driveway and turned north onto Second Street in the opposite direction of the wrecked Cadillac, the sound of automatic weapons erupted once again. This time the attackers were riding off-road motorcycles that jumped into sight from an alley north of the Hart Building. The Secret Service sharpshooter in the bell tower killed one dirt bike rider instantly. The ammo exploded within his chest with such force that he flew from the cycle. His passenger, who was firing an old Mac-10 submachine gun, sailed headfirst through the air. His body smacked against the waist-high granite wall alongside the Hart Building's entrance. His neck snapped. The other motorcycle kamikaze fared no better. A Capitol Police officer inside the glass booth by the horseshoe drive stepped outside and aimed his H&K MP-5 submachine gun at them. Several rounds hit the driver and his gun-wielding rider. Both were blown off the motorcycle and bounced across the blacktop much like flat stones skipping on a smooth pond. Since neither wore protective leather clothing, their blue denim jeans and slogan T-shirts were shredded, bloody, and embedded with peeled-back flesh and bits of asphalt.

Now it really was over. The protected witness convoy sped away, leaving the D.C. police and Secret Service to sort out the gruesome failed attack. Detectives Fred Beacon and Charles Anderson both tiptoed between the fallen gangsters looking for familiar faces.

"Stupid kids," Beacon muttered as he surveyed the carnage.

"Anyone hurt?" Anderson yelled.

No officers were, but six gang members were dead.

Kimberly Lodge asked Henry Clarke if he was okay.

"I think so," he replied. But his face was drained of color.

"Jesus Christ, that was close!" she exclaimed.

Two Capitol Hill cops climbed on top of the SUV with pistols drawn. One peered inside.

"He's a goner," he yelled, referring to the driver. "There's no one else."

Kimberly asked Clarke, "Do you need an ambulance?"

"No, I'm fine," Clark replied, but his legs crumpled as soon as he spoke those words. He collapsed and began gasping.

"I need paramedics now!" a nearby officer screamed.

Within minutes, Clark was on a stretcher and being placed in the back of an ambulance.

"Go on without me," he told Kimberly. "But keep your mouth shut at the hearing." He forced a grin. "We've had enough excitement around here for one day."

With everything that had happened, Kimberly had forgotten about the DCCI's testimony. She looked at her watch. She was going to be late. But this time she figured she had a legitimate excuse.

17

Vladimir Khrenkov watched the gun battle between the O Street Crew and federal agents with no emotion or reaction. At one point, he'd had a clear shot at the fat man being escorted by bodyguards from the Hart Building. But he hadn't fired.

The cell phone in his jacket pocket vibrated.

"You let him escape!" an angry Igor Fedorov declared.

"It wasn't Sergey Pudin. It was a decoy!"

"How do you know?"

"The police were too prepared."

Fedorov paused to think about what Khrenkov had just said. "Perhaps you're right," Fedorov said. "When one of my men went to the Senate Intelligence Committee room, there was a sign there saying the hearing had been moved."

"Where was the hearing held?" Khrenkov asked.

"Down the hallway. In a different committee room."

It was just as Khrenkov had suspected. Pudin had testified in the Senate Finance Committee hearing room where Khrenkov had seen the police officers and their bomb-sniffing dogs the day before.

"These deputies are playing hiding-and-seek with us," Fedorov said. "But if that was a decoy, then where is Pudin?"

"He's still inside the building."

"How can you be so certain?"

"I feel it."

Fedorov grunted. "You have twenty-four hours." Before Khrenkov could reply, Fedorov added, "And don't try to be clever. The cell phone you are using has a GPS tracking device inside it. I can tell exactly where you are. If you don't answer each half hour when Pankov calls you, then your family will be killed. Don't even think about coming to New York to rescue them."

Fedorov hung up.

Khrenkov was lying on his stomach on the flat roof of a row house at the corner of Second and C streets across from the Hart. From his perch he could see its main entrance, as well as watch west down the side of the three Senate buildings where they exited onto C Street.

He had crept into his sniper's lair during the night. Around ten p.m., he had left the Hyatt Hotel, carrying his rifle inside its golf bag. A taxi delivered him to Ronald Reagan National Airport. There Khrenkov waited ten minutes before hailing a cab for a ride back to Capitol Hill. He instructed the driver to drop him two blocks east of the Hart Building. Then he walked casually along C as if he were a homeowner returning from a golfing trip. About one block from his destination, Khrenkov turned left onto a narrow path. On city maps, this walkway was identified as Justice Square Road, but it really was more like a new driveway. One of the row houses on C had been demolished and a blacktop path had been paved through the gap. This new entry led to several tiny offices that an enterprising developer had built in the alleyway. The name Justice Square was chosen because nearly all of them were rented by lawyers. Khrenkov had chosen this route because it enabled him to walk behind the homes on C Street without attracting attention. The row houses were connected and shared the same flat roof.

After he got behind them, Khrenkov slipped his weapon from its case, leaving the golf bag next to a trash can. He slung the rifle onto his back and, using the cover of darkness, climbed over a high cedar fence into the backyard of one of the narrow homes that had an ivy-covered trellis attached to it. He scaled the shaky trellis to reach the second-story roof.

Carrying his shoes, he'd made his way across four houses until he'd reached the last one on the block. It was three stories tall, so he was forced to use a rooftop air conditioner as a step to reach it.

Khrenkov had brought a bundle of black fabric with him. It was four feet wide and eight feet long. He moved quickly to the roof's northwest corner and unrolled the fabric. The house was made of redbrick and had an eighteen-inch-tall crown that ran around its rim. Using a knife, Khrenkov gingerly chipped out the mortar and removed a single brick. This opening was now serving as his gun portal.

He crawled underneath the fabric and with two-inch-wide duct tape attached the material to the house's brick facade. This created a make-shift tent above him. Because the fabric was black, it blended in with the flat roof's tarry surface. He'd made the covering because he was worried the police might use a helicopter to scan the rooftops. He didn't know that it was nearly impossible—even for the D.C. police—to get permission to fly this close to the Capitol. Just the same, the fabric hid him from being seen.

His SVD Dragunov rifle was disguised with dull-black electrical tape to prevent it from reflecting light. He'd brought two bottles of water with him. After he drank one, he'd use it as a urinal. He didn't want to crawl out from under the black canopy for any reason until he'd shot Pudin.

Khrenkov hadn't known that the O Street Crew had also been hired to kill Pudin. But he had welcomed the noise and confusion their doomed attack had caused. At one point, he'd been close to joining the fray by squeezing his rifle's trigger and shooting the protected witness. But Krenkov had stopped himself because he suspected the witness was a decoy. There had been several signs.

When the noisy motorcade had first arrived at the Hart building, the deputies in the two SUVs and the Lincoln Town Car had all gotten out on the driver's side. No one had climbed out of the passenger doors, which were facing Second Street. They must've known an attack might come and had wanted to use the three vehicles as shields to protect them from any gunfire.

Khrenkov had also noticed that the Capitol Hill guard in the booth at the driveway entrance was armed with an H&K MP-5—a powerful nine-millimeter submachine gun. The day before, when Khrenkov had passed by the building, the cop had only been carrying his sidearm.

These two anomalies had given Khrenkov pause. He'd become fur-ther suspicious when deputies emerged holding a black raincoat near the witness's head. The entrance had a canopy over it. The sun was shining. He was already wearing sunglasses and a hat. And the news photogra-phers and TV cameramen were being penned at the edge of the block. Besides, Sergey Pudin's testimony had been nationally televised. His photograph had already been in that morning's *Post*. Why were the deputies so intent on hiding his face? Khrenkov could think of only one logical explanation. The man was an imposter.

Even if he'd not seen any clues, Khrenkov still would have known. He had a sixth sense when it came to such matters. It was not something easily explained, so Khrenkov rarely tried. To fully comprehend it, a person first had to know a popular Russian fairy tale and an incident from Khrenkov's past.

Shortly after he turned thirteen, Khrenkov traveled with his father to visit relatives in a rural village. Khrenkov and his cousin, Dmitri, decided to hunt birds with shotguns. En route to a forest, they'd met a skinny old woman carrying a heavy bundle of sticks for her hearth. Dmitri had mocked her, but Khrenkov had insisted on helping the old hag by toting the wood for her.

"I've nothing to pay you," she then declared.

Khrenkov replied, "I didn't want any payment."

The grandmother grabbed his head and kissed his cheek. Dmitri rolled in laughter, but rather than being repulsed, Khrenkov politely returned the kiss by pecking her withered cheek. As he did so, he noticed that her eyes were not blue, green, or brown, but a bright yellow.

An hour later, as the boys were about to ford a creek, Dmitri slipped on the mud and his shotgun accidentally fired. The pellets hit Khrenkov in the stomach. He collapsed. While Dmitri was running for help, Khrenkov passed in and out of consciousness. At one point, he felt something warm and wet touch his face. When he looked, a gray wolf was hovering over him. He assumed his bloody entrails would be ripped out next and devoured by the notorious predator. But the lupine beast continued to gently lick him.

When Khrenkov next awoke, he was in a bed at his uncle's house and a baba was saying an incantation over him. The old woman was the village's folk healer and a practicing witch. There was no doctor in their community, so Khrenkov's father and uncle had called the baba to care for him while they drove to a nearby city to get one.

"Did a wild animal appear to you?" the healer asked.

"A wolf," Khrenkov muttered.

"What color were its eyes?"

"Yellow."

And then he wondered if he had made a mistake. Maybe he was describing the old woman's yellow eyes, not the wolf's.

"Ah," the baba said, "that was no wolf then. That was the

witch Baba Yaga Kostianaya Noga, and only she knows why you deserved to be saved."

Every Russian child was familiar with the fairy tale that introduced the witch. A beautiful Russian maiden named Vasilisa the Beautiful had tricked Baba Yaga Kostianaya Noga, which means Baba Yaga bony legs, into helping her destroy her cruel stepmother and jealous stepsisters in a Cinderella-like yarn. Baba Yaga was a terrifying figure who lived in the woods, flew on a broom, ate human flesh, and had soul-less yellow eyes.

When the doctor arrived, he examined Khrenkov and became angry.

"Why have you wasted my time by making me come here to treat this boy?" he complained. "Only a few shotgun pellets hit him."

Nearly all of Khrenkov's wounds had been healed.

"It's the baba's magic!" Khrenkov's uncle shouted.

"Only ignorant peasants believe in witchcraft," the doctor sneered.

Not long after he recovered, Khrenkov noticed changes. His eyesight became keener. So did his sense of smell. His parents thought it was because he was maturing, but he knew better. Baba Yaga had saved him by becoming a wolf and licking his wounds, and for some reason she had passed on to him certain powers.

Any doubts about this were vanquished after he was sent to fight in Afghanistan. Several times, Khrenkov rescued his comrades from being ambushed by sensing danger. He could look at a trail in the Paktia Mountains and know when rebel fighters would be walking along it.

He was like a lone wolf.

Perched on the roof across from the Hart Building, Khrenkov dialed the FBI's number in New York on the cell phone.

"You're right about the Polov family!" Special Agent Bunker declared. "They're being held hostage by the Russian Mafia. I've got agents posted outside their house in Brighton Beach. But we haven't tried to get them out because we still haven't found the girl—Olga Polov."

"Did you follow Igor Fedorov? He knows where she is being kept."

"Yes, but we thought he noticed our men, so we backed off. We didn't want to bring him in for questioning and have his men harm the girl."

"We're running out of time."

"How much is there?"

"Less than twenty-four hours."

"Why don't you tell me who you are? That might help us."

"Who I am doesn't matter! You must find where they're hiding Olga."

"Listen, if you're in the Russian Mafia, we've got a protection program. It can help you get out. We can change your identity, move you to another state, hide you. We've never lost one of our witnesses. Never."

The hypocrisy of the moment struck Khrenkov. He was lying in wait on a Washington, D.C., rooftop with a sniper rifle to kill a witness who was being protected.

"I'll call back soon," Khrenkov said. He ended the call. He had to think of a way to make Igor Fedorov lead the FBI to his sister. After several minutes, he telephoned Special Agent Bunker again.

"Do you know where Fedorov is right now?" Khrenkov asked.

"No, but I can find him."

"Then do it."

Two hours later, Khrenkov once again used the phone to reach Agent Bunker.

"Fedorov's with a couple hookers in a restaurant in Little Italy," Bunker said.

"Get ready to follow him. I'll try to get him to visit the spot where they are hiding Olga. Then you can rescue her."

Khrenkov disconnected that call and quickly hit the preprogrammed button that rang on Fedorov's cell phone. "I need to speak to my sister, Olga," Khrenkov said. "I want to make sure she's still alive."

"She's fine. I'm busy. Maybe later."

"I want to speak to her *now* and I want you there with her when we talk."

"Why? Why do I need to be present?" Fedorov asked suspiciously.

"Because I want you to be looking at her when I ask you if she is safe. This is between the two of us. I want to hear you tell me that she is okay."

"Maybe after dinner," Fedorov replied. "Right now I'm with two friends. Pasta fagiole and panzerotti. That's what I'm eating—not my friends' names."

Khrenkov could hear tittering in the background, but he had no reason to chuckle at Fedorov's humor.

18

I tossed Sergey Pudin a bundle of clothes.

"Another costume?" he asked.

He was on his cot in the makeshift safe room hidden inside the Senate office building. It was late Friday night, about seven hours after the O Street Crew shoot-out.

"That clown suit got you here safely, didn't it?" I asked.

He untied the package knot.

"It's a letter carrier's uniform," I explained. "No one notices mailmen. I'll be back in the morning to take you out of here."

"And where will you be hiding me next after I leave these posh accommodations?" he asked, sweeping his hand across the spartan basement room.

"A coastal town. No casinos, but there's a nude beach."

Pudin smiled. He was enjoying his newfound celebrity. "I did well testifying before Senator Farthington's committee, did I not?"

"You were simply spellbinding," I replied sarcastically. "Women across America experienced multiple involuntary orgasms. Even Senator Farthington got a hard-on."

Pudin laughed.

"Yes, your New York senator owes me now," he said.

"First of all," I replied, surprising even myself by the irritation in my voice, "Farthington is not *my* senator. Second, that dog-and-pony show he put on resulted in eight people being killed."

Pudin said, "Are you really so naive? These men who were killed to-day, they had no value. If not today, they would've been shot later committing some violent crime. They were of no consequence."

"Tell that to their mothers."

"Their mothers already know this, my friend. I can think of many, many people in this world whose lives mean nothing."

"Sergey," I said, "what makes you think your name wouldn't be at the top of the disposable list?"

He put the blue uniform aside and said, "I'll be ready in the morning for you to take me to this new coastal hideaway. I'm looking forward to seeing this nude beach!"

19

Khrenkov peered down from his sniper's perch and watched Friday afternoon as a steady stream of police officers came and went outside the Hart's main entrance. Second Street was still closed to traffic. Bright yellow DO NOT CROSS tape was strung everywhere. The bodies of the eight dead gang members had lain for several hours where they had fallen before they were hauled away by the medical examiner. Television crews swarmed around. Reporters broadcast live from the scene that night. At dusk, the cops brought in portable spotlights powered by noisy gasoline generators to illuminate the area.

Khrenkov didn't budge in his black fabric cave. His Russian watchdog, the neanderthal Pankov, telephoned each half hour as promised to check on him. Every time the cell phone vibrated, Khrenkov hoped it was Igor Fedorov calling from the location where Olga was being held, hoped that the FBI had followed Fedorov to that hiding spot, hoped that his sister would be saved from harm and his family freed.

But each time it was Pankov's dull voice on the telephone line. Khrenkov hated Pankov a little more with each call.

"When you speak to your master," Khrenkov told Pankov at eleven p.m., "remind him that I am still waiting to talk to my sister."

At eleven thirty, Khrenkov badgered Pankov once again. At midnight, too. Then at twelve thirty. Finally, at one o'clock, Pankov said, "Fedorov says he will arrange the call for you Saturday morning. He's still busy with his dates."

Khrenkov pictured the scene in his head. FBI agents had spotted Fedorov as he ate in a Little Italy bistro. They had followed him and two prostitutes to a seedy hotel and waited, all that time wondering why they were bothering.

Khrenkov pushed the thoughts from his head. Thinking about Olga was not helpful. He needed to concentrate. He looked down at two police officers stationed outside the Hart's entrance at the shooting scene. He couldn't imagine them trying to smuggle Sergey Pudin out that same door again. Khrenkov inspected C Street. The Hart, Dirksen, and Russell buildings had six exits onto the street. No matter how many times he reviewed the different doorways, he always reached the same conclusion: Pudin would be hustled out the exit at the intersection of First and C—the same exit that Khrenkov suspected had been used to sneak him into the building.

He needed to calibrate his weapon's Russian PSO scope. He'd been pleased when he'd first examined the Dragunov that Fedorov had given him. It was a military-issued SVD, not the cheaper version manufactured in China or the Tiger model imported for a brief time through a California company. But he wasn't as thrilled when he inspected the three bullets that Pankov had given him. They were standard 7N1 rounds, which were the gun's original loads and were first designed in the 1950s. The 7N1 was a steel-jacketed projectile with an air pocket behind it, a steel core, and a lead knocker in its base. This arrangement gave it more destructive power. After the tip of the round penetrated its target, the steel core would shift forward into the hollow area, much like a crash-test dummy being thrown forward in an accident demonstration. This shifting of the round's center of gravity would cause the bullet to tumble, creating a larger wound channel and exit hole. Still, Khrenkov would've preferred a newer cartridge, the 7N14, which traveled at the same speed of 2,723 feet per second but had a lead-core projectile and was more accurate.

Khrenkov had rubbed each round with four-aught steel wool, a precaution to remove any corrosion that might make them stick in the chamber when they were fired. The Dragunov had a ten-round magazine, but that hardly mattered, since he had only three bullets. He decided to shoot one as a test. He had to make certain the rifle worked properly, and he needed to know the accuracy of its scope.

Shortly after three a.m., Khrenkov chose his target: a cardboard sign nailed to an oak tree in a park near the intersection of First and C. The area was well lit because of street lamps and bright spotlights that illuminated the grand facades of the three Senate buildings. The message tacked to the tree was a cartoon—Uncle Sam standing on suffering women and children trapped under his jackboots. Demonstrators put it about twelve feet above the sidewalk, which explained why it hadn't been taken down by the park's maintenance crews.

The Dragunov's barrel was equipped with a flash suppressor to help hide the shooter's location. But there wasn't a silencer. Khrenkov wasn't concerned. The report would actually be two distinct sounds when the rifle was fired. The initial bang, the muzzle blast, would be masked by the noisy generators on the street below. The second sound would be the sonic crack that a bullet makes as it flies through the air. Much like a Concorde jet, the slug would actually create a sonic wave as it sped forward. Fortunately, the sound of this sonic wave would radiate backward, like water at the bow of a speeding boat. This meant the reverberations would strike the ear at an angle ninety degrees off the firing point. Anyone hearing the crack would look forward, in the direction of the bullet, not back to where the shot had originated. It was unlikely that they would be able to tell from the sound where he was hiding.

The first step in "doping" his scope was computing the distance between his location and the target. In Hollywood movies, snipers simply align a scope's crosshairs on their victim. But it's really not that simple. To begin with, the PSO scope on the Dragunov didn't have crosshairs. Rather, it featured a thin red T. The top bar of the T ran horizontally across the center of the viewfinder. The vertical bar dropped down the center. On the left side of the T was a rangefinder marked off in meters. It was this scale that Khrenkov used to estimate the distance of his rifle from the "killing zone." His cardboard target was not that far away—only 250 meters, or about 274 yards. When he was in the army, he would be expected to place five sequentially fired rounds within a 1.5-to-2.5-inch circle at this close range. However, there was a slope in the terrain that meant Khrenkov would be aiming at a steep downhill angle.

He remembered most of the statistics for the 7N1 round from the ballistics table that he'd been issued during the war. The chart provided a shooter with a trajectory guide about different bullets based on each's characteristics: such as its caliber, weight, velocity, and so on. In particular, a sniper needs to understand these dynamics because no slug flies in a straight line. Rather, it travels in an arc that usually rises several inches from the muzzle of the weapon, peaks out, and then drops down until it hits the ground. After mentally reviewing this information, Khrenkov peered through his lens. He squinted at a series of chevrons—arrowhead-shaped red marks—that made up a piece of the vertical T. These chevrons helped him to compute how much the slug was likely to drop while flying toward a target. Finally, he factored in the biggest variable of all—the wind. He had to estimate how the force of any wind and its direction might push the fatal projectile off course. Because the night was dead calm, which in sailors' and snipers' parlance means there were "no-value winds," Khrenkov did not have to worry about his test shot.

Normally, a sniper would fire three to five rounds to zero in his scope. But because he had only one bullet to test, he would have to estimate any rifle adjustments after he saw the results of that single shot.

Before firing, Khrenkov used the gun's four-power magnification to get a closer look at the guards at the First and C intersection. The U.S. military used much more powerful lenses, but the Russians preferred scopes that only enlarged everything by a multiple of four because that gave their shooters a wider field of view. As usual, there were two uniformed officers on duty in the booth. One was watching a combination TV/VCR, which had a movie playing on it. The other was flipping through pages in a magazine. Both were wearing earphones—one attached to the television, the other to a CD player.

Excellent! Khrenkov thought.

He'd brought a one-pound bag of sugar with him to steady his weapon. It was under the rifle's foregrip. He grasped it firmly with his left hand and compressed the contents to bring the muzzle higher. At this short distance, Khrenkov really didn't need the prop, but he didn't want to be holding the rifle for long periods and he knew that he might have only nanoseconds to fire off a good shot. The improvised device would help reduce fatigue. Lying prone, he used the scope to take aim at the Uncle Sam poster and gently squeezed the Dragunov's trigger. The round exploded and because the rifle's stock didn't have a protective cheek piece, its butt smacked against his shoulder. To Khrenkov, the shot sounded thunderous under his fabric tent. As soon as he fired, he pointed the scope toward the guardhouse to see if the officers there had heard it. Apparently neither had. Both were still preoccupied with their entertainment.

Khrenkov next checked the two men standing watch on the street beneath his "hide site." Neither of them had heard the shot. It hadn't even caused any dogs in the neighborhood to bark.

Perhaps, he thought, *the animals here are used to hearing gunshots at night!*

Satisfied that no one had detected him, he used the scope to examine the cardboard sign. The slug had struck Uncle Sam's chest about an inch lower than where Khrenkov had aimed. He adjusted the lens accordingly.

Now he was ready.

I was still angry Saturday morning about Friday's gangland shoot-out. It had been unnecessary, especially since I'd suggested a safe way to extract Sergey Pudin from his makeshift site with minimal risk.

My plan involved running a scam on the defense attorneys who were defending Ivan Sitov. I like abusing attorneys and do it every chance I have. They had demanded an opportunity to take a pretrial deposition from Pudin. But that request was a ruse. What they had really hoped to do was flush him out of hiding so Sitov could kill him when he surfaced for the grilling. The attorneys' demand was so transparent that even the federal judge hearing the case saw right through it. He ruled we didn't have to produce Pudin for a deposition. I suggested that we tell the defense lawyers that we were now willing to have him come to their offices in Manhattan for the questioning. All they had to do was tell us the date.

I believed such an offer would have caused Sitov and his hired guns to change their attack plan. Sitov would've called off the O Street Crew and focused on assassinating Pudin in New York—his home turf. On the day when Pudin was supposed to report in Brooklyn, I would've slipped him from the Senate basement hideout. We could've gotten out of Washington, D.C., without anyone noticing. Then the U.S. attorney in

New York could've called the defense attorneys and told them that we'd changed our minds about producing Pudin for the questioning.

Like I said. Safe. Simple.

But the director of the U.S. Marshals Service had overruled me. It was his idea to use a decoy on Friday. He'd put my officers at risk, not to mention the public. Of course, none of that mattered now. The director and his cronies were giving each other high fives and celebrating after Friday's shoot-out. Because no officers had been killed, they considered the massacre a big success. After all, it had gotten them on the evening news.

The director was so confident that Pudin was no longer in any danger that he thought my idea of dressing Pudin as a letter carrier was unnecessary. They even ignored my request for a customized Kevlar vest. Because of Pudin's girth, the Marshals Service would have had to have one specially tailored, and the director didn't want to incur that extra expense. But I wasn't so sure the threat had passed.

To make Pudin's disguise as realistic as possible, I commandeered a United States Postal Service truck to drive Saturday morning. As I pulled the mail truck up to the curb at the intersection of First and C Streets, I suddenly had an eerie feeling.

I felt someone was watching.

21

From habit, Khrenkov checked his wristwatch when he spotted a mail truck at the First and C intersection on Saturday. It was 9:50 a.m. He knew the bells in the top of the Robert A. Taft monument chimed at ten o'clock and he recalled that he had seen the mail collector stop at the bright blue box on the sidewalk once before when he'd first scouted Capitol Hill.

So it struck him as peculiar when the letter carrier, whom he was now watching, marched right by the box without stopping to take its contents. Instead, the mailman went straight into the Dirksen Building.

Khrenkov's cell phone vibrated.

"*Da,*" he whispered, answering it.

"As you wished, I will visit your sister this morning," Igor Fedorov announced.

"How long before I can speak to her?"

"Maybe a few minutes, maybe an hour, maybe two hours. I'm a busy man. You'll know when I call you."

He hung up.

Khrenkov punched in the FBI's telephone number in New York. He used the one that connected him directly to Special Agent Bunker.

"Are you watching Fedorov?" Khrenkov asked.

"We've got people on him. He's in Brooklyn eating breakfast. Can you get him to lead us to the girl?"

"Yes, soon. But you must stay with him!"

As Khrenkov was speaking, he noticed another postal van arrive at the curb at the First and C intersection. Its driver walked over to the letter collection box and began emptying its contents.

Khrenkov asked Agent Bunker, "What about the Polov family? Are you prepared to save them, too?"

"Yes, but we're waiting to hear from you before we send in the Hostage Rescue Team."

"Good, I must go."

"Hold on!" Bunker exclaimed. "I'm sticking my neck out big time here and—"

Khrenkov clicked off the cell phone while Bunker was in midsentence. He checked his watch again. It was now five minutes past ten. The first mailman had been inside the Senate building for fifteen minutes. As Khrenkov watched, the second mailman finished collecting mail from the blue box, returned to his truck, and drove away.

Why are there two different mail carriers at the same place today?

At this exact moment, two men wearing U.S. Postal Service uniforms walked out of the Senate building. They were heading to the mail truck still parked at the curb. One of them was the letter carrier whom Khrenkov had seen arrive at 9:50. But he'd never seen the second man before.

In a series of split seconds, Khrenkov reviewed the scene being played out. The "unknown" mail carrier weighed at least four hundred pounds. *That was the same girth as Sergey Pudin.* Neither man had any packages. They weren't carrying letter pouches either. *Why had the first mailman gone inside the building empty-handed? If he wasn't delivering mail, then what was his purpose? What was he bringing back with him?*

Khrenkov noticed another eccentricity. A thin man in a business suit was standing at the corner only a few feet from the two mailmen. The traffic light had changed colors, and though everyone else at the corner had started across the street, this man did not budge. Instead, his head was turned to the left to watch the two mailman moving toward the parked truck.

Khrenkov knew. He aimed the Dragunov.

22

Sergey Pudin hadn't been ready to leave when I first arrived just before ten o'clock even though I'd told him that I was coming for him then.

"I've got a plane waiting," I explained.

"Fuck you!" he snapped.

I lost my temper. "No, fuck you! You can sit here for another week until we're confident no one is waiting outside to shoot your fat ass! I'm leaving."

He'd scrambled to get himself together, and within moments we headed upstairs. I peered out the glass exit doors and noticed a mail truck pulling away. Jeez, that bothered me. I hadn't checked to see when the regular Saturday driver would be picking up the letters from the blue box. It was a mistake, but I didn't think it was that big a one.

As I opened the door for Pudin, he asked, "Exactly where is this nude beach?"

I stepped with him into the sunlight and replied, "Puerto Rico."

We were about two steps from the mail truck and I was jealously picturing Pudin lounging next to a swimming pool this afternoon in the Caribbean when I felt something warm slap against my cheek. Next, I heard the sound of a gunshot. Spinning, I watched helplessly as Pudin collapsed. Nearly all of the left side of his face was missing. Those warm spurts that I'd felt were his blood.

I leaped on top of him to shield him from a second hit and screamed to Doug Chandler, a deputy pretending to be a pedestrian, still at the crosswalk. He bolted toward us. Another deputy burst out of the Senate building where he had been watching us. While they glanced around for a sniper, I checked Pudin's vital signs. He was dead.

"Shit!" I yelled.

"Look!" Chandler screamed, pointing to his right.

Another body was slumped on the sidewalk across the street.

I dashed there, shouting as I ran to the two Capitol Hill Police officers sitting inside the guard booth. Everything was unfolding so fast that I wasn't certain they realized Pudin had been shot. I grabbed my cell phone and called the four-deputy escort team that was cruising the area in two unmarked cars waiting to follow the mail truck to the airfield.

"Witness down!" I exclaimed. "Get an ambulance!"

The second man lying on the sidewalk had a bullet hole in his chest. He, too, was dead. I opened his dark blue sports jacket and fished out his wallet. His New York driver's license identified him as Petr Pankov. There was a .45 semiautomatic tucked in his waistband. He didn't look like a cop. *Russian Mafia,* I figured. *But if Pankov had been sent to assassinate our witness, then why was he now stretched out lifeless on the sidewalk? The sniper had hit them both. It didn't make sense!*

"The church tower," Chandler yelled. "The shots came from there!"

We both looked up C Street at Saint Joseph's Church. Only yesterday, the Secret Service had posted one of its own sharpshooters there. I started running toward it.

Khrenkov's first shot had pierced the obese mail carrier's skull slightly above his right ear at a downward angle and exited between his left cheek and lower front teeth. He'd died instantly. Khrenkov's second effort had struck the thug Pankov directly in his chest, literally exploding his heart. He'd been loitering across the intersection—ironically, near the tree that had the Uncle Sam cardboard poster nailed to it. He'd been speaking into his cell phone when Khrenkov fired.

Khrenkov had seen both men collapse. Then he rolled out from under his makeshift tarp and called the FBI on his cell phone.

"Go now!" he ordered Agent Bunker. "Save the family! Get the girl!"

"But Fedorov is still eating breakfast!" a flustered Bunker replied. "We don't know where *she* is!"

"Save the family then! Now!" Khrenkov disconnected the call and hurried across the flat roof. He dropped to the air conditioner on the row house next door. His cell phone vibrated. He answered as he was running across the roofs. It was Igor Fedorov.

"I can't reach Pankov!" Fedorov announced. "What's happened to him?"

"How do I know? I just shot Sergey Pudin. The police were taking him out of the Senate building. I don't know anything about your damned Pankov."

Fedorov asked, "Is Pudin dead?"

"Turn my family loose! Release my sister!"

"How can I be certain Pudin is really dead?"

"Call a newspaper! Turn on the television! I don't care. Just free Olga and my family—as you promised!"

"We'll see." The phone went dead.

Khrenkov didn't have time to argue. He'd already ditched his rifle by leaving it under the fabric. He dropped down the vine-covered trellis. As part of his escape plan, Khrenkov removed his jacket, which he tossed into a garbage can. Now he was wearing a black shirt and white cleric's collar—the uniform of a Roman Catholic priest. He'd bought them yesterday at a costume shop. He stopped in the alley long enough to retrieve a Bible that he'd hidden behind the garbage can. His "camouflage" now complete, he walked calmly from the Justice Court cutout onto the C Street sidewalk.

A few hundred yards away from him, a swarm of Capitol Hill Police had descended on Saint Joseph's Catholic Church. Rather than walking in the opposite direction, Khrenkov headed directly for them.

"Is there a problem?" he asked the first cop he encountered.

"Father, you need to get out of here! There's been a shooting. They think the sniper is still in the church tower."

"Oh, how terrible!" Khrenkov declared. "Is there some way I can help? Does anyone need last rites?"

"Two men have been shot, but they're both dead."

"This is horrible, especially after what happened yesterday."

The entire block was now teeming with police. The nearby Capitol Police headquarters had emptied itself.

"I'll pray for the poor men's souls," Khrenkov said. He turned and strolled away from the church. Within five minutes, he entered Union Station, the historic depot that serves the capital. He walked briskly across its shiny marble lobby, going directly to an Amtrak ticket counter.

"One-way to the Baltimore-Washington Airport," he said, sliding a hundred-dollar bill across the counter.

"There's an express train that leaves at eleven o'clock on track 7B," the clerk replied. "That good enough, Father?"

"How long is the ride?"

"It takes twenty minutes."

Khrenkov took his passenger ticket and started toward the boarding gates. Along the way, he ducked into a men's restroom, where he entered a toilet stall and removed the priest's collar and shirt. Underneath, he had been wearing a maroon, collarless, NFL T-shirt with a gold Washington Redskins logo stenciled on it. He wadded the collar and black shirt into a ball and jammed them in a trash can as he left the lavatory. He dropped the cell phone in another trash receptacle close to the departure gate. By the time he reached track 7B, the train was half-filled. He found a seat next to a teenager wearing stereo headphones.

No one paid any attention to him during the ride. When he reached the B.W.I. airport, he checked the flight departure board. There were no direct flights to Moscow and Aeroflot didn't operate out of Baltimore. He bought a seat on a Delta flight that left at three o'clock for John F. Kennedy Airport, where he could connect to another Delta flight to Russia.

The flight to JFK was uneventful. After it landed, he found a pub, where he bought a hamburger and waited. Just before his ten p.m. flight to Moscow was boarding, Khrenkov used a pay phone to call FBI agent Bunker.

"Did you save the girl?" he asked.

"We got the Polov family out okay," Bunker replied. "The two men guarding them were both killed. But the father, mother, and boys are safe."

"What about Olga Polov? Did you find her in time?"

Bunker hesitated. "Igor Fedorov never led us to where she was being held hostage. He stayed in the Brooklyn restaurant where we were watching him. After our Hostage Rescue Team saved the Polov family, we were able to locate the girl based on the telephone traffic between the men holding the family in their home and those holding her hostage."

"Is she okay?" he asked, although he suspected he already knew the answer.

"Listen," Bunker said, ignoring the question. "You clearly care about these people. Who are you? We need your testimony to arrest Igor Fedorov. Otherwise, we can't link him to the kidnapping."

"Tell me about Olga Polov!"

"She's dead," Bunker said sadly. "I'm sorry."

"How?"

"Does it matter?"

"Yes, tell me!"

"They shot her, and it appears, they also raped her first. Now, will you help us get Fedorov? You're the only link we have who can tie him to the kidnappers!"

Khrenkov replaced the telephone receiver and boarded his flight.

PART II

"Sir," the Icelandair flight attendant said, knocking on the door. "You'll have to return to your seat now because we're about to land."

No one replied.

"Sir," she repeated, this time rapping harder. "Is there a problem?"

"No," a voice answered. "But I need another moment."

Inside the Boeing 757 washroom, Movladi "the Viper" Islamov gingerly removed the final layer of a bandage from his abdomen and dropped it into the dark blue water of the toilet. The slug had completely penetrated his abdominal cavity and exited on the other side, but it had gone in at an angle and miraculously had not hit any major blood vessels or his liver, kidney, or spleen. Because the abdominal lining is filled with nerve fibers, the wound was extremely painful. But not fatal. He had endured the past eight hours by eating Dilaudids, an opiate painkiller. Reaching across his waist with his left hand, he grasped a red string and jerked a tampon from the wound. As the bloody wad popped free, a wave of nausea and tremors washed over him.

Don't faint! he told himself.

Soon, the bloody cavity would be sewn shut. Soon, he would be able to rest. *Amiina.* She had promised to meet him at the Baltimore-Washington International Airport. Amiina would be his nurse. In their language, her name meant "faithful," although in her new hometown of Washington, D.C., she had chosen to call herself simply Amy.

His hands were trembling as he tore open the thin paper cover of a fresh tampon. Gritting his teeth, he shoved it into the bullet hole. He gasped for breath and tried to focus on Amiina. Amy. By whatever name: Faithful. Beautiful Amy. Waiting. Waiting to help him.

Islamov placed his palms against the jet's stainless-steel washbasin and took a long, deep breath. After he had regained his composure, he removed a thin roll of gauze from his jacket pocket and once again covered his wound. Totally spent, he rinsed his hands in the sink and splashed water on his unshaven face.

"Sir!"

It was the flight attendant knocking again. "You *must* return to your seat now!"

"Yes, yes," he replied impatiently. He fumbled to button his shirt and slip on his worn jacket. Tossing the rest of his trash into the toilet, he flushed and then glanced once more into the mirror. How very old he looked. Haggard. But what did he expect? Life wasn't meant to be easy. He'd read Camus while studying in college in the United States. "Remembrance of things past is just for the rich. For the poor it only marks the faint traces on the path to death."

His mind wandered back.

He should have known it was a trap in Reykjavik! Why hadn't he walked away from the arms deal? The night before, he'd been suspicious after talking to Rafe. But he'd gone ahead. And now everyone else was dead. Mansur and the others: Tovsultanov, Sultan, Heaidar. It had been Mansur who had assured him that his plan was safe. How stupid they both had been. Hadn't there been numerous warning signs? Alarm bells should've been ringing. He was smarter than this! And yet, he had wanted to secure the bomb. His greed had blinded him.

Islamov replayed in his mind what had happened, as if it were a looped videotape, running over and over again and again, tormenting him.

Rafe had agreed to make the exchange at noon in Reykjavik Harbor and the powerboat that the arms merchant had rented had been anchored right where it was supposed to be. Mansur and Tovsultanov had ridden out in a bay taxi to the boat, where they'd been welcomed aboard by two of Rafe's goons. That's when Rafe had announced that now he was making some last-minute changes in plan.

Islamov's cell phone had rung. It was Mansur. "They are refusing to let us inspect the merchandise in the hull until you tell them where you will be delivering the first payment."

One of the goons had come on the line.

"Listen, you Chechen bastard," he'd declared, "Rafe says you ain't getting to look at anything until he knows you've got the bonds. Here's how this is going to work. You tell me where you're going to meet Rafe, and once he sees the payment, then your two associates here get to see the merchandise."

He'd realized that sending Mansur and Tovsultanov to the boat was risky. Now they were Rafe's hostages.

"Hafnarhus," he'd said.

It was the newest of the city's three art museums and located next to the harbor. He and Sultan had watched their two compatriots from the second-floor window of the museum's cafeteria as the water taxi delivered them to Rafe's powerboat in the harbor.

"Tell Rafe to meet me in the outdoor courtyard. It is enclosed by the museum."

"How will he know who you are?"

"I'll be carrying a black briefcase with his bonds. Look for two of us."

Islamov had chosen the courtyard because it was crowded and a public place. He didn't believe Rafe would risk a scene. In addition, there were metal detectors at the museum's entrance and guards. Now inside the museum, neither Islamov nor Sultan was armed. But Heaidar was stationed outside with their rental car, and he was carrying a semiautomatic pistol. The remainder of their guns were locked in the trunk.

It had been Sultan's idea to switch roles. As the two of them were walking toward the courtyard, Sultan had said, "You're too valuable to our cause to take this unnecessary risk." Islamov had reluctantly agreed and traded places outside with Heaidar. Sultan had taken control of the briefcase filled with counterfeit bonds.

Moments later, Islamov had spotted the Russians. He'd recognized them as soon as they leaped from two black sedans that had roared up to the museum. SVR. He was certain of it. They'd run toward the front entrance and immediately started conferring with the museum's security guards. Acting quickly, Islamov had telephoned Sultan.

"Get out! It's a trap! Drop the briefcase!"

And then Islamov had taken out his forty-caliber semiauto-matic pistol and begun firing at the black-suited men still talking to the museum guards. As he had expected, his gunshots had sparked a panic. He was trying to divert attention from Sultan and Heaidar so they could flee.

Caught completely unprepared by Islamov's gunfire, the Russians and museum guards had scrambled for cover, but not before two of them had fallen dead. As Islamov continued firing, Sultan and Heaidar bolted through an exit, but rather than dis-appearing into the fleeing crowd of terrified museum visitors, they'd dashed toward Islamov and the rented car. Both had been cut down in a volley of fire despite a last-ditch effort by Islamov to save them. He'd sped up onto the curb in the car. That's when one of the Russian's rounds had penetrated the car door and hit Islamov's side. Still, he managed to race away from the Haf-narhus. He'd abandoned the car two blocks later and ducked into a large store for cover. He'd attempted to telephone Mansur and Tovsultanov, who were still on Rafe's powerboat, but an un-familiar voice had answered Mansur's cell phone.

It was over, and it had been a huge disaster. He would later hear on a news report that he had been the only survivor. The Russians onboard the powerboat had executed Mansur and Tov-sultanov.

Islamov silently cursed himself for being so stupid. He felt responsi-ble, and he was. Mansur, Tovsultanov, Sultan, Heaidar had depended on him. He'd failed them.

He refocused and found himself still staring at his worn face in the lavatory mirror. It seemed like a stranger's. But his appearance no longer mattered. He'd already lived longer than he'd expected.

His mind took him back now even farther into his past, back to when he had been in college in America. He'd been a believer then, an opti-mist who had wrongly trusted in the inherent goodness of humankind. He'd thought reasonable men could resolve their differences in a civi-lized way without bloodshed. How wrong he had been! In the world of realpolitik, Machiavellians ruled.

When had he become disillusioned?

His fate had been sealed August 10, 1994—*had it really been that long ago?*—when the clan chieftains, village elders, and Muslim religious leaders had met in Grozny and voted to declare *gazavat*—a holy war—against Russia if then-president Boris Yeltsin invaded Chechnya. Fifteen days later, forty helicopters with Russian insignia attacked the airport there. The war had begun, and Islamov had killed a human being—his first. He still could recall the soldier's face. A cliché, but true nonetheless. The others since then had become a blur.

So many deaths, so many battles. He'd read on the Internet about the "shock and awe" campaign the United States had launched against Iraq when the U.S. decided to overthrow Saddam Hussein. A thousand bombs and missiles had been dispatched into Baghdad in a single twenty-four-hour period. Islamov had laughed when he first read that news account. In February 1995, during the most fierce battle for control of Grozny, the Russians had bombed and shelled the city at a rate of four thousand bombs and missiles *per hour!*

These had not been smart bombs like those fired by the U.S. military—bombs that were precisely aimed to destroy only military targets. Russia's own commissioner for human rights, who had led a five-person observation group to Chechnya to monitor the fighting, later wrote: "Every day we see planes dropping bombs on residential areas with complete impunity. Every day we see the bodies of civilians torn apart by these bombs, some without heads, others without legs. Many places in the city of Grozny resemble the section of Stalingrad left unrepaired in order to serve as a war memorial . . ."

Islamov's parents, his three brothers, two sisters, four uncles, and five cousins had been killed during the war. When everyone you love is murdered, then what is the point of life except to fight? Hatred fueled him. Revenge was his mantra.

It was during the first year of the war that he'd become known as the Viper. That December, Russian troops had launched a massive campaign to seize the President's Palace in Grozny. Back in those early days, there was still a Chechen army, and its commanders had cleverly allowed the Russians to advance through the city facing only minor resistance. And then the Chechens blocked all possible avenues of escape. The Russians had been surrounded inside an urban canyon. Snipers had rained bullets on them. Dozens of Russian soldiers were burned to death inside their armored personnel carriers. The enemy had been crushed, and so the Russian generals responded by unleashing their bombs and missiles on Grozny until there were no more tall buildings left standing. Without American-made, handheld Stingers or equivalent Russian antiaircraft weapons, the Chechens were easy targets for helicopter gunships. The fighting for the palace went on for an entire month and was so deadly that both sides finally agreed to a forty-eight-hour cease-fire to permit the exchange of prisoners and the recovery and burial of their dead. It was during this brief interlude that Islamov had slipped into a pocket of the city surrounded by Russian troops. Somehow he was able to bring two dozen women and children through the enemy lines back to safety. He had left their brothers, fathers, and lovers behind to fight. They had chosen to stay even though they knew they'd be killed. It was Islamov's ability at slithering in and out of Russian-controlled areas that had earned him the Viper moniker.

In the beginning, Islamov had been confident of victory. Allah was on their side. Right would triumph over Evil. But for some reason Allah had not responded to their prayers. The Chechen military couldn't stop the endless stream of Russian soldiers who had flowed into their home-land. Nearly all of Islamov's comrades had been hunted down like rabid dogs and executed. As time passed, Islamov underwent a transformation. He was no longer a soldier, no longer a freedom fighter. Now, he was a self-admitted terrorist. And proud of it!

Did he really have a choice? How else can you fight an overwhelming force?

Islamov shoved open the Icelandair's bifold lavatory door and looked unapologetically into the stern face of the flight attendant who'd been hounding him to take his seat. Without either saying a word, he walked down the aisle. As soon as he sat down, he felt the urge to vomit. But he resisted and gulped down two more Dilaudids without water. Soon his mind would feel dull.

Nearly there now, he told himself. *Amiina will be waiting. She'll sew my wound closed. She'll hide me until I can think straight, until I can formulate a new plan.*

The firefight outside the Reykjavik museum again popped into his mind. He watched it as if he were standing to one side, a casual observer, seeing himself firing at the Russians. Wait! Back up the reel! He'd missed something earlier that he now was seeing. When the carloads of Russians had arrived outside the museum, another sedan had been following them. Only none of its riders had gotten out at the museum. Islamov forced himself to remember, to isolate the scene. *Think, think! Remember!* There had been three men sitting in the car watching the Russians. They had neither moved to help nor to stop them. They'd simply observed.

Americans! He felt certain of it.

He again thought about Mansur, Tovsultanov, Sultan, Heaidar. They had been his close friends. Despite the narcotic-induced stupor into which he was now falling, he was coherent enough to understand that the Russians in Reykjavik had not acted alone. The Americans had been ad-vising them. No other country had the Big Brother capabilities to inter-cept telephone communications as effectively as the United States. Its CIA must have tipped off the Russian SVR.

Islamov smiled.

It was good that he was landing in the United States. Its CIA had chosen to enter his war now, and he would teach the Americans that they had made a fatal mistake. He would reduce one of their greatest cities to ashes and teach them not to interfere.

Dala atto boila vain! Allahu akbar!

25

"In the entire history of the U.S. Marshals Service, we've never lost a protected witness!" William Jackson boomed. "Never!" He was furious. "Sergey Pudin was *your* responsibility. *You* were opposed to hiding him in a federal prison. *You* insisted on personally calling the shots! Now, the son of a bitch is on a slab in the morgue."

I started to defend myself, but Jackson raised his hand to stop me before I had a chance to speak.

"I've been fighting all morning to save your sorry ass," he explained. "You've got any idea how many people you've pissed off over the years? And now you have the gall to march in here and tell me you don't want to go to the Counterterrorism Center?" He jabbed his finger at me. "Hey, bucko, here're your two options: CTC or pack your bags and turn in your badge!"

He stopped. I waited a second to make certain he was done. When he didn't speak, I started to respond, but as soon as I opened my mouth, Jackson started up again. "Even if you weren't in deep shit, which you are, you know damn well that the U.S. Marshals Service doesn't investigate murders. Finding Pudin's killer is the FBI's problem now. Our job— no, *your* job—was to keep him alive to testify, which *you* failed to do!"

"I'd like to explain—"

"Explain? You don't get to explain a goddamn thing! You lost that right when your witness got his brains splattered all over the sidewalk. Have you seen the New York newspapers this morning?"

I'd been too busy being questioned by the FBI to read any news account of Pudin's assassination. Jackson held up the front page of the tabloid *New York Post*.

STOOLIE SHOT!
Russian Godfather Freed After Star Witness Gunned Down!

"All criminal charges against Ivan Sitov have been dismissed," Jackson said. "Without Sergey Pudin, the government's got no case! The U.S. attorney is furious! He wants you fired!"

"I want to help catch Pudin's killer."

"The hell you say! Well, I got news for you. You aren't going to get involved. This is an FBI investigation now! Is that clear? You're going to report to the CTC. Period. Either that or I'm sending you to Minot."

One of the lesser known tasks of the Marshals Service is safeguarding nuclear missiles while they're being transported across country. Deputies were frequently assigned to the air force base in Minot, North Dakota—our own personal Siberia.

I said, "I thought I only had two choices: the CTC or resign. Now you're saying I can go to Minot?"

Jackson leaped up from behind his desk.

"Goddamn it, Conway, that mouth of yours is your own worst enemy. I'm trying like hell to save your ass and you're making jokes!"

"Bill," I said, "I appreciate what you've done for me. I'll go over to the CIA—just like you've arranged. But will you at least tell me who in our department is assisting the bureau in the murder investigation. Maybe I can help."

"Forget it! You're going to lay low at the CTC, and in a year I'll try to get you transferred back here."

A year!

Fucking up in the government is different from fucking up in the private sector. That's because it's damn near impossible to fire a civil servant. So the suits play a little game with employees they want to get rid of. They "detail" them to another agency. I was being banished to the Counterterrorism Center.

I knew that Jackson really was doing me a favor. So I thanked him and walked out of his office. In the past twenty-four hours, I'd retraced my actions over and over again, searching for mistakes I'd made, signs I should've recognized, precautions I should've taken. How had the sniper known the decoy on Friday wasn't Pudin? How had he figured out which exit we were using? We'd only been exposed for less than a minute while walking from the Dirksen to the mail truck. How had he known that Pudin was posing as a letter carrier?

The sniper had made a fool of me.

My secretary, Marcella Penbrook, was teary when I arrived at what soon would no longer be my office.

"You've been a great boss," she stammered. She made it sound like I had terminal cancer.

"Who's our liaison with the bureau on the Pudin murder?" I asked.

"I knew you'd want to know," she said. "It's Breeden."

"Thanks, now get out of my office," I snapped. She'd worked for me long enough to know that I was only rude to her when I wanted to show her affection. I'm not one of those touchy-feely guys who can share his feelings with the opposite sex or his buddies in a nice way.

I rang up Deputy Scott Breeden. I knew him from a training class I'd taught a few years back. We'd never been buddies, but a lot of these younger guys look up to me. Or at least I thought they did.

"Breeden," he said, answering his phone.

"I hear you've been assigned the Pudin case," I said.

He didn't answer, which meant he was either in awe because I had called him or he was trying to decide if he really wanted to talk to the Marshals Service's newest in-house leper.

"Jackson warned me that you'd call," he finally said. "And he told me *not* to tell you anything."

"So much for esprit de corps!" I replied good-naturedly. "Look, if one of your witnesses was bushwhacked, wouldn't you want to help find the killer?"

"None of my witnesses has been."

Ouch! So much for me being a mentor.

"Breeden," I said sternly, "the reason why Jackson told you *not* to talk to me is because that's exactly what he wants you to do." I wasn't completely certain where I was going with this reverse logic, but I tried to sound convincing. "Jackson is just covering his ass and now he expects you to cover your ass by officially telling me 'no comment.' Then you and I are supposed to have an off-the-record chat, and during it, you're supposed to tell me everything you know about the case because we're all on the same team here. Trust me, that's what Jackson wants. You've just got to read between the lines."

There was another long pause as Breeden pondered what I'd just said. I wondered if he was reviewing old cop movies in his mind, trying to decide if what I was telling him was accurate according to the teachings of Starsky and Hutch. I've always suspected that most of these younger guys got their ethical training by watching television reruns.

"*Anything* I say will be completely off the record?" Breeden asked. "You'll deny I ever told you anything?"

I couldn't believe he was falling for this. "That's right! It will be as if we never talked. Mum's the word! Now, what can you tell me?"

Once again Breeden took a deep breath and then he said, "The FBI crime lab dug a pair of unusual slugs out of both Pudin and that other dead Russian—the one on the sidewalk—Pankov. The slugs are Russian military—7N1 rounds—the type used by snipers."

"Any of Ivan Sitov's crew ever serve in the military as a Russian sniper?"

"As far as we know, none has any military training."

He paused and I was afraid he was having second thoughts about telling me anything more. Then he said quietly, "The FBI is pursuing a different theory."

"Really, what's that?"

"A New York special agent got a series of anonymous telephone tips just before your witness was shot. The caller told 'em a Russian family named Polov was being held hostage by Ivan Sitov's crew."

"So what's the connection?"

"Sitov's thugs were holding the father, mother, and two sons in the family's house in Brooklyn. They had the daughter stashed in a different location. The caller knew all about the kidnapping—so he had to be an insider—but he didn't want any of the hostages harmed."

"A wise guy with a conscience?"

"No, the bureau doesn't think the caller was part of Sitov's crew. In the past, the Russian Mafia has kidnapped Russians in Brighton Beach and then made them contact their relatives in the old country. Rather than extorting ransom money, they forced them to come to the United States and commit murders."

"Contract killings?"

"Yeah. The relatives can't go to the cops, and the cases are nearly impossible to solve because there's no direct link between the killer and his victim. If the cops do figure it all out, they still have to track down the shooter in Russia and try to get him extradited. Good luck with that."

"There's just one problem with your theory," I said. "The sniper who killed Pudin was not just someone's Uncle Joe from Russia. That guy was a damn good shot. He'd been trained."

"The FBI has questioned the Polovs to learn if they still have relatives back in Russia," Breeden continued. "Of course, they're claiming they don't have anybody left there."

"They're obviously lying to protect someone?"

"Probably. And the authorities in Moscow are refusing to help."

"Where's the family now?"

"The bureau rescued the parents and brothers, but the Polov girl was killed. The rest of them are currently in our safesite. They're going into the witness protection program. The U.S. attorney wants them to testify about their kidnapping. Wait a second . . ."

I could hear Breeden shuffling several sheets of papers. Returning to the line, he said, "The alleged mastermind behind the families' abduction is Igor Aleksandrovich Fedorov—one of Ivan Sitov's capos."

Pudin, Sitov, Pankov, Polov, and now Fedorov—all these Russian names were beginning to jumble together in my head. Detective work was simpler when the suspects were named Smith or Jones or after dead presidents.

"Look," I said, "if this Polov family is covering up for a relative, then threaten to throw their asses out of the protection program. That should get them talking."

"No can do. The D.A. wants to use them to get this Fedorov character. Besides, maybe they're telling the truth. Maybe their abduction and the murder of your witness is a coincidence."

I don't believe in coincidences. "How about physical evidence?" I asked.

"The sniper didn't leave any fingerprints, but the lab boys recovered trace evidence on a jacket—a couple hairs."

"That's enough for a DNA sample."

"Not much good if the killer is hiding in Moscow."

"Did the bureau check airline manifests?"

"There were no passengers named Polov."

"Do me a favor," I said. "Get me a computer printout that lists the names of all passengers traveling with Russian passports who departed from the East Coast on the Saturday when Pudin was murdered."

"Ah, we're just having a friendly chat here, remember?"

"Just do it, okay? Now, you said the Polovs are at the safesite, right?"

"Hold it, I'll get you the list, but I'm not helping you get inside the safesite to question the family."

I'd pushed Breeden as much as I could. We ended the call.

About an hour later, I drove my car up to a metal speaker under a remote-controlled camera at the front gate of the CIA's main entrance.

"Wyatt Conway, federal Marshals Service," I said when asked to identify myself.

"What's the purpose of your visit?" a voice asked.

"I'm being banished," I said, but the person apparently didn't understand my wry humor. I explained, "I'm here to see a Ms. Kimberly Lodge at the Counterterrorism Center. She's expecting me."

In Washington, D.C.'s politically sensitive and correct world, you can't question the wisdom of assigning women and men to work together as cops. I know plenty of women who are smart and tough enough to carry a badge. Just the same, putting me with one as my partner is stupid. It's not that I'm a male chauvinistic pig. The problem is that men from my generation were never raised to be "just friends" with women, especially attractive ones. Unless it's my mother or some other next-of-kin, if you team me with the opposite sex, at some point I'm probably going to try to bed her. Who am I kidding? There's no probably about it. Ever see *When Harry Met Sally?*

I'll admit my attitude is behind the times, but the truth is, deep down, I don't believe I'm much different from any other red-blooded American law-enforcement officer. Unless he's gay or happily married, every male cop I know will try to make it with his female partner. I'm not gay. And I'm no longer married.

I was thinking about this when I first saw Kimberly Lodge. She struck me as being self-confident, professional. And yet, I sensed an undercurrent of raw sensuality. I don't find women who pretend to be helpless or who flaunt their sexuality very appealing. I had both the first time around during my marriage, and I soon discovered my bride was an extremely manipulative bitch.

Kimberly Lodge was straightforward. A what-you-see-is-what-you-get kind of girl. I was intrigued. The fact that she was pleasant to look at helped. She had caramel-colored skin and a knockout figure. For the first time since I'd been banished to the Counterterrorism Center, I felt a spark of interest. Or maybe it was just the rush of blood from my brain into a lower part of my anatomy.

We shook hands in the lobby of the CIA's main building.

"Call me Kimberly. We like to use only our first names here for security reasons."

"I'm Wyatt," I replied, wondering how many of our nation's enemies were so inept that they couldn't discover a person's full name.

"A federal marshal named Wyatt. Let me guess, after Wyatt Earp?"

"Yes," I replied sheepishly. "My father's idea."

She said, "I'll get you a temporary security pass. It'll take a few days to push all of the paperwork through. Use the temp one until then. Before I show you around the CTC and make introductions, let's get coffee."

I liked how she thought. I also liked how she walked as I followed her through the agency's security turnstile and up a short flight of steps. She led me into an employee cafeteria where she found a table away from everyone else.

"I was on Capitol Hill last Friday during that gang shoot-out," she volunteered. "The newspaper said you were using a decoy. But the actual Russian witness got killed Saturday anyway. Shot, right?"

This was not a subject that I wanted to discuss. But she apparently did. I decided to be polite.

"You were inside the Hart Building when the shootings on Friday occurred?" I asked.

"Actually, my boss and I were at the corner of Constitution and Second Street when that SUV flipped over. It nearly hit us!"

"I'm glad you weren't hurt."

"It's unfortunate you didn't smuggle the real witness out on Friday. Maybe he'd still be alive."

The *Washington Post* had called the melee "the Friday afternoon massacre." Sergey Pudin's murder had been splashed across the front page, too. Somehow, in the retelling, I ended up being portrayed as the deputy marshal responsible for both fiascos. Meanwhile, Senator Parrish Farthington and the director of the Marshals Service had both escaped criticism, even though Farthington was the idiot who had insisted that Pudin come out of hiding and testify, and the director had thought up the deadly decoy idea. Ms. Lodge's comment about how Pudin might still be alive if we'd done things differently irked me. I'd spent most of the weekend justifying my actions to the FBI, and I was not in the mood to chew them over again with her.

"We'll never know, will we?" I said, trying to dismiss the subject.

"May I ask a personal question?" Then, without waiting for me to reply, she continued. "I'm guessing you'd rather be looking for the sniper who murdered your witness than being stuck working here with me at the CTC, isn't that correct?"

"Since we're being frank here," I replied, "that's exactly right. I'd much rather be hunting the killer. Also, the CIA isn't my favorite agency."

"I'd assumed as much, based on the fact that you never bothered to return my telephone calls last week." Now *she* sounded irritated.

"I was a bit preoccupied trying to keep Sergey Pudin alive," I replied.

"Yes, and now he's dead," she said. "Which makes me wonder if I can really depend on you or if we—the CTC team—can depend on you to pull your weight around here?"

Now she was being downright rude. Continuing, she said, "I've read your personnel file, and you're a cowboy—someone who prides himself on not sticking to the rules and not being part of the team. That attitude may work in the Marshals Service, but not at the CTC. Our success depends on complete cooperation. Teamwork. Most of us work either for the FBI or the CIA, two agencies which historically haven't gotten along. It's taken us a lot of hard work to build up our trust in one another. The White House wants to shut down the CTC and put the Homeland Security Department in charge of all terrorism investigations. None of us here wants that."

She leaned forward and whispered: "Everyone knows you're being assigned to us because you fucked up big time. So here's some friendly advice from all of us: Check your cowboy boots at the front door!"

Ms. Lodge apparently didn't believe in sugarcoating.

I took a sip of coffee and thought about how I wanted to respond.

"Having this little heart-to-heart has made me feel real welcome," I said, as sarcastically as I could. "But I'm not much of a coffee drinker." I put down my cup, stood up, and said, "So let's dispense with the social pleasantries and get right to the part where you introduce me around."

I'd only known Ms. Kimberly Lodge for a few minutes, but in that short time she had single-handedly caused me to rethink my attitude about bedding female partners.

Neither of us spoke again until we reached the CTC, where Kimberly took me around to meet other employees with names such as Roger, Evan, Elsie, and a bunch of others. She then led me to a my "cubicle," where a stack of reports and files was waiting.

"I thought you'd like to read these," she explained. "To get up to speed around here."

"I'm not much on reading files," I replied.

She raised an eyebrow and left.

I made a token effort. I glanced through a few of the reports. They were about various terror organizations that I'd never heard of. About an hour later, my new Ice Queen partner reappeared and announced she needed me to join her for a briefing by Todd—the second in charge after Henry Clarke, who still happened to be in the hospital recuperating from his scare at Friday's shoot-out. I recognized Todd Markley as soon as we were introduced. He was an FBI agent and we'd worked together a few years earlier during a mob trial. But Todd either didn't remember me or he didn't want anyone to know we already knew each other because he didn't say anything.

There were six of us in the briefing when Todd began. "The SVR attempted yesterday to apprehend five renowned Chechen terrorists in Reykjavik, Iceland. Four of the terrorists and two SVR operatives were killed. The fifth Chechen terrorist escaped, although he was wounded. Kimberly has been monitoring the cable traffic on this."

Kimberly glanced around the room, looked directly at me, and then said, "Some of you may not be familiar with what we've been doing at the CTC to prevent another 9/11 disaster." Having made it clear with her eyes that I was the newcomer who needed a history lesson, she continued. "One of our primary goals is to help Russia deal with its so-called loose nukes problem. These are poorly protected nuclear weapons that could easily fall into the wrong hands. Before it collapsed, the Soviet Union had more than twenty-seven thousand nuclear weapons and enough plutonium and uranium to build triple that number. Since 1991, our government has spent more than $10 billion helping the Russians protect their remaining nuclear devices."

How odd, I thought. *We're paying the Russians to safeguard nuclear weapons that they might someday use on us.*

Kimberly said, "I'm happy to report that, overall, we've been extremely successful. In the past decade, there have been 175 nuclear smuggling incidents reported and only 18 of them have involved highly enriched uranium. Working closely with foreign intelligence agencies, we've been able to thwart all of these attempted thefts, most of which have been tried in Russia or its former satellite republics."

She paused and once again gave me a superior glance. It was one of those "are-you-keeping-up-with-this" looks—the sort that my high school teachers used to send my way. She said, "Sixteen months ago, we decided to take a proactive step. We launched Operation Beartrap—our nation's first international counterterrorism sting operation. We put out word through sources that we had a hydrogen bomb for sale."

Kimberly paused again, only this time, I suspected it wasn't so that I could catch up. It was so everyone in the briefing would understand the apparent brilliance of the operation.

"To make our trap believable, we baited it with falsified top-secret documents that described an actual event—the 1968 crash of a B-52 bomber just off Thule, Greenland. At the time of this mishap, the U.S. reported that the downed B-52 bomber had been armed with four hydrogen bombs. The U.S. assured the world that all four had been recovered from the ocean. But as part of our ruse we leaked falsified documents to the media so that it now appeared that one of the bombs had never been found. We then had a black marketeer announce that the bomb was for sale to the highest bidder."

Apparently, the CTC had gotten more bids than most items offered on eBay. "We thought we would attract an al-Qaida member. We never imaged the highest bid would come from Chechnya," Kimberly said.

Once again she paused to look at me. She then said, "It was made by Movladi Islamov."

Moe had tried to buy an H-bomb?

It was difficult for me to imagine. When he was one of my students, Moe had been antiviolence.

"As Todd just explained," Kimberly continued, "two of Islamov's cohorts were killed during a gun battle outside the Hafnarhus Museum, and another two were fatally shot while aboard a powerboat in the harbor, where they believed the bomb was being stored. However, Islamov escaped. We've learned through a source that he'll be arriving in the U.S. today."

"How are you handling his arrest?" someone asked.

"As soon as he is positively identified, the FBI will apprehend him and he'll be immediately turned over to the SVR."

"You're turning him over to the Russians after he's landed on U.S. soil?" I asked, interrupting.

"Yes," Kimberly answered. "Does that surprise you? As a deputy marshal, you should know the U.S. has made plenty of arrests in foreign countries. Federal deputies have kidnapped drug dealers in Mexico and Colombia and forcibly returned them to the U.S. for trial."

"And every time we've done that, it's caused an international furor,"

I replied. "Besides, I can't ever remember an incident where the United States has permitted a foreign government to kidnap someone from *our* soil. Why isn't he being arrested by the FBI and then extradited through the proper channels?"

"This has already been decided," she replied coldly.

"By whom? Because I'm new here, I'm not familiar with the chain of command. But if this is a CTC operation, then I want it put on the record that I'm opposed to having the FBI simply turn him over to the SVR."

"Why? Because the two of you are friends?"

"No!" I replied sternly. "Because it's a stupid precedent. The Russians will kill him before he ever lands in Moscow."

"This is no different from what we would expect if one of our allies captured a known war criminal, the likes of Osama Bin Laden," Todd said, intervening. "Moscow is calling the shots here."

"What happened in Iceland?" I asked. "How did Islamov escape?"

"That's still being investigated."

"In other words," I continued, "someone blew it. My guess is the SVR never intended to capture him alive. They came in shooting."

When no one responded, I said, "If you know what flight Moe Islamov is on, then you've obviously got a mole feeding you information."

"This discussion is going outside the necessary parameters," Todd announced. "Thank you, Kimberly, for the briefing. What's important here is that Operation Beartrap has helped identify and capture a terrorist. Kimberly will prepare a background paper for us to release to the appropriate congressional committee. I'm certain it will buttress our position that the CTC is doing excellent work and should not be put under the Office of Homeland Security."

Todd was obviously thinking politics—keeping the CTC operating inside the CIA. He wasn't worried about Moe Islamov. But that's who I was thinking about. It had been a long time since we'd talked. People change, especially during wars. But I was still having a tough time picturing Moe as a terrorist who was capable of detonating a nuclear bomb. Then another thought hit me. Someone close to Moe was an informant. He was about to be betrayed. He was about to enter another trap. Plus, he was wounded. This could get deadly fast, real fast.

Before Movladi Islamov first set foot in Reykjavik, he'd arranged several escape routes just in case something went wrong. After he fled in the rented car from outside the Hafnarhus, he'd contacted a friend, who'd provided him with rudimentary first aid and safe passage to the Keflavik International Airport.

The riskiest part of his escape had come once he'd entered the airport. All travelers at Keflavik are secretly scanned by video cameras. Their images are then relayed to a computer that compares their photographs to mug shots of known terrorists and other criminals. The airport's "biometric face recognition system" is one of the most sophisticated in the world and is not easily fooled by ordinary attempts. That's because it is based on an algorithm that literally transforms human faces into mathematically computerized templates. The Keflavik computers use between twelve and forty different spots on a face to create each person's template. These checkpoints are unique facial characteristics, such as the distance between a person's eyes. They are features that can't be easily changed. The template taken by the video security cameras is then compared to the information in the computer's data system, much as fingerprints are matched.

Islamov knew about the biometric system, but he thought he could fool it. A good template could be made only if the computer had a sharp mug shot in its files. And Islamov hadn't allowed anyone to take his picture in more than fifteen years. Whenever he appeared on television as the Viper, he'd hid his face behind a ski mask. Any pictures of him that had been entered into the computer's data bank had to be of poor quality. Even more important, he'd been badly injured during a mortar attack five years earlier. The explosion had left him so disfigured that he'd been forced to undergo reconstructive surgery in France. His Parisian plastic surgeon, who'd been aware of his patient's actual identity, had used the opportunity to alter Islamov's features.

The only question was: Had the surgeries changed his face enough to fool the machine?

Islamov had spied one of the video cameras as he passed through a security checkpoint. He'd stayed calm. None of the security guards manning the magnetometer had questioned him. Nor had they realized that he was wounded and wearing bandages under his shirt. He'd walked to the departure gate without arousing any suspicion.

He'd beaten the machine!

Still, Islamov hadn't relaxed. Before boarding, he'd telephoned Amiina in Washington, D.C., and asked her to meet him at the Baltimore-Washington International Airport. Although he trusted Amiina, he'd lied to her about his travel plans. His flight from Iceland was not actually bound for Maryland. It was scheduled to land at New York City's J.F.K. Islamov would go through international customs there and then board a domestic flight for the next leg to B.W.I. It was a maneuver that he hoped would help cover his tracks. Amiina did not know what flight he would be arriving on at B.W.I. He'd simply told her that he would arrive around ten o'clock at night and would meet her in the baggage claim area where customers traveling on Delta Airline flights picked-up their checked items. Once again, this was subterfuge. He actually was arriving at B.W.I. three hours earlier on a flight operated by U.S. Air.

There was another bit of deception in his plans. He'd not told Aminna that he'd radically changed his appearance. Over the years, he'd learned that even his closest friends might betray him. It was a fact that he lived with daily. His survival depended on his being suspicious, especially now that he had nearly been captured in Iceland.

Amiina. He wondered what she now looked like. They had grown up together in Grozny. Their parents had been close friends. She was the only woman with whom Islamov had ever made love. It had been at her initiation. They'd planned on marrying, but the war had started and

Amiina's parents had fled to the United States. Being an obedient daughter, she'd gone with them. Amiina and her family were not the only Chechens to flee. As time passed, fighting the Russians seemed futile. In March 2003, voters overwhelmingly approved a new constitution that made their republic a permanent part of Russia. Officially, the war was over. The Kremlin promised amnesty to Chechen rebels who surrendered and to eventually withdraw its eighty thousand troops.

But Islamov and his followers claimed the elections were nothing but a publicity sham. Most of the votes had been cast by Russian soldiers fighting in Chechnya. Two months after the much-ballyhooed elections, Islamov sent his first suicide bomber—a woman whose husband had been killed during the war—to blow herself up during a prayer meeting in the country's second-largest city. She'd managed to get within six feet of the new Chechen president, whom Moscow had installed. Incredibly, the puppet hadn't been injured. Fourteen others were—enough to spark international headlines. Two weeks later, Islamov dispatched another suicide bomber—this one driving a truck filled with explosives. The vehicle rammed through a guard post into a Russian military camp, killing forty-one and injuring two hundred more.

After the election, it was no longer enough to kill Russian soldiers. Islamov needed to shock the world. He needed headlines in the media to keep his revolution alive. This is what had led him to Reykjavik. A nuclear bomb was the ultimate threat, and it would give him the ultimate headline.

Amiina. He thought about her often. In his mind, she had come to symbolize what he was fighting to preserve. She was the human face of this war. She was his past and his future. He'd been excited when they spoke. She'd sounded genuinely happy that he was coming to see her. Of course, she would meet him at the airport. Of course, she would make certain that she wasn't followed there. Of course, she would nurse him back to health.

Islamov arrived in New York City without incident, easily passed through security, and boarded a U.S. Air flight. By the time the aircraft's wheels touched down at B.W.I., the painkillers had buoyed him. The arrival gate was on the airport's second level. A sign directed him downstairs to the baggage claim site on the ground floor. It was already swarming with other newly arrived passengers when he rode down an escalator and began wading cautiously through the crowd, scanning the ceiling for security cameras and mentally noting the number and location of guards and exits. Not wanting to call attention to himself, he returned to the second level and took a seat in a fast-food eatery. An hour later, he merged into a new wave of arriving passengers heading downstairs. This time, Islamov noticed there were six additional uniformed security officers in the luggage collection area. A man in a pinstripe suit was giving them instructions. He had a flesh-colored earpiece tucked into his left ear. Its wire disappeared under his lapel. Islamov quickly returned upstairs to the restaurant.

About fifteen minutes before ten o'clock, Islamov blended into yet another throng of new arrivals. They were from a Minnesota flight. He walked with them downstairs and joined them at a luggage carousel. It was about fifty feet from the one used by Delta flights.

He saw her. Amiina was already waiting in the Delta luggage area. She didn't see him because he was intermingled with the Minnesota crowd. He studied her. She looked as beautiful as when they'd last been together. He controlled his desire to run and embrace her. But he knew, if he had, she wouldn't have recognized him because of his facial surgery. Instead, he surveyed the room. Each exit was now being guarded by two security people, rather than one, as had been done earlier. Two officers were casually walking through the crowds. But their supervisor in the pinstripe suit was nowhere to be seen.

Islamov felt uneasy. He checked the time. It was now ten o'clock. The Minnesota passengers gathered around him began to disperse. For a moment, he considered sliding over to a different, nearby baggage pick-up point. But he was afraid that might look suspicious. Instead, he reached down and grabbed a black carry-on that already had gone past him several times on the revolving belt. A sharp pain shot across his abdomen and nearly caused him to buckle. But he heaved it up anyway.

"Excuse me," a man said, hurrying up behind him. "I think you've got my suitbag."

"Sorry," Islamov replied cheerfully. "It looked like mine. Do you know where I can report a missing suitcase?"

"There's an airline agent down that hall," the stranger said, pointing to a narrow corridor on his right. "The airlines lost mine last week. I filed a claim there."

Islamov thanked him and made his way into the hall, where there was a door marked "Lost and Found." Before he opened it, he looked back at where he'd been standing. All of the bags from the Minnesota flight were gone. If he hadn't gone on this "errand," he would have been the only person remaining and Amiina would have noticed him.

"May I help you?" the woman inside the office asked.

"Oh, I apologize. I'm looking for a men's restroom."

She gave him directions. He went back toward the baggage claim area once again. Had anyone been observing him, they would have assumed that he'd just reported his luggage as being lost.

Amiina was still waiting at the Delta carousel. He ducked into a public toilet and entered a stall. He was still wary, especially about the man in the pinstripe suit. His uncle had been a tailor, and Islamov had worked summers in his shop. He could tell the stranger's clothing had been hand-tailored and expensive.

How could an airport security guard afford such a fine garment? It was more in keeping with an FBI or CIA officer.

Caution and paranoia can be twins.

Islamov remained in the bathroom cubicle about fifteen minutes. As soon as he stepped from it, he returned to the baggage area and melted into yet another newly arriving crowd of passengers. Amiina was still standing at the now-deserted Delta carousel.

Faithful Amiina. Waiting. Waiting for him.

For the first time since he'd landed, he allowed himself to feel some happiness. Still, he did not call out to her. He didn't know why he was uncertain, he just was. *Five more minutes,* he told himself. *Be patient.*

Amiina glanced to her right and then to her left. He followed the direction of her eyes—her beautiful brown eyes—toward a wall of public telephones.

It was him!

The supervisor in the impeccable suit was standing in front of a pay phone, but he hadn't bothered to pick up its receiver. Islamov had overlooked him earlier because the man had his back to the claim area. But now this man's attention was on Amiina, and he returned her glance.

As Islamov watched, Amiina shrugged her shoulders, as if to say *What now?*

The man pointed to his wristwatch and held up five fingers. A signal: *Five more minutes.*

Islamov had been deceived.

He nearly collapsed. Thinking about Amiina was what had been helping him endure the pain. *Why? How could she betray him?* As quickly as those questions popped into his head, he knew the answers. The Amiina whom he'd loved no longer existed. She was a traitor. She'd been corrupted by the United States and its wicked Western ways. Suddenly, it was as if blinders had been torn from his eyes. He should've known. Amiina was wearing provocative denim pants. Her blouse was too revealing. Her face was made up with lipstick. It was not only Amiina whom he now was seeing clearly. Islamov noticed a chauffeur positioned near an exit with a placard with the name "Johnson" written on it. The chauffeur was not watching passengers, he was focusing on Amiina. He had a square head, strong jaw, close-cropped hair. A Russian. Another man was staring at Amiina, too. He was fifteen feet away and wasn't paying any attention to the bags whirling by on the carousel. His shoes gave him away. They had a European cut.

For a moment, he considered confronting her. He would walk directly up to her, slap her face, and call her a traitor. He'd loved her and this is how she had repaid him! But what was the point? She had sold her soul to the devil. If anything, he needed to pray for her. She would suffer in Allah's hands.

He moved nearer the carousel and continued to pretend that he was watching for a suitcase. Still shell-shocked, he watched the man in the pinstripe suit stroll from the pay phones to where Amiina was waiting. Seconds later, the chauffeur joined them, and so did the man with the European shoes. Amiina began to cry. They escorted her out an exit.

Islamov rode the escalator upstairs. He couldn't risk trying to pass through an exit on the ground floor, so he walked the length of the terminal until he found a pedestrian bridge that connected it to the airport's main parking garage.

Amiina. Why? Why?

There was a solitary phone on the fourth level of the garage. He dialed information.

"Dr. Paul Custis," he said when the operator came on the line. "It's a Baltimore number. It could be listed under his business."

"Is he a medical doctor?"

"No, a veterinarian."

A few seconds later, she said, "There are two numbers for a Dr. Paul Custis at the Dogs and Cats Animal Clinic. One is the main number and the other is for emergencies."

"Please connect me to the emergency one."

After several rings, a man answered. "Hello?"

It was a raspy voice, a voice that Islamov still recognized.

"Wheezer," Islamov said, "it's Moe calling!"

"Jesus H. Christ!" Custis exclaimed. "Or should I say, Jesus H. Mohammad?"

"It's been many years since we've talked."

"You've got that right! College. Goddamn, I'd forgotten my old nickname—Wheezer."

"The asthma is gone then?"

"Yes, well, no, not really, but I've not had a serious attack in years. I think it's the exercise program I'm on. I'm still hoarse because I've got messed-up vocal cords. But I'm in much better shape than I was in college."

"Does this mean you've stopped drinking beer?" Islamov asked teasingly.

"Hell no! A man's got to have a few vices. We can't all be a goody-goody Muslim like you, Moe!"

Turning serious, Islamov said, "I'm at the B.W.I. airport. The airline has canceled my flight. I'm stranded. Can you recommend a hotel?"

"Like hell you'll stay in a hotel. I'm only a half hour away."

"I'd appreciate your hospitality. I'm on a tight budget but was afraid to ask. I don't wish to inconvenience you."

"When weren't you on a tight budget?" Custis replied. "Listen, any chance you can change your flight—put it off a few days so we can catch up. Julie and the kids have gone to New Orleans to visit her parents for ten days and I'm leaving first thing in the morning for Chesapeake Bay and my boat. Why don't you come with me?"

"Fishing? Are you certain it wouldn't be a problem?"

"As long as you don't mind living on a boat. I'm gonna be gone ten days, but I could run you back to shore anytime you wanted. You still a devout Muslim?"

"Yes, of course."

"Great, I won't need to buy any extra beer then!"

"If you're certain I will not be intruding on your holiday, I will go change my ticket."

"Fantastic! Hey, it will be just like the old days when we were college roommates."

A half hour later, Custis pulled up at the arrivals gate but he didn't recognize Islamov because of his plastic surgery.

"Jesus, Moe!" Custis exclaimed, after Islamov approached him. "Your face—"

"It's from the war," Islamov said. "But underneath it, it's me—Moe!"

Custis said, "I decided there's no point in us driving back to my place and waiting until tomorrow to drive back this way to the boat. We'll go there tonight. There's plenty of room."

"An excellent idea," Islamov said.

"Yep!" Custis said. "Once we get out into the bay, there will be no ringing phones, no interruptions, no other people. Just the fish and us."

"And your beer!" said Islamov.

"That's right."

"Then it really will be perfect."

Dr. Paul Custis's boat was a thirty-six-foot Grand Banks trawler with twin diesel engines and two staterooms. Although it had been built in 1989, it was in immaculate condition. The teak and stainless steel in its galley gleamed, and it was equipped with cutting-edge radar and communication gizmos.

"I bought it from its original owner and only had to make two improvements," Custis bragged as they cast off. "I installed a cold storage box. When I pack it with ice, I can keep fish a week without having to dock. I also changed its name."

"Isn't changing names unlucky?" Islamov asked.

"Some think so, but *Cats and Dogs* is more fitting than *Gay Waves*! That could've been open to misinterpretation."

The trawler glided effortlessly east through a narrow inlet into Chesapeake Bay.

"Know much about the bay?" Custis asked.

"No!" Islamov replied sharply. His pain medication was wearing off, and he was exhausted.

"A fascinating body of water. It's the largest estuary in the nation, with four thousand four hundred miles of shoreline."

Unaware of his guest's growing discomfort, Custis continued. "At the bay's widest spot—near the mouth of the Potomac River—you can barely see land. It feels as if you're out in the middle of the ocean. Miles from anywhere!"

"How deep is it?" Islamov asked, trying to be polite.

"Not deep at all. The bay's shaped like a serving tray. Most of the water is less than thirty feet but there are troughs that go much deeper."

"I remember sailing with you here before when we were in college," Islamov replied.

"That's right! I'd forgotten."

"You forced me to go with you to a boat show once, too. There were hundreds for sale."

Custis laughed. "Yes, in Annapolis. Now I remember. You did some sailing as a boy, isn't that right?"

"Only on a lake and in a small sailboat, not a powerboat like this. Tell me, is your boat hard to pilot?"

"Naw, it's simple. Here, take the helm while I get another beer."

Islamov took the controls. They were moving southeast, away from the Maryland coastline. The water stretched out before them black, lit only by the moonlight. Raising a beer in toast, Custis declared, "Here's to old friends, a great boat, a tubful of ice-cold beer, and—to steal a line form the movie *Jaws*—'swimming with bowlegged women.'"

Islamov thought about Amiina, which made him even more irritable. "Are beer and women so important in your life?" he suddenly asked.

"C'mon, Moe. I'm on vacation. Julie is gone with the kids and I've got an entire week to do nothing but fish, drink, eat, sleep, and forget about my problems."

"Do you have a lot of them—problems?"

"Doesn't everyone? There're always bills to pay and everyday headaches, especially if you've got kids. You'll understand after you settle down and marry."

Once again the image of Amiina came into his mind. "I will never marry. Do you know what is happening in my country?" Islamov asked.

Custis grunted. "Well, not really. The truth is I'm not even sure I could find Chechnya on a map. I doubt most Americans could. I know you're fighting the Russians. Or, at least, I think you still are. I thought I read somewhere the war was over."

"You Americans look at the world like a rich person standing inside a beautiful house who occasionally glances out a window. You don't see yourself as being part of what's outside unless you choose to step out there. Do you have any idea how the rest of the world perceives the U.S.A.? We see you at the Olympics chanting 'U.S.A. is number one!' We see your president going to war because you do not like the president of a country. We see your McDonald's restaurants invading our homelands with your cheap french fries and greasy hamburgers."

Custis opened another beer. "Okay, okay, I'll admit we can come off as arrogant at times. But let's face it. The truth is that we are number one. We're the world's only superpower and you should be happy that we are and not the Russians or the Chinese. We use our strength to bring stability to the world. We're not like Hitler invading other countries!"

"You are doing nothing to help my people win their freedom," Islamov snapped. "All you care about is your Jewish friends in Israel."

"Wow!" Custis said, genuinely surprised. "Where's this coming from, Moe? I don't remember you being this critical when you came to the States to get your college education."

"I'm sorry," Islamov said. "I'm your guest and I'm being rude. But it's frustrating for me to listen to you worrying if there will be enough beer on this boat while my country is being destroyed by Russia."

Continuing, Islamov said, "You have lectured me about your precious bay, now let me educate you about my country's history. In 1991, we declared our independence and chose a general by the name of Dzhokhar Dudayev as our first president. Three years later, Russia invaded. You see, Moscow accused our president of transforming our country into a marketplace for drugs and weapon trafficking. But it was an excuse. What Russia really wanted was our oil."

"Dig deep enough and all of the world's problems are tied to oil," Custis volunteered, as he took another sip of beer.

"We killed ten thousand Russian soldiers, and after two years they gave up and went home like dogs with their tails between their legs."

"So, the war is over then, right?"

"No, you must understand almost everyone in Chechnya is a Muslim. There are a few Russians, but not many. After the Russian army left, my people decided to form a new country with our Islamic friends in Dagestan—a place you probably have never heard of. We were going to create a new Islamic nation. But the Kremlin was afraid we'd control the oil, so they sent troops to liquidate us. Tell me, do you know the word *zachistki*?"

"No, I've never heard it."

"It means 'cleansing.' It's what the Russians are doing. They came into my neighborhood early one morning and went house to house searching for Chechen soldiers. They forced everyone outside, and they began shooting them. Women, children—it didn't matter. Old, young— no one cared. If you were a Muslim, you had a death sentence. The girls, they raped first, and then they used machine guns to shoot them with so many bullets that they were blown into pieces."

"That's terrible," Custis said.

"No one in the West cared. Why? Because we're Muslims and you hate us because of that. America loves only the Jews."

"Moe," Custis said, "maybe we shouldn't be talking about this. We've come out here to have fun, remember? To fish, and reminisce about old times."

"My sister was thirteen when she was gang-raped and slaughtered," Islamov continued, ignoring his host's comments. "They forced my father and my mother to watch. Then they raped my mother. Eight men. Everyone in my family—my father, my brothers, my sisters—has been murdered by the Russians. From that day forward, there has never been a time for me to 'have fun' and 'reminisce' about the past."

Neither spoke. They looked across the bow at the smooth bay waters that parted as the boat sped forward.

Islamov said, "Eighty thousand Chechens have been murdered, and your great country—your superpower—is doing nothing but watching us be massacred."

"But it's over now, right? I saw a report on television. A new constitution was passed. There's been a cease-fire."

Islamov said, "The new constitution is a lie. There is no cease-fire!"

"There's something I should tell you, Moe. I saw you interviewed on CNN. The reporter called you the Viper, and I remember you telling the reporter that you'll never stop fighting—you'll never surrender."

"That's correct. For me the war will never end."

Custis dropped an empty beer bottle into a recycling bin. "Moe," he said, "we were really good friends in college. But that was a long time ago. We've both changed. That's obvious. I admire your courage, I really do. I admire your dedication. I've never been as dedicated about a cause as you have. I've never risked my life for a cause. And I'm really, really sorry about what happened to your family, especially your mother and sister. But you know, there's really not much we can do about the world's problems right now, is there? I say, let's try to put all that horrible stuff aside and just turn back the clock to when we were college kids."

Custis checked his wristwatch. "Time to stop and get some sleep. Tomorrow, after we start catching fish, I'll guarantee you'll feel better about all this."

Islamov fought the urge to scream. *How could catching fish make me feel better?* Instead, he said, "Moe, you're right."

A few moments later, after the engines had been switched off and the boat was gently rocking, they sat on the deck looking at the lights from the shore.

"Before we retire," Islamov said, "there's something I need you to do for me. It's a personal favor." He began unbuttoning his shirt. "I require medical attention."

"Good god!" Custis gasped, when he saw the bandage wrapped around Islamov's waist. "What the hell happened?"

"I've been shot by the Russians. It happened about thirty hours ago. Lucky for me, the slug passed entirely through. But it has left a hole here."

"You got shot in Chechnya?" Custis asked. "You've been shot this whole time and you haven't said a damn word about it?"

"I was not shot while I was in Chechnya. It is a long story that doesn't really matter now. I've put a tampon in the wound to slow the bleeding." Islamov started removing the bandage.

Custis was horrified. "I can't believe you aren't dead," he said. "If the bullet didn't kill you, shock should have. We've got to get you to a hospital. Now!"

"No!" Islamov replied. "I want you to treat me."

"I operate on dogs and cats, not humans!"

"Are they really that different?"

"Dogs and cats usually don't shoot each other! Are the cops chasing you? Is that why you don't want to go to a hospital?"

"I've just arrived in your country," Islamov said. "I've not had time to break any of your laws."

"I'm sorry, Moe. But I can't treat you. I could lose my veterinarian license or even be sent to jail. I'm a vet, for God's sake, not a surgeon. We've got to get you to a hospital and notify the authorities!"

Islamov spoke in a deliberately calm voice, "Wheezer, we're old friends here. I don't want you to have any legal problems because of me. But it's after two a.m. and we're far away from help. There isn't time to get me to a hospital. All I want you to do is treat my wound. First thing in the morning, you can pilot your boat to shore and I will go to a hospital and you can talk to the local police."

Custis thought about it. "Okay," he finally said. "If that gunshot was going to kill you, it already would have. I guess we can wait until tomorrow morning to get you medical attention. But you've got to promise me you'll go."

"I've got no reason to fear the authorities in the U.S.," Islamov said, lying. "Think about it. If I did, why would I come to your country?"

His reasoning placated Custis. To further reassure him, Islamov placed his hand gently on his friend's shoulder. "I'm exhausted," he said. "And in pain and in need of your help. For old time's sake, just help me tonight."

"I've got an emergency medical first aid kit on board. Let me go get it." After he had examined the wound, he said, "Moe, you're damn lucky. The bullet missed your solid organs and didn't tear the intestines. There's no leakage, which means you haven't gotten peritonitis. You're also hemodynamically stable."

"Please speak English."

"Your blood pressure is okay. Truth is, there's not much for me or even a doctor to do. We need to pack the wound, just like you did with that tampon. And I got some strong painkillers I can shoot you up with."

"Are you going to sew it shut?"

"No, that wouldn't be wise right now. You don't want to trap oxygen inside. All you need to do is gradually pack it with less and less so the body can mend itself."

"I don't need a doctor to recover?"

"If that bullet had gone in a little to the left or to the right, then you would have needed a good surgeon. All a doctor can do now is give you pain medication. But I'd still like to get you into an emergency room tomorrow morning first thing. You're damn lucky, Moe!"

"It wasn't luck. My life is in the hands of the great one, Allah, bless his name. There is a reason why I'm alive. I'm on a mission."

"Oh yeah, what sort of mission?"

"A mission to open the eyes of the world."

"Moe, I think world politics and religion are probably subjects we should avoid."

"Yes, you've been an excellent host and I'm ruining your fishing trip with all of my talk about war, and death, and politics. I'm sorry for being such a burden."

"You've changed," Custis said quietly. "You didn't used to be so goddamn serious."

"If you'd seen what I've seen, you, too, would've changed."

"In the CNN newscast, they called you a terrorist. Are you a terrorist?"

"My old friend," Islamov replied, "do you know what the word 'Islam' means in Arabic? Islam means 'surrender' or 'submission.' A follower of Islam surrenders himself totally to Allah, the most blessed one, and to the teachings of the Prophet Muhammad. Did you know that Islam recognizes Jesus Christ as an early prophet? It's true! So you see, you and I are not so different when it comes to our religious beliefs." He hesitated and then added, "I ask you now this question: Can a man who surrenders himself to the only true God and submits himself to His will—can that man ever really be a terrorist?"

Custis looked Islamov in the eyes and replied, "Moe, you're trying to get me into one of your philosophical arguments—just like you did when we were living together in college. I was the one who always wanted to talk about women and sports and you wanted to talk about religion and philosophy! I'm too old to stay up arguing with you all night about whether or not a tree makes a sound if it falls in a forest and no one's there to hear it!"

Islamov said, "You Americans believe all Arabs are Muslims and all Arabs are terrorists, therefore anyone who is a Muslim is a terrorist when, in fact, there are more than a billion followers of our Islamic faith and only fifteen percent are Arabs and only a few of them are fundamentalists and fewer are terrorists. You believe Muslims are intolerant but that's not true either because—"

Custis cut him off. "Moe, I'll show you where the guest stateroom is."

He led Islamov to his sleeping quarters. They said good night and Custis retired to the master stateroom. After he was inside, he bolted the door, something he rarely did when he was aboard. The more he thought about his exchange with Moe, the more worried he became.

This was not the Moe he'd known. He seemed radical. He'd also showed up with a gunshot wound—a fact he'd hidden until they were already out in the bay. As Paul Custis slipped on a pair of pajamas, he'd wished that he'd not invited his former pal to join him.

But I'll be rid of him tomorrow, he thought. *And then it will be just me, the beer, the bay, and the fish.*

29

Vladimir Khrenkov had no idea why he had been summoned as he waited outside the office of GRU general Valery Yablokov. *Had General Yablokov learned about his unauthorized trip to the States? Had he discovered that Khrenkov had killed two men in Washington, D.C.?*

An hour ticked by and then half of another. Finally General Yablokov's aide appeared and announced, "Follow me." There was no friendly chitchat or inflection in his voice that gave Khrenkov reason to hope or to fear what was about to happen. The general was seated behind his desk in a spacious room. Yablokov had always favored Khrenkov, but now there were no visible signs of their earlier relationship. He neither acknowledged nor greeted Khrenkov. Instead, he stared at a single sheet of white paper.

"Colonel Khrenkov," Yablokov said stiffly, without glancing up. "We have a complication."

Protocol demanded that Khrenkov remain silent until he was told to speak.

Yablokov said, "Is there something you wish, at this moment, to disclose voluntarily to me?" As he asked, he finally made eye contact with Khrenkov.

"No, sir," Khrenkov answered. He was not about to confess, at least not until he had some idea exactly how much Yablokov already knew.

The general released a loud sigh, expressing his obvious disappointment.

"Many of your comrades are lazy," Yablokov said. "They show no initiative, lack motivation, and have no courage. But you always have been different from them, and this is why I have promoted you and why I chose to keep silent about your parents' treason in abandoning their homeland to emigrate to the United States."

Khrenkov remained quiet.

"Because I believed at the time that you were an excellent and loyal officer," Yablokov continued, "I did not reveal your parents' treachery. And now I fear this cover-up has put me at risk."

"It was never my intention to harm or hurt you," Khrenkov said, interrupting.

"How dare you say such a thing!" Yablokov exclaimed. He held up the paper that he'd been studying. "How dare you make that comment when I have this evidence right here in front of me!"

He knows everything! Khrenkov thought.

"Why has General Lev Stepanovich Rodin written this note to me?" Yablokov demanded. "What have you told him about me?"

About you?

Khrenkov was confused.

Yablokov tossed the paper at him. He picked it up and read it:

General Yablokov, by my order, you are to immediately assign Colonel Vladimir Mikhailovich Khrenkov to my personal staff for an indefinite period.
Signed, General Lev Rodin

Everyone knew General Lev Stepanovich Rodin. Under the Russian constitution, the president exercised sole control over the nation's security agencies. In addition to the SVR, he oversaw the Federal Security Service (similar to the FBI in the United States), the Federal Border Guard Service, the Federal Tax Police, the Federal Guard Service, and the Presidential Security Service. But no Russian president had time to actually manage these huge police bureaucracies. That job had been given to General Rodin. It made him the ultimate keeper of government secrets in a country that still had many secrets to hide. Rodin's specialty was exposing corrupt military and Russian political leaders, nearly all of whom, incidentally, turned out to be opponents of the president. As soon as Khrenkov read the paper, he understood why General Yablokov was nervous. It wasn't Khrenkov's secret trip to Washington, D.C., that had caused the general to fret. He was afraid that Rodin was investigating him!

"May I speak freely?" Khrenkov asked.

"I suspect you already have—to General Rodin!" Yablokov snapped. "Why else would he demand that you be moved to his personal staff?"

"I have no idea why General Rodin is transferring me, but I have not betrayed you, and I will have only praise to tell him about your leadership."

Yablokov leaned back in his chair. "Khrenkov, you are naive. Ours is a history of betrayal, of lies told by friends to save themselves."

"Sir, I have only respect for you."

"And I believe you. But this will not matter. General Lev Rodin sees himself as a future Beria. Do you understand the significance of what I am telling you?"

Lavrenty Beria.

Although Beria had been executed in 1953, long before Khrenkov was born, his name was still uttered in hushed voices with a reverence reserved only for the most horrific of tyrants. It was as if Russians today were still afraid that Beria would reach out from hell and close his bloody fingers around their necks. As Stalin's police chief, right-hand executioner, and commander of the Gulag slave-labor network, Beria was a mass murderer who enjoyed raping young girls snatched from Moscow streets. Stalin reportedly once bragged that Beria was Russia's "own Himmler," a reference to Heinrich Himmler, the head of the Nazis' dreaded SS, and the madman in charge of implementing Hitler's Final Solution. What made Beria even more frightening was that he could be utterly charming. He was known for deceiving his friends and enemies alike, both of whom he was quick to execute at the slightest provocation without any sign of remorse.

There was a knock on the door.

General Yablokov's aide entered and whispered in the general's ear.

"It seems," the general announced, "that General Rodin is sending a car to pick you up outside in exactly ten minutes."

Yablokov stood up.

"Here is my advice to you, Colonel Khrenkov. Choose your words carefully because you are holding both of our fates in your hands."

Ten minutes later, a white Volga limousine pulled up to the sidewalk where Khrenkov waited. A military officer stepped from the car.

"Welcome, Colonel," he said. "My name is Mikhail Artyukhov. I'm one of the general's military aides. Please join us."

Khrenkov entered the Volga, taking a seat in the rear across from two other passengers. Neither spoke to him. Although Khrenkov had never met Rodin, the general's face was well known from television newscasts and photographs in the media. He was always shown standing behind the president. Khrenkov knew that neither of the passengers in the car with him was Rodin. He also noticed that both were handcuffed.

Artyukhov slipped onto the seat beside him and said, "I understand, Colonel, that we share a common interest."

"What's that?"

"The unfortunate unrest in Chechnya. I recently returned from a very interesting visit there."

Khrenkov had assumed the limo would take them directly to the Kremlin, but instead it headed away from Moscow's inner city toward a suburb that Khrenkov considered an architectural eyesore. During communism's heyday, party leaders had decreed there would be no homeless in the city. Every Russian citizen, even destitute drunks, would be assigned an apartment. Giant construction cranes and earthmovers had transformed pastures outside Moscow into miles of high-rise apartment complexes. All of these buildings were made of gray concrete slabs. All were identical in design. All were erected side by side, one as ugly as the next.

It was into this maze of tenements that the limo drove, weaving between the structures like a mouse searching for cheese. When the Volga finally stopped, Artyukhov stepped out and waited for Khrenkov. The other passengers then got out. Artyukhov led them into an apartment building identified only as 112. An elevator took them to the ninth floor, where the three men again fell in behind their guide. The first door where they stopped was answered by a woman in her early thirties.

"Colonel Khrenkov, please go inside," Artyukhov said.

Khrenkov did, and Artyukhov and the two handcuffed men continued down the hallway.

"Welcome, Colonel Khrenkov," the woman said with forced enthusiasm.

She escorted him into what had once been a living room, but was now a dining area. There was a wooden table there with two chairs, one on each side. His hostess told him which seat to take. She excused herself, disappearing through a door on his left. Khrenkov did not sit down. He remained standing. He didn't want to risk insulting the general by sitting at the table before he arrived. He surveyed the flat. Two ornate china plates sat atop a lace tablecloth. The serving ware was polished silver, the glasses, cut crystal. A bowl of fresh fruit was the table's centerpiece. There were no decorations of any sort on the walls. But directly across from his seat at the table was a large mirror. Khrenkov looked at his own reflection. He was wearing his military uniform. He straightened his tie. He also assumed that General Rodin or one of his minions was watching him from behind the one-way glass.

The woman returned with two vodka glasses and a decanter on a silver serving tray. He noticed she was wearing a black wool skirt and white blouse. She was pear-shaped and had white, almost poreless skin. Though one of her shoes had been built up higher than the other to compensate, she still had a slight limp. She didn't speak or look straight at him. Instead, she placed the tray near the chair opposite Khrenkov and then stepped back two feet from the table. Like Khrenkov, who was now directly across from her in the room, she waited in silence.

He wanted to check the time, but he didn't. After several uncomfortable minutes, General Rodin entered.

"Colonel Khrenkov," he said, as he walked toward the table.

Khrenkov saluted while the woman pulled out Rodin's chair and he sat down. "You may be seated, Colonel," Rodin said. "Please relax. You're my dinner guest tonight. I'm afraid I rarely eat in public, for obvious security reasons."

The woman poured two vodkas. The first she served to Rodin.

"A toast to our great motherland," Rodin declared, lifting his glass.

Khrenkov immediately shoved out his chair and rose to his feet, but the general waved him down. "If we leap up each time we take a drink tonight, we'll both be exhausted."

Khrenkov brought the vodka to his lips, but unlike the general, who threw the glass back, emptying it with one gulp, Khrenkov barely sipped the liquor.

"Is there something wrong with the vodka?" Rodin asked.

"No, sir."

"Then drink like a man."

Khrenkov downed the shot. The woman poured them another.

"And now a toast to our president," the general said.

They drank it quickly and she moved to refill their glasses. But just as she was tilting the spout, Rodin stopped her. "Serve dinner in five minutes," he said. She left them alone.

Rodin was solidly built, but short, standing only five feet, three inches. The top of his head was completely bald. The hair on each side was cut close. He had black bushy eyebrows, wire-rimmed glasses, and a wide nose that was slightly crooked, a sign that it had once been broken. Khrenkov seemed to recall that Rodin had been a successful boxer.

"Did you speak with the two other men in the car during your ride here?" he asked.

Khrenkov assumed that Rodin already knew the answer from querying Artyukhov.

"No, sir!"

"But you saw they were prisoners."

"Yes, sir."

"Weren't you curious as to why they were handcuffed?"

"If the general had wanted me to know why, the general would have told me or had his aide tell me. It was not my place to inquire."

Rodin pondered this response for a moment. Then he reached under the table. When he raised his right hand, he was holding a pistol.

"Do you recognize this?" he asked.

"Yes, sir," Khrenkov replied. "It is a PSS—a silent self-loading pistol. It was created specifically for Russian special operations. It fires 7.62×41-millimeter silent SP-4 ammunition."

The general looked down at the handgun. "What this is, Colonel Khrenkov, is a marvel of Russian technology. This gun is much quieter than regular pistols, even those with noise suppressors. Even the cartridge has been manufactured to be quiet. None of the exploding gases from the bullet ever leave the chamber when it is fired."

"Yes, sir!"

Rodin said, "I admire efficiency, whether it comes from a fine pistol or a soldier such as yourself."

Khrenkov still had no idea why Rodin had summoned him.

"What would you do, Colonel Khrenkov, if I handed you this pistol and said I wanted you to execute the two men who were brought with you here tonight in the limousine?"

"I'm a soldier. You're a superior officer. I would follow your orders and execute them."

"You wouldn't question me? You wouldn't ask why these men should be killed? What crimes they had committed?"

"I'm certain you would not order me to execute them unless you had a justifiable and legal reason."

Rodin raised an eyebrow and then said, "Colonel Khrenkov, one of these men has been sentenced by a military tribunal to death. He has been found guilty of committing a number of crimes. But the other man, quite frankly, is an ordinary citizen who has broken absolutely no laws and has been brought here by me solely because of *you*. Now, knowing this man is innocent, would you still execute him if I commanded you to shoot him?"

Khrenkov didn't understand why Rodin was asking him these questions. Even worse, he didn't know how the general expected him to respond. If he refused to shoot the man, he would be disobeying an order. But if he shot an innocent man, he would be committing murder. He decided the wisest answer was the simplest one. "Sir, you are my commander. I am a Russian soldier. If you give me an order, I will carry it out."

"Yes, you've said that, so I take it that the fact this man has not broken any Russian laws is immaterial?"

"I've been taught that my commanders are men of wisdom and integrity. If you order me to execute both men, I will do it." Khrenkov paused, and then added, "I am certain that a general of your importance and stature would not ask me to commit murder."

Rodin grunted. "So you would put the responsibility back on me?" He raised his right hand and waved, as if he were signaling someone unseen. Artyukhov entered the room. Now Khrenkov was certain the mirror behind the general was a one-way glass. Artyukhov handed a brown file folder to the general who removed two eight-by-ten photographs from it. He slid them across the table to Khrenkov, who looked down at the grainy, poor quality images. One showed Khrenkov passing through customs at Sheremetyevo Airport en route to Washington, D.C. The next was of him when he returned.

Rodin said: "Colonel Khrenkov, you spoke earlier of integrity. Are you a man of integrity?"

So Rodin knew about his illegal trip!

Before Khrenkov could reply, the woman entered carrying two bowls of steaming soup.

Rodin's mood changed instantly from serious to jubilant. "Ah," he declared. "It's time for our feast." As they were being served, Rodin said, "I was not born in Moscow. I was born in the country, far away from the city, in a very tiny village where my mother was a schoolteacher and my father a carpenter. My parents worked hard and believed in the collective. They were avid Communists who were absolutely convinced they were helping build a perfect society that existed without social class distinctions."

Rodin tasted the *rassolnik*, soup with pickled cucumbers.

"When I first arrived in Moscow, I discovered my parents had been ignorant. I earned extra cash fighting with my bare fists in boxing matches. I had to work hard to overcome my peasant past because I learned that in our classless society there were actually many different social classes." He sipped the soup. "I became sophisticated, worldly, but I must admit that now, even though I have traveled many places, seen many things, and dined in many expensive Western restaurants, deep down, I still crave the simple rural dishes that my mother cooked."

He put down his spoon. "Tonight, you will not eat Russian caviar and smoked salmon. You will have wild rabbit baked in sour cream."

The general nodded toward their server. "This woman is my cook. She is Lubmila, the daughter of a man from my village who once humiliated my father by disrespecting my mother. He's in prison now. I had him arrested."

Khrenkov glanced at her. There was no expression on her face. He looked down at the soup. Rodin noticed and chuckled.

"You think she will poison us?" the general asked.

She left the room.

Continuing, Rodin said, "Lubmila despises me. You are correct about that. But I'm not worried that she will poison me. I'm not afraid because if she ever works up enough courage to season my soup with rat poison—that is the moment when I will know I no longer have any power in this city."

Khrenkov looked confused, but Rodin wasn't in a hurry to explain. Lubmila reappeared, cleared their soup bowls, and set down plates of rabbit cut into chunks. "You see," Rodin continued, "Lubmila has three brothers, and a mother, in addition to her father. She understands that if I were to get even an upset stomach after eating a meal, one of them would be tortured. All of them will be instantly executed if anything worse happens to me."

Rodin tasted the rabbit and declared, "Delicious!"

Once again, they were alone. Rodin said, "But then, you already know how vulnerable a person is if they care about their family, don't you?"

Khrenkov sat silent.

Rodin said, "Colonel, you had three options when the Russian Mafia first sent you that videotape of your sister, Olga. You could have gone to the United States and murdered Major Igor Aleksandrovich Fedorov the moment you first realized he was responsible for kidnapping your family. Chances are you would have been killed. Fedorov is not a fool. And your family would have died."

"And my other two choices?"

"You could do what Fedorov asked you to do. In fact, this is what you did. You shot the Mafia criminal, Sergey Pudin. Of course, you knew Fedorov was planning on killing you and your family, too, anyway. So you killed Petr Pankov, who was waiting to murder you. Apparently, you also somehow contacted the U.S. authorities and had them rescue your parents. Your sister, however, was raped and murdered."

"And what was my third option?"

"You could've stayed in Moscow. You could've told the Mafia and Fedorov to go fuck themselves. Of course, he would have tested you, probably by murdering your sister, since she was the most vulnerable. But there would've been no reason for him to kill your parents or your brothers. At that point, Fedorov would have realized that he couldn't control you. And he would have been afraid that you would come seeking revenge. Unfortunately, your sister, Olga, would still be dead—regardless of which option you selected. But you would not have been controlled by him."

"Did I make the wrong choice?"

Rodin replied, "Rarely in life are there wrong choices, rather each choice brings with it a different reward or punishment. By leaving Moscow with a fictitious passport, you have committed treason and are now, yourself, a common criminal."

Rodin's comments had ruined Khrenkov's appetite. But not Rodin's. He continued chewing stewed rabbit as he talked.

"Did you know," Rodin asked, "that the Germans captured one of Stalin's sons during the war? They sent word to our leader and announced they were ready to negotiate for his son's release. And our great leader sent them this message: All Russian soldiers are my sons! He told the Germans: Go ahead! Execute him! I will not negotiate. Why? Because he wasn't going to let anyone control him."

Rodin added, "For what you've done, you can be arrested and executed. But before I decide your fate, we must first deal with the two men who rode here with you tonight. The criminal is named Geronti Pavlovich Pekhomov. I want you to go into the apartment next door and execute him. This is a direct order given by your superior officer to you. Do you understand?"

"Yes, sir. And the other man?"

"Ah, the innocent one. Interesting. Kill him if you wish or free him." Artyukhov reappeared.

Rodin said, "But you need to understand this, Colonel Khrenkov. While this innocent man's future is of no consequence to me, the decision you make about him will have an immediate impact on you. It will determine whether you return here to join me for dessert or are handcuffed and taken to Lubyanka to be interrogated about your illegal visit to Washington, D.C., and the murders you committed there."

Khrenkov's mind was swirling. Artyukhov said, "Please follow me and don't forget the pistol." They walked into the hall and the flat next door. The handcuffed men were both blindfolded and sitting stiff on wooden chairs in the center of the room. Artyukhov walked behind them and removed their blindfolds.

"Geronti Pavlovich Pekhomov," Khrenkov said. "Stand up!"

The taller of the two men rose. Artyukhov withdrew his own gun from its holster.

"Step forward," Khrenkov commanded Pekhomov. He moved one pace in front of his seat as the other prisoner watched. "On your knees," Khrenkov ordered. Incredibly, Pekhomov did as he was told without protest. He showed no fear and made no attempt to argue or plead for his life. But the other man began shaking so violently that the legs of his chair began rat-a-tatting against the oak parquet floor.

Khrenkov moved behind Pekhomov.

"Is your name Geronti Pavlovich Pekhomov?"

"Yes," the kneeling man replied. He seemed so calm that Khrenkov wondered if this was some sort of demented game. *Was the PSS pistol actually loaded? Were these men part of a charade—actors in some bizarre test that General Rodin was giving him?*

Khrenkov put the pistol behind Pekhomov's head and declared, "For crimes against the state, you are being executed." He squeezed the trigger. The pistol's recoil surprised him. It was no game, no dramatic test. Although the weapon was extremely quiet, there was a smacking sound as the slug entered Pekhomov's skull. Blood, bits of bone, and brain splashed back onto Khrenkov's hand.

As the body keeled forward, the innocent man waiting for his turn began to wail in his chair. Tears gushed from his eyes. "Please, please," he pleaded. "I've committed no crimes. I have a wife, children, grandchildren. I'm a good man. There's been a horrible mistake!"

"Get down on your knees!" Khrenkov ordered.

Why would the general want me to kill this man? Had everyone on Rodin's military staff been forced to shoot a prisoner and then given the choice of freeing or killing another man? What was he supposed to do?

Khrenkov reviewed the facts. *Rodin had said there was no legal reason to execute this man. But if he was released, how would Rodin react? Would he think that Khrenkov was fair-minded or think that he was squeamish and untrustworthy? Would he congratulate him for having a conscience?* Khrenkov had another thought. *The weapon held six rounds. But Rodin might have put only one bullet in its magazine. What if there were no second bullet? Or maybe it was a blank!*

"Please," the man cried as he moved down onto the floor. "Don't kill me."

Another idea came to Khrenkov. *Rodin had said that his fate was*

*tied to this decision. He would either be taken back into the dining room
to have dessert with Rodin or he was going to be handcuffed and driven
to Lubyanka. That was probably why Artyukhov had his own pistol
drawn. The military aide didn't want to risk having Khrenkov shoot him
in an escape attempt. This was sheer madness! What did Rodin expect
him to do?*

He stepped behind the cowering man and aimed the pistol at his
head. Then he turned the gun to the side. The most logical action was to
free the innocent man.

Khrenkov said, "It appears a mistake has been made."

Artyukhov said, "Before you free this prisoner, you should ask his
name."

Khrenkov peered down at him, "Who are you?"

"A nobody. A simple Russian."

"Tell me your name."

"Yevgeni. Yevgeni Aleksandrovich Fedorov."

Fedorov!

"Do you have a brother?"

"Yes, he lives in America. His name is Igor."

"A retired major—who fought in Afghanistan?"

"Yes, yes! Do you know him? He once was a Russian hero. Is that
why I am here? Is this about him? What has he done?"

Khrenkov was not listening. He was thinking about Olga. He was
thinking about Igor Fedorov on the videotape, ripping open Olga's
blouse, pushing up her bra, tweaking her breast. He imagined Olga being gang-raped and murdered.

Khrenkov squeezed the trigger.

The man's head exploded. He fell forward in the throes of dying. His
body twitched on the floor. Khrenkov handed his pistol to Artyukhov. He
felt numb. He didn't care if Rodin arrested him now.

"Wash up in there," Artyukhov said, pointing toward a bathroom.

Khrenkov went inside and splashed water on his face. The soap foam
was pink with the diluted blood running from his hands. Although he had
killed men before, they'd been enemy soldiers. He'd shot Sergey Pudin
and Petr Pankov, but they were criminals. Yevgeni Aleksandrovich
Fedorov was the first man whom he'd killed solely for revenge. Yet he felt no
guilt or remorse. He also felt no real satisfaction, and that surprised him.

General Rodin had already started to eat his dessert when Khrenkov
was led back into the dining room.

"Look!" the general said enthusiastically. "It's one of our famous
Russian cakes, Praga. Sit, eat, enjoy!"

Khrenkov wasn't in the mood. Artyukhov returned the silenced pistol to Rodin.

"Colonel Khrenkov," the general said. "What am I to do with you? You have just compounded your problems. You have now murdered an innocent man. Luckily, I am a very forgiving man, and now that I'm in control of your fate, I will give you a way to climb out of this horrible hole."

Khrenkov waited in silence.

Rodin said, "Your records indicate you are assigned to a special task force monitoring Chechnya. Therefore you are familiar with the terrorist Movladi Islamov. Is this not true?"

"I am familiar with the rebel leader known as the Viper."

"The SVR has learned that Islamov is currently hiding somewhere inside the United States. I am sending you there to track him down and arrest him. You will leave tonight for New York City. There you will be provided with whatever tools and intelligence you may need. You will report only to me, and you will be denied nothing that you require to complete this assignment. You will cooperate fully with CIA and FBI officials, who are also hunting him. And you will stick with this search until he is either dead or arrested."

"What should I do if I capture him or the Americans arrest him?"

"Your job is to bring him back to Moscow. You will do this personally. Is that clear?"

"Yes, sir!"

"No, I do not believe it is. We do not need to put him on trial in Moscow and invite more terrorist acts. We do not need him to become a Chechen martyr. You will bring him back in a military aircraft, but at some point Islamov will attempt to escape and you will be forced to kill him. This is what I mean when I say you will escort him home."

"I understand, sir!"

"Good. Now there is another private matter we need to discuss. There is another reason why I'm sending you to the United States. You want revenge. Fortunately for you, we have a mutual goal. I want you to kill Igor Aleksandrovich Fedorov and his Russian Mafia boss, Ivan Ivanovich Sitov."

Why would General Rodin want them dead?

Rodin seemed to read his mind. "It's no concern to you why I am encouraging you to eliminate Fedorov and Sitov. It's enough for you to know that during these difficult economic times, our government and certain wealthy and influential Russian businessmen here in Moscow sometimes find it beneficial to perform favors for each other for the greater good of the entire Russian people."

Obviously someone in the Russian Mafia in Moscow wanted Fedorov and Sitov killed. Rodin was helping them, most likely in return for favors or cash.

Continuing, Rodin said, "Because you are my special envoy, you will be shielded under diplomatic immunity laws while you are in the United States hunting the international terrorist Movladi Islamov. If he resists arrest, you can shoot him and the Americans will not be able to prosecute you. However, if you are caught carrying out your vendetta against Fedorov and Sitov, I will insist that Moscow knew nothing about your actions. You'll not be protected by diplomatic immunity."

Rodin had finished his dessert and, apparently, his instructions. "A final comment," he said. "Do not underestimate me. Do as you have been told and with any luck you will be returned to General Yablokov's staff after your mission is completed. But if you fail or you betray me, then I will release the evidence that shows you are a traitor. I will help the Americans prosecute you for the murders of Sergey Pudin and Petr Pankov. I will testify to prosecutors here in Moscow about how you have tonight murdered Yevgeni Fedorov. You will be disgraced."

Rodin stood and said, "You should be happy. I am helping you take your revenge."

Khrenkov, however, did not feel at all fortunate.

CIA HEADQUARTERS,
LANGLEY, VIRGINIA

I hate meetings. It takes an hour to accomplish what you can usually do in five minutes. There's always someone who wants to demonstrate how clever he is by offering an opinion on every subject, often repeating the obvious. I hate the phrases that people use in meetings, too. Everyone has to be "on the same page." All decisions need to reflect a "collaborative effort." There's got to be "team spirit." But the most irritating one is when a boss talks about how we're "one big family." Hey, I work for a bureaucracy in a nation that's based on capitalism—you remember—supply and demand, goods and services, profit and loss, survival of the strongest. When did "meeting the bottom line" have anything to do with being part of "one big family"?

Because I was the new guy at the Counterterrorism Center, I was required to attend a series of "orientation meetings" to get me "up to speed." This involved sitting around with several other new employees discussing terrorism with an academic egghead who'd probably never spent a day outside the confines of Langley. On day two, I was listening to a scholarly, dandruff-speckled analyst with really awful yellow teeth explain the differences between the Islamic Jihad, the Jaish-e-Mohammed, and the Hizballah, when Kimberly Lodge thankfully interrupted his mind-numbing speech to rescue me.

"Wyatt," she said, sticking to our policy of using first names, "you're needed."

Gosh, I suddenly felt warm and fuzzy all over. Kimberly Lodge, who'd made it very clear that she considered me a first-class pain in the ass, needed me. I said goodbye to the lecturer with bad teeth and my fellow prisoners and followed Miss Lodge into the hallway. She was wearing one of her nonsexual, gray wool-blended suits, but as we were walking stride for stride, her white blouse gapped open at the buttons enough that I could see her bra. It was one of those sateen, push-up underwire types from Victoria's Secret. This was a side of her that was much more intriguing. I preferred to think of her as a woman who was hiding a smoldering side under all that tough exterior and tailored fiber. Hey, it's fantasies like these that make most days interesting.

Of course, Miss Lodge was all business.

"Todd wants to speak to us about Movladi Islamov," she said. There was a tension in her voice. She added, "There's a problem."

"With Moe—the dreaded Viper?" I replied sarcastically. "How can that be? Remember Operation Beartrap? Selling him an H-bomb? I thought you had it all under control. Yesterday you said he was going to be captured when he landed at the Baltimore-Washington Airport. You were gearing up to turn him over to the Russians."

Kimberly didn't reply, but her cheeks grew red. I didn't think it was because of the brisk pace. Someone, I was sure, had screwed up.

Todd welcomed me with an extended hand, and he shook mine briskly. Apparently, his amnesia had evaporated since our meeting yesterday, because he said, "Wyatt, it's great to be working together again.

"I'll get right to the point," he continued. "Islamov never showed up at B.W.I. last night. Our guys were waiting, but he never came down to the baggage claim area where he was supposed to meet our informant. There was an international flight to Germany that left at eleven o'clock so we think he might have simply gone from one gate to another and is now back in Europe. Meanwhile, there's a slim possibility he's hiding on our soil. He didn't contact you, did he?"

I wanted to smack the guy. "Actually, Todd," I said, "he rang me up last night and we met for coffee this morning at Starbucks. I was going to tell you, but somehow it slipped my mind."

Todd, who had never struck me as being particularly bright, almost went for it. Then he scowled and said, "The Russians are putting a lot of pressure on the State Department. He's their version of Osama Bin Laden, and they want him caught."

"No," I volunteered. "The Russians want him dead. It makes life simpler."

He ignored my combative attitude. "You and Kimberly are going to be part of a joint task force being organized to capture Islamov. You'll be our liaison with both the FBI and the Russians. The fact that you're a deputy U.S. marshal should help, since you've been trained to track down criminals. You also know Islamov personally."

Todd paused and waited, presumably for me to say something about how excited I was to be on this assignment. I didn't, because I didn't have anything to say and I knew he was expecting me to respond. I didn't like him and I was enjoying being difficult.

After a few very long seconds, Todd said, "Wyatt, do you think Islamov caught that flight to Germany or is he here in the U.S.?"

"If I remember correctly, Miss Lodge said yesterday that Moe had been wounded during the shoot-out. If that's accurate, I doubt he flew to the U.S. just to catch another six-hour flight to Frankfurt. How reliable is the informant who told you that he was coming to B.W.I.?"

"She's someone Islamov trusts. He called her from Iceland," Kimberly interjected.

"Maybe he was using the woman to preoccupy us while he was changing flights," Todd said.

Kimberly thought about that for a moment. "I don't think so. Why would he want to call attention to the airport? I think he figured out somehow that our guys were waiting for him."

Todd said, "The joint task force is scheduled to hold its first meeting downtown in about two hours at the FBI building. You need to be there—both of you."

As soon as we left Todd's office, I said, "I've got an errand to run. See you later."

"Wait! We're supposed to be partners. Besides, we've got a meeting in two hours."

I said, "I need to go to B.W.I."

"The FBI was there last night and a report has already been filed about what happened."

"Did they look at the airport's surveillance tapes?"

"What tapes?"

"That's what I thought. You see, Miss Lodge," I said in my most patient tone—I was also intentionally calling her by her last name—"the FBI is just as worried as the CTC about losing turf to the new Homeland Security Department. I'm guessing its agents didn't tell the Transportation Security Administration officers at the airport much about what was going down last night."

"I don't know how much they told the TSA."

"I do. The FBI never likes to tell anyone *anything*. Now if I'm right, the TSA probably felt snubbed, which means it didn't tell the FBI squat. That's how we operate in federal law enforcement. You screw me, I'll screw you."

"Oh, that's so mature."

"No, it's not mature. But it's reality in this town. There's a good chance the TSA didn't offer the FBI access to its surveillance tapes."

I could tell from her expression that Kimberly still didn't understand.

I explained. "After September 11th, the TSA began placing cameras in airports, just like banks hide cameras in their lobbies. I'm guessing there're several cameras in the baggage area, and if that's the case, maybe one of them got a picture of Islamov passing through there."

"We don't have time to drive to the airport now, look at tapes, and then make the trip downtown for the joint task force meeting."

"Right, that's why you're going downtown while *I'm* driving to B.W.I."

I started toward the elevator, leaving her standing outside Todd's office. But by the time I'd reached it, she'd caught up to me.

"Okay, I'm going with you to B.W.I., but you'd better be right about those goddamn tapes," she said.

Because of traffic, which is always congested on the Beltway, it took us more than an hour to reach B.W.I. As soon as we entered the main terminal, I flashed my identification and asked to see the TSA security chief. When I saw who he was, I broke into a huge grin. The Homeland Security Office had been in such a rush to tighten airport security that it had raided other federal law enforcement agencies and had recruited recent retirees to fill its TSA security roster. Bill McHenry was a retired deputy marshal. I'd known him forever. In the 1970s, he'd been involved in the Sky Marshal program when the Justice Department had begun putting plainclothes deputies on airplanes to prevent skyjackings.

"What the hell are you pestering me for?" McHenry declared grumpily when he saw me.

I introduced Kimberly and explained what we were after.

"Hoover's boys came rushing in here last night with two Russian goons tagging along," McHenry said. "Acting like real *big* shots. An agent named Rodney Ames in charge. Wouldn't tell me a damn thing because my guys are only good enough to look through people's underwear in suitcases!"

"I'm familiar with Rodney Ames," I said. "He's a jackass."

"Yeah, when I saw his nose I thought of you."

Kimberly asked, "What's his nose got to do with this?"

"Wyatt broke it for him," McHenry replied. "Everybody in the Marshals Service knows the story."

I changed the subject. "I'm guessing you never mentioned your security cameras to Ames."

"Don't blame me. He never asked!"

I gave Kimberly an I-told-you-so wink. McHenry led us to his office. He had three TV monitors, each attached to a separate VCR. "I set this up this morning. Each tape is from a separate camera located in the carousel areas. Now, your terrorist was supposed meet someone at ten o'clock in the baggage claim area so I've keyed up all three to show us what was happening starting at ten o'clock."

All three screens came on.

"We've got a four-second delay," McHenry explained, "which means our cameras take a picture every four seconds. It helps us save on tapes. Anyway, this will seem a bit jumpy."

A black-and-white image of a woman appeared on the first television set, which was showing the video from the ceiling camera in the Delta baggage claim area. She was obviously waiting for someone. I assumed she was the FBI's contact. The other two videos were from lenses farther away and were filming events taking place at two other pick-up sites. As we watched, the woman at the carousel was gradually joined by passengers from arriving Delta flights. One by one, each claimed their bags and left, leaving her behind to wait. McHenry stopped the tape.

"See your guy?" he asked.

"No," I replied. "But let's keep watching."

He turned the video back on. For five minutes, nothing much happened, and then three men approached the woman. I recognized Special Agent Rodney Ames. He was wearing a distinctive pinstripe suit.

"Those other goons are Russians," McHenry said.

"Can you rewind all three so we can see what happened in the baggage claim areas, say, two hours earlier?"

"Sure."

While he rewound the tapes, Kimberly asked, "You think Islamov knew he was walking into a trap?"

"I don't think he's survived as long as he has by trusting people."

McHenry began the three tapes again, and in herky-jerky movements, throngs of people appeared. They gathered around the three separate islands, collected their belongings, and then left. I didn't see anything unusual. Meanwhile, Kimberly was becoming antsy.

"We're going to be late to the meeting," she complained. "We've seen what you came to see."

"Go without me. I'll catch a cab."

"Todd isn't going to like this," she said. But she didn't leave.

I kept watching. Several painful minutes later, I said, "Hey, rewind the video on the second set."

"Why?" Kimberly demanded, sounding even more frustrated.

"Because I'm pretty sure I just saw a guy who was at that same carousel about an hour earlier."

McHenry rolled back the tape. It confirmed what I had suspected. A man who had first entered the baggage claim area around eight p.m. returned an hour later to that same place.

"Is that Islamov?" Kimberly asked.

"I'm not sure. He's the right height and weight, but his face looks different. Let's speed up the reel and see what happens next."

McHenry synchronized all three cassettes so we could see what the man was seeing while he loitered in the baggage area.

McHenry cued the tapes so that each began at exactly 9:02. On the number-two monitor, the same man was lingering at a carousel. On the number-one set, FBI special agent Rodney Ames was standing near the Delta carousel briefing a group of uniformed guards.

"Those aren't actually TSA employees," McHenry clarified. "They're FBI agents dressed in our uniforms. Ames wanted his own people stationed at all of the ground floor exits."

Kimberly said, "If that man is Islamov, then he *saw* Agent Ames giving out assignments. That's how he knew it was a trap!"

"Maybe not," I said. "Moe wouldn't be aware of TSA security procedures. He might have assumed that he was simply watching a shift change."

The playing continued. Our suspect disappeared but then resurfaced at 9:55 p.m., once again at the same place. This time he bent down and retrieved a piece of luggage. But another passenger confronted him. After they spoke, the suspect willingly handed the bag to the stranger. Then he disappeared.

"Where'd he go?" I asked.

"It looks like he went to the Lost and Found office just down the hall," McHenry replied.

"So he's *not* Islamov," Kimberly said. "He's just some guy who's lost his suitcase."

A few moments later, the man reappeared. As we examined the image, he ducked into the men's room.

"He wasn't in Lost and Found very long," McHenry noted. "It takes a good five to ten minutes to file a claim."

We continued watching.

"My god," Kimberly said. "It's been ten minutes and he's still in the bathroom!"

Another five minutes passed before he emerged. He immediately inserted himself into a new group of arriving passengers.

"He's either your terrorist or he's looking for something to steal," McHenry announced.

I glanced from screen to screen to screen. Finally, Ames appeared again on the first one, along with the two Russians. They were speaking with the woman informant waiting at the Delta carousel. On monitor number two, our suspect was watching them. He immediately strode to the up escalator.

That's when I knew.

"He's done something to his face," I said. "But *that's* him. I remember now that he lowers one shoulder when he walks. He's badly pigeon-toed, too."

"So Islamov is still in the U.S.?" Kimberly asked.

"There's no way he could've caught that German flight. He was in the baggage claim area too long."

I asked McHenry to make an enlargement of Islamov's new face from the videotape.

"I'll circulate it through the TSA," he offered. "If he shows up at an airport, we'll detain him."

"What about the FBI?" Kimberly asked.

"You can take a copy of Islamov's photo to the joint task force meeting," I said. "That'll impress 'em."

She checked the time. "You're talking about a meeting that started ten minutes ago."

We hurried out to the car. As we walked, I asked, "Who was the woman at the baggage carousel—your bait?"

"Her name is Amiina Asaev. She called the FBI immediately after Islamov called her from Reykjavik. She's married now, only Islamov doesn't know it. She was frightened she'd get into trouble with immigration if she helped him."

"Where's she now?"

"The FBI is guarding her at her house. They're still hoping Islamov will contact her. They've also notified all the hospital emergency rooms in case he shows up with a gunshot wound."

I tried to put myself in his place. What would I do if I'd landed at B.W.I., realized I'd been betrayed, and needed medical help?

A name suddenly popped into my head. I dialed information on my cell phone.

"I need a number in the Baltimore metro area for Dr. Paul Custis," I said.

A few moments later, the phone at his animal clinic rang.

"Dogs and Cats Veterinarian Clinic. This is Angel speaking. How can I assist you?" a woman said.

"I need to talk to Paul Custis," I explained. "I'm an old friend." That wasn't exactly true. I barely knew him. He'd been Islamov's roommate in college and had tagged along a couple of times when Islamov and I had met up after class to discuss the criminal mind. I remembered that he'd graduated and set up practice in Baltimore because he'd sent me a few Christmas cards.

"The doctor is on vacation this week," Angel said.

I explained who I was and asked her how I could reach him.

"He never leaves us a number because he knows our patients' owners will insist that we call him if there's an emergency. But I can call his wife, Julie, and speak with her. She's in New Orleans and probably knows how to reach him."

I gave her my cell phone number and stressed that it was extremely important.

"Who's Custis?" Kimberly asked.

"A long shot. He and Moe were really close. Call the CTC and get his home address so we can check out his house."

I turned north on Interstate 95 while Kimberly called. As soon as she got the address, Todd came on the line.

"The FBI's called three times demanding to know where you are," he announced.

"Todd, we've found a photograph of Islamov at B.W.I, something the FBI missed," Kimberly said. "We've been at the airport looking at surveillance tapes."

I could almost hear the wheels in his head spinning.

"Wyatt thinks Islamov might have contacted an old friend from college, a veterinarian," she continued. "We're heading to Baltimore right now to check it out."

"No!" he replied. "Turn around and get down to that meeting. I'll call and tell 'em what you've found. We're part of a team here. We've got to tell the FBI what's happening."

I snatched her phone from her hand.

"Todd, this is Wyatt. We can't quite hear you!"

"Knock it off, Wyatt. You heard me perfectly!"

"When we get to Baltimore, we'll call from a land line." I clicked off the connection.

"That was *really* lame," Kimberly said. "It wasn't even original."

"Look, if I can get to Islamov before the FBI, maybe I can talk him into surrendering without anyone getting killed. But if we let the FBI handle this, they're going to involve the Russians, and I can guarantee you the SVR isn't going to want Islamov taken alive."

Her phone rang. We both knew it was Todd. She hesitated and then switched off her cell.

"I owe you an apology," Kimberly said. "I assumed you were a screw-up because of what happened on Capitol Hill to your witness. But you were right about the surveillance tapes, and you were also right about the FBI and the Russians. I'm willing to back you on this, but remember, we're partners. Don't hide anything from me."

"Sure. Partners. Only I'm not real good at working with other people."

"Really?" she replied. "Gosh, that's a real surprise!"

31

Paul Custis awoke to the aroma of steak and eggs. He slipped into faded blue jeans and an Old Navy T-shirt, unbolted his stateroom door, and entered the galley of the *Cats and Dogs*. Movladi Islamov was manning a skillet atop the electric range.

"I remember how much you like eggs with meat for breakfast," Islamov said.

"How does your bullet wound feel?" Custis asked.

"It hurts, but it is much better than yesterday, I think."

Islamov turned off the burner and walked to the boat's saloon, where he had placed a steak knife, fork, and spoon. He said, "I was up early this morning for prayers and have already eaten, but I'll have hot tea with you."

Custis sat and Islamov slid onto the cushion beside him.

Taking a bite, Custis said, "Hey, these are really good! I don't eat eggs as much as I used to because my cholesterol got high, but these are really tasty. I didn't know you were a short-order cook?"

"A soldier quickly learns many trades," he said. Then he asked, "Where will we fish today?"

"Moe, we agreed last night that we're going ashore so you can be seen by a medical doctor."

"And this doctor will call the local authorities, I assume, when they see that I have a bullet hole in me—yes?"

"That's the normal procedure, I believe."

Islamov leaned across the table and picked up the empty plate. He scooped up the utensils, too.

"It looks as if this is going to be a beautiful morning," Custis said, turning his head away from Islamov to glance toward the stern. As he was swinging his head back around, Islamov plunged a steak knife into Custis's chest. The blade went directly into the heart. Pulling out the knife, Islamov jabbed it again, and then again, until Custis slumped sideways onto the thick cushion. Islamov checked. Paul Custis was dead.

He calmly walked into the master stateroom and removed the sheet from the double bed there. He spread it out on deck and rolled Custis onto it. He dragged the sheet to the cold storage box used to preserve fish. It had double doors. Islamov crammed the body into the ice-packed cooler. It was four feet long, three feet wide, and a yard deep. That was enough space for Custis after his knees were pressed up against his chest. Islamov used towels to wipe up the blood. Then he turned his attention to the boat's controls. He used the trawler's compass to sail south. He would follow the shoreline to Annapolis, the capital of Maryland.

As he started the trawler's engines, he thought about what he'd done, and he told himself that he hadn't really had a choice. He couldn't risk being detained by the police.

"I'm sorry, good friend," he said out loud. "You should not have been so insistent about going ashore."

32

When I think of veterinarians, I picture someone who lives in the country in an old two-story farmhouse with horses and dogs and cats running freely in a tree-shaded and vast front yard. But Dr. Custis owned a Victorian, four-level town house built in 1870 in downtown Baltimore. It was made of ruby-red brick with a solid front door painted black that opened directly onto the concrete sidewalk. No grass here.

I knocked. No one answered. I rang the doorbell. No one came. Kimberly said the obvious, "I don't think he's home."

"Let's play detective," I said. I tapped on the door of the adjoining town house to the left. No one answered. I banged harder. No one responded. This was getting repetitious. I went down the street in the opposite direction and tried the neighbor who lived on the right side of the Custis house. Someone called out, "Who's there?"

I took a step back so the homeowner could see me through the security peephole.

"U.S. marshal," I announced, holding up my badge.

An elderly woman opened the front door, but she kept the chain fastened. She asked, "What do you want?"

"We're looking for Dr. Custis, your neighbor. Seen him recently?"

"Did he do something wrong?"

"No," I said. "He takes care of our K-9 police dogs and one of them got hurt this morning. Hit by a car. The doc's secretary said he was on vacation so we were trying to catch him at home."

A worried look came over her already wrinkled face. "I've seen police dogs on television do fantastic things," she said. "But I'm afraid the doctor is gone. I heard him leave last night a bit after ten o'clock when I was getting ready for bed. I think something's wrong with his car's muffler because it's too loud. That's why I know when he went out."

"And he didn't come home?"

"I don't think he did. I'm a light sleeper. I would've heard his muffler. I sure hope your police dog is okay."

When Kimberly and I returned to the car, she said, "You're a good liar. For a second, you almost had *me* believing a police dog had been hit."

I wasn't certain she meant that as a compliment.

As we drove away from the curb, I said, "Since we're partners now, I think you should tell me your story. Your background."

"You're the detective. You guess."

"Wealthy parents. Silver spoon. Ivy League. Career woman. Blindly ambitious. Don't think men can keep up with you. No wedding ring. Got a boyfriend?"

She didn't answer, which meant she didn't have one or, if she did, she didn't think he was important enough to mention. Or maybe she didn't feel it was any of my business.

"My father was a career State Department employee," she finally said. "Diplomatic corps. He met my mother in Ankara. That's in Turkey. She was born and reared there. Yes, they sent me to boarding schools. But the fact that I was of mixed blood didn't sit well with the Anglophiles. Tell me, are you always this insulting?"

"Brutally honest," I said, correcting her.

"Okay, then it's my turn. You're clearly blue-collar. You watched way too many John Wayne movies as a kid. You're suspicious of authority and you're proud of it. You're bullheaded, think you're smarter than anyone else, and cocky around women, even though you're actually insecure when it comes to them. You especially don't like aggressive women. They threaten you. You'd be loyal to your friends—if you had any. Your wife divorced you because you cared more about work than her. In a nutshell, you're a relic, and psychologically dysfunctional."

"Ouch!"

"What?" she asked coldly. "Did my brutal honesty hurt your feelings?"

"No. Not really. But let me ask you something: That comment about no friends, are you counting pets?"

"Why, you got a dog?"

"No, but I've been thinking about it."

My cell phone rang. It was Julie Custis.

"Paul is fishing on his boat, the *Cats and Dogs,*" she explained. "He was planning to leave first thing this morning for the bay."

"How can I reach him?"

"You can't, unless you swim out to wherever he's fishing. He refuses to answer his phone on trips like this. I guess you could have the Coast Guard contact him on his ship-to-shore radio if it's an emergency. Can you please tell me what's going on here?"

"We're not sure. Has he ever mentioned the name Moe Islamov to you?"

"That's one of his old college friends. He's not talked about him for years and then we were watching CNN a few weeks ago, and this masked figure came on. Paul said, 'Oh, my god! That's Moe!' Only the CNN reporter called him 'the snake' or something."

"Viper."

"That's right! But what's he got to do with my husband?"

"Probably nothing. Has your husband heard from Islamov recently?"

"Heavens no! Isn't he fighting in Chechnya? Why would he call us?"

I asked her for specifics about their boat.

"Paul keeps it docked at a marina south of the harbor tunnel." She gave me the name and address.

"When you hear from him, please have him give me a call," I said before hanging up.

Kimberly and I drove to the marina. It was a large operation with at least a hundred various kinds of boats moored along its slips. The owner operated out of a combination office, mini grocery store, and bait shop, but he wasn't around. The only employee on duty was a skinny, unshaven clerk who was thumbing through a well-worn *Hustler* magazine from the sales rack when we walked in.

"The animal doc came by here around midnight," he volunteered. "He just popped his head in to let me know he was taking his trawler out. Sometimes high school kids prowl around here looking for a joyride."

"I thought they did that in cars, not boats," Kimberly said.

"Boats got beds in 'em."

"Was anyone with him?" I asked.

"I didn't go outside and look. Why, you think the doc was with a woman?"

I didn't like the implication, nor did I like the lustful glances he was giving Kimberly.

"No," I said. "I thought he might've had a fishing buddy with him."

"Listen, all I know is he bought a bunch of ice and bait from me earlier and said he'd be out fishing all week. I didn't ask who he was taking with him."

Looking down at the *Hustler,* Kimberly said, "Yeah, it looks like you've got your hands full in here at night."

Her comment took him by surprise. He grinned stupidly, revealing teeth stained by tobacco juice, but couldn't think of anything clever to say.

When we returned to the car, I called the Coast Guard and asked them to try to reach Custis. A dispatcher promised to call me back as soon as they did.

Kimberly asked, "What now?"

"Time to head back to the CTC and face the music for skipping out on that joint task force meeting."

"You hungry?" she asked.

I hadn't eaten all day. When I'm busy on a case, I often forget to.

"There's a great crab house not far from here," she offered.

"What about Todd?" I asked. "He's going to be furious at us."

"He'll blame you. He likes me. Besides, another hour isn't going to make a difference."

Moe Islamov slowed the trawler's twin engines as he guided the *Cats and Dogs* gently into the Annapolis harbor. As it neared the public dock, Islamov could see tourists strolling between the souvenir shops and restaurants beside a narrow inlet that was just wide enough for a dozen boats to dock. These slips were rented by the hour and it wasn't unusual for a boat owner to sail into the harbor for a relaxing lunch. Despite his inexperience at the controls, Islamov was able to maneuver the vessel up to the pier. A sandy-haired kid helped tie it up.

"How long you gonna be, mister?" the youth asked.

"Only a few hours," Islamov replied. He'd gone through Custis's billfold, helping himself to $355 that he'd found there.

He paid the docking fee, stepped onto the dock, and disappeared into a crowd of sightseers and shoppers.

34

My hour-long lunch with Kimberly stretched into two hours. She was clearly enjoying herself, and neither or us seemed in a hurry to return to CIA headquarters and have our knuckles rapped by Todd for missing the FBI meeting. Over her order of soft-shell crabs, she began talking about overseas assignments that she'd had. Kimberly struck me as a natural-born storyteller. It also became clear that she felt more comfortable living outside the United States than being stationed at home. I asked her why and she seemed surprised.

"Isn't it obvious? Look at me," she replied.

"Sorry, but I'm not following you."

"My parents thought that because my father was a white American and my mother was Turkish café au lait that I could choose between being Caucasian and being Middle Eastern. Overseas, that's true, but not here. If you have a drop of nonwhite blood, you're colored."

"I think your brown coloring is perfect," I said, before I realized what I was saying.

"Thanks," she said. "But being a woman at the CIA, especially a non-white woman, doesn't exactly help your career. It's still very much a good-old-boys' network, and all of those good-old-boys are lily-white. I just feel more comfortable abroad."

My cell rang. It was the Coast Guard.

"We've found Dr. Paul Custis," the dispatcher said. "He's been stabbed to death."

The Coast Guard had launched a search for the *Cats and Dogs* after Dr. Custis didn't respond via his ship-to-shore radio. When the trawler was spotted at the Annapolis dock, a crew had been dispatched to investigate. They'd boarded the craft after the dock attendant told them that a foreigner had sailed it into the harbor. A quick search had turned up Custis's body in the ice storage box.

Kimberly and I drove to Annapolis. The local police were in charge. I flashed my deputy marshal credentials and we made our way to the *Cats and Dogs*. A patrolman was standing guard while the forensic team gathered evidence.

Because no one knew there was a possible link between Custis's murder and Moe Islamov, we were the only federal agents at the scene besides the Coast Guard. The two Annapolis homicide detectives investigating the murder wanted to know why we were interested in what seemed to them to be a local case.

I didn't want to tell them. I was afraid they'd leak information to the media. Anything that involves terrorism is guaranteed to make national headlines, especially if we had a homicidal Chechen running loose. So I conveniently forgot to mention the CIA, CTC, and terrorism. Instead, I explained that Ms. Lodge and I were deputy marshals hunting for an escaped ex-con who liked to steal boats and stab people. When they asked me the name of our suspect, I made one up: "Ketchum."

"And his first name?" the detective asked.

"Todd," I replied. "Todd Ketchum."

Kimberly shot me a nasty look, but the detective didn't find anything suspicious about my explanation.

"If your ex-con did this," he said, "we'll know real soon. The murderer left plenty of fingerprints and trace evidence. He obviously wasn't too concerned about his tracks."

We chatted with the investigators and then headed back to our car.

"Ketchum?" Kimberly said. "I can't believe you told them we were looking for an ex-con with a name that's pronounced 'catch-'em.' And then you threw in *Todd's* name!"

I didn't respond. I was thinking about Moe Islamov. The last time I'd spoken to him, we'd been sitting in a pub and he'd appeared as harmless and ordinary as any man I'd ever known. I was contrasting that memory with the cold-blooded stabbing that I'd just seen. Paul Custis had been Moe Islamov's roommate. They'd been friends! And yet Islamov apparently had stuck Custis in his chest with a knife and stuffed him like a caught fish into an icebox.

Kimberly said, "Have you ever heard the term 'the banality of evil'?"

"Yes," I replied. "But I don't think that really fits Moe."

"Why not? You said he was a regular guy—someone you'd never suspect."

"Because this really isn't about banality. It's about fanaticism. If you genuinely believe you are God's chosen instrument, then everything and anything is permissible that helps you achieve your mission. Anyone who gets in your way is expendable—even best friends. That's how a man such as Moe Islamov rationalizes what he is doing."

Dead bodies normally don't affect me. I've seen a lot of them. After a while, you find yourself thinking about them not as people but as pieces of evidence. Of course, when the corpse is someone you know, it's tougher. It's not because you feel sorry for the person who's dead, even though you clearly do. It's upsetting because it's a reminder of your own vulnerability. If Moe Islamov had shown up unexpectedly at my front door late one night and I'd been unaware that he was hiding from the FBI, I would've invited him inside, too. And I was pretty certain that despite our friendship and past camaraderie, Moe would have skewered me with a knife in the morning. It would all have been part of some misguided, divinely inspired "master plan," and I would have been the corpse chilling in the ice chest.

35

BRIGHTON BEACH,
BROOKLYN, NEW YORK

"Come here!" Ivan Sitov declared.

The seventeen-year-old girl crept forward. He was sitting on a metal folding chair in her bedroom and was wearing only his white boxer shorts. The girl's fourteen-month-old baby daughter, Lana, short for Svetlana, was crying in the adjoining bedroom inside the upstairs apartment in a two-story house off Coney Island Avenue.

"Do you know this bitch's name?" Sitov asked his bodyguard, who was standing near the door. Sitov explained, "It's Afim'ia."

The bodyguard grinned. Translated into English, the Russian name Afim'ia means "the unkissed."

The girl said nothing. She was petite and weighed less than ninety pounds. She wore a gold Charmeuse silk robe Sitov had given her. The gown was knee-length and had French seams, but could be bought over the Internet for less than forty dollars.

"You can wait outside now," Sitov said. "We won't be too long."

The bodyguard left, walking down a hallway that took him by the nursery, where Lana was clutching the side of her crib and staring out the open door. When the infant saw him, she stopped crying, but only until she realized he was not coming to comfort her. The bodyguard exited through another door and descended a flight of covered steps that had been attached to the side of the older house. A black Mercedes-Benz S600 with tinted rear windows was parked in the center of the street. It was well after midnight, and there was no traffic. The car had its caution lights flashing. It was raining hard.

"Damn!" the bodyguard cursed. He could remain under the covered stairway or he could make a run for the car, which was about fifty feet away. He checked his Rolex. Based on past visits, the bodyguard knew Sitov would be upstairs another fifteen or so minutes. He decided to make a dash for the car. The rain pelted him as soon as he stepped out from the protective cover. He nearly slipped as he ran. The front passenger's door was locked, so he pounded angrily on the glass and the driver pushed a button unlocking it.

Meanwhile, upstairs, Sitov said, "I'm ready."

Afim'ia tugged off his boxer shorts so that he was now sitting naked on the chair.

"You left Russia when you were still a baby," he said, "but there is a saying there your mother knows. 'A chicken is not a bird and a woman is not a person.' Do you understand this?"

Afim'ia didn't answer. She was afraid he'd slap her if she offered the wrong response.

"Of course, you don't know," he continued, "because you're an ignorant cunt—a stupid Russian whore."

There was a twin bed in Afim'ia's bedroom. A white teddy bear leaned against the pink bed pillow. The bedspread also was pink and cheap. On the bedside table was a clock radio and last month's *Seventeen* magazine. The lamp there had a plastic cutout of Elvis attached to its stem. A battery behind the singer's hips caused them to swivel back and forth when the light was on.

Afim'ia dropped her gown to the red-and-black-speckled linoleum floor. Her parents lived in the apartment downstairs. Whenever Sitov came to see her, Afim'ia's father turned up the volume on their CD player to cover the sounds. Her father always played the same album. She could hear it rising up now: the voice of Novella Nikolaevna Matveeva, a Russian folksinger whose songs were about romance. Afim'ia preferred Smash Mouth's *Pacific Coast Party* album. California! That's where she and her baby would flee someday.

Her parents had fled once. From Russia to America. They'd come to give her a better life. What a cruel joke! Sitov had first spotted her one afternoon when she was walking home from public school. That night he and two men came to talk to her parents. That's when everything changed. There was no schooling now.

Afim'ia knew what he wanted. He came here two days a week. She stepped beside him and bent over his lap so she was now looking directly into the linoleum. Her bare buttocks were over his thighs. She could feel his limp genitalia underneath her. He slapped her hard with his open palm.

"Russian whore!" he declared, as he hit her again. Her father turned up the volume. Matveeva was singing: "Cinderella."

"Bitch!" Sitov shouted, striking her. She did not cry out. Instead, she dug her fingernails into the palms of her clenched hands, knowing that if she screamed, it only encouraged him to hit harder. Underneath her soft belly she felt his penis beginning to stir. He was sixty-four years old, fat and saggy. Mats of thick black hair covered much of his white skin, which was pocked from old pimple sites. He began smacking her faster, and with each blow his penis became a bit firmer until it was semierect. Now ready, he pushed her from his lap. She hit the floor but spun to her knees and grabbed his penis with her hands. She began massaging it. *It was almost over,* she told herself.

"Ahhhhhhhhhh!" he cried moments later. He shoved her away with both hands. She stayed on her knees, afraid to move, waiting for his next instruction. Lana was still crying next door.

Sitov's eyes were shut, his head tossed back. His round face was covered with sweat, and for a second she hoped he'd died from the excitement. How easy it would be to tuck a knife under her bed, grab it, and stab him in the chest at this very instant. But what if she missed? What if he didn't die?

She heard her father lower the music. *Why was she the one who had to suffer?*

He opened his eyes. "I thought I saw two people on the street once in Moscow," he said, more to himself than to her. "But I was wrong. It was just a man and his wife." He shook his head in disgust. "You don't understand, do you? It's another joke. Ask your mother. Every Russian woman knows it. I'm doing you a favor, training you."

He nodded his head toward the bedroom door, and she rushed to her feet and ran down the hallway. The apartment's bathroom was directly across from Lana's bedroom, and as soon as the infant saw her mother, she wailed louder. Afim'ia hushed her: "Quiet! He'll hurt you!"

At the bathroom sink, she warmed a washcloth and grabbed a towel. She carried both back to her room and reached down to clean Sitov's thighs, but when the warm cloth touched him, he yelped and backhanded her. She was knocked to the floor.

"Bitch!" he screamed. "It's too hot."

She went to cool the cloth.

"Why does that brat make so damn much noise?" he complained.

Afim'ia didn't answer.

"If you'd given me a son, he wouldn't bawl constantly h.

She returned and washed him gently. Satisfied, Sitov stoo,

She scrambled to the bed, where she'd carefully stacked h. in a neat pile. She carried them—one article at a time—back to th and dressed him.

With her head bowed, she said, "The baby. She needs clothes."

"Don't I give you and your parents enough?" he complained. He raised his open hand to strike her, but she cowered and he stopped himself. "You're a worthless cow," he said. He removed a dollar bill from his pants pocket and tossed it on the floor.

It was still raining hard when Sitov made his way down the covered stairwell. He'd expected to see his bodyguard waiting there, but he wasn't. Sitov peered into the evening darkness at his Mercedes-Benz. It had cost $300,000 because of the executive protection package that he'd ordered. It was supposed to be as impenetrable as an M1A1 Abrams tank. He waited for his driver and bodyguard to notice him and hurry out with an umbrella.

But no one came.

Sitov called his bodyguard on his cell phone. There was no answer. He tried his driver's number. No answer. He saw lightning. Perhaps the storm was interfering with the signals. Just the same, they would pay for their laxity. He scanned the street. No one was in sight. The block was lined with parked vehicles. Nothing seemed out of the ordinary. If someone had wanted to attack him, they would've done so already. He'd been standing under a bare bulb at the bottom of the exposed stairs for several moments.

Afraid that he might slip on the wet concrete, Sitov moved cautiously toward his car. By the time he reached it, he was both soaked and furious, so much so that he didn't hesitate when neither his bodyguard nor his chauffeur made any effort to help him. Instead, he jerked open the rear passenger door and dropped inside, unleashing profanities as he slammed the door behind him.

It was only then, after he had plopped on the plush leather seat, with rainwater dripping off him, that Ivan Ivanovich Sitov leaned toward the two figures seated in front of him. The man in the passenger seat was his bodyguard, but his head was hanging down. Now his chin rested against his massive chest. He didn't move. The driver, meanwhile, was someone Sitov had never seen.

"Who the hell are you?" Sitov demanded.

"My name is Vladimir Mikhailovich Khrenkov," the man replied, as he turned sideways to face his backseat passenger.

Sitov thought for a moment, but didn't recognize the name. He glanced down and saw that Khrenkov was holding a pistol in his left hand. It was pointed directly between the car's bucket seats at him.

"My sister was Olga Polov," Khrenkov continued.

"Is this someone I'm supposed to know?" Sitov replied. There was no fear in his voice.

"You had her murdered."

Sitov considered this and then said, "I don't know who gave you this information, but they lied."

"Your lapdog, Igor Aleksandrovich Fedorov, kidnapped my sister and held my family hostage. He did this so I would assassinate Sergey Pudin."

Now Sitov understood, and for the first time, fear shot through him.

"Listen," he said, "Fedorov acted on his own. It's true, I wanted Pudin dead. But I did not wish you or your family any harm. We are reasonable men. Killing me will accomplish nothing. But if you spare me, I will help you take your revenge on Fedorov."

When Khrenkov didn't immediately respond, Sitov mistook his silence for interest in his proposition. "I will show you where Fedorov lives. We can drive right now and I can call him out to the car for you!"

"The only way you can help me," Khrenkov replied, "is by dying." He pulled the trigger.

Sitov screamed in pain when the bullet hit him in his stomach.

"My sister was raped," Khrenkov said.

Sitov gasped. "Don't shoot—"

Before he could finish, Khrenkov shot again, this time taking aim at Sitov's face, knocking his head backward and then forward. Khrenkov stepped outside and opened the car's rear door. He fired three more rounds into Sitov. Certain now that the mobster was truly dead, Khrenkov slammed the car door, raised the handgun again, and fired it into the Mercedes-Benz's window. Because the glass was bullet resistant, the slug didn't pierce it. But the window shattered and the car's alarm began blaring. Lights in the houses along the block came on. Residents peered out.

Khrenkov tucked the pistol in his jacket and calmly made his way to the sidewalk. He'd parked a few blocks from here. He glanced at the upstairs window of the house where Sitov had been. A young girl there, holding a baby, looked down at the noisy car.

Khrenkov wondered: *How long will it be before Fedorov hears that Sitov has been murdered? How deep will Fedorov try to burrow to escape the same fate?*

"Ivan Sitov is dead," deputy U.S. Marshal Scott Breeden announced. "Someone murdered him last night in Brighton Beach."

Breeden was still serving as the service's liaison with the FBI while it was investigating the sniper shooting of my dead witness. He was also my own personal Deep Throat. He'd telephoned me this morning seconds before I was to leave my apartment for work, where I was supposed to meet Kimberly Lodge and attend a joint task force meeting. That session was being held to review the stabbing murder of Dr. Paul Custis aboard his trawler and our continued pursuit of Moe Islamov.

Whew!

Two different killings. Two different cases.

I mentally placed Islamov on hold and focused on what Breeden was now telling me about the Russian Mafia.

"The FBI thinks a pro killed Sitov because his limo driver and bodyguard were also whacked," he explained. "All three were shot at close range. The driver's body was found stuffed in the car trunk. The other stiff was still sitting in the front seat. And here's the best part. They were murdered with 9×18 mm slugs fired from what appears to be a PM Makarov semiautomatic pistol."

"A what?"

"It's a Soviet military handgun."

I took a moment to digest this. A notorious crime godfather is gunned down with a Soviet-made military handgun. The sniper who killed my witness on Capitol Hill had used a Soviet-made military rifle. It didn't take a rocket scientist to see a connection.

"The bureau still believes the mob had the Polov family kidnapped as part of an extortion attempt," Breeden continued. "So now they're convinced one of the Polovs' relatives is seeking revenge."

"And what do the Polovs say about all of this?"

"They're still insisting they don't have any relatives living in Moscow."

"Does the FBI believe them?"

"Absolutely not!" he exclaimed. "The Russian authorities have sent us a cable that states there are no relatives of the Polov family in Russia and the FBI believes that's a lie. The Russians have never—ever—responded with a cable like this one, and the fact that they're now going out of their way to deny there are any relatives living there means the Russians are protecting someone. He must be important."

"Or politically well connected."

"Hey," Breeden replied nervously, "we're still off the record here, right? You aren't going to tell anyone we've talked?"

"Yes, yes," I answered, impatiently. "Now tell me, where have the Polovs been relocated?"

"I can't reveal that! I'd lose my job!"

"Breeden," I snapped, "we've been over this before. The Marshals Service wants you to keep me informed, remember? It wants me to help the FBI catch Sergey Pudin's killer. Don't turn into a chump now."

"Yeah, but—"

"Listen, I'm driving over to headquarters. Think up an excuse to leave your office and meet me in the underground parking garage on the fourth level near the elevator in about thirty minutes."

I wasn't certain that Breeden wouldn't lose his nerve, but he was waiting when I arrived there.

"Colorado," he whispered as I stepped up to him. "Pueblo." He handed me a yellow sticky pad with an address scrawled on it. "They're in an older subdivision called Belmont Estates."

"Thanks."

"Just remember, this meeting never happened."

As soon as I exited the parking garage, I telephoned Kimberly. She was fuming. The joint task force meeting had already started—without me.

"Sorry, but I'm heading to the airport," I said. "Family emergency. Real sudden. Make excuses for me, will you?"

"I didn't think you had a family."

"A father. He's real sick, cancer." Actually, both of my parents died a decade ago in a freak accident, but I was fairly certain Kimberly didn't know that.

The tone in her voice changed. "Oh, no. I hope he's okay."

"I'll be back as quickly as I can."

Within a few hours, I was landing at my favorite airport: Denver. From there, I caught a puddle jumper to the regional airport in Pueblo, which is a working-class city located in the southern part of Colorado. I used a pay phone to call Russ Armengol, the deputy marshal whose jurisdiction covers this area. We'd worked together earlier when I'd hidden Pudin in Central City.

"I thought you got dumped into another agency," Armengol said.

"I've been detailed to the CIA, but I've been sent to Pueblo to help the FBI. We've got a good lead on Sergey Pudin's murder." I added, "This is a black-bag job."

"Oh," Armengol said quietly. "Whaddaya have in mind?"

"I need to break into a protected witness's house, and I need you to keep them occupied while I'm searching it. Say about eight tonight. I'll need two hours."

Like me, Armengol had been a deputy for all of his career. He knew about black jobs and he knew enough to know that the fewer questions he asked, the better.

"I'll have them drive up to Colorado Springs to meet me," he said. "That should give you enough time."

I rented a car and drove into Pueblo via Highway 50. When I reached Bonforte Boulevard, I turned off. A few blocks later, I took a left onto Horseshoe Drive. The Polovs were living in a three-bedroom house on Kickapoo Street, named after an Indian tribe. It ran parallel to Zuni and Iroquois streets. We'd changed the Polovs' last name to Shapkin. The Marshals Service, as a routine, doesn't mess with a person's first name. We've found that it's difficult for witnesses to get used to completely new first and last names. By changing only his last name, a witness still had time to catch himself and not make a mistake when he's signing documents. There's also a psychological advantage to permitting a witness to retain at least some of his identity.

As soon as I saw the bright blue house at the corner of Kickapoo Street, I knew how I could slip inside without being spotted. It was November and dark by eight o'clock. That would help. But another factor in my favor was a six-foot-high slatted fence around the backyard. Once I ducked in behind it, I'd be out of the neighbors' sight. There was a gate that opened into the backyard. It was one of those double openings, large enough for a vehicle to pass through. I parked a block away and walked alongside the fence. When I got to the gate, I reached over, lifted the metal latch, and eased through.

The Polovs' house was a one-story ranch style that had been built on a concrete slab. There was no deadbolt on the rear door. I forced it open with my pocketknife and entered a mud room that led into the kitchen. I checked the icebox first. I've never figured out why, but people always hide things in their refrigerators. There was nothing out of the ordinary there.

We require protected witnesses to destroy all family photo albums, diplomas, personal letters, school yearbooks, marriage and baptismal certificates, and anything else that could link them to their pasts. Before they are relocated, every witness signs a statement swearing they've gotten rid of their personal mementos. But I've never met one yet who didn't keep something—usually a picture.

The living room, next to the kitchen, had a bay window with closed curtains. I continued my exploration down the hallway. The first room on my left was a bathroom. Across from it was a bedroom. At the end of the hall were two more bedrooms, one on each side. I began my search in the master bedroom but didn't find anything. The other two rooms belonged to the Polovs' sons, I deduced, based on the porno magazines and X-rated videotapes that I found tucked in their closets. An hour of searching brought me back to the living room empty-handed. It was my last hope.

The Polovs had furnished it with a sofa, two overstuffed chairs, a coffee table, two bookcases, a pair of end tables, and various electronics: a big-screen television set and stereo CD player. I checked the shelves first and noticed there was one volume that seemed out of place. One bookcase contained popular bestsellers by Mary Higgins Clark, Sue Grafton, Patricia Cornwell, and other notable women crime and mystery writers. The other was filled with volumes by Nelson DeMille, John Grisham, Tom Clancy, Scott Turow. There was only one nonfiction book on display, and it was on the bottom shelf. *Blind Ambition: The White House Years,* by John Dean, whose testimony helped bring down President Richard Nixon during the Watergate scandal. I'm not much of a reader, but I recognized this specific title because the U.S. Marshals Service had once protected Dean. The deputy in charge of keeping him safe had been my mentor when I first joined the service, and he used to tell me stories about his experiences. I remembered him saying that John

Dean always felt strangers were staring at him whenever he and his wife went out in public. But the gawkers were actually checking out his blond and curvy wife, Maureen, who became famous during the Watergate hearings for her strikingly good looks. The TV cameras always showed her sitting faithfully behind her husband as he testified.

Dean's nonfiction account of Watergate didn't fit with the novels, so I removed it first. *Surprise!* The text inside was Cyrillic. Dean's book jacket had been wrapped around a Russian Orthodox Bible. I found two photographs tucked between the pages. The first showed a family standing in front of the Pushkin Café. There was a man, a woman, two young men, a girl, and then another man. I assumed this was a snapshot of the Polov family and that the girl in the picture was Olga. The extra man was probably a relative or business partner. There was a GRAND OPENING banner nearby strung across the restaurant's door. The second image was of a teenager dressed in Soviet military green camouflage pants and shirt. An armored personnel carrier could be seen in the distant background along with two men wearing traditional Afghan clothing. The youth was holding a cigarette in his left hand, which dangled casually at his side. In his right hand was a Dragunov sniper rifle.

I flipped the photograph over and on its back found several Russian words, which I couldn't translate, and the date: 1981.

I compared the two snapshots and noticed that the soldier was not with the family members posing in front of the Pushkin Café.

This must be the missing relative!

I tucked the family photograph back in the Russian Bible and returned John Dean's "book" to its spot on the shelf. But I kept the photograph of the lone soldier. I had a feeling the man in this 1981 picture was the same sniper who had waited patiently for me to escort Sergey Pudin out of the Dirksen Building. I also suspected that he was the same murderer who had gunned down Ivan Sitov and his two miscreants in Brooklyn.

I exited the Polovs' house the exact same way I'd entered it. I still didn't know our assailant's name, but I now knew what he looked like—or used to look like more than twenty years ago. I also had a hunch. If the assassin was out to get even, then I knew who his next target would be. The FBI had said that a mobster named Igor Aleksandrovich Fedorov had orchestrated the Polov kidnappings and Olga Polov's rape and murder.

If we found Fedorov, then the revenge killer would come to us.

PART III

37

The two rented Ford Broncos crept eastbound in jammed traffic caused by commuters streaming from the downtown office buildings that line K Street Northwest, the unofficial main street of Washington's business district. Movladi Islamov sat dispassionately in the front seat of the first Bronco. He'd selected his wardrobe with television and terrorism in mind. Everything was black: his leather jacket, his turtleneck shirt, his trousers, his combat boots, even the ski cap on his head. The mask was one of those that had holes in it only for the eyes and mouth. Islamov intended to pull it down as soon as the assault began. Not only would it conceal his identity, but it would give him a tremendous advantage. Viewers would be forced to use their imaginations, and Islamov understood that evil left undefined is always more terrifying than evil that can be seen.

Three other Chechens were riding with him, including the driver. The SUV following them was carrying his second in command, Aslan Akhman, two women, and another man, bringing the total number in the two vehicles to eight. As the Fords inched across the intersection at Connecticut Avenue and K Street, Islamov spoke over the intercom on his cell phone to Akhman.

"We'll be taking a left ahead!"

Two blocks later, the lead SUV turned onto Sixteenth Street. The second followed, staying close to prevent anyone from separating them. When they reached the next crosspoint—at Sixteenth and L Streets—the caravan stopped. They wanted to distance themselves from the cars traveling in front of them. They needed room to accelerate so they could reach maximum horsepower. The drivers in back of their impromptu roadblock began leaning on their horns. But the rented Fords stayed put. After several moments, Islamov took off his sunglasses, lowered his ski mask into place, and commanded into the intercom: "Now!"

Both vehicles lunged forward.

Islamov's plan was simple. As they neared the stone mansion at 1125 Sixteenth Street, the head SUV swung right into the northern entrance to a half-circle drive. The second went in the southern entrance. Both collided with ornate wrought-iron gates. But those barriers, installed in the early 1970s, had never been reinforced, and neither could stop the duo of Fords from wrenching them off their hinges.

Leaping from their trucks, Islamov and his team ran across the blacktop courtyard and burst through the mansion's double front doors. Just inside the foyer was a glass-enclosed security booth, but its panes were not bullet resistant. Islamov fired his Bizon submachine gun, a Russian-made antiterrorist weapon that he had plucked from a dead soldier who'd been sent by Moscow to Chechnya to eliminate him. Five of its rounds easily cut through the glass and pierced the guard's chest, killing him instantly.

Islamov and his crew had spent hours studying a set of floor plans of the U.S.S.R.'s old embassy. Each terrorist knew exactly where to go. The women ran down a corridor at the left of the lobby and forcibly began to round up the workers in the basement and first-floor offices. Another of Islamov's soldiers stationed himself at the entrance. Islamov and the remaining ones bolted up the marble stairs to the second floor.

From a disgruntled employee, Islamov had learned there would be two armed guards posted here. The gunfire would've already been heard, so Islamov had assumed the men would be ready to fight. But when he reached the landing, he quickly realized he had overestimated his opponents. One of them was peering out a window at the abandoned Broncos now blocking both ends of the embassy compound's courtyard. The other guard was trying to phone the security desk downstairs to find out what was happening. Islamov and his warriors fired, dropping both. This left only one embassy security guard inside the building. He was stationed on the third floor.

Two of Islamov's men stayed behind to collect hostages. Islamov and the last of his attack team proceeded to the next floor. Like his comrades below, the Russian guard on the third floor had heard gunfire. But he'd turned over an old gray metal desk and was now crouching behind it to thwart the attackers. As soon as he saw the masked Chechens, he opened fire. One of his slugs struck the man standing next to Islamov. It sent him tumbling backward down the stairs. He didn't fall far because Akhman was right behind him. Akhman tried to catch his wounded comrade without dropping his own semiautomatic weapon, and this caused both of them to fall down the stairs. Islamov, meanwhile, ducked for cover and, in a well-practiced move, retrieved a hand grenade from his jacket pocket. It bounced long and hard across the marble floor before it blew up, killing the Russian crouched behind the desk.

Now confident that the embassy was under his control, Islamov motioned to Akhman and they bolted down the marble staircase toward the basement. Once there, they moved quickly along a narrow east-west hallway, and Akhman removed a map from his pocket as they ran. It had been sketched by Andrei Bobkov, the Russian physicist who had sought them out in Chechnya, and although both men had memorized it, Akhman wanted to make certain they knew exactly where they were going.

Bobkov's drawing showed the location of the atomic bomb, which Bobkov and his scientific team had secretly built in 1954.

"It's in the last room on the right!" Akhman shouted.

Islamov tried the steel door there. It was unlocked. But when he entered, he found himself inside an oblong room divided by shoulder-high partitions into a series of cubbyhole offices. Each contained a metal desk, computer work station, and chair. There was no bomb.

"His map must be wrong!" Islamov exclaimed.

Followed by Akhman, Islamov darted into the hallway and tried the door directly across from them. This room was identical to the one they'd just inspected. It also contained partitioned offices. The only difference was that its westernmost wall was lined with a series of huge metal filing cabinets.

"We've been betrayed!" Akhman declared. "The old man lied!"

"Maybe they dismantled the bomb. Maybe it's gone now," Islamov said, as he turned his head once again, scanning the second room they had entered.

Suddenly, he realized their mistake.

He swung around and reentered the hallway. About halfway down the passageway, there was a coiled water hose and a bright red firefighter's ax for emergencies. He hurried toward them and grabbed the ax. With it firmly in hand, he returned to the first room they had inspected. This was where Bobkov had claimed the bomb was hidden.

Islamov hoisted the ax above his right shoulder and brought it crashing down into the room's western wall, which was decorated with a large map of the world. By chance, the blade ripped into the diagram almost directly on Moscow.

"The room across the hall is the same as this one," Islamov explained, "but it's filled with big file cabinets. There are none here. This is a false wall!"

He swung the ax again and again with such force that it easily punched through the wallboard. Within seconds, he had knocked a hole large enough for them to peer inside.

Inside the cubicle was a metal cylinder that Islamov estimated was eleven feet long and six feet in circumference. It was resting on a reinforced steel cradle with metal wheels that held it about two feet above the floor. Islamov had never seen a nuclear bomb up close, nor would he have assumed from first glance that this was a bomb. Bobkov had told him that it had been designed to look like a storage tank that holds propane or some other fuel. Because it had not been made to be dropped from an airplane, it did not have fins nor had it been built in a teardrop shape. Islamov moved into the chamber to examine the device more closely. He'd been told to look for a metal plate located near the center of the device. He found it quickly. It was five inches wide and seven inches tall and engraved with Cyrillic letters. He scanned the markings and found what he'd been seeking:

РДС-6с

Islamov broke into a grin. He had it!

There was a metal safe welded to the side of the cradle. It was about twelve inches tall, ten inches wide, and five inches deep. A thick cable ran from it to the end of the cylinder. Islamov had been told that the safe contained the Emergency Operating Procedure for the bomb. It explained how to detonate the device and schematics about its inner workings.

Andrei Bobkov hadn't lied. This was the nuclear sleeper device that he and his long-dead teammates had secretly built in the very heart of Washington, D.C. It had simply been cocooned behind a facade of two-by-fours and plaster.

"It exists!" Akhman exclaimed.

Islamov handed him the ax. "Finish ripping down this wall," he ordered. "I'm going upstairs."

One of his fellow terrorists was waiting. "We have thirty-two hostages," the woman reported. "We've lost one of our own."

"Take them upstairs as planned," Islamov said.

Stepping into the embassy's lobby, he dialed 911 on his cell phone. When a voice answered, Islamov triumphantly declared, "Chechen freedom fighters have just seized control of the old Soviet embassy on Sixteenth Street!"

"I'm sorry but all of our operators are busy. Please stay on the line and your call will be answered in the order that it was received." A recording.

Islamov dialed 202-456-1414, the published number for the White House. An actual human being answered. "Listen carefully, because this is not a prank," Islamov said. "My name is Movladi Islamov. I'm a Chechen freedom fighter and we have just taken charge of the old Soviet embassy on Sixteenth Street. Tell your FBI and CIA there are two Ford Broncos parked on the embassy grounds. Both contain explosives. We have taken hostages. Any attempt to rescue them will result in their deaths and the detonation of the bombs in the vehicles. Do you understand?"

"Yes, but could you tell me your name again," a woman's voice replied.

He hung up and punched another number on his cell phone: 202-334-6000. It was the main switchboard of the *Washington Post*.

"How may I direct your call?" a pleasant voice answered.

"News desk," Islamov said.

A man answered and Islamov repeated the exact speech that he had given to the White House switchboard operator. He added, "Since *Post* is located directly behind the embassy, it should be easy for you to verify my claims. You may also wish to evacuate your employees in case we are forced to set off the bombs in our trucks!"

He disconnected the call before the editor could ask any questions. There would be lots of time to talk to the media later and plenty of time to negotiate with the authorities.

38

"Wyatt!" Kimberly exclaimed as she stuck her head into my work cubicle. "CTC conference room. Now! We've got an emergency!"

Sure, I thought. Everything around here is an emergency. That's why we have to attend so many meetings. My obviously less-than-enthusiastic reaction was noted by Ms. Lodge.

"This really is a crisis!" she said. "Moe Islamov has just overrun the old Russian embassy in downtown D.C. near the White House!"

That tidbit made me move a bit faster. We joined about twenty other CTC employees hustling into the meeting. The CTC head, Henry Clarke, was adjusting a slide image that he'd just projected on a screen when we walked in. It showed a four-story, stone, Tudor-style mansion.

"The Russians have two embassies," he explained. "This is the older one. It's less than four blocks from the White House and was built at the turn of the twentieth century by Mrs. George M. Pullman, the widow of the railroad sleeping-car magnate. She never lived in it. Instead, she sold it to the last czarist family, the House of Romanov. When the Communists seized power, they claimed the deed."

Clarke pointed to the top floor. "The KGB operated from here during the cold war. It's where we believe Islamov is probably holding the hostages."

"Why there?" someone asked.

Kimberly whispered, "That's Lansing Schaeffer who asked that question. He's an assistant to the DCCI."

I'd figured he was someone important, otherwise he wouldn't have interrupted Clarke.

Clarke replied, "The KGB installed thick shields in front of the windows on this floor to prevent electronic eavesdropping. There's also only one entrance to the floor, and the KGB installed a heavy door there for security. If there was a fire in the embassy, for example, they'd seal the door to keep us from sneaking inside dressed as firefighters—which is exactly what they tried to pull on us once at our Moscow station."

"Can the hostages be rescued?" Schaeffer asked.

"That floor is a fortress. We can't land a helicopter on the roof because of all the various antennas the KGB installed and there's no way for them to escape out a window because they are covered. The FBI Hostage Rescue Team is working on possible scenarios right now."

Returning to his slide show, Clarke pushed a switch causing a different view of the embassy to appear. "During the cold war, there was always a D.C. police officer positioned outside the curved driveway. The Soviets also kept an armed sentry inside the courtyard. But even back then, security was rather lax. This is where two of our most destructive spies—retired naval officer John Walker Jr. and CIA traitor Aldrich Ames—simply walked in and asked to speak to the KGB chief."

Clarke clicked the control again and a new image flashed on the screen. "In the 1970s, we agreed to let the Soviets build a new and bigger embassy," he continued. "But we rejected their first two choices for sites. Finally, we agreed to let them build at Mount Alto in the District, which happens to be the third-highest point in the entire city. The White House said yes without ever asking us, and, of course, we immediately complained that the KGB was going to be able to intercept all sorts of secure communications from its new high ground. I'm sure you all remember what happened next."

I didn't, but wasn't going to ask. I was still trying to figure out what idiot had approved the Soviet's request to build their new embassy on a hill!

"The White House refused to let the Soviets occupy their new embassy after it was completed," Clarke explained, "and for more than ten years, both sides bickered back and forth. After the Soviet Union collapsed, we finally let the Russians move in." The slide on the screen showed a white rectangular stone building with narrow slits for windows. It looked a lot like most prisons I'd seen.

"What happened to the old embassy—the one the terrorists have seized?" Schaeffer asked.

"It's been used mostly for ceremonial dinners and cultural events. The Russians never bothered to update its security. They only had four guards stationed there. We believe the hostages are low-level employees assigned rather mundane jobs—arranging visas, running student-exchange programs, that sort of thing. Islamov was clearly after the building more than anyone inside it."

"What's Islamov want?"

"We're assuming this is a rather reckless and dramatic publicity stunt to attract world attention. The State Department, the FBI, and the Russians are handling this right now. But there's more at risk here than just the hostages."

Clarke paused, apparently to emphasize the seriousness of his next disclosure. Then he said, "Islamov telephoned the White House and claimed there are explosives packed inside two vehicles the Chechens used to crash through the embassy's gates. The FBI believes they contain something heavy, probably bags of fertilizer, based on how close the rented Fords are sitting to the ground."

"Isn't that what Timothy McVeigh used in Oklahoma City?"

"Yes," Clarke answered. "Bags of fertilizer are not dangerous by themselves, but when mixed with nitromethane, which is used in drag racers, or with some sort of diesel fuel, they can become lethal bombs. McVeigh reportedly had forty-eight-hundred pounds of the stuff crammed into his rental truck. We doubt Islamov has that much, but there's enough out there to cause serious damage to nearby buildings."

"Is the president safe?"

"The Secret Service wants to move him away from Washington just to be sure. But I've been told the president doesn't want to leave. He's afraid it might set off a panic. Plus, he doesn't want to give Islamov that much power—making it appear as if a terrorist has driven him from the White House."

Clarke turned off the projector, and when the lights came up, he spotted Kimberly and me. "Wyatt Conway is a deputy U.S. marshal who's recently joined us," he announced, nodding in my direction, "and I'd like to suggest that he be assigned to work as a liaison with the Russians and FBI. He's the only person here who actually knows Islamov, having once taught him in a university classroom."

Everyone, including Schaeffer, turned to look at me.

"I'll be happy to do whatever I can," I replied, "but I'd appreciate it if you could also assign Ms. Lodge to assist me. She's an expert on the situation in Chechnya, and I'm not up on all of the political dynamics there."

"Sounds like an excellent idea," Schaeffer decreed. "I'd like as many eyes on the Russians as possible. They've always elected to use brute force rather than patience in situations such as this." He stood up, a sign that he'd listened to enough. But before leaving, he addressed Clarke. "Henry, the president doesn't want a bloodbath in the streets of D.C. He doesn't want a terrorist setting off two truck-bombs in the middle of our nation's capital. But he *also* doesn't want the Russians launching some crazed Rambo rescue mission either. Somehow we've got to resolve this thing fast, but let's do it diplomatically if possible, without bloodshed. Let's find out exactly what Islamov wants first."

"I thought we didn't negotiate with terrorists," I said.

Everyone looked at me. I was out of line addressing him without first being invited to join in.

Henry Clarke glanced at Schaeffer and then at me. "The United States *doesn't* negotiate with terrorists," the CTC head replied. "But at this moment, this is the Russians' problem. It just happens to be taking place in downtown D.C. Therefore, our role would be as a go-between with Islamov and the Russians. That's different from direct negotiations and would not violate our country's no-negotiation stance."

That sounded like diplomatic bullshit to me, but I'd said enough.

"Who have the Russians put in charge?" Schaeffer asked.

"The Kremlin has ordered a GRU colonel to fly down from New York to take control of the situation here until it can send in a more senior government official from Moscow."

"What do we know about this man?"

"Very little. He's a member of a special GRU group that was created to oversee the war in Chechnya. We've been told his name is Vladimir Mikhailovich Khrenkov."

As soon as the meeting ended, Kimberly and I left for the Jefferson, a ritzy hotel located on Sixteenth Street, about two blocks north of the embassy. The Russians had rented a floor of suites there to use as their on-site command post. As I sped along the George Washington Parkway toward the city, my cell phone rang. It was Scott Breeden, from the Marshals Service.

"You hear what happened?" he asked.

"Let me take a guess," I replied sarcastically. "A group of Chechen terrorists has seized control of the old Soviet embassy and they're threatening to blow up two Ford Broncos filled with explosives."

"Really?" Breeden said, clearly surprised.

"Turn on a television," I said. "Where the hell have you been—in a hole somewhere?"

"Well, yeah, sorta. I've been inside our orientation safesite all night," he said. "We've been debriefing our newest protected witness. That's why I'm calling you."

"This call has nothing to do with the embassy takeover?" I asked.

"No! But it's something you're gonna want to hear anyway. Guess who showed up in New York last night asking for help?" Without waiting for me to reply, Breeden said, "Igor Aleksandrovich Fedorov—the Russian mobster who kidnapped the Polov family and got your witness murdered on Capitol Hill!"

"I know who Fedorov is," I replied. "Why'd he come to us for protection?"

"He's scared. He panicked after that other Russian mobster got murdered in Brooklyn—Ivan Sitov. Anyway, Fedorov wants to switch sides and tell the D.A. the name of every Russian criminal he knows in Brighton Beach. Everyone is really excited!"

"Did he tell you last night the name of the sniper who murdered my witness?"

"Yes! That's why I'm calling. He gave us his full name."

"Well, what the hell is it!"

"Hang on." I could hear Breeden flipping through sheets of a notepad. "Sorry, but all these goddamn Russian names are confusing." After more shuffling, he said, "According to Fedorov, the sniper is a relative of the Polov family—just like we suspected. He's also the same shooter who gunned down Sitov, his chauffeur, and his bodyguard in Brooklyn, and, oh, I forgot to tell you, Fedorov says the killer is on a revenge kick because Olga Polov was raped and murder. She was his sister!"

"His sister? It was his sister who was murdered?"

"Yeah, his sister. This guy's an officer in the GRU. A colonel. His name is Khrenkov Mikhailovich."

"What?" I asked. "You sure you've got that name right?"

"Oh, sorry. I got it switched around: It's *Colonel* Vladimir Mikhailovich Khrenkov."

"Spell his last name for me," I said. I motioned to Kimberly and she reached over to steady the steering wheel as I took out pen and notepad.

"Khrenkov," he repeated. "K-h-r-e-n-k-o-v. Colonel Vladimir Mikhailovich Khrenkov."

I wrote that name directly under another Russian name—the one that I had recorded earlier during our CTC conference. I handed my notepad to Kimberly.

Colonel Vladimir Mikhailovich Khrenkov
Colonel Vladimir Mikhailovich Khrenkov

She raised her eyebrows, clearly puzzled.

I thanked Breeden for calling me and hung up.

"Kimberly," I said, "the top name on my notepad is the GRU officer who the Russians have sent to Washington to deal with the Russian embassy crisis. The bottom name is the sniper who killed my witness and is on a revenge murder spree."

"That's impossible!" she replied. "They can't be the same person. Someone's made a mistake. Is it possible there are *two* Colonel Khrenkovs in the GRU?"

I pushed down on the car's gas pedal.

I know how I can tell if they're the same, I thought. The clue is the photograph of the young soldier in Afghanistan that I'd taken from the Polov family during my secret trip to Pueblo. But I didn't say anything to Kimberly. I wanted to be sure.

What were the chances? Was it possible that we were about to meet the sniper who had patiently lain in wait for me when I was responsible for keeping Sergey Pudin alive? Was it possible that he had been forced to kill Pudin and was now carrying out a vendetta against the Russian Mafia?

My two cases—the murder of my protected witness and the capture of Moe Islamov—suddenly seemed to be merging together.

"Before we meet the Russians," Kimberly said firmly, "you need to understand that Colonel Khrenkov is probably protected by diplomatic immunity, which means you can't just walk into his hotel suite and slap the cuffs on him like he's some lowlife criminal."

We'd already driven past the D.C. cops' street barricades, parked our car, and were now riding upstairs in the Jefferson Hotel's elevator.

"Save your speech," I said. "I've already had a run-in with the State Department about this subject."

"Diplomatic immunity?"

"A few years ago, a diplomat's kid got drunk in Georgetown. He raped a college girl. She happened to be the daughter of a protected witness. The girl's old man wanted him killed, but we got him to play by our rules. The State Department got the punk deported, and we were promised he'd be arrested as soon as he set foot back in his native country. But his diplomat father pulled strings and his son was never arrested or charged."

"I'm sorry, but there's not much the State Department can do in situations like that. Our people need diplomatic immunity, too; otherwise Americans overseas would be in real danger all of the time."

"No reason to feel sorry. Our witness paid two thugs to track the kid down and castrate him. He died a few days later. Apparently, they bungled the operation."

Kimberly frowned. But it was one of my favorite stories. It was poetic justice, and it had actually happened.

"Wyatt," she said, her voice lowering to a whisper as the hotel elevator came to a sudden stop. "No cowboy antics here, okay?"

When the doors opened, we were greeted by a portly Russian wearing thick glasses and a rumpled, ill-fitting suit. "I'm from the Russian embassy. My name is Petr Shpigelglas. But please just call me Peter. I'll take you now to meet with Colonel Khrenkov."

He led us into a nearby suite, where we waited for about ten minutes before he reappeared and escorted us into an adjoining room. A fit man wearing a Russian military uniform was leaning over a table studying blueprints. As soon as he looked over at us, I recognized him. Although he was now much older than when he'd posed with his sniper's rifle in Afghanistan, he was definitely the same man. The telling factor was his eyes. How many men do you know who have yellow eyes?

This was Sergey Pudin's killer.

The three of us shook hands, and I wondered if he remembered seeing me through his sniper scope. If he did, he didn't reveal it.

"General Lev Rodin will be taking charge once he arrives from Moscow," Khrenkov explained. "Until then, my orders are to keep the terrorists contained within the embassy grounds. Your FBI and local police are providing the necessary manpower to accomplish this until our Spetsnaz team arrives."

"I assume the FBI has posted snipers at strategic points," I said.

It was an odd comment, and Kimberly shot me a dirty look, but if Khrenkov realized that I had mentioned snipers for a specific reason, he chose to ignore it.

"The FBI has not briefed me on its containment tactics," he replied. "But I'm confident it has taken whatever precautions are necessary."

"The reason we're here," Kimberly began, "is—"

Khrenkov interrupted. "I've already been told that Mr. Conway knows Islamov personally. You once taught him at a Virginia university, correct?"

"Yes, he was a student of mine."

"And tell me, was he a good student?"

Now he was the one asking what I thought was an odd question. Why did he care? But I answered it anyway. "Moe was very passionate about ideas. He was very smart, too. He apparently still is, judging from how easily he overran your embassy."

Khrenkov took out a cigarette and lit it. "A man who believes so passionately in a cause that he is willing to die for it is a fanatic, and that makes him an extremely dangerous opponent," he said. "Such a person is incapable of compromise, and without compromise, there can be no meaningful negotiation. There can only be one resolution for such a person—victory or death."

He was studying Kimberly and me, and I think all three of us understood what he was saying. General Rodin and his goon squad would be attacking Islamov inside the old Russian embassy once they arrived.

Khrenkov said, "An American eyewitness, who was walking by the embassy at the time of the attack, has told your police that there were eight or nine hooded figures." He handed me a sheet of paper with a list of names on it. "These are the employees who were inside the embassy during the attack. They are now hostages." The sheet contained forty-two names.

Petr entered the room and Khrenkov said, "The FBI special agent in charge is expecting us to join him at his mobile command post. I believe he wishes for you to telephone your friend Islamov now."

"Excuse me, Colonel," I replied. "Moe Islamov was one of my students and, yes, I liked him very much and, at one point, did consider him a close friend. But he is now the chief suspect in a murder investigation and he's threatening to blow up an entire block of Washington, D.C., with explosives in two SUVs, so I'm having a bit of a problem thinking kindly toward him. Let's just say we're acquaintances."

"As you wish."

Kimberly and I followed Khrenkov and Petr out into the hallway and to the elevator. We left the hotel and went around the street corner to where a large double-wide trailer was parked. The words FBI MOBILE COMMAND CENTER were stenciled on its side. Dozens of antennae and three satellite dishes were attached to its roof. As we neared, a door opened and I saw a familiar face: Special Agent Rodney P. Ames. He was chewing a wad of gum with such ferocity that I thought his jaw might snap. He looked in person no different from when he'd appeared on the video security tape at B.W.I., only he was now wearing black military fatigues rather than a tailored pinstripe suit.

He shook Kimberly's hand. "Ms. Lodge," he said formally, "welcome to our command center." He nodded respectfully toward Colonel Khrenkov and then looked directly at me and said, "I thought you'd been fired."

"Thought?" I asked. "Or wished?"

"Hoped," he responded. He turned and we followed him into the trailer. Ames quickly explained that in 1995, the White House issued

Presidential Decision Directive 39, known in FBI parlance as PDD-39. It laid out how the federal government is supposed to react during a "domestic terrorist threat or terrorist incident." The directive, he said, designated the FBI as the "lead law enforcement agency" in charge of all "operational response and crisis management" during such an incident. It was slightly modified after the Office of Homeland Security was created in 2002. But the FBI still remained the "primary agency" in charge of "responding to everything except consequence management" during a terrorist attack.

I didn't know what "consequence management" meant, but I also didn't really care or wish to waste time by asking.

"Even though the FBI is in charge," Ames continued, "part of our mandate is to work simultaneously and collectively with other federal, state, and local agencies which have counterterrorism responsibilities."

I'd heard enough of Ames's bureaucratese. I said, "Which in plain English means you've got the D.C. cops helping you."

Ames glared at me and replied, "It's a bit more complicated. Besides the D.C. Metropolitan police, we're working closely with FEMA, Homeland Security, the State Department, *and* with Colonel Khrenkov, because this particular attack is taking place on Russian soil." He paused for a moment, apparently to collect his thoughts, and then added, "I'm assuming you both understand that embassy grounds are not legally part of the U.S., which means we have no authority to enter them without the colonel's permission."

"The fact there're two Fords crammed with explosives that could blow up, kill Americans, and cause millions in damage—that doesn't give you the authority?" I asked rhetorically. "Oh yeah, we both understand that, perfectly."

Ames bristled at my sarcasm, but checked his anger. Stepping over to a table, he picked up a headset. "My orders are to arrange telephonic telecommunication between you and the terrorists. But first I've been told to remind you that you are not speaking on behalf of either the Russian government or the U.S. government."

Khrenkov interrupted. "This is correct. You do not represent Russia and cannot make any legally binding promises on our behalf."

"The same is true of the U.S.," Ames reiterated. "You'll be talking to him on his cellular phone. It's not a secure line, so the media might be listening in. We've kept their television satellite vans parked about five blocks from here, but they've got some pretty sophisticated equipment. Before we make the call, I'd like you to talk to our hostage negotiator so he can give you some basic dos and don'ts."

I'm not big on having armchair coaches tell me what to do. I started to object, but Kimberly shot me one of her "no cowboy antics please" looks.

"Ur, sure, no problem," I said.

For about five minutes, the FBI's chief hostage negotiator gave me pointers that were painfully obvious. One was: Don't say anything that might make Islamov feel as if the FBI wasn't taking him seriously. Duh? I mean, he'd already blasted his way into the embassy and rigged two trucks with explosives. Plus, he'd butchered his old college pal, Dr. Paul Custis. Add in the fact that he'd been fighting the Russians for more than a decade and I think Moe Islamov had pretty much proven to everyone just how serious and dangerous he was.

Once Ames was satisfied that I'd been sufficiently schooled, he handed out headsets so they could listen in to my "intimate" conversation with Islamov. As he was giving me my pair, Ames said in a quiet voice that only the two of us could hear: "You're a smart-ass and I think having you call Islamov is a total waste of time. But I've been ordered to do it, and unlike you, I obey my orders."

"Your enthusiasm is simply overwhelming," I said.

Ames signaled one of his technical support agents and I suddenly could hear a telephone number being dialed and ringing, followed by a man answering, "Yes?"

Despite the passage of years, I recognized Moe's voice. It was his accent: a blending of Eastern European with proper British English.

"Hello, Moe. This is Wyatt Conway."

I realized at that moment I should've had something clever in mind to say, but I didn't, so I ad-libbed. "What've you been doing lately?"

A look of sheer horror swept across Kimberly's face. Ames looked physically disgusted. Only Khrenkov remained unreadable.

Islamov laughed.

"*Professor* Conway," he replied, "you're still as flippant as ever."

"Sometimes a tiny bit of humor helps, especially when there're dead bodies involved. You've managed to get quite a few folks around here pretty excited. I'm assuming this doesn't have anything to do with the marks I gave you back in college."

Once again he chuckled. "Sometimes humor does help, but I must confess it's been a long time for me when it comes to laughing. Am I correct in assuming we're not alone when we are talking on this phone?"

Ames began shaking his head furiously, which I assumed meant that he wanted me to lie.

"The entire gang's here," I said. "The FBI, State Department, even your Russian buddies."

"In that case, Professor, why don't you come see me in person so we can catch up in private?"

I glanced at Colonel Khrenkov, who returned my stare.

"I'll have to check my schedule. I might have a lunch date today. When's a good time?"

A red-faced Ames flipped a switch so he could speak into the telephone receiver. "This is FBI special agent Rodney P. Ames. I'm in charge here and Deputy Conrad is overstepping his bounds. He doesn't have permission from the Russian government to enter their embassy grounds."

"Why does he need the Russians' permission? In case you haven't noticed, we've taken control of this embassy."

The hostage negotiator, who had urged me not to question Islamov's power, began whispering to Ames.

"What guarantees do we have that you'll not take Deputy Conway hostage if he meets with you?" Ames asked.

"Professor Conway has my word," Islamov replied.

"That's enough for me," I volunteered.

"Well, it's not good enough for me," Ames declared. "The only way I'm willing to allow this is if you release one of the hostages as a sign of good will."

Islamov didn't respond for several moments and then he said, "Professor Conway, this FBI agent is a fool. First, he claims he is worried I will take you hostage. Then he demands that I release a hostage in return for allowing you to come inside the embassy. By making this a condition, he is, in effect, suggesting a prisoner swap—you for a hostage—which puts you on the same level as a hostage and makes you vulnerable."

"Wait," Ames protested. "You're twisting my words!"

"No, *you* wait!" Islamov said. "You want a sign from me? Here is one for you. If you don't send Professor Conway into the embassy to see me during the next twenty minutes, I'm going to kill a hostage and throw her body into the courtyard for the world to see."

Ames looked at the hostage negotiator, who was clearly exasperated by what had just transpired. When the negotiator didn't offer him any guidance, Ames looked at Khrenkov.

"You have my permission to let Mr. Conway enter Russian soil," Khrenkov said, "as long as he understands that if he's taken hostage, he'll not receive any special consideration."

"Fine by me," I added.

Ames spoke to Islamov: "Okay, let's all relax here. There's no need for such drastic action."

I jumped in before Ames stuck his foot farther down his throat. "How do you want me to do this?"

"Just knock on the front door," he said. "But there is something I must ask. When you first enter the compound, you'll need to stop and strip down to your undershorts. This way, we can be certain you're not armed and that the FBI and CIA haven't asked you to sneak in any microphones or other listening devices."

"Moe," I said, sounding hurt, "your lack of trust is disturbing. But understandable. I'm going to need a few minutes to take care of something personal first before I can meet with you."

"Need to cancel that urgent lunch date?"

"No, if you must know, I'm not wearing undershorts. Since you want me to strip down, I'll need the FBI to buy me a pair." I added, "Are you sure you're not trying to embarrass me because of the grade I gave you?"

"Professor Conway, you gave me an A. I'll expect you in no more than thirty minutes." The line went dead.

Ames stormed up to me. "What the hell do you think you're doing? Everything is always a big joke to you, isn't it?"

"I'm trying to keep you from getting hostages killed!" I replied. Our noses were only an inch apart.

"Gentlemen," Kimberly said, "this is counterproductive. There are better ways to spend thirty minutes than having you two engage in this little mano a mano dance."

"I agree," Khrenkov announced. "Once you are in the embassy, please try to ascertain where his men are positioned, how many there are, and how heavily armed they are. In the past, Chechens have attached bombs to their hostages. Try to see if he's done this or booby-trapped the embassy."

Ames barked out an order. "Get an APC brought up here ASAP."

"I don't need an armored personnel carrier to drive me down the street," I said. "I don't think Moe is going to shoot me before I get inside."

Ames and I were still standing eyeball to eyeball. He didn't like having his orders challenged.

"Ah, excuse me," Kimberly said, "but what about buying you undershorts? I'm certain the media have telephoto lenses aimed at the embassy's front door and CNN is broadcasting this live. I don't think Mr. Conway needs to be showing his butt to the entire world."

Several off-color comebacks popped into my mind, but for once I decided to keep them to myself.

Ames ordered a female agent to dash down the street and buy me a pair. Before the embarrassed twenty-something agent left, I told her that

I wore "extra large" and preferred boxers. By this point, Ames was so irked that he excused himself and disappeared through a doorway in the command post. Khrenkov took advantage of the absence to ask me, "What did you teach Islamov in college?"

"As funny as it may sound, it was a class about the law and ethics. Most of the course was about specific legal issues, such as how to avoid entrapping a witness during an undercover operation or how to obtain legal confessions—stuff like that."

Khreknov looked confused, which didn't really surprise me, because I assumed that the Russian police, GRU, and KGB didn't recite Miranda warnings before they started beating a confession out of their chosen suspects. Continuing, I said, "But what really got Moe going were discussions about situational ethics."

"That's not a term I'm familiar with," Khrenkov replied.

"Here's a classic example of a situational ethical problem. A group of western settlers is making its way across the country when they stumble upon a wagon train that has just been destroyed by Indians."

"Native Americans," Kimberly interjected. "That's the correct name."

"Let's just call them an indigenous tribe," I replied. "There are dead bodies everywhere. Men, women, children. No one has survived the attack. Suddenly, the settlers hear the Indians, er, indigenous tribe, returning. So the settlers hide. You following me so far, Colonel?"

"I'm familiar with western cowboy-and-Indian movies."

"That's correct, only by now it's nighttime and the settlers are hiding under this small cliff and the Native Americans are standing right above them. Suddenly, a baby being held by one of the settlers starts to cry. The mother immediately covers the infant's mouth, and that causes the baby to begin to fuss even more."

Kimberly interrupted me. "The question becomes: Is it better to kill the baby or to let it scream, in which case, the Indians will hear the cries and slaughter everyone?"

"Native Americans," I said, correcting her.

"I always hated that hypothetical," she continued. "Because there could be other options. Couldn't the mother just muffle the baby's sounds? Why does she have to slay her child? And who's to say the Native Americas would kill everyone if they heard the noise? Maybe this was a friendly group that is just riding by."

"You're missing the point of the exercise," I said. "This is a question about life and death, and when—because of a strange situation—a person might be ethically justified in killing another person. It's the old choice between the 'lesser of two evils' argument." I turned to

Khrenkov. "I'm curious, Colonel, when do you feel murdering someone is justified?"

Khrenkov didn't flinch. "What I think isn't the issue here. How did Islamov respond to your situational illustration?"

"Obviously," I said. "He believes the end justifies the means."

I'd begun walking from the FBI mobile command post along Sixteenth Street toward the old Soviet embassy when I heard footsteps running up behind me. It was Kimberly Lodge.

"You going along to be taken hostage with me?" I asked.

I could see FBI special agent Ames, Colonel Khrenkov, and a handful of others watching us from the sidewalk about thirty yards away.

"Two quick questions," she said. "One. What's going on between you and Ames? You two obviously dislike each other."

"Hate would be a more accurate term. But why ask me? Ask him."

"Because you're my partner."

I liked how that sounded. I said, "I broke his nose."

"I already know that. It got mentioned at B.W.I. when we were looking at the security videotapes. Why did you break it?"

"I wanted to."

"Could you possibly tell me a bit more, such as *why* you wanted to?"

"Look, Ames and my ex-wife are now a couple, okay? She cheated on me when we were married. You figure it out. Now, what's your second question?"

"Is there someone you'd like me to call, you know, if you really are taken hostage? A relative, a girlfriend?"

"Relative, no. Girlfriends? Sorry, but that list is classified information, and even your clearance isn't high enough."

She smiled. "So tell me, how does someone get added to this list of yours?"

Now I was the one who was grinning. "Are you applying?"

"If promising to go on a dinner date with you will be an incentive for you not to get taken hostage, it seems the least I can do for my country." She suddenly turned serious. "Wyatt, be careful. I saw what Islamov did to Paul Custis, and they were college friends. Don't think for a second he wouldn't stick a knife in you."

"I'll keep that in mind. Meanwhile, I need you to tell Special Agent Ames something for me. Tell him he can kiss my naked white ass."

"The boxers!" she gasped. "You put them on, didn't you? I saw that girl give you the package."

I turned and continued walking toward the embassy. When I reached the northern entrance to the courtyard, I stopped. The Ford that had crashed through the embassy's iron gate was parked so that it was blocking the driveway. I had to turn sideways to slip between the vehicle's bumper and the embassy's security fence. The gap was so narrow that only one person at a time could scoot through, which meant General Rodin's antiterrorism troops were going to have one slow time storming into the courtyard.

I crossed the courtyard and paused, as directed earlier, directly in front of the mansion's massive front doors. I began undressing. My pants were the last article to drop. As soon as I stepped free of them, the right embassy door opened a crack, and I heard a voice say, "Step forward with your hands above your head."

I did as told, and when I was within reach, two sets of arms grabbed me and pulled me in. I didn't resist and was thrown to the floor. Two hooded figures held me down while a third aimed his automatic rifle directly at my chest. They slipped a black hood over my head so I couldn't see.

"Get him up!" one of them exclaimed.

They hoisted me to my feet.

"Did I come to the right house?" I asked. But no one laughed.

"Get him some pants from one of the guards," one of them commanded.

I heard footsteps click against a hard marble floor. The two men holding me lifted me up onto my toes and half-dragged me down a hallway. A door opened. I was pushed in and shoved onto the leather seat of a chair. The door slammed.

"You can take off your hood, Professor Conway," Moe Islamov said.

I removed it. The two of us were seated inside a large embassy conference room. I was at one end of an oblong mahogany table. He was at the other end and was wearing a black ski mask so I couldn't see his face. There was a Russian flag and oil portraits of former Soviet officials hanging on the walls. The only two leaders I recognized were Leonid Brezhnev and Vladimir Putin. There wasn't one of Mikhail Gorbachev, which I thought was odd, but when you are sitting butt-naked in a leather chair facing a former student-now-turned-terrorist, room decor isn't something you dwell on. I was about to speak when the door opened and another hooded figure came in carrying a pair of dark blue trousers.

"Put those on," Islamov said.

I stepped into them though they were several sizes too big. They were also stained with blood.

The pants deliverer left us and Islamov said, "I thought you bought undershorts?"

"I decided not to wear them—as a favor to you!"

"To me?"

"Yes. You want to call attention to the war in Chechnya. You're after headlines. Having a naked man come see you has got to be a bigger story than if I'd simply arrived wearing boxer shorts."

"Are you managing the news for me now, Professor?"

"I helped you for a purpose. I want you to free one of the hostages after I leave. It will guarantee you more headlines and also demonstrate you can show mercy."

Islamov didn't reply. Instead, he sat quietly for several moments simply staring at me, waiting for me to speak.

I said, "Moe, I never pictured you as a terrorist."

"Terrorist?" he replied. "That is such a subjective word. Was your George Washington a terrorist? Didn't terrorists throw tea into Boston Harbor?"

"I don't remember George Washington sending women with dynamite strapped to their bodies into crowds of innocent British men, women, and children to blow themselves up."

"In today's wars, there are no morals."

"Bullshit!" I replied. "There are always morals."

"There is an Arabic proverb that says, 'She accused me of having her malady, then snuck away.' Do you understand this?"

I did, but said I didn't. I wanted to hear his interpretation.

"Terrorism can be commendable at times," he continued, "and it can be reprehensible. Terrifying an innocent person is objectionable and unjust, but terrorizing oppressors, and criminals, and thieves, and robbers is necessary for the safety of people. Every state and every civilization and culture has to resort to terrorism under certain circumstances for the purpose of abolishing tyranny and corruption. Every country has its own security system and its own security forces, its own police, and its own army. They're all designed to terrorize whoever even contemplates attacking that country or its citizens."

"Look, Moe, I didn't come here to get into an intellectual debate. The truth is that I think the Russians should get the hell out of your country. But I don't believe killing innocent people in Moscow—like you've done—is the best way to go about it. And I really resent how you've brought your war into my country now. Your fight is with Russia and doesn't have anything to do with Washington, D.C."

"Professor, don't be so arrogant," he replied. "Your president is the one who declared that no country can simply stand by and do nothing when another country is being victimized. Yet your country chooses to stay silent while my people are killed. It was your president who decided to make your country the policeman of the world. He should've known that a policeman can't pick only the battles that suit him."

Islamov hesitated and then said, "When you were my professor, you loved to use the hypothetical, so let me now give you one. If you are a weak boy in school and a bully is picking on you by stealing your lunch money every day, what should you do?"

"You should get help," I answered. "But the last time I checked, threatening to blow up a square block of prime downtown Washington, D.C., real estate and possibly kill hundreds of innocent people is not an endearing way to recruit a knight in shining armor to rescue you."

"We've tried to appeal to your various presidents over the years on moral grounds. We've asked them to help us fight this bully who is tormenting us. But your country has refused because you do not wish to risk irritating Russia. You're also afraid of us—that if we become independent, we will create another Islamic nation."

"Moe, I'm not a diplomat, okay? But I still don't see how attacking the embassy here is going to persuade anyone in the U.S. to come to your rescue."

"Remember my hypothetical? When a weak schoolboy needs help and no one will help him voluntarily, he must find a way to pressure someone to assist him." At this point, Islamov reached into his jacket and removed a standard-size white envelope, which he slid across the table. I caught it but saw that it was sealed and addressed to "President: United States," so I didn't open it.

Islamov said, "A few minutes ago, CNN announced that the Russians are sending General Rodin and a team of antiterrorists to deal with us. This general knows only one way to resolve a crisis. Attack. You should know from history that Russians don't care about hostages. Their generals think in terms of the collective. But I'm warning you now, this attack will not be in the best interest of the U.S. and its people. Your president needs to be made aware of this."

"Moe, what do you expect the U.S. to do?"

"I want your president to order Russia to remove its troops from Chechnya. If the Kremlin refuses, then I want the U.S. to use its military might to force Moscow to withdraw."

"Moe," I said, as if I were lecturing a small child, "do you really believe that threatening to blow up those two vans outside and kill the hostages will make our president join your team and agree to use the U.S. military against the Russians if they don't withdraw? C'mon, there's not a chance in hell that's going to happen. If anything, blowing up those trucks will drive the U.S. farther onto the Russians' side."

"You're wrong, Professor. Once your president reads what I've just given you, he will begin immediate negotiations on our behalf with the Kremlin. I am confident of this."

I looked at the envelope and asked, "What if I refuse to accept this letter? If I take it, then I will be obligating the president to get involved, and he may not want to even read it."

"If you refuse to deliver my letter, I'll kill a hostage, pin it to her chest, and toss her corpse in front of the embassy for your television cameras to broadcast. The choice is yours."

I didn't doubt he would. I also didn't think arguing with him would change his mind. I decided to change subjects. "Why did you murder Paul Custis? He was your closest college friend and a good man."

"This is true," he said sadly. "But he was going to turn me in to the authorities. I had no choice. I am on a sacred mission." He paused and then said, "Professor, you sit here and judge me to be a cold-blooded killer. But, in fairness, you should look at the world through my eyes. The Russians murdered my father, my mother, my sisters, my brothers, my uncles, my aunts, my closest friends. They destroyed my home. They arrest and torture people without reason. Their victims' only crime is they believe in Islam and they live on a patch of dirt which the Russians need for an oil pipeline. Would you not fight such tyranny?"

"I'm certain the Russians are committing atrocities, but that doesn't justify murdering Paul Custis."

"How dare you make such a statement? You admit in one breath that the Russians are engaging in atrocities and yet you do nothing to stop them. In your next breath, you condemn me because I dared kill one man!"

"But that man was your friend. He trusted you."

Islamov said, "You are still a deputy U.S. marshal, is that not correct? If one of your prisoners attempts an escape, you will shoot him, won't you?"

"I'd try to stop him first, but yes, if I couldn't, I suppose I would shoot him."

"And yet this man might be a complete stranger to you. Still, you would kill him even though he has never harmed you or your family. You would kill him simply because it is your job, something you are paid to perform. It is not personal. It is not intellectual. It is simply about money."

"Let's not forget that he's a criminal, and if he escaped, he might hurt someone else."

"And who declared him a criminal? I kill men who have murdered my family and are destroying my country. I fight for freedom. I fight for my religious beliefs. The fact that I murdered a good friend simply shows how dedicated I am to this cause. I would not kill a man simply because I was paid to shoot him and he was trying to run away. Now, who between us is a cold-blooded killer—the man who kills for what he believes in or the one who does it for a weekly paycheck?"

Continuing, he said, "You Americans are experts when it comes to rationalizing murder. You dropped bombs on Baghdad that killed women, old men, and children. Was that murder? Or was it simply the reality of war? When a U.S. soldier fights in a battle, is he a murderer? I am a soldier, but you label me a terrorist."

"This discussion is pointless," I said. "You'll never be able to convince me that killing Paul Custis was necessary—or that killing these hostages is justified." I picked up the envelope he'd given me. "Let's say I do take this letter and deliver it to the president. What if he chooses to ignore its contents? Is there some room for compromise here? Is there a way I can negotiate a peaceful end to this standoff?"

"Professor," he replied, "your president will not be able to ignore what is in the letter. And my advice to you is that you deliver it to him as quickly as possible before General Rodin launches his suicide attack. If you really are concerned about American lives, then you will run from here directly to the White House."

41

"You didn't learn how many terrorists are in control of the embassy or what floors they are hiding on?" Special Agent Ames asked.

"I've already told you that I was blindfolded as soon as I was pulled inside," I replied. "I didn't see anything after that—not the hostages, not the terrorists, nothing except the interior of a conference room and Islamov, who was wearing a ski mask."

His questions had been annoying the first time he'd asked them. This was at least the fourth time.

Ames unwrapped another stick of chewing gum. He was trying to stop smoking and needed something to keep his mouth occupied.

Colonel Khrenkov, his aide Petr Shpigelglas, Kimberly, Ames, and I were inside the mobile command post. I'd gotten dressed in my own clothes, and the FBI had taken the blue pants that Islamov had given me to its lab to examine. Khrenkov had already verified that the trousers were the same type worn by the embassy's security guards.

Ames had debriefed me for about a half hour and I'd provided him a near verbatim account of my encounter with Moe Islamov. I'd left out only one tiny piece of information. I'd not mentioned the envelope that Islamov had given me for the president. I didn't trust Ames. I also didn't want the Russians to learn about the letter—not if it was as important as Islamov insisted.

"The bottom line here," Ames declared, "is you really didn't learn jack shit during your face-to-face with Islamov."

Just then one of Ames's underlings interrupted us. "We've got movement," he announced. We looked at the bank of television screens hanging from the ceiling. The FBI had set up video cameras at key locations outside the embassy so the command post could monitor every angle of the mansion. A woman with her hands raised high above her head walked out of its front doors.

"He's freeing a hostage!" Kimberly exclaimed. "Just like Wyatt asked him to do!"

"We can't be certain she's not a terrorist pretending to be a hostage," Ames said.

The woman moved across the courtyard to the sidewalk, where she was quickly engulfed by heavily armed FBI agents.

Ames addressed Khrenkov. "Colonel, I'll have my men bring her to your hotel suite so we can question her together." He looked at me and added with much disdain, "I'm sure she will be more helpful than Deputy Conway."

Khrenkov checked his wristwatch and said, "General Rodin should be arriving at Andrews Air Force Base in two hours. He will expect me to greet him."

"You're allowing an armed Russian Spetsnaz team to land at a U.S. base?" I asked.

"Conway," Ames replied, "your job was to make contact with Islamov and learn as much intel about his operations as you could. Unfortunately, all you and he talked about apparently was philosophical bullshit."

"Agent Ames," Kimberly interrupted, "being rude is not going to accomplish anything constructive."

Ames smirked, as if to suggest "What's wrong, boy? Need a woman to fight your battles?" Then he said, "If we need to send Deputy Conway in again, we'll let you know. Meanwhile, the colonel and I have work to do here."

Kimberly was about to argue, but I cut her short. "Actually, I think Ms. Lodge and I will return to the CTC. We need to brief our bosses."

Kimberly looked puzzled. Ames was estatic. He raised his right hand and wiggled his fingers toward me. "See you later!"

As soon as we were outside the command post, Kimberly asked, "What the hell are you doing? We're supposed to watch Khrenkov."

"We'll talk in the car."

Fifteen minutes later, as we were speeding north on the George

Washington Parkway toward CIA headquarters, I removed Islamov's letter from my pants pocket.

She read the envelope. "Islamov wants you to deliver this to the president?" she asked, and then, before I could answer, she exclaimed, "Oh my God! You didn't tell Ames about this!"

"I didn't want the Russians to know until we have some idea what it says. Besides, Ames is an asshole. He'd probably open it in front of Khrenkov."

"But Ames is in charge, and you deliberately withheld information from him!"

"So what? I'm sure one of your Office of Technical Service wizards can steam this open so we can get a peek at what's inside. I can always turn it over to Ames later. That way, I'm not really keeping it from him, I'm just taking my time delivering it."

"You're not only going to get us both fired, you're going to get us arrested!"

"C'mon. There's no love lost between the CIA and the FBI. Besides, I think your director will want to make certain the contents of this letter are worth bothering the president about. For all we know, Islamov could have filled it with anthrax spores."

Kimberly suddenly placed the packet down between us on the car's bench seat.

"It feels like there are photographs inside it," she said. "You know, maybe Polaroid snapshots."

"Yes, I felt them, too."

We reached the CIA's main entrance. Both of us flashed our ID badges so the guard could read them.

"I can't believe you didn't tell Ames about this," Kimberly repeated as we were pulling away from the security gate. "I hope like hell you know what you're doing!"

So did I.

42

Colonel Khrenkov stood silently on the tarmac and watched the IL-76 Russian military transport plane as it made a final descent toward Andrews Air Force Base, a sprawling complex about ten miles southeast of Washington, D.C. He and Special Agent Ames had been joined by two other U.S. officials. As commander of the 89th Airlift Wing, Brigadier General Thomas Jacks was the base's ranking military officer. Standing next to him was Randolph Fletcher, the head of the State Department's counterterrorism office.

At this particular moment, Khrenkov wasn't tuned in to his hosts' friendly banter. His mind was on Wyatt Conway and the seemingly unproductive encounter that the deputy marshal had had with the terrorist Moe Islamov. Khrenkov had a hunch that Conway was holding something back. It was one of those feelings on which he could always rely. What had Conway not shared with them? And why was he keeping it a secret from his own people?

When the lumbering IL-76 touched down, Khrenkov and the Americans entered their separate limousines to ride in a line to a hangar that had been reserved for the Russians. The vehicles parked near the stopped IL-76 that had been towed there and waited for the aircraft's engines to completely wind down. Stepping from their cars, the men formed a reception line.

General Lev Rodin descended from the airplane wearing his full-dress military uniform. There was only one large star on his shoulder boards, which in the Russian army outranked the four smaller stars that the generals under him wore. He strutted forward, halting a few feet directly across from General Jacks. Colonel Khrenkov saluted his Russian superior and then made the introductions.

"Please let me know if there is anything we can do for you while you are here," General Jacks said, offering his hand. "We've arranged housing for your men on the base."

Although General Rodin both understood and spoke excellent English, he chose to speak Russian and have Khrenkov translate. He thanked Jacks, but said that he would prefer that his antiterrorist squad accompany him to the Jefferson Hotel, where rooms had been reserved for them.

"I'm sorry, General," the State Department's Fletcher interjected, "but our government would rather your men remain here. All of this was communicated to your ambassador while you were still in flight."

Rodin listened to Khrenkov translate and then rubbed his clean-shaven chin slowly with his left hand as if he were considering his options. He'd already been informed during the flight by the ambassador over a secure telephone line, but he pretended that this was the first time that he had heard the news. He said through Khrenkov, "As you prefer. I will require only my two top officers to accompany me to the hotel. When can I expect a briefing by your people?"

Fletcher looked over at Ames. "We're ready as soon as we return to your hotel," Ames announced.

As if on cue, three stocky Russians dressed in black fatigues emerged from the aircraft. General Rodin barked out a command. Khrenkov explained that one of the Russians would remain at the base with the Spetsnaz team. The other two would travel with Rodin.

Having taken care of the formalities, General Rodin, Khrenkov, and the two Spetsnaz leaders entered the black stretch limo that the Russian embassy had sent. Ames and Fletcher climbed into a State Department car, and both vehicles left the base, leaving General Jacks behind. As they pulled away from Andrews, they were joined by several other cars carrying various Russian security guards and FBI agents.

En route, General Rodin quizzed Khrenkov. He kept his answers short and offered only facts, no opinions. At one point, Rodin asked, "Did the terrorist Islamov give this deputy—what's his name?"

"Conway," Khrenkov replied. "Wyatt Conway."

"Yes, did the terrorist Islamov give this Wyatt Conway any documents, photographs, or other written materials?"

"Deputy Conway did not mention that he'd been given anything."

"And do you believe he was telling the truth?"

"No," Khrenkov replied. "I believe Deputy Conway is holding something back. However, this is merely speculation."

"Why would he not tell the FBI if Islamov gave him something?"

"He doesn't get along well with Ames."

"A rivalry? Dislike? How interesting," Rodin said. "This could be useful. But for now, tell me, did Deputy Conway say anything about why the terrorist Islamov chose the old embassy to attack?"

"No. The Americans are assuming he selected it because our security at the mansion was minimal."

"Think very carefully before you answer my next question," Rodin said. "When this Conway was being questioned, did he mention anything about the basement of the old embassy? About being taken down into it?"

"No. I would've remembered such a comment."

"Did he use the term 'layer cake'?"

Khrenkov thought for a moment and then replied, "No. He never used that term."

As was his way, Khrenkov's face showed no emotion. But his mind was racing. *Now he understood!* A key piece of the mystery had suddenly come together in his mind.

Sloika—which means "layer cake."

Now he realized why Islamov had selected the old Soviet embassy as a target. He also understood why someone as powerful and important as General Rodin had been dispatched to Washington to personally handle the reclaiming of the embassy.

How long, he wondered, *would it be before the United States comprehended what was really happening?*

43

I knew I'd receive a stern lecture from CTC chief Henry Clarke after I handed him the letter that Moe Islamov had given me. Clarke didn't disappoint. For about ten minutes, he droned on and on about the importance of interagency cooperation and abiding by the correct chain of command, especially during a crisis. He said I should've informed the FBI. But after Clarke had delivered his pro forma lecture, he kept the envelope and dismissed both Kimberly and me from his office. This is exactly what I thought would happen. Despite the scolding, the CIA was not going to tip off the FBI without first reading the contents.

"Wanna get a cup of coffee?" I asked Kimberly.

"No," she replied, sounding hurt. Apparently, she'd taken Clarke's dressing-down personally. "Clarke ordered us to write individual reports about what happened today, and I'm going to get started on mine. I've worked too hard to see my career go down the toilet because of you!"

"Kimberly, you're overreacting," I replied. "First, you didn't do anything improper. Second, you can just blame me. And third, I know how Washington bureaucrats think. No one is going to be disciplined because of this."

"Really, oh, well, thank goodness. I feel so much better now," she said sarcastically. "It's so reassuring coming from a deputy who's been detailed to the CTC because the U.S. Marshals Service wants to get rid of him."

"Ouch! I'm guessing this isn't the best time to remind you of your promise—about our date?"

She gave me an exasperated look and huffed away.

I went to get coffee. After about an hour of pretty much wasting time, I decided I should also write a report for Clarke since he was expecting both by the end of the day. But when I got to my cubicle, my mind kept wandering back to Colonel Khrenkov. I pulled out the snapshot that I'd taken from the Polovs' family Bible and studied it. There was no doubt in my mind that the young, yellow-eyed sniper in Afghanistan and Colonel Khrenkov were the same.

I heard footsteps, and when I glanced up, two CIA security officers were hovering over me.

"Mr. Conway," the taller one said. "Please come with us."

"Where to?"

"Please," the shorter one replied. "No questions."

Rather than slipping the photograph of Khrenkov back into a file, I tucked it into my pocket and fell into step with the officers. We rode the elevator down into the lobby of the CIA's main building.

Great, I thought. *I'm being escorted out of the CIA and booted from CTC!*

But when we reached the front doors, neither of the guards asked me for my identification badge. Instead, they showed me to a limousine—one of three parked in a line outside the entrance. Kimberly and Clarke were already in the backseat.

"Get in!" Clarke ordered.

I heard a commotion behind me and saw four security guards bustling CIA director Richard Starkweather into the lead car. His aides jumped into the second.

"C'mon!" Clarke declared. "He won't wait!"

I got in just as the motorcade started to pull away. Several black SUVs fell into position in front and in back of us. They were carrying the security detail.

"Either of you want to tell me where we're going?" I asked.

Kimberly looked at Clarke, who was perfectly happy to ignore me. After several intentionally uncomfortable moments, he said, "The White House."

Our caravan sped down the parkway, crossed the Potomac, entered Washington, and eventually turned north onto Fifteenth Street. We stopped outside the White House's southeastern gate. It was a short walk to the president's residence, but I fell behind because the U.S. Secret

Service agents at the security checkpoint required me to lock up my handguns in a firearms cabinet. I generally carry a nine-millimeter Glock semiauto on my hip and a good old-fashioned snubnose .38 on my ankle. Clarke and Kimberly waited impatiently for me to catch up. Neither of them had been armed.

We hustled up a flight of worn marble stairs and entered the famed West Wing.

"This is the Roosevelt conference room," Kimberly whispered.

"Which Roosevelt?" I asked.

"Didn't realize you knew there'd been two," she replied. She nodded toward bronze plaques near the door. One had a bust of Theodore Roosevelt on it. The other was of Franklin Roosevelt.

"Both," she answered.

"How diplomatic, and politically correct."

There was an enormous table in the center of the room. But Clarke, Kimberly, and I didn't sit at it. We found chairs near a colorful display of military service flags adorned with battle ribbons. I scanned the group of mostly white, older males seated around the long table and recognized most, but not all of them. They were various governmental leaders from the Justice Department, FBI, CIA, State Department, Homeland Security, and a smattering of other federal agencies. I noticed that Special Agent Rodney Ames was not sitting at the table, but was perched on a chair behind FBI director Travis Davenport. As soon as Ames saw me, he looked away.

We'd been seated about five minutes when a side door opened and the vice president of the United States came in, trailed by four aides. Everyone leaped to their feet and remained standing until the V.P. sat down. He was holding the white envelope that Islamov had given me, only now both it and its contents were sealed in clear plastic sheets.

"Travis," the vice president said, addressing Davenport, "what can you tell me about these photographs?"

"Sir, our lab has reached the same conclusion as the CIA's Office of Technical Service," he replied. "They were taken within the last forty-eight hours based on the freshness of the chemicals used in the instant picture-making process."

"George," the vice president said, "can you add anything new to this?"

I didn't recognize George, but assumed he was some honcho from the Department of State—a hunch quickly confirmed by his wordy answer.

"While none of our people has ever actually been inside the basement of the old Soviet embassy," he said, "we've discreetly shown copies of the shots to several of our Russian sources and they've confirmed to us that the characteristics of the room—the office shown in the picture—are consistent with the characteristics of an office in the basement area of the embassy as well as they remember—although we can't be absolutely positive."

I didn't recognize the next person the vice president called on. He was in his early sixties and looked scholarly. He was slightly bald, a bit portly, with white, closely trimmed hair, a full matching beard, and a round face.

"Who's he?" I whispered.

"Don't know," Kimberly hissed back.

The man removed his half-glasses and slowly surveyed the table, as if he were about to lecture a classroom of college students. "We've confirmed," he began in a deep, sonorous voice, "that the snapshots from this packet could be photographs of a fusion device."

"An H-bomb?" I murmured.

"Shit!" Kimberly uttered in a hushed tone.

Clarke frowned at us.

"Thanks, Dr. Colter," the vice president said quietly. He next looked at CIA director Starkweather and asked, "How in the hell did Chechen terrorists smuggle a weapon of mass destruction into our city?"

"Well, sir," Starkweather replied, "they aren't the ones who brought it here."

"Then who did?"

"To adequately explain that, I need to go back a few years. The former Soviet Union began trying to create a thermonuclear bomb in an aggressive fashion in 1948. Five years later, the Soviet press announced the Soviet military had successfully tested a hydrogen bomb. Having now developed a nuclear device, the Soviets turned their attention to solving the same problem that our scientists were trying to resolve: how to develop a rocket powerful enough to carry a nuclear warhead across the Atlantic and Pacific oceans. We still hadn't developed one dependable enough to transport a hydrogen bomb the distance that we needed to attack Moscow. At the time, the only successful delivery device we had was our B-52 bomber. And it wasn't totally reliable because it was vulnerable to attack."

"Let's cut to the chase here," the vice president said. "Are you telling me someone in the Kremlin came up with the idea of what—secreting a hydrogen bomb in our capital?"

"Yes, sir, that's exactly what happened. But they didn't actually smuggle it in. They built it here. As early as 1955, we began hearing rumors that the Soviets were using diplomatic couriers to bring parts and materials into Washington that they needed to assemble a bomb within the safe confines of their own embassy."

"Rumors or facts?"

"We couldn't confirm it because we didn't have any moles inside the Soviet embassy and there were no monitoring devices in place at our major ports and airports that would have detected radioactive materials. We've since been told by defectors that the KGB brought in most of what its scientists needed by concealing materials in Soviet-manufactured vehicles that were imported here for embassy use."

"Was President Eisenhower told?"

"I apologize, sir," Starkweather said sheepishly, "but I'm not certain everyone in here has a security clearance that allows me to discuss any further information about this subject because it's classified. Let me simply say the appropriate authorities were made aware of our suspicions and concerns, and a course of action was taken to stop the importation of items that could've been used by the Soviets to construct an atomic bomb."

"Damn it, this is no time to speak in generalities!" the vice president snapped. "If the Chechen terrorists have an actual goddamn bomb in the basement of the old Soviet embassy, then we need to get all of our facts on the table now." He scanned the room. "The simplest way to do this is by asking everyone here who does not have a top-secret clearance to leave right now. I'll then have one of my aides record the names of those who stay so we can verify their security clearances while we continue our discussion."

About five people immediately left. Neither Clarke, Kimberly, nor I moved, since all of us had been issued top-secret clearances as part of our jobs at the CTC. I noted that Ames was also still with us.

"With all due respect, sir," Starkweather continued, "I'm still reluctant to go into details because much of this information falls under a 'need to know' basis."

"Well, I need to know!" the vice president replied curtly. "Get on with it."

"Yes, sir," Starkweather said. "President Eisenhower elected to keep silent about our concerns and never publicly confronted the Soviets. Let me add that he had a very, very good reason for this."

"I've been around long enough to read between the lines," the vice president replied. "Eisenhower didn't say anything because the CIA had decided to do the exact same thing to the Soviets that they were doing to us!"

Starkweather didn't comment.

Good god! I thought. *We were assembling a nuclear bomb in our embassy in Moscow at the same time they were building one here.*

Starkweather said, "The construction of the so-called Soviet basement bomb was feasible only for a short window of time. You'll remember that in 1962, we caught the Russians attempting to install medium and intermediate-range ballistic missiles in Cuba. By the midsixties, both sides had successfully built intercontinental ballistic missiles capable of hitting overseas targets. There was no longer any need to hide a bomb in Washington, D.C., or in Moscow. In fact, until we saw what you'd received today, we weren't really positive the Soviets had ever bothered to finish the project."

The vice president once again turned toward the white-haired academic sitting nearby. "Dr. Colter, can you tell from these photographs exactly what sort of bomb is in the Soviet basement?"

"Obviously, we can't tell from these photographs what, if anything, is inside this cylinder. But the terrorists took a picture of a metal plate welded onto this device and that plate contains Russian markings. They translate into 'RDS-6s'—that's the designation the Soviets used to identify their first thermonuclear bomb. They also called it the 'Sloika' bomb."

The vice president appeared confused, so Colter said: "Sloika refers to a Russian pastry or layer cake. Without getting too technical, a Sloika bomb uses a fissile core surrounded by alternating layers of fusion fuel, usually lithium-six deuteride spiked with tritium, and a fusion tamper, such as uranium, placed inside a high explosive implosion system. The small fission core acts as the trigger."

"Thanks for keeping it simple," the vice president replied. A few officials seated at the table chuckled. It was an obvious attempt to ease the tension that had seized the room ever since Starkweather had announced there was a nuclear bomb in our city. One of the vice president's aides whispered in his ear. The vice president said: "I have been remiss in not introducing Dr. Irwin Colter since many of you might not know him. He is our nation's preeminent nuclear expert. He's a professor at MIT and often advises the White House."

Dr. Colter nodded appreciatively and then said: "If these terrorists had only sent photographs of this mysterious cylinder, then I might be skeptical, but in addition to the RDS-6s inscription, there are pictures of schematics from a Soviet Emergency Operating Procedure. The Soviet military attached an EOP document to each of its nuclear weapons. The diagrams in the photographs are of a layer-cake bomb. So, Mr. Vice President, if you are asking my opinion, which you obviously are, then, yes, the terrorists do, indeed, have possession of a layer-cake nuclear bomb in the basement of the old Soviet embassy."

The vice president asked: "Can they explode it and if they do, how much damage will it cause?"

"It is entirely possible that the layer-cake bomb is obsolete. Deuterium and tritium are hard to store and tritium has a short life. But we don't know what the terrorists might have done to replenish this bomb. We have no choice but to assume it will explode."

"And the damage?"

"This bomb appears to be a copy of a layer-cake device exploded by the Soviets on August 12, 1953. We know that bomb had a yield of about four hundred kilotons."

"You'll need to translate that," the vice president said.

"Let me give you some perspective. The bomb detonated over Hiroshima was an atomic bomb and had a blast equivalent of ten kilotons, or 12,500 pounds, of TNT. The layer-cake bomb exploded in 1953 had a yield of four hundred kilotons—making it forty times more destructive than what we dropped on the Japanese."

"What would a blast like that do to our city?"

"It would destroy it. It would create a crater more than a hundred feet deep and a thousand feet in diameter. Within a one-mile radius, only the strongest buildings—those made of reinforced concrete—would have bits of their skeletons standing."

The V.P. looked from one official to the next. He said, "I don't need to tell any of you that the old Soviet embassy is less than three-tenths of a mile from where we are now sitting." Then he asked: "What about human casualties?"

Dr. Colter said, "When we do hypothetical blast estimates, we use rings for illustrative purposes. The first ring from this explosion would reach out an entire mile from the embassy in all directions. Inside this ring, there would be no survivors. The White House, as you correctly pointed out, would be inside that ring. The second ring would extend from the first, one-mile ring, out to, say, ten miles. This ring will become a wasteland, although the twisted steel beams from some extremely well-built structures would be visible. In addition, thick marble structures, such as the U.S. Capitol, might still be recognizable. At best, however, the odds of human survivors would be well under fifty percent, depending on whether these victims happened to be in some protective shelter, such as an underground subway car."

Continuing, Colter said, "As we move farther and farther away from the embassy blast site, the destructive power of the explosion weakens and the survival odds improve. Even so, I'd predict that buildings up to fifteen miles away would be substantially damaged by the blast."

"Tell me if I'm wrong, but just because someone survives the initial blast—that doesn't mean he or she would escape unharmed, correct?" the V.P. asked.

"That's true," Colter said. "If there is a wind speed of about fifteen miles per hour, within seven days, everyone who lives within seventy miles of the nation's capital would receive a lethal dose of radiation. They would die from two to fourteen days later. A conservative estimate would be about five million persons dead."

"Including the president, Joint Chiefs of Staff, Congress, the judiciary, and the president's entire cabinet," the vice president interjected, "if they were inside the city."

"It would take about ten years before anyone could return to the capital without becoming seriously ill," Colter explained. "Washington, D.C., as we know it, would no longer exist."

"Director Starkweather," the vice president said, framing his next question to the CIA head, "surely the Soviets took steps to prevent this layer-cake bomb from exploding by accident. It *must* have some built-in safeguards."

"This is mostly speculation, but after conferring with Dr. Colter, and Russian nuclear scientists who have fled here and now teach in the United States, we're convinced the Soviets did implement safety devices. We know, for example, that all U.S. nuclear weapons stored abroad are protected by what's called 'permissive action links,' known as PALs. This has been true since the 1950s."

"You call them PALs?"

"Yes, sir," Starkweather continued. "Seems like an appropriate acronym since their purpose is to prevent unauthorized use of a nuclear weapon. Most of these PALs began as simple combination locks, but over time they evolved into sophisticated antitampering devices. Some permit only a few tries to arm the weapon before disabling the entire physical package should an intruder persist in attempts to defeat the PAL."

"Did the Soviets equip their nuclear weapons with similar PALs?" the vice president asked.

"Yes, sir," Starkweather said. "We've analyzed the photographs the Chechen terrorists sent, but, unfortunately, it appears the terrorists have overridden the KGB's original PAL device and, ironically, replaced it with their own. Actually, there seems to be two safeguards on this layer-cake bomb. One is an older detector the Soviets installed. It was designed to keep the bomb from being transported out of the basement. If anyone tries to move it without first disarming its motion detector, the bomb will explode. We're speculating the KGB was afraid the U.S. might learn about the embassy bomb and try to airlift it out of Washington."

"And the other?"

"It appears to have been added to the bomb by the Chechen terrorists. It's connected to a laptop computer. We believe the computer is being used to control the detonation of the bomb."

The V.P. uttered a loud "Goddamn!" Then he said, "This madman—Movladi Islamov—has in his hands the power to detonate a four-hundred-kiloton nuclear bomb in the very heart of Washington, D.C. And what you're telling me is there isn't a goddamned thing we can do to stop him. Is that what you're saying?"

"If the bomb is still active, then he certainly has the ability to detonate it," Starkweather replied.

For several moments, the only noise in the Roosevelt Room was the vice president's fingers drumming against the conference table. Then he asked, "Where's the deputy U.S. marshal who delivered this letter to the CIA from the Chechens?"

The CIA director turned and looked at Clarke, who then looked at me. I stood up, and for once in my life I didn't have any smart-ass comments in mind. What I'd just heard was too horrible for even me to joke about.

"My name is Wyatt Conway, sir. I once taught Moe Islamov while he was an exchange student taking night classes at a local university."

"I realize, deputy," the vice president said, "that you're not a trained psychiatrist or a mind reader, but you're the only person in this room who actually knows this man. Do you believe he is capable of detonating a nuclear device and destroying our city?"

I thought about Moe. Then I thought about how he had stabbed Paul Custis to death. I said, "Sir, I believe Moe would do it in a heartbeat if he believes he's been backed against the wall or he has no other alternatives."

"Dr. Colter," the V.P. said, returning his attention to the scientist seated near him. "Can this terrorist simply push a button, like they do in the movies, and set this thing off?"

I sat down while Colter explained the various types of triggering devices which the Soviets used in the 1950s. Most required two separate keys to be turned simultaneously. "But the Chechen terrorists appear to have jury-rigged a new trigger through the laptop," he concluded.

"Mr. Vice President?"

It was FBI director Travis Davenport. "If I may, sir, we've done some theorizing about this that may be useful to our discussion."

"Go ahead."

"The Chechens don't want this bomb to go off by accident. But if the embassy is attacked by the Russians, Islamov can't be positive that he'll have time to run downstairs and do whatever he needs to do to detonate the bomb. He also knows he might be killed during an armed attack. Based on these assumptions, we believe Islamov has programmed the laptop computer attached to the bomb to detonate at a specific time. We're guessing that he's using an incremental time line."

"What exactly are you saying?"

"Let's say Islamov sets the bomb to detonate in eight hours, then he goes down into the basement after, say, seven hours, and restarts the clock. This way, even if he is killed, the bomb will still go off and the most time that we'd have to disarm it would be less than eight hours."

"If your theory is correct, then, it would be possible for us to storm the embassy and possibly disengage the bomb before it goes off."

"Excuse me, sir," CIA director Starkweather interrupted. "This is a theory the FBI has come up with. We can't be certain Islamov is using a time delay."

"Mr. Vice President," Davenport said in slightly irritated voice. "To answer your question: I firmly believe there's a good chance that we can storm the old Soviet embassy, neutralize the Chechens, and disable this bomb. The CIA director is accurate in arguing that this is speculation, but we believe it's an accurate theory based on conversations we've had with our Russian sources and our examination of the photographs."

"What if you're wrong?" Starkweather insisted. "What if we can't disconnect the laptop or break his computer code?"

"Starkweather," the vice president said, "are you suggesting this Chechen rebel has developed a computer program that is so sophisticated the best minds in America might not be able to override it?"

"Sir, there's no doubt in my mind that we have the technical expertise to break any code the Chechens have put into place," Starkweather said. "But that's really not the issue. The question is: Will we have enough time? What if Islamov is resetting his timer every hour or every two hours?"

"Deputy Conway," the V.P. said.

Once again, I stood up.

"Are you willing to return to the Soviet embassy and talk to this terrorist?"

"Of course I am, sir."

"Maybe you could calm him down, stall him for a while. I don't know—maybe you could get him to actually show you the bomb. Or even get him to brag about how smart he's been at attaching this laptop and arming it. We're going to need time to discuss this with the Russians and develop a mutual game plan."

He addressed Starkweather and Davenport next. "Has either of you relayed any of this information to the Russians? Hell, they *built* this goddamned bomb, so they should know how to dismantle it!"

"Mr. Vice President," Starkweather interjected. "My gut reaction, sir, is the Russians are going to stonewall and deny knowing anything about the basement bomb. I'm guessing they'll insist the Chechens brought it with them. They'll want to be able to deny all knowledge of it in case Islamov sets off the device."

"I agree," Davenport chimed in. "I don't think we can count on the Russians for much help."

The V.P. asked, "What other options do we have except to attack? Diplomatically, is there any chance we can get the Russians to agree to begin pulling their troops out of Chechnya?"

The State Department's honcho said, "Sir, the current Russian president was elected largely on his get-tough stance toward the Chechens. Polls show their people have no sympathy for the Chechens, and they oppose giving them any freedoms. But we will try to reason with the Russian president—just the same."

"How are we going to handle the U.S. media?"

"I'm opposed to revealing anything to them at this time," Davenport said. "News of the bomb could spark mass hysteria, traffic jams, looting, and a complete breakdown in law and order inside and outside the Beltway."

The V.P. released a loud sigh.

"I'll brief the president," he finally said. "He's currently aboard Air Force One. The Secret Service insisted he leave Washington, D.C., as soon as it learned there was a possible nuclear device inside the city. He was scheduled to deliver a speech in Los Angeles tomorrow, so the public is being told his decision to leave town has nothing to do with the Chechens and the embassy standoff. I'm certain he'll want the secretary of state to begin talks with the Russians immediately. Maybe we can get them to withdraw some of their troops as a token gesture—enough to appease Islamov. If that doesn't work, we might have to get tough with them."

He rose from his seat and everyone stood. "It might be a good time for all of us to start praying," he said.

Talking to God was the last thing on my mind. I was thinking about Moe Islamov and how he'd assured me that he'd found a way to force the

United States to use its military muscle to pressure Russia into withdrawing its troops. It looked as if he was going to get his wish. Moe Islamov was a murderer, but he was also damned smart. He really had deserved that A grade that I'd given him back in college years ago when everything in life seemed so much simpler.

44

FBI director Davenport, followed by his lapdog, Rodney Ames, rushed over to complain about how I'd ignored the chain of command in my handling of Islamov's letter. Even though I was standing a few feet away, I could discern CIA director Starkweather shrugging off their grievance.

"Deputy Conway hasn't worked very long at the CTC," Starkweather said. "I'm not certain he understood that your agent was supposed to be given the letter. It won't happen again."

Of course, this was nonsense, and all of them recognized it. But his comments sounded credible enough to put the matter to rest. In Washington, few federal employees are actually disciplined, and, in my case, the simple airing of Ames's complaint was sufficient to placate everyone—everyone, that is, except Special Agent Rodney Ames.

All of us had more pressing matters to resolve now.

"The State Department is reluctant to call in the Russian ambassador for an official sit-down," Davenport declared. "The media would ask why. Luckily, both men are scheduled to attend the same Georgetown party tonight, so arrangements are being made for them to speak privately at that time."

Kimberly and I slowly shouldered our way into the ring with Davenport, Starkweather, Clarke, and Ames.

"What about General Rodin?" I asked. "Does someone have him under control?"

Davenport ignored me. I was a lower-ranking federal employee, and that meant I didn't have enough clout to address the FBI director. But Starkweather said, "Good question! How *do* we want to handle General Rodin and his Russian goons?"

Davenport replied, "Let's let Ames monitor General Rodin."

Ames perceived this as his cue. He said, "The general checked out of the Jefferson Hotel and is now operating from the new Russian Federation embassy. I'm scheduled to meet him and Colonel Khrenkov there in about an hour. I'll grill 'em about the bomb at that point."

"I'd like Deputy Conway and Ms. Lodge to accompany Ames to the Russian embassy," Director Starkweather said.

A look of shock came over Ames's face. But before he could object, Davenport said, "As long as Conway understands that we're all on the same team here and Ames is in charge, then I see nothing wrong with the two of them tagging along."

Davenport then asked me, "You do understand that this *is* an FBI operation? Ames *is* in charge and *he* will be calling the shots."

"That's what I've been told," I said, which I thought was a good answer because I wasn't acknowledging that I'd submit to Ames. I was simply stating that I had been told he was in charge. After all, Washington is a city of nuances.

It was eight p.m. when our motorcade arrived at the Russian Federation's new quarters on Wisconsin Avenue in Mount Alto. Ames was riding in the first limousine with two aides. Kimberly and I were sitting together in a second car. An armed Russian security guard stopped the motorcade at the gate and began arguing with Ames.

I got out to learn why. It turned out the sentry was refusing to allow Ames and the rest of us in because we were carrying firearms. Ames was balking at surrendering his hardware to a Russian. Hence, the standoff.

"For God's sake, let's just lock 'em in the car trunks," I suggested. I'd once delivered a Mafia prisoner to the Italian embassy and I'd learned way back then that putting weapons out of reach in a trunk was the diplomatically acceptable way for U.S. law enforcement officers to resolve this issue. Apparently, no one had ever told Ames.

The Russian immediately agreed, but rather than thanking me, an embarrassed Rodney P. Ames snarled in my direction and sped off.

Colonel Khrenkov was at the front entrance with disappointing news.

"We have a diplomatic problem here," he said. "General Rodin is our highest-ranking military officer in the Russian Federation. He answers to our president."

"Yes," said Ames, "we realize this, and we fully appreciate the opportunity to meet with him."

Although Ames said he understood, he really didn't.

"Ames," I said quietly, "what the colonel is trying to say politely is that none of us is important enough in diplomatic status and rank to be talking to him."

Ames's jaw tightened. I didn't know if it was because I'd had to explain what Khrenkov was saying or if he felt insulted by General Rodin's stance. Either way, Ames was clearly not having a good day.

"Perhaps your FBI director would like to join us for this briefing," Khrenkov volunteered.

Ames hesitated and then returned to his car to use a cell phone to call FBI headquarters. Had the stakes not been so monumental, I would have thought this entire scene was hilarious. We had every reason to believe there was a fully armed nuclear bomb in the hands of Chechen terrorists in the basement of a downtown Washington building. We'd just left a White House briefing where we'd been told that this nuclear instrument was powerful enough to destroy the nation's capital. And yet, despite this ominous threat, we were still getting hung up on diplomatic etiquette and ego trips.

When Ames reemerged from his car, he said brusquely, "The director is on his way."

Khrenkov excused himself and disappeared inside the embassy, leaving us to wait outside.

"Gosh," I said sarcastically, "this is going swimmingly so far!"

"You've got a big mouth," Ames said, "and someday I'm going to enjoy putting my foot in it."

I was about to make a witty comment about how he'd have to take both of his feet out of his own mouth first, but Kimberly intervened. "Let's wait inside our separate cars," she suggested.

Forty-five minutes later, Davenport, flanked by light-flashing lead and rear vehicles, arrived at the compound. He wasn't pleased. Ames immediately ran over to him while Kimberly and I fell in behind. At that same moment, Colonel Khrenkov reappeared and escorted us inside. We passed a security desk and walked along an ornate hallway into a conference room.

"General Rodin will be with you momentarily," Khrenkov said.

"Wanna bet he lets us cool our heels here for at least ten minutes?" I asked Kimberly.

She was studying Davenport, who'd taken a head seat at one end of the conference table and was conferring in hushed tones with Ames.

"That would take some pretty big balls," she replied.

I was wrong. General Rodin didn't make us wait ten minutes. He made us wait a half hour. Davenport was purple-faced by the time the general came breezing in.

"I was detained because I was speaking to the president in Moscow," General Rodin announced offhandedly through an interpreter.

I suspected he was lying and had simply wanted to impress us, but, hey, maybe he really had been talking to Russia's top leader.

"The only practical response to the Chechen terrorists is the immediate reclaiming of our embassy by force," the general stated before Davenport could utter a sound through his dropped jaw.

"General Rodin," Davenport replied, checking his anger, but visibly uncomfortable, "under normal circumstances, I'd agree. But these are not normal circumstances."

"Our embassy is on Russian soil," Rodin said through his translator. "All hostages are Russian citizens. Your point of view, while welcome, is nevertheless not overriding."

"My government isn't questioning your ability or your legal authority to reclaim your embassy," Davenport asserted. "But a special situation has arisen, and the risk that our capital city now faces has made this standoff much more than a Russian Federation problem."

I can't stand bureaucratic gobbledygook or political posturing. General Rodin had to know there was a nuclear bomb in his embassy's basement, especially if the KGB had built it. But neither he nor Davenport wanted to be the first to spill the beans. Both were dancing around the issue.

I decided to ignore the diplomatic bullshit and help them out by jumping into the fray.

"Moe Islamov has a nuclear bomb," I said, "so let's get to the point here, shall we?"

Davenport turned his face toward me. I'd never seen a public official so angry. Without help from his interpreter, General Rodin said in English: "Deputy Conway, I've heard much about you. You are the deputy who met face-to-face with the terrorist, Movladi Islamov?"

"Yes, he was once my student and friend."

"You Americans," Rodin said, "are both naive and romantic when it comes to world affairs. Islamov belongs to a fundamentalist Islamic religious sect that teaches it is better for nonbelievers, such as you and me, to be murdered than for you to continue living in darkness. Tell me, why would you befriend a man whose religion teaches him to kill you because you are an infidel?"

I opened my mouth, but General Rodin wasn't finished. "When the Russian Federation was first formed," he said, "we allowed the Chechen people to elect their own president. They chose a president who was totally corrupt."

"Still, it was their choice," I said. "Maybe they'd get a better one if you hadn't invaded."

Rodin replied, "And perhaps they would get a worse one. You must understand there are primitive, uneducated people in this world, and such people are not capable of governing themselves. The Chechens are this way. Would you allow a small child to drive a speeding car? A fanatic such as Movladi Islamov would turn against your country if Russia was not standing in the way. Don't forget that the terrorist Osama Bin Laden was once fighting on your side against my country in Afghanistan. As soon as our troops pulled out, he began biting you."

Davenport moved to put an end to my interruption. "I think it would be more expedient if the general and I continued this conversation in private," he said. He pushed a manila envelope across the table to Colonel Khrenkov, who gave it to Rodin. The general removed an eight-by-ten photograph from the packet. While I couldn't see the picture, I assumed it was an enlargement of the layer-cake bomb.

General Rodin spat out a command in Russian. All of his aides, except for Khrenkov, immediately left the conference room. Davenport then looked at Kimberly and me.

"That's our cue to go." Kimberly nudged me.

"No, not yet," I replied. "If the general is going to let his top aide stay, then we can, too."

I'd said this loud enough for both Davenport and Rodin to hear. The Russian general was watching Davenport, as if to say, "This guy is your problem. You deal with him."

"Deputy Conway and Ms. Lodge," Davenport said, "you both need to wait outside now."

Kimberly stood, but I touched her elbow as she started to move past my chair and said, "With all due respect, sir, Ms. Lodge and I are with the Counterterrorism Center, which is headquartered at the CIA, and we have orders from the CIA director to stay put. I'll call him, if you'd like, to see if he'd like us to leave, but I'd just as soon stay."

My blatant insubordination caught everyone by surprise. General Rodin decided to intervene.

"Deputy Conway," the Russian general said, "you are obviously a man with no patience, a man who prefers actions to proper channels, a man who speaks his mind, no matter what the consequences."

"I've been told that before."

"Sometimes this sort of frankness is a very good thing, but when it comes to diplomacy, it isn't. How do you Americans say it? 'Fools rush in.'" He smiled. "In this case, I believe your country and my nation will be best served if Director Davenport and I can now speak frankly without an audience."

I looked over at Colonel Khrenkov. General Rodin followed my eyes and understood that I wasn't going to leave as long as Khrenkov was allowed to stay. "Colonel Khrenkov," the general said, "would you please accompany our guests outside for refreshments so the director and I may speak privately?"

Without hesitation, Khrenkov stood.

I began to rise, too, but still couldn't keep my mouth shut. "Since I'm the only one here who actually knows Moe Islamov, I'd like to pass along an insight about him. He fully expects you to attack the embassy, and he will not hesitate to detonate the basement bomb."

Having said my piece, I turned away to leave, but just then realized that Ames was still sitting beside Davenport. General Rodin noticed, too, and said, "Perhaps your FBI agent would enjoy having refreshments also?"

Davenport nodded at Ames, who rose slowly from his seat. All four of us—Khrenkov, Ames, Kimberly, and I—marched into an adjoining chamber where a table had been prepared with an urn of freshly brewed coffee, hot water for tea, and finger sandwiches.

"You nervy son of a bitch!" Ames exclaimed, as soon as the conference door closed behind us. "Director Davenport is going to fry your ass! How dare you embarrass him and the FBI! How dare you challenge his authority!"

"Rodney," I replied, in a patronizing tone, calling him by his first name as if we were best friends, "let's not get our noses bent out of joint."

He wanted to hit me, but not in front of Kimberly or Khrenkov.

"I'm going to the men's room," he announced.

Khrenkov called an aide, who was told to escort Ames to the closest bathroom. This left Kimberly, Khrenkov, and me in the lounge.

I knew Ames was right. I'd insulted Director Davenport and he was going to see to it that I was fired or, at the very least, returned to the U.S. Marshals Service and banished to Minot, North Dakota. Having little left to lose, I decided to dig my grave even deeper.

"You've spent your entire career in the GRU, isn't that correct, Colonel?" I asked.

Khrenkov considered the question and then replied, "Yes. And you've been a deputy all of yours, is this not accurate?"

For a moment, I thought we were replaying a scene from a James Bond movie in which Bond and one of his rivals show off how much they know about each other.

"I joined the Marshals Service directly out of the military in 1991," I volunteered, "just after I got home from Operation Desert Storm. You did some time fighting in the Middle East, too, didn't you?"

Kimberly, who knew exactly where I was going with this, attempted a segue to sidetrack the conversation.

"These sandwiches are terrific," she declared. "What's inside them?"

Khrenkov said, "I don't know."

I reached into my pocket and removed the snapshot of a youthful Khrenkov posing with his sniper rifle in Afghanistan. I said, "Colonel, you might find this picture interesting."

He was adding sugar to his coffee with one hand and balancing his cup and saucer with the other. He made no effort to take it from me, so I held it up so that both he and Kimberly could see it.

"That's you, isn't it, Colonel?" a surprised Kimberly asked.

"Yes," Khrenkov replied without betraying any emotion. "Only I was much younger."

"You were fighting in Afghanistan when this photo was taken, weren't you?" I said.

"That's correct," he answered.

"And if I'm not mistaken," I said, "that's an SVD Dragunov sniper rifle you're carrying."

Khrenkov lifted the spoon from his cup and rested it on the saucer. "It's one of several weapons I was trained to fire, just as I'm certain you, too, have been trained to use a variety of weapons."

"I've never had the pleasure of shooting a Dragunov," I continued. "Tell me, is it fairly accurate?"

"It can be. In the right hands."

"Is this is your first trip to the United States?"

"Yes."

"So you weren't here, say, in October?"

"No."

"Ever been to Washington, D.C., before?"

"No."

The fact he was answering my questions with one-word replies was significant. As a trained interrogator, Khrenkov knew the most common mistake suspects make is to volunteer too much information during questioning.

I continued, "In October, a Russian mobster named Sergey Pudin was killed by a sniper in Washington, D.C."

Khrenkov sipped his coffee.

"I happened to be protecting Pudin at the time, and the sniper left his rifle behind when he escaped. It was a Russian-made Dragunov, just like the one you used in Afghanistan."

Kimberly interrupted. "Wyatt, are you certain this is the proper time to talk to Colonel Khrenkov about this matter?"

"Yes, actually, I do," I said firmly, keeping my eyes locked on Khrenkov's. "This sniper escaped after he murdered my witness. The FBI believes he rode a train to Baltimore where he caught a flight to New York and then boarded another to Moscow. The airline manifest said his name was Vadim Tolomasin."

"I do not know him," Khrenkov said.

"I don't think Tolomasin is his actual name. Just before the sniper boarded his Moscow-bound flight, he telephoned the FBI in New York to ask about a young woman named Olga Polov. She'd been kidnapped along with her parents and two brothers. The FBI managed to rescue the others, but Olga was murdered."

I studied Khrenkov's face for the slightest acknowledgment. There was none. I said, "The mobsters took turns raping Olga before they killed her."

Again, no reaction.

"We are currently hiding the surviving members of the Polov family in a new city. We've given them new names to protect them."

Khrenkov took another sip of coffee. I'd never seen anyone who'd kept his emotions so well hidden.

"Would you like to know where they are being hidden?" I asked.

"This matter is of no concern to me," he replied.

"Oh, really? Does that mean you don't know them—the Polovs?"

Khrenkov didn't reply.

I said, "Because this photograph of you in Afghanistan—I got it from the Polovs. I found it tucked inside a family Bible, even though they insist they don't have any relatives still living in Moscow. Now why would the Polovs keep a picture of you in their Bible?"

No reaction, not even a raised eyebrow.

"Tell me, Colonel," I said, "have you ever heard of a Russian gangster named Igor Aleksandrovich Fedorov? He likes to smoke expensive Cuban cigars."

Khrenkov continued drinking his coffee.

I said, "Fedorov—actually, he likes to be called Major Fedorov—is now being protected by my government. It's ironic, actually, because he's in the same witness protection program as the Polov family."

Again, nothing.

I said, "Major Fedorov has admitted it was his idea to abduct the Polov family and arrange the murder of Sergey Pudin. He's also told us that you are the Russian sniper who shot and killed Sergey Pudin. He says Olga Polov was your sister."

Khrenkov slowly set his cup onto its saucer and placed both on the serving table.

Just then Ames came back into the room. He stepped past Khrenkov and got himself a cup of coffee. I tucked the photograph of Khrenkov into my pocket to keep Ames from seeing it.

"This is a conversation," Colonel Khrenkov said calmly, "I think we will need to continue later, Deputy Wyatt Conway. I didn't know Major Fedorov was now under your government's protection."

"Major who?" Ames asked.

A phone rang. Khrenkov got it. After he finished speaking in Russian, he said, "General Rodin and Director Davenport have requested Agent Ames and me to join them in the conference room. You and Ms. Lodge are to remain here."

A door opened and four bulky Russian security guards stepped into our area.

"Is this going to be a problem?" Khrenkov asked me.

Ames gleefully said, "Not for me. I'm ready to go inside, Colonel."

I looked at the muscled knuckle-draggers he'd summoned and said, "You and Ames have a good time in your meeting. We'll stay here and enjoy the eats."

Khrenkov and Ames exited, but the goons stayed put. Kimberly said, "You're fucking unbelievable! You insult Director Davenport and then you accuse Colonel Khrenkov of murdering Sergey Pudin. What did you expect Khrenkov to do? Burst into tears and confess?"

"I wanted Khrenkov to know that I know."

"Why? We don't have time for this macho bullshit! You've got to look at the big picture here! No one gives a damn about Sergey Pudin. He was a vicious criminal. You're just angry because he got killed on your watch and now you're on a personal crusade to expose Colonel Khrenkov!"

"I prefer to think of it as bringing a criminal to justice. It's what we do in law enforcement."

"Don't give me that bullshit! Khrenkov has diplomatic immunity!" she said. "We've got terrorists threatening to vaporize Washington and you're baiting him!"

The door opened and Ames's head popped in. "You two can come in," he smirked.

Kimberly and I entered the conference room.

"Deputy Conway," Director Davenport said, "we have just agreed it's time for you to pay another visit to your Chechen terrorist acquaintance—just as the vice president suggested earlier."

The friendliness of Davenport's demeanor made me uneasy.

"When do you think I should do this?" I asked.

Davenport looked at his watch. It was nearly eleven p.m. "I doubt he's sleeping," he said. "Why not make it tonight? We can have Special Agent Ames call him after the three of you drive down to the mobile command post and discuss a few things. Tell Islamov you'd like to come see him at five in the morning—before daybreak. Say you want to meet him then because you're trying to avoid having American television crews see you."

"And, Deputy Conway," General Rodin added, "please wear boxer shorts this time."

Rodin laughed, and Davenport and Ames joined him. But Khrenkov stared straight ahead, without any hint of what he was thinking.

"You've been duped," Rodney Ames triumphantly announced as soon as Kimberly and I entered the FBI's mobile crisis command post parked near the Jefferson Hotel. He'd arrived there a few minutes before we had. Colonel Khrenkov had stayed behind at the Russian embassy, but was supposed to be joining us shortly.

"What are you talking about?" Kimberly asked.

Ames couldn't suppress the huge smile on his face. He was clearly enjoying this. "Those photos that your terrorist pal gave you—the ones of the layer-cake bomb—they're fakes! General Rodin says the bomb in those pictures is in the Russian Museum of Nuclear Weapons in Arzamas, which is where the Soviets designed most of their nuclear weapons."

"The pictures are of a bomb in a museum?" Kimberly repeated.

Ames wet his lips with glee. "That's what the general says. And he's assured Director Davenport and the White House there is absolutely no threat of a nuclear bomb being in the basement."

"Did he admit the KGB built a bomb there in the 1950s?" I asked.

"Hell, no!" Ames said. "He says Islamov is playing you for a complete fool. And you bought it—hook, line, and s-u-c-k-e-r!"

"Oh my God!" Kimberly said. "We've gotten the entire White House and cabinet worrying about a bomb that's on display in a Russian museum!"

"That's right," Ames said. "I'm thinking you both have just kissed your careers goodbye."

"Hold on," I said. "The State Department confirmed the pictures had been taken inside an office in the basement of the Soviet embassy."

"Any high school kid with a computer could've doctored those museum pictures to make them look like they were shot in their basement," Ames replied. "Besides, Islamov apparently pulled a similar stunt a few months ago. He mailed photographs of a suitcase bomb to the SVR in Moscow and claimed he'd hidden it near the Kremlin. General Rodin says his specialists were able to prove the bomb was a computerized fabrication that looked real in pictures but didn't actually exist."

"How do you know Rodin isn't lying?"

"The Russians are contacting museum officials right now in Arzamas to get duplicate shots of their museum bomb display sent to Rodin so he can compare them to Islamov's pictures."

"I don't trust Rodin," I said. "We expected the Russians to deny knowing about the embassy bomb. What's to keep him from doctoring the museum photograph to make them look the same as Islamov's bomb?"

"Okay, I want to make certain I'm understanding what you just said. You don't trust General Rodin, but you do believe Islamov is telling the truth?" Ames said. "Listen, Conway, the cold war is over. Done. *Finito!* Besides, it's not just General Rodin who's saying this. The Russian ambassador has assured the secretary of state that the images are fake and there never was a covert KGB plan to build a bomb in Washington, D.C."

"Golly gee," I replied sarcastically, "the Russians say there's no bomb, so we automatically believe them. How silly of me to think they could be shittin' us to cover their own asses!"

"Wyatt, we're talking about the Russian ambassador," Kimberly said. "Would he lie about something this lethal?"

"*Absolutely,*" I answered. "Ever since the Soviet Union collapsed, the Russians have been licking their wounds. It's difficult to give up being a superpower. Do you think Moscow would care if Washington were suddenly destroyed—especially if the world blamed it on Chechen rebels? There are plenty of nations out there who'd love to see another 9/11 disaster. Vaporizing D.C. would help level the playing field, and it would give the Russians a free hand to sweep into Chechnya and do anything they wanted without the United Nations or anyone else complaining."

"We are talking about killing five million human beings," Kimberly said. "I don't think even the Russians would sink that low."

"Read your history books. Stalin killed seven million in just four years during purges in the 1930s. And those were his own people! I don't think killing five million Americans is going to cause anyone at the Kremlin to lose a night's sleep."

Ames chimed in. "I happen to believe General Rodin. But the White House wants to make certain. That's why we're sending you back into the embassy to confront Islamov. We want him to actually show you the bomb."

We were interrupted by a knock on the door. An aide announced, "Colonel Khrenkov has arrived." When Khrenkov joined us, Ames said, "Colonel, I was just explaining to Ms. Lodge and Deputy Conway here our plan."

"You've told them there is no bomb?" Khrenkov responded.

"Yes, of course," Ames said. "But Mr. Conway here thinks you might be fibbing about that."

Ames asked one of his aides to fetch Dr. Irwin Colter, the nuclear scientist whom I'd first seen at the White House briefing. Colter was carrying a bag in his hand when he joined us. Ames introduced Dr. Colter and then said, "We believe we have come up with a foolproof way to prove whether or not there is a layer-cake bomb in the embassy basement."

Dr. Colter pulled a pair of men's gray boxer shorts from the bag that he was carrying and tossed them to me.

"Please, inspect these," he said.

They looked like ordinary underwear to me.

"Feel under the label," Colter said.

I did. There was something hard hidden there.

"It's a microchip sensor that can detect the presence of radioactive elements and transmit a reading to us here in the command center," Colter explained. "If the terrorists have a layer-cake bomb on the premises, the detector will let us know—as long as you can get within ten feet of it."

I was impressed, but I couldn't believe there wasn't a more practical way than sending in bugged boxers to detect whether the Chechens actually had a bomb. Besides, I was wondering what all this was going to do to my sperm count!

Apparently, Dr. Colter read my mind—about the bomb, not the sperm count. "The Nuclear Emergency Search Team, called NEST, has flown over the embassy in a helicopter with a gamma ray sensing device," Dr. Colter said, "but the KGB has installed so many shields in the building over the years, that it was impossible for us to get a reading."

"What happens if Islamov refuses to show me the bomb?"

"Then we'll know he's bluffing, just like General Rodin says he is," Ames replied.

"What happens if this is a bluff?" Kimberly asked.

Khrenkov replied, "General Rodin already has a plan in place to end the standoff."

"In other words," I said, "he'll send in his Spetsnaz team and we'll end up with dead hostages on the nightly news."

"Dead terrorists," Khrenkov said, correcting me. "Obviously, General Rodin will do his best to save as many hostages as possible, but even if some die, they are not Americans, and therefore are not your concern."

"Last time I checked," I said, "a hostage's blood was red no matter what his nationality was."

"Did you deliver the letter I gave you?" Moe Islamov asked when I called his cell phone.

"Yes, that's why I've been ordered to pay you another visit," I answered.

"That's good news!" Islamov exclaimed. "I'm waiting here to greet you."

A few minutes before five a.m., I began retracing my steps down Sixteenth Street to our rendezvous. I eased by the Ford SUV blocking the gateway, entered the mansion's courtyard, and began stripping just outside the doors—only this time I left on my electronically bugged Joe Boxer underwear. When a set of hands appeared from behind the doors and pulled me inside, none of the terrorists seemed concerned that I wasn't completely naked. As before, a black hood was dropped over my head and I was jostled off to the same conference room where I'd met Islamov earlier. When my hood was removed, Islamov was sitting across from me. He was wearing a ski mask but had changed out of his all-black "terrorist" outfit. He was now dressed in blue gabardine pants, like the ones that he had given me during my last visit, and a white shirt.

"Was your president impressed by my photographs?" he asked.

"What?" I snapped. "No small talk? No 'How ya doing, Professor Conway? Glad to see you again.' " Even I was surprised by the sharpness in my voice. I'd managed to suppress it during our first meeting, but not now. If Islamov actually had a nuclear bomb in the basement, I was angry about it. And if he didn't have a bomb and had slipped me doctored photos of a museum relic, I was mad about that, too. Either way, I was pissed off.

My attitude caught him off guard. "In a war, friendship, even admiration, is of no consequence," he said.

"Moe, you aren't my friend anymore. And despite all your philosophical bullshit that you keep spouting to rationalize your actions, you're nothing but a cold-blooded fanatic."

He seemed hurt, and the thought hit me that this might not be the best time to be verbally attacking him.

"Putting my personal feelings aside," I said, "there's a problem. The good news for you is the White House is prepared to use its diplomatic and its military might to force the Russians to negotiate and, hopefully, to begin withdrawing its troops from Chechnya. The bad news is General Rodin and the Russian ambassador are insisting the photographs that you gave me are fake."

"Fake?"

"Yes, as in 'not real.' Doctored. Computer enhanced. They claim the pictures are of a layer-cake bomb that is currently on display in the Russian Museum of Nuclear Weapons in Arzamas."

Much to my utter amazement, Islamov grinned through the cutout in the ski mask that he was wearing. "This would be something General Rodin and the old KGB might attempt—to fool you with doctored images from a display," he said. "But there is a nuclear bomb in the basement underneath us, and it is very, very real."

"Sorry, Moe," I replied. "But no one out there is willing to take your word for it. Something about your reputation, I suppose."

"Perhaps," he said, "if I were to snap a shot of you standing in front of the bomb, *that* would convince them that it is here and I am serious about my threat."

Wow, I thought, *this is almost too easy.*

"Especially," he continued, "if I then shot you and put both your body and the photograph outside for the FBI."

Okay, I thought, *this isn't going as well as I had hoped.*

"I think the Polaroid will be enough to convince them," I said. "Besides, you don't want to kill me. I'm the only person on the outside who is arguing in favor of forcing the Russians to get out of Chechnya."

"Of all the Americans I know," Islamov said, "I really thought you would understand why I am fighting this war."

Apparently my earlier remarks about his character had hurt his feelings.

"I'm a moral man," Islamov continued. "How dare you judge me? How dare your president demand more evidence, more photographs?"

For a moment, I wondered: *Maybe there isn't a bomb. Maybe General Rodin and the Russian ambassador are right! He's bluffing!*

Islamov suddenly stood up and went out the door, leaving me alone. Minutes later, he returned with two of his compatriots. They, too, were wearing ski masks, but they were dressed in all-black clothing. Based on the silhouette, I knew one of them was a woman. She was carrying a Polaroid camera.

"Put your hood on," Islamov ordered.

I placed it over my head while asking, "Where to?"

"Downstairs."

Someone grabbed my arm and led me into the hallway. We entered an elevator. Moments later, my bare feet were chilled by concrete as we walked into a room. When we finally stopped, the grip on my arm was released.

"Remove your hood," Islamov said.

It took my eyes a moment to adjust to the fluorescent lighting, which cast a garish glow throughout the office. When they came into focus, I saw before me exactly what I'd seen in the photographs that Islamov had sent to the White House. A big metal cylinder was sitting in front of me. The photographs had made it look ordinary, but standing there, staring at it, I felt a sense of dread.

"Get closer," the woman commanded. She raised her camera as if she were a paparazzo. I stepped over the rubble where the fake wall had once been, entering the cubbyhole next to the bomb. I turned my back toward it so that the Joe Boxer label in my underpants was only inches from the metal casing.

If this thing is emitting radiation, the detector should be sending back one hell of a signal just about now, I thought.

"Put your hand on the bomb," she barked. "Then they will know you were actually here touching it."

I reached over and placed my palm against the cool steel. I'd never touched an actual nuclear bomb or any kind of bomb before, and as I did, a tremendous sense of awe and horror flowed through me. It seemed implausible, *impossible,* that this one thing could destroy our capital. And yet, I'd been told it could. This mammoth, evil creation of man was capable of killing five million human beings and reducing the most powerful and important city in the world to rubble.

As the camera flashed, another thought hit me: *Is Islamov going to send these pictures back with me alive—or dead?*

The woman took a second shot, waited for it to appear, and then grunted something to Islamov.

"If they didn't believe our first photographs," Islamov said, "why will they believe this. The Russians will simply claim that we have doctored these. We must do more to convince them."

I didn't like how that sounded.

But rather than ordering them to shoot me, Islamov stepped over to a telephone mounted on the wall.

"Cell phones don't work down here," he said. "Too many KGB-installed shields." Islamov dialed the FBI emergency command post. Special Agent Ames had given him the number when the bureau had first contacted him.

"This is Special Agent Ames," a voice answered.

Islamov brought me the telephone. Its long cord uncoiled across the room.

"Ames, this is Deputy Conway," I said. "I'm standing in the embassy basement right now and I'm calling to tell you that General Rodin, Colonel Khrenkov, and the rest of those Russian bastards are lying."

Islamov smiled. So far, he liked my report.

"Watch your mouth, Conway," Ames said. "This is being automatically tape-recorded."

"Good," I replied, "because I want this on the record for everyone to hear, especially the president. There's a nuclear bomb down here—just like Islamov says."

"You're sure?"

"I'm standing next to it. I have touched it with my own hands."

"What sort of bomb is it? Can you describe it?"

"Rodney," I said, "it's a goddamn big bomb!"

"And you say you're standing next to it?"

"It is only inches away from me!"

Islamov took the receiver from me and hung it up.

"That should convince them," he declared.

I was about to agree when we heard an explosion upstairs. The noise was so loud that all of us instinctively ducked, as if we were afraid the ceiling was about to fall. Islamov's eyes met mine, and I could tell that both of us had been caught completely off guard.

"It's General Rodin!" Islamov screamed. "Upstairs! Now!" His two cohorts ran out of the room, leaving just the two of us behind. In an effortless move, Islamov pulled his .40-caliber semiautomatic pistol from his waistband and aimed it squarely at my chest.

I thought: *I'm not supposed to die this way.* But then, who really ever expects to die?

"You've betrayed me!" he said. "Why? Why have you done this?"

"No, Moe," I replied. "We've both been betrayed."

"You called me a cold-blooded killer, but it's General Rodin and your FBI who must now bear responsibility for what is about to happen here."

"Moe, is this bomb really programmed to explode?"

"Even you still don't see what should be obvious," he snapped.

"Moe," I said, trying to appear calm, "you can stop this madness. You can choose not to detonate this bomb. You don't have to die, and neither do the innocent men, women, and children in this city. Do you really want to be remembered in history as a fanatic who destroyed all of Washington, D.C.? How can this possibly help Chechnya?"

"I have no choice," he replied. "We must show the world how serious we are about driving the Russians out of my country."

"If you set off the bomb, the world will say Russia is justified in wiping out your people."

"My friend," he said sadly, "the world has already said that."

He slowly lowered his handgun and said, "You will die, Professor. But not by my hand."

He turned and hurried out the door.

I ran after him, but he shut the door and bolted it from the outside. I dashed over to the layer-cake bomb and examined the laptop computer that the terrorists had attached to the bomb through wires in the cylinder. I didn't have a clue as to how to disarm it.

As I looked at the computer screen, I wondered: *If you are standing next to a 400-kiloton nuclear bomb when it explodes, does your brain even have time to compute that you no longer exist?*

The windows in the old Soviet embassy are made of bullet-resistant glass. None can be opened and many of the upper-floor windows have been covered by heavy shutters. The KGB put in these security safeguards because it was worried that angry protestors might someday storm the mansion and attempt to break inside.

No one in the KGB apparently considered, however, how these barriers would prevent those inside from firing their weapons at approaching attackers. Because of this poor planning, the Chechen terrorists were helpless when a six-man FBI Hostage Rescue Team bolted into the embassy courtyard and raced up to the front doors.

Although General Lev Rodin had been consulted, he was not in charge of the assault that was now under way. The White House had ruled that the FBI's specialized HRTs would reclaim control of the Russian embassy. In tense negotiations, Moscow had reluctantly agreed. The Russian Spetsnaz squad under Rodin's command had been ordered to stay put in the guest barracks at Andrews Air Force Base.

The HRTs, as they are known, are part of the Tactical Support Branch of the Critical Incident Response Group, both referred to by their bureaucratic acronyms, TSB and CIRG, respectively. Formed in 1982, the HRTs are based at the FBI Academy in Quantico, Virginia, and are considered to be the most elite tactical assault unit in American law enforcement. Their leaders had elected to launch a four-pronged assault on the embassy. The attack was being coordinated by senior FBI officials from inside the Strategic Information Operations Center on the fifth floor of the J. Edgar Hoover Building.

It had been tacticians at SIOC who had first realized that Islamov and his fellow Chechens wouldn't be able to fire their automatic weapons at an approaching assault team unless they opened the mansion's front doors, which would have been foolhardy. The FBI had positioned snipers around the institution, and they could easily have killed anyone who showed himself. Although the terrorists didn't have any ammunition that could pierce the windows' thick glass, the sharpshooters did. They were armed with Barrett Model 82 sniper rifles, which fired a .50-caliber slug capable of punching through two inches of steel plate.

Wearing black Nomex flight suits, tactical vests with the letters FBI marked in bright yellow on them, and body armor, the first HRT team reached the embassy's double doors in a matter of seconds. A Chechen stationed on the second floor had tried to alert Islamov on his cell phone intercom, but the embassy's basement shields had blocked his transmission.

At that point, a terrorist attempted to detonate the explosives inside the two SUVs abandoned in the embassy's courtyard. Both vehicles had been packed with ammonium nitrate, fuel oil, and boxes of nails, bolts, and ball bearings to increase the explosion's lethalness. But when the Chechen pushed the button on his remote detonator, the SUVs didn't react. FBI technicians were using electronic-jamming devices to disrupt the radio signal between the firing button and the SUVs. Having failed to set off the outside bombs, the terrorist raced down a hallway where he paired up with another Chechen standing watch on the second floor. They ducked into an office.

The moment the initial HRT unit reached the embassy, the "breacher" on the team slapped a two-inch square of C4 explosive onto the heavy front doors. It was this blast that Islamov and Conway had first heard in the basement. As soon as the portals blew open, another HRT team member pitched flash bangs into the foyer. They blew, causing a loud noise, blinding flash, and a shock wave designed to disorient and confuse.

At the same time the frontal attack team was barging through the entrance, a second HRT squad was darting across the courtyard. Its job was to neutralize the two SUVs, a task they accomplished by using high-pressure water hoses to soak the potentially explosive fertilizer inside, making it nearly impossible to ignite.

At the rear of the embassy, a third HRT team used a larger charge of C4 to blow open a reinforced entry. It had been used primarily for deliveries, and it led directly into the mansion's basement. This team was in charge of locating and disarming the device.

A fourth HRT team, meanwhile, was making its way to the embassy's roof. This four-man squad used steel "zip" wires, which had been fired down from a taller building next door. They slipped down the anchored wires. Once safely on the roof, their breacher fired two-and-three-quarter-inch shotgun shells filled with double-aught buckshot into the hinges of a rooftop access. He fired his twelve-gauge shotgun quickly but methodically, as he had been trained, beginning with the middle hinge and then aiming at the top and bottom hinges. Each gunshot contained nine .30-caliber balls, and he fired exactly three shots into each. The breacher then kicked open the dangling door—and whirled out of the way so that a fellow HRT team member could shoot at the "tangos"—the slang that HRT members use to describe bad guys—who might be inside. There were none in sight. This roof team was responsible for freeing the hostages being held on the top floor.

Although each of the teams had specific, individual assignments, their actions were being meshed together by the SIOC. Each squad's progress was monitored on a wall of giant plasma screens. The television images came from tiny cameras attached to each man's helmet. Their voices were broadcast via microphone mouthpieces. Earpieces allowed them to hear each other and SIOC commands.

The frontal assault team immediately began searching for the seven terrorists. They knew that an eighth terrorist was already dead, having been dispatched earlier by a Russian security guard. The FBI had gleaned this intel from the lone hostage whom Islamov had released as a goodwill gesture at Deputy Conway's request. The FBI also had discovered from this source that the other employees were being held prisoners inside what used to be the KGB offices and were being guarded only by a single man. He was posted outside a steel door. They were locked behind it.

"Police! Get down!" the frontal attack team's leader yelled as he burst through the embassy's entryway into the lobby. One of the two female terrorists had been standing guard near the entrance when its double doors were blown to pieces. She'd been knocked to her knees by the blast and stayed there, still disoriented.

The attacking HRT special agent aligned the red dot from his H&K MP-5 submachine gun on the tango's chest in a spot formed by a triangle between the woman's nipples and the notch of her throat. He shot two rounds, just as he'd been trained. The first slug kicked the tango backward, causing her own submachine gun to begin firing wildly. The second toppled her completely over. She was dead in midair.

By chance, the doors of the embassy's elevator opened at the same moment the last member of the frontal HRT entered the lobby. The two terrorists who had been downstairs with Islamov stepped out of it. Although they were clad in solid black—just like the HRT team—their similiar attire didn't fool anyone. The unit leader yelled, "Tangos!" and before the terrorists could respond with their weapons, they were cut down in a barrage of two-shot bursts.

Now only Islamov and three of his Chechen freedom fighters were still alive.

"Clear!" the HRT team leader yelled, indicating the mansion's foyer was now safely rid of tangos. His team moved stealthily and deliberately through the first-floor rooms. Finding no more threats, they started upstairs. The second-floor hall was empty, and all of the doors to the offices were open, except for one. The unit's lead slipped a flexible, pencil-thin camera under the closed door so that he could see what was happening inside. Two terrorists were heaving over a huge conference table to use as a shield. Using hand signals, the agent motioned for the breacher, who stepped forward and fired two ferret rounds through the door. The plastic slugs broke apart as they emerged on the other side spewing an almost invisible mist of liquid chemical irritant, similar to pepper gas, into the room. Both terrorists screamed and tried to wipe their eyes, as a patch of C4 explosive tore away the door. In a reckless move, the Chechens remained standing rather than dropping to the floor. They were killed instantly.

"Five tangos down!" the unit leader reported in his shoulder microphone.

On the top floor, Aslan Akhman had listened to the approaching gunfire. Curious why the SUVs parked outside had not yet exploded, he'd stepped up to the wall and made his way to an exterior window where he carefully peeked at an angle through the slit in the heavy gray shutters. He was careful not to stand in front of the window, and because his back was leaning against an interior wall, he felt safe.

But Akhman had underestimated the FBI's technological weaponry.

Not all of the top floor was protected by shields, and Akhman had unknowingly edged outside of the KGB's fortified cocoon. The stairway that led to the top floor opened into a lobby, and it was here that the KGB had constructed its steel door to protect its corridor of offices. The KGB, however, had never bothered to fortify the adjacent walls of this outer room. While the bulk of the embassy was made of heavy blocks of stone hauled in from a local quarry, the top floor's exterior walls were made of bricks overlaid with pale green slate to give the building a distinctive Tudor facade. Because of this, these walls, composed only of slate, bricks, insulation, and wallboard, were not nearly as thick and strong as the hewn stones below.

An FBI sniper on the roof directly across the street from the embassy noticed the outline of a human appear on a motion detector that he'd positioned near his rifle. The instrument utilized concrete-penetrating radar and three-dimensional imaging to "see" through the exterior wall. Because all of the hostages were known to be contained behind the impenetrable door inside the KGB wing, the FBI sniper knew the aberrant figure now on his screen was a tango. Without pausing, he pointed his weapon and a .50-caliber slug punched effortlessly through the slate facade, brick, and wallboard. It pierced Akhman's chest, killing him instantly, and continued across the room until it embedded itself in a wall.

The reclaiming of the embassy had taken under four minutes. There was now only one tango unaccounted for, and that was Movladi Islamov.

47

Locked in the basement with a nuclear bomb, I kept asking myself: Why?

Why had the FBI allowed General Rodin to launch an assault on the Russian embassy after I'd clearly warned Ames there was a nuclear bomb here? It was insanity!

When I heard voices coming from outside the door, I immediately got down on the floor. I don't speak Russian and I wouldn't have been surprised if Rodin's squad had been told to execute me. I wasn't going to give them the excuse that I'd acted like an armed terrorist.

I braced myself for the worst.

"Police! Get down!" someone yelled in English as the door swung open.

It was an American voice.

"I'm a friendly!" I yelled, using the FBI's own terminology.

The first HRT agent through the door kept his submachine gun aimed directly at me.

"I'm Wyatt Conway, U.S. Marshals Service," I shouted. But I didn't attempt to get up. I remained on the floor wearing only my bugged undershorts.

The unit leader pulled a photograph from his vest and compared it to my face.

"What's your social security number?" he demanded.

I called it out.

"He's Conway," the agent confirmed.

They helped me stand.

"The basement is clear," the HRT unit leader announced. Then he saw it. "Jesus Christ!"

All of the HRT members were now frozen at the sight of the cylinder behind me.

"What's wrong with you guys?" I yelled. "I told Rodney Ames there was a bomb and it was real!"

Dr. Colter, Kimberly, Ames, Colonel Khrenkov, and four men wearing vests that said BOMB SQUAD appeared. The scientist pushed by me. He swept a handheld radiometer across the bomb.

"It's active!" he declared, clearly surprised, as he read the sensor's reading. Spinning around, Colter looked at my crotch and yelled, "Your boxers? The sensor? What happened?"

I asked, "Didn't you get a reading? I was less than an inch from it!"

"No! There wasn't any reading. We didn't think there was anything down here! We thought it was a hoax."

I suddenly understood what had happened. "This entire room is shielded," I said. "That's why you couldn't see into it using a gamma detector on a helicopter and why you can't use cell phones down here. The transmitter in my boxers couldn't send you a signal because of the shields!"

I thought the doc was going to collapse. His already pasty-white face was now really devoid of any color. His mouth hung open. The shields should have been an obvious barrier. He couldn't believe he'd not factored them in. Now the enormity of his blunder flattened him.

I glared at Colonel Khrenkov. "You had to know it was real!"

He didn't reply.

I started toward him, but one of the HRT team members stepped in front of me.

"There'll be time for finger-pointing later!" Kimberly exclaimed. She asked Dr. Colter, "Why didn't Islamov detonate it during the attack?"

"There's a timer controlled by the laptop," Colter said. "He's done what the FBI thought. He's scheduled the bomb to go off at a specific time each day and then he apparently comes down here and resets it."

"How long do we got?" Ames asked.

"Three hours," one of the bomb-disposal agents, who was examining the laptop with Dr. Colter, replied.

"Is that enough time to disarm it?" Ames asked.

The bomb-disposal technician looked hesitantly at Colter and then back at Ames. "I'm afraid it's not quite that simple," he replied. "The terrorists have encrypted this computer with codes that we'll need to key in correctly to stop the detonation. If we try to disconnect the electrical current or circumvent the codes, the bomb will explode."

"Then you'll have to break the codes," Ames said.

"I'm not sure we can," the expert replied.

"Not sure you can do it in three hours?" Ames asked.

"Not sure we can do it at all. They've programmed the bomb to explode if we try a wrong number. One mistake and bingo, the bomb blows."

"Then how can you shut it down?" Kimberly asked.

The technician didn't reply for several moments as he studied the display. Then he said, "We can't stop it from exploding. This bomb is going to go off!"

"Whatever happened to picking between a red or green wire and cutting one of them?" I asked, only half joking.

"I wish that were the case," he said, "but I'm trying to be as clear and frank about this as I can. The odds of us figuring out the code without making an error are not good."

No one said anything. Each of us was trying to fathom what we'd just been told. A nuclear weapon was going to explode in less than three hours and there was nothing we could do to prevent it. People were going to die. *We* were going to die.

"If we can't disarm it," Dr. Colter said, "then we've got to find a way to move it out of the city."

"Let's drop it in the ocean!" Ames volunteered. "We can get a helicopter in here to fly it away from the capital."

Kimberly asked, "How are you going to move it? The KGB built it inside this basement room. It's not going to fit through the doorway."

"We can blow a hole through the wall, drag it to the rear exit, and use a crane to haul it outside. A helicopter can swoop in here and pick it up."

I noticed Khrenkov hadn't uttered a word.

"Wait," I said. "You're forgetting the White House briefing. We can't move this bomb without setting it off, isn't that right, Colonel?"

Kimberly spoke before Khrenkov could answer. She said: "Oh my God! You're right! At the White House briefing, they said the KGB had installed some sort of motion detector on the bomb to prevent us from carting it out of Washington!"

"My instructions are strictly to observe what is happening and to make no comments," Khrenkov said. "I need to report this situation to General Rodin."

"C'mon, Colonel!" I snapped. "We don't have time to play diplomatic games here. Can we move this godforsaken thing or not?"

Khrenkov didn't reply.

"There's no use in pretending," I continued. "We know the KGB built this damned thing. Islamov and his followers couldn't have brought it into the basement. They couldn't have gotten it through the door!"

"If the KGB made this bomb," Kimberly said, "there's got to be someone in Moscow who knows how to disable it!"

Khrenkov repeated, "I must consult the general."

At that point, Colonel Khrenkov started to leave the room. I blocked his exit.

"I don't think you should be going anywhere just yet," I said.

Much to my surprise, Ames agreed. Two HRT agents raised their weapons and moved in front of the exit.

Khrenkov stopped. "Are you holding me against my will?" he asked.

Ames said, "Colonel Khrenkov, no one is going anywhere until I check with my superiors. Since my headset doesn't work down here, I'll have to ask you to wait." He walked over to the wall telephone and dialed a number. After a few moments of hushed conversation, he said, "SIOC has just informed me that your general is being consulted as we speak. I've also been told that the FBI would prefer it if you'd stay here with us in case we have other questions."

"Am I being held captive?" Khrenkov asked.

"Let's just say we'd enjoy your company awhile longer," Ames replied.

I'd been so focused on the bomb that I hadn't realized that I was still wearing only boxer shorts. Kimberly finally noticed, too, and handed me a bag that contained my clothes, my U.S. Marshals shield, and handcuffs, but my two handguns were missing. Ames apparently had locked them in a drawer in the command post.

"Did you catch Islamov?" I asked, as I was getting dressed. "If he's still alive, then he'll know how to disarm this."

Everyone seemed surprised, and I assumed that none of them had thought about using him to stop the laptop's countdown.

Ames said, "It's a bit too late for that. Islamov's dead. The HRT teams got eight terrorists upstairs."

They watched to see my reaction. But I was intentionally stone-faced. I wasn't certain how I felt about Islamov being killed. I'd expected it and so had he. Just the same. These were feelings best sorted through later.

"Have they gotten the hostages out okay?" Kimberly asked.

"Yes, the only casualties are the Chechens and the guards they killed when they took over the embassy."

"Were all the guards killed?" she asked.

"No, we found one wounded on the second floor. He's on his way to the hospital. It's a miracle he's still alive."

"Good for him," Kimberly said.

But I was suddenly suspicious.

"Why wasn't he being held with the other hostages?" I asked.

"He was hiding in a closet. He crawled inside it after he was wounded, apparently while the Chechens were killing the other guards," Ames replied.

"I want to look at the bodies," I announced. "And I want Colonel Khrenkov to come with me."

"They're on the first floor," Ames said.

"I'll go with you," Kimberly offered.

"We'll all go," said Ames, motioning to the two HRT agents guarding the doorway.

Ames took the lead. Kimberly, Khrenkov, and I followed, and the two HRT agents fell in behind us. The HRT agents had gathered all of the Chechen corpses in the same conference room where I'd met earlier that morning with Islamov. The agents had removed the terrorists' ski masks and I was surprised when I saw how young they were. Four appeared to be teenagers. As soon as I examined the bodies, I knew Islamov wasn't one of them.

I asked Khrenkov, "Which one of these bodies is your Russian security guard?"

"What!" Ames exclaimed.

"Islamov isn't here. He's escaped," I said calmly. "He's pretending to be a guard—the wounded one you're taking to the hospital!"

"How can you be sure?"

"The last time I saw Islamov, he was wearing blue pants. All of these bodies are dressed in black. At some point, he obviously changed clothes with one of the dead Russian security guards."

Ames didn't want to admit the FBI had made such a rudimentary mistake.

Khrenkov said, "The last man in this line is our security guard. His name is Yuri. I know him from Moscow."

"Shit!" Ames shrieked. Speaking into the headset's microphone, which now worked fine because we were out of the basement, he said, "Islamov is not dead! He's posing as a Russian security guard and is en route to the hospital." Then he said to us, "I've got two D.C. cops riding in that ambulance with him. We'll have them bring him back to the embassy."

"Maybe we can get him to agree to stop the countdown," Kimberly suggested.

I didn't think it was going to be that easy. Nothing ever was. Within a few seconds, Ames yelled, "Islamov is *gone!* SIOC says the ambulance never made it to the hospital. It was found empty two blocks away. Islamov killed the cops and the EMTs."

Spinning toward Khrenkov, Ames said, "There's something else you need to know. General Rodin and his Spetsnaz team have just taken off in their aircraft from Andrews Air Force Base. The Russian ambassador went with them."

"I guess," I said looking at the colonel, "they've left you holding the bag."

This seemed as good a time as ever.

"Colonel Khrenkov," I said, getting closer to him in the conference room with eight corpses at our feet. "I'm arresting you for the murder of a federally protected witness, Sergey Pudin."

"Wyatt!" Kimberly exclaimed. "Not *now!*"

"Murder? Who?" Ames asked.

Khrenkov showed neither surprise nor concern.

I pulled out a set of handcuffs.

"You can't arrest him," Ames declared. "Deputy U.S. marshals hunt, transport, and protect prisoners. They aren't authorized to arrest anyone. That's the FBI's job. You're not authorized."

"Actually, U.S. marshals have the broadest authority of any law enforcement officer in the nation. We can arrest anyone who has committed a felony in *our presence*. That's the key phrase, and Colonel Khrenkov shot Pudin while I was standing right next to him on the sidewalk. The colonel also murdered a Russian criminal named Pankov who was watching us from across the street."

"But he has diplomatic immunity," Kimberly protested.

"I don't think so. In addition to killing Pudin and Pankov, the colonel is suspected of shooting Ivan Sitov, along with his driver and bodyguard.

That's five dead Russians—all Mafia figures. I don't believe that even the Russian government is going to let him hide behind diplomatic immunity on five murder cases." I turned to Khrenkov. "Besides, your ambassador just hopped on an airplane, and by the time he gets to Moscow and learns you're under arrest, there's a good chance this bomb will have exploded and we'll all be dead."

"Then why arrest him?" Ames asked.

"Because I can." Focusing back on Khrenkov, I said, "Igor Fedorov has told us everything—how he forced you into coming here to kill my witness and even how he intended to kill you. But you outsmarted him, and now you've come back to the United States to take your revenge."

Surprisingly, Khrenkov didn't deny the accusations. Instead, he said, "What would *you* do if your sister was raped and murdered?"

"I'd probably do exactly what you're doing. But that wouldn't make it legal. No one in our country is above the law. If we survive here today, I'll be putting you in jail. You're not going to simply walk out of here."

Ames said, "Those handcuffs won't be necessary. No one is leaving the embassy anytime soon. SIOC has just ordered me to put the entire mansion under lockdown. No one comes or goes."

"Do you mean us, too?" Kimberly asked.

"I said no one leaves."

"What about the hostages?"

"They're already gone. They've been flown by helicopter to a hospital where they'll be kept isolated from the media."

"But why can't we leave?" Kimberly asked.

"Don't you understand what's happening?" I said. "They're not going to tell the public about the bomb. They can't risk having us leak word to the media."

"It would spark a panic," Ames explained. "We can't afford to lose control of this city."

"But there's still time for people to get out alive," Kimberly said. "We can start evacuating."

"Kimberly," I replied, "all of the right people *are* being evacuated. It's the rest of us schmucks who are being left clueless. Right, Ames?"

"A federal evacuation is under way based on rank. It was developed during the cold war," he explained. "Members of Congress are currently being withdrawn discreetly from the danger area."

"Where are they going?" Kimberly asked.

"I guess there's no harm in telling. To an underground shelter in West Virginia called Project Greek Island."

"I know where that is. It's the bunker underneath the posh Greenbrier Resort," she replied. "They built it in the Eisenhower administration. I've been there. I've even taken a tour of it."

"A tour?" I asked. "Of a top-secret bunker?"

"The government officially opened it to the public several years ago, after the *Washington Post* revealed its location. No one thought we'd ever need it after the Soviet Union collapsed."

Now curious, I asked Ames, "What about the White House staff?"

"The president is still out of town, so he's safe. The vice president is being flown to the Mount Weather Emergency Assistance Center, code-named High Point."

"Hey, I've been there, too!" Kimberly declared.

"Were you on some underground secret-bunker tour?" I asked.

"The Federal Emergency Management Agency teaches several training courses at Mount Weather's aboveground facilities. The agency sent me to one of them."

"Never heard of it," I replied.

"Obviously," she said, "no one was real interested in protecting you in case there was a nuclear attack." Continuing, she explained, "The bunker at Greenbrier is tiny compared to Mount Weather. The Greenbrier one was built much like a parking garage. Workers dug a big hole, constructed two concrete buildings, and then buried them under about sixty feet of dirt. There's no way it would survive a direct hit by a nuclear missile. But Mount Weather was designed to take a direct blast. It's an incredible structure—a self-contained underground city that literally was gouged from stone. It's burrowed deep inside a mountain, and it contains everything our government needs to continue operating during a nuclear war. It's by far the safest bunker for the president."

"There are more?" I asked.

"Actually, there are. There's an emergency bunker directly under the White House where the president and his staff can stay if there's a sudden threat, like the crashing of an airplane into the White House à la the September 11 attacks. The Federal Reserve Board also has its own radiation-proof relocation center in Culpeper, Virginia. And the Pentagon has a large bunker in Gettysburg, Pennsylvania. But none of them is as formidable as Mount Weather."

"What happens after all of the big shots are safely outside the city?" I asked Ames.

"I'm certain the public will be informed and an orderly evacuation will begin," he replied. But from the sound of his voice, I wondered if he was trying to convince us or himself.

"So you're going to let the government decide when to tell Maggie that she should start driving west on Interstate 66?" I asked. Maggie was my ex-wife. Personally, I didn't really care if she was warned, but I figured he would.

Ames spouted the official line, but I detected some fear in his voice. "My orders are to keep everyone in this building, let no one leave, and let no one use the telephones."

"If I tried to call Maggie, you'd stop me—even though I was trying to save her?"

"You don't care about her. Besides, all cell phone signals are now being jammed and the lines to the embassy have been shut down. The only communication between us and the outside world is through my headset to SIOC."

Kimberly dialed a number on her cell phone. It didn't work.

I put away my handcuffs. Colonel Khrenkov was still my prisoner, but none of us was going anywhere.

"Let's all go back downstairs," I suggested.

When we entered the bomb room, Dr. Colter said, "We're not even going to try to disarm this bomb. The odds of breaking Islamov's computer code are too high and the risks too great."

"Then what are you trying?" Kimberly asked.

"We're working on deciphering the code that controls the bomb's motion detector. If we succeed, then we can move it out of the basement before it explodes."

I checked the time. We had two-and-a-half hours.

"Exactly where are you going to take it?" I asked.

"SIOC's got a military chopper standing by, ready to fly it away from the city. We can ditch it in the ocean. Right now, the HRT guys are figuring out which interior walls we can blast through in the basement so we can haul it out of here."

"How far at sea will they be able to get?"

"Not that far, but away from the center of Washington. The Pentagon and SIOC are computing the best drop zone in the Atlantic. But we can't lift it until Dr. Colter disables the motion detector."

"If the KGB built the bomb and installed the motion detector, then it should know how to disengage it," Kimberly reasoned.

"That's right," Dr. Colter agreed, "but the Russians are still insisting the terrorists brought the bomb with them into the embassy."

"General Rodin and his Spetsnaz team had to have known about the bomb," I said. "That means Rodin must've had an emergency plan formulated in his head. He either was planning on disabling the bomb or possibly moving it."

Everyone stared at Khrenkov. I asked the obvious, "Do you know the KGB code to disarm the motion detector?"

Khrenkov replied, "My government's stance is that we do not know anything about this bomb. Until that changes—if it does—that is my stance, too."

Clearly, he knew more than he was telling.

"You know the code, don't you?" I said.

Kimberly agreed. "Colonel," she said, "we're talking about saving the lives of five million people. Where's your conscience? Don't you realize that you'll die, too, unless we move this bomb out of here?"

"I'm not afraid to die."

I decided to try a different tactic. "If you die, you'll never be able to exact your revenge. You won't be able to punish Major Fedorov."

I saw a flicker in his yellow eyes. "Tell me," he replied, "am I still under arrest? Do you still intend to take me to jail?"

Before I could answer, Ames jumped in. "If you know the KGB code to unlock the motion detector, and you tell us, I can guarantee you the Justice Department will overrule Deputy Marshal Conway and allow you to leave the United States without being detained or charged with any crimes. Those five Mafia murders will be forgotten!"

Khrenkov quickly considered what Ames was offering and just as quickly rejected it. "Letting me return to Moscow isn't enough," he explained. Khrenkov looked squarely at me and said, "Do you remember your story—the one you told about ethics—where the western pioneers were traveling by wagon train and the Indians were trying to find and kill them?"

"I do," Kimberly interrupted. "We were discussing ethics. The mother on the wagon train had to choose between suffocating her own baby or risk having it cry and the Native Americans discover where the settlers were hiding and kill them all."

"That's correct," said Khrenkov. "Now tell me, Deputy Conway, what is the answer? Is killing one person ethically acceptable if that one murder saves others' lives?"

"What are you trying to say?" I asked, although I thought I already knew.

"Ms. Lodge just said I could help save five million lives if I told you the KGB code. Every second you save dismantling the motion detector is a second farther you can fly the bomb out over the ocean."

"What's that got to do with a crying baby and Indians?" Kimberly asked. "Er, I mean, Native Americans."

Khrenkov said, "Where is your government hiding Igor Fedorov?"

I replied, "If I tell you, you'll kill him."

"I certainly will try. But then that's part of the deal here. You let me go now and agree to not prosecute me for murder, including Fedorov's—assuming I find and kill him. In return, I tell you the code."

"Then you do know it!" Kimberly exclaimed.

Ignoring her, he said, "You decide, Deputy. Are the lives of five million innocent people worth the sacrifice of a ruthless and disgusting Russian criminal?" He paused to gather his thoughts and then asked, "What will it be, *Professor*—now that your little intellectual, ethical exercise has suddenly become real?"

"Dr. Colter!" It was one of the bomb disposal technicians calling. "We've deciphered the first symbol in the motion detector's combination!"

Ames interrupted. "What is it?"

But before the techie could reply, Colonel Khrenkov answered, "It's the Russian letter pronounced *zeh*."

"He's right!" the expert exclaimed.

Obviously, Khrenkov knew the KGB code.

I said, "We could torture you. Slicing off a man's balls is a pretty effective way to get him to talk."

Without any sign of fear, Khrenkov replied, "Why is it so important to you to protect a criminal such as Igor Fedorov?"

"Because my government promised to keep him safe. It's also against the law for me or any other deputy to reveal where a federally protected witness is being hidden."

"Doesn't your law also forbid you to cut off a prisoner's testicles? Or is this another example of your situational ethics?"

He got me. But I wasn't going to admit it. I asked, "How can you be certain I'll actually let you leave here once you've told us the code?"

"The KGB combination lock contains seven characters. I'll tell you five more right now if you let me go and also tell me where Major

Fedorov is hiding. After I'm safely away, I'll telephone you with the last character."

"Sure you will," I said sarcastically. "But what if you 'forget' to call?"

A nervous Dr. Colter spoke up. "Deputy Conway, please! Having to decipher only one character in the code will be much quicker than having to figure out the last six! Even if he doesn't call us, we might have the time we need."

"You'll have to trust me to call," Khrenkov said. "Just as I must trust you to tell me the truth about where Fedorov is hiding."

One of the HRT agents from upstairs came into the bomb room and quietly gave Ames a message. When he was finished, Ames said to Khrenkov, "The attorney general of the U.S. has agreed *not* to charge or prosecute you for the five murders you've allegedly committed. I've also been told that the attorney general has decided that Deputy Conway will immediately tell you the whereabouts of Igor Fedorov."

Khrenkov addressed me. "It seems you've been spared making the decision. Your superiors are ordering you to tell me. Now, where is Fedorov?"

I stood there contemplating. Even though Fedorov was a Mafia scumbag, this was dirty. I didn't appreciate the attorney general betraying him or, better put, forcing me to play Judas. But then I realized I had a trump card. Fedorov was in Arizona and there was no way that Colonel Khrenkov could get to him quickly. "Okay, Colonel," I said. "You win. I'll tell you, but I want you to go first. What are the next five characters in the lock?"

Khrenkov said, "A Russian letter pronounced *zheh*. It's followed by the number three, and then the letter *ehl*. After that is the letter *tesh*, and finally the number five."

Almost immediately, Dr. Colter declared, "They work! We only need one more to disable the motion sensors!"

"Now, Deputy Conway," Khrenkov said, "please fulfill your part of our bargain."

"Igor Fedorov is in Phoenix, Arizona. He lives in the Pergate Apartments under the name Igor Kukin. You'll find him in Apartment 56."

Khrenkov turned to speak to Ames. "I'll be leaving now." The two HRT agents guarding the door stepped away to let him pass.

"Don't forget to call us," I said.

"Deputy Conway," he replied, "you judge me harshly. I'm curious, if I were not seeking revenge, what would happen now to Fedorov—the man who destroyed my family's happiness by having them kidnapped and my sister raped and murdered?"

"You already know. He'd go unpunished. Fedorov has been granted immunity for his past crimes in exchange for his testimony against the Russian Mafia."

"What's fair about that?"

"Absolutely nothing, but no one said life is fair."

"The men whom I have killed in your country were criminals. My conscience is clear. It's your own government which has lost its moral compass."

After nodding respectfully to Kimberly, Khrenkov left.

"I need to speak to your bosses," I told Ames. The three of us— Ames, Kimberly, and I—went upstairs into the lobby away from the basement security shields so I could use Ames's headset to speak directly to SIOC.

"This is Deputy Conway, I need you to telephone Deputy Marshal Byron Fitzsimmons in Phoenix. Tell him that Fedorov's security has been compromised. Tell him to move Fedorov immediately."

I handed the headset back to Ames. He said, "I'm going back downstairs to help the HRTs decide which walls we can blast through. As soon as the motion detector is disabled, they'll set the charges and we can get this damn thing out of here. All we have to do now is wait for Colonel Khrenkov's call."

"*If* he calls us," I said.

"He will," Kimberly reassured me. "He's after revenge for his sister. He doesn't want innocent people murdered."

Ames left us in the embassy's front lobby. We collapsed in two over-stuffed chairs under a large painting of the Russian Federation's president. An HRT agent was keeping an eye on us from the open doorway about fifteen feet away. It was nearly seven a.m. and even though the embassy was sealed off from the rest of the city, we could hear the familiar noises from outside as Washington awoke to another day. The grinding gears of a distant UPS delivery truck, brakes squealing to a sudden stop at a red light, an occasional car horn honking, street vendors rolling their rickety metal hot dog and pretzel carts down the streets—all this everyday cacophony usually went unnoticed. Not now. Not by us. We both knew it could be the last time we'd hear them.

"I really do believe Colonel Khrenkov will call," Kimberly said. "We'll get the motion sensors switched off. We'll get the bomb hauled out of here and dropped in the ocean. Someday we'll be telling this story at parties and laughing about it."

I wasn't so confident. But I didn't say anything.

Continuing, she said, "I love mornings. It's when I run. My mother used to tell me each new day is a gift from God, an opportunity to begin your life with a clean slate."

"A few blocks from here," I said, "people are going about their daily business without a clue that in less than two hours, they could be dead and this city will be nothing but atomic ash. Now that's what I call really cleaning the slate."

"Hey, we're the good guys here. And in the end, the good guys always win."

"Only in Hollywood."

My skepticism annoyed her. We sat without speaking and then she said, "I know the September 11th attacks should have taught us that we aren't invincible—that this sort of horrible event can and will happen. But I believe it's the American public's nature to rise and triumph over every kind of adversity. I'm not being a Pollyanna. I believe in our country's spirit. I believe in the goodness of other people. If I didn't, then I wouldn't want to even bother getting up in the morning."

"I get up each day mostly because I'm curious how God is going to fuck with us," I replied. I thought I was being witty, but Kimberly didn't.

"Is your life that empty?" she asked, peering in my face. "What do you really know about suffering? We Americans fuss about trivial inconveniences while others in the world are starving." She was becoming emotional. "When my mother was a child, the secret police butchered her parents. She and her siblings lived in the streets. They picked through garbage. Her brothers died in prison. Her sister was killed. Yet she survived. Her secret was that she has always believed tomorrow will be a better day."

An HRT agent came in and said Ames wanted us to go back downstairs. When we got there, he was talking into the telephone that was attached to the wall next to the bomb.

"SIOC is letting us use this phone line," he explained, "because Colonel Khrenkov is calling. They're patching him through to us." He handed me the receiver.

"You kept your word," Khrenkov said. "Now I'm keeping mine. The last character in the combination is the Cyrillic letter pronounced *geh*."

I repeated it out loud, and Dr. Colter quickly tried it. The KGB lock opened.

"We've disarmed the sensors!" Colter shouted. "We can move the bomb!"

Khrenkov said, "Deputy Conway, there's something more you need to know. The bomb can now be transported from the basement, but you should not attempt to fly it out of Washington."

"Why not?"

"The KGB installed a unique safeguard that you will not be able to dismantle or recalibrate without causing the bomb to explode. Nuclear bombs made in the 1950s contained internal altimeter devices that told the bomb when to detonate. They were installed because a nuclear bomb is most effective if it explodes before it hits the ground."

"And your point is what?"

"The KGB found a way to invert this procedure."

"I don't understand."

"They reversed it."

"Goddamnit, speak clearly, okay?"

"The bomb in the embassy is set to explode if it is raised higher than a certain altitude."

"You mean if we put it in an airplane that takes off, it will explode?"

"It will detonate when the airplane reaches a predetermined altitude. The KGB thought this would make it more difficult for your air force to fly the bomb out of Washington if it was discovered."

"How high can the bomb be lifted before it detonates?"

"General Rodin couldn't find an exact measurement in the KGB's records, but he guessed it was about five hundred and eighty meters."

"Why that figure?"

"That was the altitude you Americans used when you dropped a bomb on Hiroshima. The KGB thought it ironic."

The image of a KGB goon squad yucking it up popped into my head. I said: "Okay, if we try to lift this thing above five hundred and eighty meters, it's going to detonate, right?"

"Perhaps it will explode at a much lower distance. I'm not certain."

I tried to think of just how high 580 meters is. I knew one mile was the equivalent of 5,280 feet and that a meter was about three feet and three inches. It took me a moment to do the math in my head but I came up with 1,902 feet. I tried to picture that distance in my mind. I knew the World Trade Center towers had stood thirteen hundred feet tall.

"I don't see why a helicopter couldn't carry this bomb out of here and over the Atlantic Ocean," I said. "There's enough distance at five hundred and eighty meters."

"That's a risk for you to decide," Khrenkov said. "Our scientists warned the general not to use *any* aircraft to transport the bomb."

"Jesus H. Christ!" I snapped.

"I wanted to be frank with you, even though you haven't been completely honest with me," he continued. "I'm assuming your fellow deputies are moving Igor Fedorov out of Phoenix as we speak?"

There was no reason to lie. "I warned them that he is no longer safe in Phoenix."

"I assumed you would. My main objective was accomplished just the same. Your government has agreed not to arrest me for the other killings. I was able to leave the embassy. Finding Fedorov will not be too difficult."

His certainty surprised me. "The U.S. is one big place," I replied, "and we've got lots of experience when it comes to protecting witnesses."

"But I have something you don't working in my favor," he replied. "Have you ever heard the name Baba Yaga Kostianaya Noga?"

"No."

"She's famous in my homeland," he said. "She is a fairy-tale character. Perhaps someday I'll send you her story."

The line went dead.

50

"We've got eighty-seven minutes to get this bomb as far away from Washington as possible!" Ames exclaimed.

The three of us had moved upstairs to the main-floor conference room because the HRTs had begun blasting holes in the reinforced basement walls. SIOC had listened to my conversation with Khrenkov and had heard him warn me not to use any sort of aircraft to fly the bomb out of Washington. They had sent a military truck to carry it away from the embassy.

Ames scoured a large map of the Washington area. "We can't drive this thing north. We'd run into Baltimore. The major routes east lead through Annapolis. If we drive south, we'll get stuck on the heavily populated I-95 corridor to Richmond."

"That leaves west," Kimberly said.

"No, all routes west are out," Ames replied. "Remember, the vice president and White House staff are being moved into Mount Weather and it's west of here."

"I thought they were inside a bomb-proof mountain?" I said.

"They are, but SIOC doesn't want to risk putting them in harm's way. They aren't going to allow us to move a bomb in the same direction as the V.P."

"Then where in the hell can we take it?"

"The Pentagon has suggested we transport the bomb to the Washington harbor, load it on a U.S. Customs speedboat, and race it down the Potomac into the Chesapeake Bay. At that point, a decision will be made. It will either be dropped into a deep trough that goes down about a hundred feet or a helicopter will be flown in and will lift it off the boat and race it over the ocean."

"Why not just bring in a helicopter now?" Kimberly asked.

"The Pentagon doesn't want to risk having it explode while there are still vital U.S. officials in the city. The further away from Washington, the better before they try to lift it."

"There's got to be a better solution," Kimberly said.

"Miss Lodge," Ames said coldly, "right now, this goddamn bomb is headed for the bay. That's where the best minds in the Pentagon want it dumped."

Kimberly studied the map.

"How long will it take to load the bomb on the truck?" I asked.

"Five minutes," Ames answered. "D.C. cops are already blocking the streets to the harbor. The speedboat is ready. It will take us fifteen minutes to get there. Five more to unload the bomb. That will give the boat about an hour to get into the bay."

"What's the damage estimate?"

"We'll save Washington, but the Pentagon believes the Virginia Beach and Norfolk areas will be devastated, even if we can airlift it out to sea at some point."

"Human casualties?"

"Virginia Beach is one of the most densely populated areas in the state. Eight hundred thousand to a million dead."

"A million people," Kimberly repeated.

"Hey, that's four million less than if we don't move it."

"This can't be happening," Kimberly declared. "There's got to be a better choice."

"It's reality," Ames snapped. "You can thank Moe Islamov—Deputy Conway's buddy—for this."

Ames got a call on his headset. "The HRTs have gotten through the final basement wall," he announced. "The bomb will be on the truck in four minutes. I'm going to supervise."

He left us in the conference room.

"Kimberly, we both knew this was going to happen. There's no way to disarm the thing."

"Damn it!" she snapped. "We're missing something. Something obvious. I can feel it!"

"The Pentagon has been all over this. North, east, south. This is the best idea they've come up with."

"It's a *million* human lives. Since when has that become acceptable?"

"When there's no other alternative."

She placed her right index finger on the map and began to turn it clockwise in a circle around the circumference of Washington, D.C. "This is how far we can drive in about seventy minutes. With help from the police, we could go up to sixty miles away." Her finger passed close to Baltimore, a bit farther than Annapolis, midway to Richmond, and finally came back to where she had started. It seemed pointless to me, but she began tracing her digit in an arc again.

"Wait!" she exclaimed. I glanced down at the map. Her finger had stopped *west* of the city. "Quick! We've got to stop Ames! I know a better place!" She bolted from the room, clutching the map in her hands as she ran. I ran after her. We dodged the debris in the basement to where the bomb was being carefully poked through a hole in the foundation toward the bed of a waiting truck.

"Ames!" she screamed. "No one has to die! Listen to me!"

Kimberly was so frantic she climbed out of the hole the HRTs had made in the wall. I followed.

She waved the map in front of him. "Tell SIOC to change the route!" she yelled. "Don't go south toward the Bay! Go west!"

"I told you the vice president is there."

"Yes, he's at Mount Weather!" she exclaimed. "He's underground! He's in a bomb shelter! That's the solution!"

I suddenly understood. But Ames didn't. He turned his back to her to watch the bomb being securely strapped into place.

"She's right!" I said. "Give me your headphones!" He glanced back at us as if we were both crazy, so I jerked them from his head.

"This is Deputy Conway!" I announced. "You've got to send this truck toward Mount Weather. I repeat: You've got to take the bomb to Mount Weather!"

"You're nuts!" Ames said.

"Move the vice president and his staff out of the bunker *now*," Kimberly said, "so we can put the bomb *inside* the mountain! We can seal it behind the blast door!"

A stunned look came over his face.

"If Mount Weather was constructed to withstand a direct hit by a nuclear bomb then it should be able to protect the outside world from a bomb that explodes inside it," I explained into the headset to SIOC. "It's a brilliant idea!"

"We can't make it there in time," Ames declared after examining the map. "Mount Weather is seventy-five miles away. There isn't enough time."

"The map's wrong!" Kimberly exclaimed. "The government claims it's seventy-five miles away, but it's actually only fifty-four miles. They intentionally lie on maps. I've been there. We can make it."

"What about the change in altitude?" Ames asked. The map showed Mount Weather as being 1,725 feet above sea level.

"What are you worried about?" I asked. "That is nearly two hundred feet less than five-hundred-and-eighty meters."

"It's much too risky," said Ames. "It could explode while we're driving up the mountain."

"But if it doesn't and we get it inside Mount Weather, we could save a million lives!" Kimberly replied. "We've got to try it!"

I heard a voice in the headset that I was still wearing. I shouted to Kimberly: "SIOC says we can go for it!" But Ames didn't trust me. He took the headset and asked for confirmation. A moment later, he yelled to the HRTs guarding the truck. "It's a go! We're heading to Mount Weather."

"What about the vice president?" I asked.

"He's being moved."

Ames leaped into the military truck with its driver.

"Hurry, Kimberly," I said. There was a black limo parked behind the embassy. It was owned by the Russian Federation. I called to one of the HRT agents. "You drive!" Kimberly and I climbed into the rear seat and we pulled directly behind the bomb-carrying truck. As soon as we reached the street, we were surrounded by police cars with their red and blue lights flashing. We sped toward the George Washington Memorial Parkway. I checked my watch. "We've got exactly seventy-five minutes—at the most."

Kimberly looked pale, as if she were about to vomit. "What if I'm wrong?" she agonized. "What if we don't reach the bunker in time or if the blast door can't withstand the explosion or if the bomb explodes halfway up the mountain?"

"Hey, you're supposed to be the optimist here, remember? It's going to work—just like you said."

But she was racked with worry.

"Kimberly, what you've suggested makes perfect sense. You're going to save one million people's lives!"

She looked up at my face and I could see how anxious she was. She slid across the seat and hugged me. It was not a sexual hug. She wanted to be held. So did I. We grasped each other tightly. Neither of us was in a hurry to let go. And then Kimberly Lodge completely shocked me.

With a lone tear slowly making its way down her face, she released me and without saying a word, touched the controls on the side panel of the car. A black screen rose between our rear compartment and the driver's seat. It matched the tinted dark windows that were now shielding us from the outside world with its alarming lights and piercing police sirens.

"Make love to me," she whispered. "Please." She began unbuttoning her blouse. "For the next few minutes, I want to believe there is nothing else going on in the world except for you and me, right here, right now. I don't want to think about a nuclear bomb, Moe Islamov, Mount Weather, the CTC, or Agent Ames. I don't want to think about the Russians, or the Chechens, or anyone else. All I want to do is be here, with you, making love. Please make me forget about everyone and everything else."

I started to speak, but she held her finger up against my lips.

"You don't have to really love me. Just pretend that you do. If we're going to die, then I want to die after having made love to you and having you make love to me."

She slipped off her blouse and unhooked her bra.

This was madness. And yet, considering the circumstances unfolding around us, I understood. And I wanted her. Desperately. I wanted her more than I had ever wanted any woman. Like her, I needed to be lost in the moment. I wanted only to feel the warmth of her skin and the passion between us.

"Kimberly," I said hoarsely. "There's no need for me to pretend."

51

In a heavily treed mountain ridge, Mount Weather looms suddenly along County Road 601 behind a ten-foot-tall, chain-link fence topped with six strands of razor wire. Armed guards patrol the 434-acre compound round-the-clock. The aboveground facilities sit quietly amid manicured lawns. They include a dozen government office buildings, a sewage treatment plant, and two water towers. There's a helicopter landing pad, an air traffic control tower, and powerful electric generators. But it's what's beneath the surface that provides this outpost with its real raison d'être.

In 1936 the U.S. Bureau of Mines began digging a tunnel a quarter of a mile long and three hundred feet deep to test various drills and bits. But no one else really paid any attention to the mine shaft until the Soviet Union exploded a nuclear weapon. America took notice and the Eisenhower administration began looking for a safe place to protect the president, the cabinet, and the Supreme Court in case of a war. Mount Weather seemed a logical choice. In a preliminary April 1953 government study, the Bureau of Mines noted: "The rock in the area . . . is exceptionally hard and tight." It went on to report that the mountain contained few faults. Most of its rock is epidosite and greenstone, a local name for a Precambrian basalt that metamorphosed into an extremely dense formation. With Ike's okay, the government began expanding the mine shaft. Crews worked nonstop for three years, burrowing ever more deeply into the mountain's belly, hollowing it into an underground shelter.

Although specific details are classified, an enterprising investigative reporter for *Time* magazine named Ted Gup revealed many of Mount Weather's secrets in the 1990s. But even with Gup's reporting, much about the bunker still remains top secret. What is known is it has its own massive supply of water stored in man-made pools inside the mountain. Some are as deep as ten feet and as wide as two hundred feet. Side accesses dug from the main shaft branch off into twenty separate office buildings, most of them three stories tall. Separate living quarters are maintained for the president, the cabinet, and the Supreme Court justices. For everyone else, there are male and female dormitories large enough to accommodate two thousand people. The city has its own television broadcasting station, air filtration system, and crematorium. To withstand the severe shock of a nuclear blast, the ceilings have been reinforced with twenty-one thousand steel bolts sunk eight to ten feet into the rock. The entrance is protected by a five-foot thick, ten-foot high, and nearly twenty-foot broad blast door made of solid steel. In front of that entry is a thinner steel-guillotine gate that can be dropped within seconds.

The truck carrying the layer-cake bomb sped through the gates of Mount Weather and braked to a stop at the tunnel entrance. We'd made it without tripping the KGB's reversed altitude trigger. The bomb had not detonated midway up the mountain, although Kimberly and I both had had our own private explosions in the limo's rear seat. Exactly twenty minutes remained before the bomb would blow. Although Mount Weather is under the command of the Federal Emergency Management Agency, its politically appointed director had fled with the vice presidential party. Agent Ames, Kimberly, and I were greeted instead by Prescott Jones, a former air force pilot who had flown bombing raids during the Vietnam conflict and had done a stint in the Hanoi Hilton after being shot down. From the moment we met, I liked Jones. A onetime NFL hopeful, he was chewing an unlit cigar and greeted us with an all-business, can-do attitude that I've often seen among the country's best combat officers.

"Everyone's been evacuated," he reported, as a FEMA crew scurried to unload the bomb. It was being settled onto a steel trailer pulled by an electric-powered cart.

Ames said, "I've just been told the vice president has arrived at

Camp David and is being moved into an underground command center there. We've gotten a go-ahead on dumping this package inside the mountain."

"I've been in charge of the Mount Weather facility for twelve years," Jones said. "We'll stick this doomsday device into a separate vault that's as deep inside the mountain as it can go. Originally, it was installed there to protect the Declaration of Independence and other historical documents. That'll give us three doors—the vault's, the main blast door, and the guillotine gate—to protect the outside."

Glancing at Kimberly, Jones asked, "You the woman who came up with the idea of blowing up *my* bunker?"

"Yes. Do you think the doors will hold it?"

"In the 1960s, everyone was damn confident this place could withstand a direct nuclear bomb hit. But that was before today's more powerful weapons and bunker-penetrating technology. Some politicians have been trying to close down this site for years because they say it's outlived its usefulness."

"But will the blast door hold?" she asked impatiently.

"Your bomb was built in the early 1950s," Jones answered. "I think our blast door will do its job. But no one ever thought about what might happen if a nuclear bomb went off *inside* Mount Weather. All of our projections were based on an outside attack." He thought for a second and then added: "If this works, everyone will think you're one damn smart woman. If it doesn't, you'll have destroyed a billion-dollar installation!"

"And saved Washington, D.C.," I added.

"How're we getting this into the mountain?" Ames asked.

"Electric carts," Jones said, indicating with his cigar the two golf cart–like vehicles. "I'll need a volunteer to drive the one carrying the bomb. I'll also need someone to ride ahead with me in the lead cart to jump out and open the doors we'll be encountering in the tunnel."

"I'll go," I volunteered.

"Me, too," Kimberly chimed in.

"Whoa, little lady!" Jones replied, sounding a bit like John Wayne in an old western movie. "I admire your guts, but I'm not taking a woman into the shelter."

Before Kimberly could react to his sexism, Jones addressed Ames, "Why don't you steer the bomb cart? I'll lead the way, and Deputy Conway can open the doors for us."

"Hey!" Kimberly snapped. "You can't—"

Jones cut her off. "Oh, yes, I can, and I will. Mount Weather is under my command. I'm the highest-ranking official here. Besides, I've got a different job for you."

"What? Fetching coffee?"

"No. I want you to stay here and close the blast door." He pointed toward a control panel and took a key from his pocket. "My people will show you how to work the controls. But I want you turning the switch—not them. You! And only you! Is that clear?"

Kimberly seemed a bit surprised, but she took the key. "Okay, when do I do it?"

"This blast door takes exactly six and a half minutes to shut and lock. It takes five minutes for the door to actually swing closed. The remainder of that time is needed for the door's steel bolts to extend into the mountain. If they don't fully embed themselves, the door may pop open during a blast."

He was focused entirely on Kimberly. Continuing, he said: "No matter what, you must start closing the blast door a good seven minutes before this bomb explodes. You've got to begin the process even if we're still inside and not within eyesight. Otherwise, the blast door will not have time to fully seal. Do you understand me?"

Kimberly said, "Yes."

But Jones wasn't taking any chances. He said, "We should have plenty of time to get out of the tunnel even if you've already started the door closing. We'll just slip between the blast door and its frame. But regardless of what happens, you *must* start the closing procedure seven minutes before detonation. Are you sure you can do this?"

"Yes," she repeated. "I'll begin the closing of the blast door even if you are still inside."

Jones ordered us to synchronize our watches.

One of the men loading the bomb yelled, "We're ready!"

Kimberly looked longingly at me. "Good luck," she said, but her eyes said much more.

"I'll be back," I replied in my best Arnold Schwarzenegger voice.

Ames climbed behind the wheel of the cart attached to the bomb while Jones and I jumped into the first cart. We sped down the compound's twelve-foot-wide and ten-foot-high, gunmetal-gray tunnel. About two hundred feet inside, we came to the first barricade. I leaped from the cart as we were approaching it and sprinted ahead. Jones had given me a key to unlock a switch on the wall. Then I pushed the red OPEN button and the double steel doors silently parted. Jones crossed through the opening. Rather than getting back into the cart with him, I ran as fast as I could down the tunnel to a second set of closed doors about twenty yards away. This was a sally port. The first set of doors could only be opened if the second set was shut. The opposite was also true. The double doorway system ensured there would always be at least one set of steel doors closed.

As soon as Ames entered the sally port, the first set of doors shut behind him, and I used the key to unlock and open the next ones. Both carts ran by me. I had to hustle to catch up and jump on board.

"This sally port is supposed to be part of the decontamination process," Jones said. "But the double doors are actually part of a compartmentalization design that enables us to seal off the mountain in various stages to prevent mobs from overrunning the shelter and reaching the president if they somehow got by the blast door. More than nine hundred federal employees work aboveground, and most have families. If there were an attack, the employees would be expected to report inside Mount Weather, but their families would be left behind, outside, totally unprotected. How many employees do you think could really abandon the people they love? I've always wondered how many of my own people would actually follow our doomsday protocol."

I noticed he was wearing a .45-caliber semiautomatic pistol, and he saw me glance at it.

"Inside this mountain, I'm authorized to shoot and kill anyone who attempts to enter without permission or otherwise interferes or disobeys my direct orders during a nuclear catastrophe. Some officers have started carrying a forty caliber. But I'm old fashioned, I trust a forty-five."

I checked my watch. We hadn't gone far, but we'd already used six minutes.

"I'm afraid I lied to Ms. Lodge," Jones said. "I told her we'd have plenty of time to return and get outside. But the truth is I don't have any idea how long it's going to take us to get the bomb into the vault. I lied because I had to make sure she would close the blast door seven minutes before detonation."

"Why did you ask her to do it, instead of your own people?"

"I don't trust politicians and generals. I learned that in Vietnam," he said. "You're right, I could've assigned one of my own guys to shut the blast door. But if someone in the White House or the Pentagon ordered him to slam it as soon as we carted the bomb inside, my man would obey that order." He looked me in the face and said, "Then the three of us wouldn't have a chance of getting out of here alive."

"You think Kimberly would disobey a presidential order?"

"She's your girlfriend, isn't she? If she loves you, she will!"

"Girlfriend?" I repeated. I hadn't told Jones anything about us.

He said, "I saw how she looked at you when you volunteered to help me with the bomb. I've also been inside enough whorehouses to know what sex smells like, and you, my boy, reek of it."

I hadn't known our lovemaking session was so obvious.

Jones said, "I consider myself a good judge of character. I had to be to survive in Vietnam. I'm betting your girlfriend will do whatever is necessary to give us every possible second." He smiled, revealing five gold front teeth.

We were quickly approaching a large service elevator. Jones pulled our cart into a side tunnel so that Ames could drive by us and park his cart and the bomb in the room-size lift. As Ames breezed by, Jones leaned over and asked, "Do you trust Agent Ames?"

"Why? You're the one who says he's an excellent judge of character."

"Because one of us needs to stay here and turn this cart around so we can exit pronto. There's no point in all three of us going down into the vault. I can take the bomb cart downstairs. You can open the doors— since you've been doing that. But I need to know. Do you trust Ames?"

I was still confused.

"Jesus Christ!" Jones snapped. "I'm asking you a simple question. When we come back up here, we'll be on foot. We'll leave the cart attached to the bomb in the vault. It'll take too long to disconnect it. Will Ames desert us if we're a few seconds late or will he stand his ground at the elevator and wait until we return before fleeing?"

I thought for a second and then said, "Ames is a complete asshole. I don't like him and he doesn't like me. I'm the guy who broke his nose. He ran off with my wife. I wanted to break her nose, but I didn't."

"Conway, I didn't ask to hear your life story. Do you think he'll leave us?"

"No! He'd be too afraid of what might happen to him if he escaped and left us behind."

Jones said, "I hope you're right."

"If you're that worried, leave me here. Ames can open the doors."

"No," he replied. "I need you to be with me when we go into the vault. There's something you'll need to do for me down there."

I checked my watch. Time was wasting.

52

It had taken us more than seven minutes to reach the service elevator. Prescott Jones and I left Ames behind in the tunnel with instructions to be ready to leave as soon as we returned.

"How far down do we have to go?" I asked, as the lift began its descent.

"To the very bottom."

Until your life is hanging in the balance, you'll never know how fast time ticks by. We had less than thirteen minutes before the bomb blew up.

"You got kids?" Jones asked, offering me a fresh cigar.

Taking it, I said, "Bad habit."

"Kids or cigars?"

"Both."

He lit his and handed me the match. "It's against regulations to smoke anywhere inside Mount Weather," he announced. "But I don't think anyone is going to complain."

The elevator finally groaned to a stop, and when the doors opened, I was stunned to see the vault directly in front of us with its door wide open. Jones drove the cart into the large safe. I looked around as we pulled inside. Stacks of U.S. currency were everywhere. The bills were shrink-wrapped in clear plastic and piled on wooden pallets. Each bundle was at least six feet wide and six feet tall.

"There's two billion dollars in here," Jones said. "That's *billion*. Not million. It's why this safe was actually built. To protect the money."

"Why's it down here?"

"To replenish our federal reserves if there ever was a nuclear war. There's every denomination here. Ones, twos, fives, tens, twenties, fifties, hundreds, etcetera."

He checked his watch. There was ten minutes left.

"I wanted you to come into this vault with me so I didn't do anything foolish that would waste time—like trying to open one of these packets and taking a few stacks for myself. Now let's get the hell out of here!"

We ran toward the elevator through the gauntlet of currency. When we reached the vault door, Jones rapidly punched a series of buttons. The safe began humming shut as we entered the lift.

I began doing the math.

"We've got under ten minutes to make it outside. How long does it take for the blast door to close?"

"Five minutes to shut tight and another minute and a half for its bolts to move into the mountain."

"That means in three and a half minutes, Kimberly will begin the closing procedure." I tried to focus. Three and a half minutes. The door begins to shut. Another five minutes before the door completely seals itself. Three and a half minutes plus five minutes equals eight and a half minutes. That's how much time we had to ride up the elevator, rejoin Ames, and make a frantic dash to the entrance.

"We can make it!" I exclaimed. "It's going to be damn close, but we can make it out!"

Jones was thinking about something else. "Two billion dollars!" he said, taking a long puff on his cigar. "If we die in this bunker, at least we'll die wealthy!"

Jones smiled and I noticed his gold teeth again. He noticed me noticing them.

"I lost the real ones in Hanoi, courtesy of the NVA," he said. "I had 'em put in gold to remind me of those days."

"Of being a POW?"

"Yeah, I got a gold tooth for each year I was held in that North Vietnamese stink hole." Then he said, "I've done the math, too, and I figure we've got a thirty-to-forty-five-second window of opportunity to escape."

I said, "In the NFL, thirty seconds is enough time for both teams to score touchdowns."

"In the NBA, it's a lifetime."

"I hear when a guy gets to be your age," I said, "thirty seconds is about all he's good for in the sack!"

Jones slowly removed his cigar and shot me a dirty look. "Well," he said, "your mama's never complained!"

Sports and sex! It's funny how macho bullshit helps you pass the time in a slow, creaking service elevator when there's a nuclear bomb warming up beneath you.

When the elevator finally bumped to a stop, I checked my watch. Right on schedule! The doors parted.

Ames was gone.

"That muther . . ." Jones exclaimed.

I couldn't believe it. He'd left us!

"You're a lousy judge of character," Jones snapped. "We've got to run for it!"

The fastest I've ever run a mile is seven minutes. That's not even close to being a world record, but it wasn't too shabby in a ten-mile footrace. Unfortunately, I'd run at that pace years ago when I was much younger and in much better shape. Within a few steps, I was puffing and a sad reality sank in. Neither of us was going to make it out alive.

"Look!" Jones yelled.

It was Agent Rodney Ames in the electric cart. He was flying backward toward us in the tunnel. He was in reverse because the corridor wasn't wide enough for him to turn the cart around. Jones and I gave it one extra sprint and fell into the rear bed. Ames switched gears so the cart would now go forward and stomped on the pedal.

Whipping out his handgun, Jones pointed it directly at Ames's temple. "If that blast door's already shut, I'm gonna kill your ass!"

Ames, who was clearly panicked, exclaimed, "It won't matter!"

"You'll die knowing you were a coward!" Jones replied.

"I thought something had happened down there. I thought you weren't coming back," Ames weakly explained. "I left but I also came back to get you. That should count for something. I didn't leave you."

"Bullshit!" Jones replied. "You came back because you remembered the sally port and knew it would be locked. We've got the key."

I looked at my watch. We'd lost nearly a minute.

No one spoke as the cart propelled us closer to the next barrier. I ran to unlock the sally port. Keeping his semiautomatic pointed at Ames, Jones ordered him to slow down so I could catch up and get back on. A few seconds later, the blast door was in sight. It was in the process of shutting.

"It's not closed yet!" I yelled. "Kimberly must have waited longer than you told her!"

"Never met a woman who was on time!" Jones joked.

Ames kept his foot pressed against the cart's accelerator, and in the excitement he forgot to brake. The cart smashed into the blast door, sending all three of us flying forward. Because Ames was in the driver's seat, he flew at the metal headfirst, his skull smacking hard against the smooth steel. Jones and I also hit it, but we both twisted in the air and collided against the door with our collarbones. Of the three of us, Ames looked the worst. His forehead was badly gashed, and he appeared to have broken his nose again. Jones was scrambling to his feet and holding his left arm. I did a mental inventory. Nothing was broken.

"You okay?" I asked Jones.

"Yeah, nothing major! Just a banged-up shoulder."

I pulled Ames to his feet. He was confused and leaned against me as the three of us stumbled toward the narrowing gap between the blast door and its steel frame. Kimberly's face peered through the slit that was shrinking by the second.

"Hurry!" she screamed.

The hole was now so narrow that there was only enough room for us to scoot through it one at a time. Without warning, Ames shoved away from me and turned so that he was now facing us. He raised his hand. He was holding a .38 pistol that he'd apparently snatched from his ankle holster while he was getting up from the floor. Jones, meanwhile, had let go of his .45 as he was being thrown from the cart. Ames said, "I'm going first!"

I'd once been told by a convict, whom I was transporting to a murder trial, that the average person can slap a gun out of a robber's hand quicker than he can pull the trigger. I'd taken the convict's word for this, although I'd had my doubts. Now, I hoped like hell my prisoner had been telling me the truth. I whisked my right hand up and slapped at the pistol.

Shocked, the gun flew from Ames's fingers. Jones leaped forward, grabbing Ames around his neck. They both landed on the floor.

"Get out of here!" Jones yelled at me. "Now!"

"Not without you!"

Ames began kicking his feet, trying to break free, like a drowning man who pushes his would-be rescuer under the water. But try as he might, Ames couldn't break loose from Jones.

"This is my bunker!" Jones snapped. "I'm still in charge! Get out so I can push Ames through to you! Then I'll come!"

I slipped into the sliver of space between the blast door and wall. The door was hinged on its right side and was moving inward in a slow, but certain motion. Pushing my back against the frame, I inched toward Kimberly. As I squeezed by, I could feel the door's edge pressing against my chest, scraping my shirt buttons off. I sucked in and tried to move faster. But I got stuck. I was going to be crushed. I couldn't budge. Kimberly reached in and deftly grabbed my belt with her fingers. She jerked hard and I practically popped through the space.

"C'mon!" I yelled back through the opening, but I already knew that neither Jones nor Ames was going to make it out.

Jones released his choke hold on Ames and the bloody-faced FBI agent lunged forward. He tried to jam himself into the narrow divide but he was too big. The door would crush him if he continued to press.

"No!" he screamed. "Stop it from closing! Save us! There's time!"

As I peered into Ames's face, I could hear Jones talking behind him. "Relax, Ames. We're not going anywhere, and you aren't going to feel a thing!"

The massive door shut with a loud boom.

A siren began to wail and red lights outside the blast door flashed.

"Watch out!" a FEMA security guard called to us. Kimberly and I stepped away from the entrance just as the guillotine gate came whooshing down.

We ran toward a waiting Hummer. The FEMA guard, who'd been standing next to Kimberly, dashed into the front of the SUV. We bolted into the back. The driver pounded the pedal. Kimberly hugged me. "You made it! You made it! You're safe!"

I began to reply, but the ground under us suddenly quaked with such a violent force that the Hummer bounced off the blacktop as if it were a kid leaping on a trampoline. The vehicle lifted completely off the pavement going down a steep embankment. Once again, the earth rumbled and the SUV flew upward and then back down, this time landing on its side. It began tumbling like an acrobat doing somersaults. Because none of us was wearing a seat belt, we were tossed inside the cab like seeds in a bag of exploding microwave popcorn. Kimberly and I collided while the driver and guard smacked into one another in the front seat. Another shock wave caused the vehicle to bounce completely off the ground for a third time. When it came down, it began sliding down the mountain. It ricocheted off several trees and finally came to an abrupt stop when it wedged itself between two large trees.

Kimberly was under me, lying now on the overturned Hummer's roof. The two guards were sprawled in the front. I smelled gasoline. We had to escape.

"Kimberly! Can you move? Are you hurt?"

"Really bruised. You?"

"The same." I called to the guards. "You okay?"

The driver replied, "Dave's unconscious!"

As Kimberly went toward the rear door, I crawled forward and helped the driver pull Dave free.

"Did it hold?" Kimberly screamed. "The blast door! Did it hold?"

Our SUV had rolled so far down the mountain that none of us could see the entrance to the bunker. But we were still alive and there was no burst of fire or mushroom cloud. Kimberly and I clambered up the steep slope by grabbing stems of trees, making our way toward the pavement. We reached the crest together. The smooth guillotine gate outside Mount Weather's entrance now looked as if it were aluminum foil that had been crumpled and reused several times. The outline of the main blast door had been imprinted on its formerly smooth surface.

I looked up. The sky was still blue. The earth reverberated again, so roughly, both of us were knocked off our feet. Great groans like a monster dying came from the guillotine door, which was twisting and buckling from the pressure against it. With a volcanic bang, it sprang forward as if it were a twig being bent between a child's thumb and forefinger, and then it was sent sailing.

The blast door was now exposed. It was so hot that it burned a brilliant gold color. I wondered if it would melt. And then I thought of Prescott Jones and Rodney Ames who were inside.

"It held," I said. "The blast door is holding."

Neither of us spoke. We simply stared mesmerized and uncertain if it, too, would come off.

"Hey!" a male voice called.

It was the FEMA driver who'd stayed with the comatose Dave. "He's waking up!"

I looked into Kimberly's eyes and said, "Are you really okay?"

"I hurt all over. But I'm alive. We're alive and that's all that matters!"

"I didn't think I was going to make it out. You know, Jones chose you to shut the door because he thought you'd wait as long as possible before closing it."

"I didn't start seven minutes before—like he told me. I gave you another thirty seconds."

It had made all the difference.

She said, "What you did was heroic. Jones and Agent Ames, too. They gave their lives to save the rest of us."

"Yes, Prescott Jones was a brave man."

"Ames, too," she added.

I realized then that she didn't know about Ames and how he had deserted us and had fled to be first through the closing gap. Only I knew the truth about what had happened among the three of us inside the shelter. I thought about Ames. I thought about my ex-wife and how she'd left me for him and how much I had hated both of them because of that, and how good it was going to feel to tell her that Ames had been a coward. I had gotten out alive. He hadn't. I thought about that ugly truth. And then I lied.

"Yes," I said. "Jones and Agent Ames are *both* heroes."

53

As soon as Kimberly and I helped the Hummer's driver and Dave climb up the mountainside to the road, we were surrounded by ambulances and other emergency vehicles. EMTs swarmed over us, but I took Kimberly's arm and said, "We've got to go!"

She didn't know why, but didn't protest. I commandeered one of FEMA's unmarked Ford Crown Victoria cars and drove down the blacktop and out of Mount Weather's entrance.

"What's the rush?" Kimberly asked. "We're safe now! There's nothing to run away from!"

She must've thought I was suffering from post-traumatic shock. "I'm not running away. I'm running toward—not something, but someone." I flipped on the car's flashing lights that were concealed in its grille and picked up speed. There was a 12-gauge shotgun attached to the dash. No other weapons were visible, and I was unarmed, since my two handguns had been locked up downtown by the recently deceased Agent Ames.

"Where are we going?" Kimberly asked.

"Baltimore. We've got unfinished business. Moe Islamov."

By the time we reached the port city, it was midafternoon. Kimberly had telephoned the CTC on her cell and convinced a coworker to discreetly give us an address that I'd requested. At my insistence, Kimberly wouldn't answer repeated phone calls from CTC chief Henry Clarke, who was trying to learn where we were. I didn't want him or anyone else in law enforcement to know. Moe Islamov had proven to be an expert at escaping, and we risked tipping him off if he'd somehow gotten hold of a police scanner.

Otherwise, I didn't have much of a plan in mind. I wasn't even sure Islamov was in Baltimore. The FBI and Office of Homeland Security had alerted every airport, train, and bus station along the East Coast to be on the lookout for him. U.S. Customs border checkpoints had been put on notice, too. Everyone assumed Moe would try to flee the United States as quickly as he could.

But I had a different idea.

Amiina!

Islamov had been betrayed at B.W.I. by a woman he had loved. He'd asked for her help and she'd called the FBI. Years ago, I'd discovered as a deputy U.S. marshal, that the old proverb "Hell hath no fury like a woman scorned" applied equally to men.

In her interviews with the FBI, Amiina had admitted she and Islamov had once been lovers. She suspected he was still in love with her. Which was why she'd never told him that she was now married. Nor had she revealed that her husband was an American named Carlos Hanover.

The bureau had stationed agents at the couple's house after Islamov failed to show up for the airport rendevous. But after Islamov and his fellow Chechens seized control of the old Soviet embassy, that government protection squad had pulled off. My guess was that no one had remembered to send in a new team of federal watchdogs.

Amiina and Carlos lived in a white brick ranch-style house built in the 1960s in a lower-middle-class suburb near Towson, a Baltimore suburb. Just before we reached their neighborhood, I switched off our flashing lights. We drove by their house to see if anything seemed out of place. There was a yellow plastic duck on wheels, sized for a toddler to ride in, near the driveway. But no one was in the freshly mowed front yard. The door to the one-car garage was shut. The living room's picture window faced the street, but its drapes were drawn. A woman with one of those three-wheeled strollers made for runners was jogging on the sidewalk. A neighbor armed with a deafening gasoline-powered blower was making piles of leaves.

"The FBI report says that Carlos drives a bus for the city during the day," I explained. "Amiina is a stay-at-home mom. They have a two-year-old daughter."

After we had driven by the house, I made a U-turn and parked across from Amiina's driveway.

"What now?" Kimberly said.

"I guess we knock on the front door." I unlatched the dashboard shotgun.

"You can't just walk up there with a shotgun," she declared, "especially if everything is fine. You'll scare her to death."

"What if Islamov is inside?"

"He'll recognize you. And he might kill Amiina and her child."

While I was mulling that over, Kimberly said, "He doesn't know *me*. I can knock on the door, and if she answers, I'll be able to tell if she's alone or frightened. If everything is okay, I'll tell her that she and her daughter need to come with us to FBI headquarters. If she acts oddly, I'll signal you."

"Signal?"

"I'll brush my right hand through my hair like this." Kimberly ran her fingers through her short dark hair.

"Okay," I said, "but stand to the side of the door in case Islamov decides to shoot first and ask questions later."

"Thanks," she replied sarcastically.

Kimberly began to get out of the car. "Wait," I said. "Be careful. Okay? I don't want anything to happen to you."

"Conway," she told me. "You're going soft."

I watched her cross the street and wished I'd called the bureau for backup. Kimberly rang the doorbell. I observed for a moment how beautiful she was. I thought about her naked in the rear seat of the limo. Then I refocused on what we were doing. Kimberly rang the bell again. This time, the door cracked, but only an inch. From the car, I couldn't see who had answered.

Kimberly turned and looked at me. But she didn't run her fingers through her hair. She waved. The door widened, revealing a woman in the door frame. It was the same woman I'd seen before on the security videotapes from B.W.I. It was Amiina. Kimberly entered the house. The woman glanced across the street at me and then shut the door.

What the hell was Kimberly doing? I hadn't expected her to go inside. Then again, if Amiina was okay, why shouldn't Kimberly go in to help pack up her daughter for the trip to the FBI office.

Where was the baby? Why wasn't Amiina holding her two-year-old? Or why wasn't the child standing next to her when she answered the door? A mother can't leave a child that age alone for very long. Of course, it was midafternoon and the tot could be taking a nap. Another thought hit me. Maybe Islamov was inside the house and maybe he had the baby and maybe that's why Amiina had gone to the door and invited Kimberly into a trap.

It's demonic thoughts like these that drive you mad. Your imagination can run wild and create all sorts of horrible scenarios. Of course, this same creative thinking process can also give one a much-needed edge. I kept my eyes locked on the front of the house. About two minutes later, the front door opened again and Amiina stepped out onto the concrete stoop. She waved at me, indicating that she wanted me to come inside, too. But rather than waiting for me to walk over, she retreated back inside, leaving the door ajar. Then I noticed something odd. The edge of the curtain in the living room's picture window had moved. It wasn't much, but enough to notice. Someone was peeking to see if I were coming.

I reached for the police radio, but pulled my hand back. Once again, I remembered my worry that Islamov might have a police scanner. If he was inside and he heard me calling for help, he might harm Kimberly.

I checked the shotgun to make certain it had a shell in the chamber and stepped out of the unmarked car. I kept low and scooted across the street. The curtain didn't move. Rather than going to the front door, I slipped around to the side of the house. There was a child's swing set and sandbox next to the garage. When I reached the back corner, I took inventory of what was behind the house. There was the usual concrete patch and two inexpensive chaise longues about halfway down the back of it. I crept along the rear of the garage wall to the patio. When I reached the sliding glass doors, I peeked inside.

Moe Islamov was standing in the kitchen looking directly at me. He had positioned himself so that he was shielded by Kimberly, who was sitting on a high kitchen stool. Her hands were tied behind her and her mouth was gagged with what looked to be a drying cloth. In his right hand was a semiautomatic Glock 9-millimeter pointed at her temple. The glass doors were open. Apparently, he'd seen me duck around the side of the house and had closed the front door and waited for me to go around back.

"Welcome, Professor," he called out.

I hesitated, but then I walked up onto the slab, slid the flimsy screen aside, and entered the compact kitchen.

"Lay the shotgun on the floor and kick it toward me," he demanded.

Amiina was standing to his right on the other side of a waist-high

Formica counter that extended out from the wall and served as a break-fast bar. In her arms was her daughter, asleep on her shoulder.

"You'll kill us if I give up this shotgun," I said. "But only one of us is going to die if I shoot you right now."

Islamov said: "No one has to die. All I need is a few more hours and I'll be leaving your country."

"I'm not putting down this shotgun. Why don't you give up? Spending the rest of your life in an American prison is a better alternative than being laid six feet under."

"And what of your woman partner?" he asked, glancing down at Kimberly. "Are you prepared to sacrifice her?"

Kimberly was looking directly into my eyes.

"Perhaps you're right," Islamov said. "I'm tired of running." And for a moment, it seemed as if he were actually going to surrender. He started to lower his right hand and turn the Glock away from Kimberly's head. Instead, he suddenly swung its nose upward and pulled the trigger. The sound was obliterating. The slug slammed into my left breast, catching me completely off guard. It sent me flailing back into the screen door, which collapsed under my weight. I landed on the patio slab. As I fell, the shotgun's barrel raised skyward, but I didn't shoot because Kimberly was in the way. My head hit the aggregate hard. Now I was sprawled with my feet still inside the house, but my upper torso outside.

I was dazed and feeling as if I might black out at any second.

"Give up the shotgun," Islamov barked. "Or she's next!"

I pitched my weapon forward and it slid across the kitchen's linoleum floor, stopping under the table. My shoulder hurt like hell. So did my ego. I'd let Islamov get the drop on me.

Amiina's baby was now wailing. The blast had scared her awake.

"How did you know I'd be here?" Islamov asked.

"A hunch," I replied. I tried to get on my feet, but my left arm wasn't obeying and I fell back clumsily in my attempt to push myself up.

Islamov said something in his native tongue to Amiina, and she and the hysterical child disappeared down the hallway. With his Glock 9-millimeter still aimed directly at me, he said, "Your little Miss Genius here found a way to dispose of the KGB bomb. I was counting on it to cause sufficient havoc for me to escape." He released her gag.

"You okay?" she cried.

"He'll live," Islamov replied. "I've seen much worse in Chechnya."

I wasn't so sure. While the shot had missed my heart and lungs, I was losing all sensation in my left arm and having a difficult time concentrating on what was happening.

Stay alert. Think. Focus.

"Let me help him," Kimberly said.

Islamov untied her hands. She jumped off the stool, dashed to my side, and squatted down next to me.

"He threatened to kill her daughter," she explained. "That's why Amiina told me everything was fine in the house. She invited me in. He was waiting. I'm so sorry."

"It's my fault," I said. "Sending you to the door was stupid."

"Wyatt," she whispered. "He's waiting to kill Carlos. Then he'll kill us. I know it."

"Get him into the kitchen," Islamov ordered.

Kimberly helped me onto my feet and I staggered in. I felt faint as I leaned against the kitchen's breakfast bar for support. Islamov backed up slowly from the kitchen into the living room, which was connected by a wide opening. When he reached the front picture window, he turned to check outside from behind the curtain. He wanted to see if anyone had heard the pistol shot above the racket of the neighbor's leaf blower. Apparently, no one had. Satisfied, Islamov returned to the kitchen.

"I need something to stop his bleeding," Kimberly said.

Islamov tossed her a green hand towel from a hook near the kitchen sink. "That's not sterile," she complained. "Plus he's going to die from shock if we don't get him to a hospital."

"A casualty of war."

"We aren't at war!" she shrieked. "You're a goddamned terrorist! Wars have heroes and there's nothing gallant or brave or heroic about anything you've done!"

Amiina rejoined us. She'd evidently put her child in a crib because the baby wasn't with her. She said something to Islamov and they began arguing. I looked down at the shotgun, still on the floor under the kitchen table. Kimberly followed my eyes and seemed to read my thoughts. So did Islamov. He walked over, bent down, and picked it up. He carried the weapon into the living room where he leaned it against the wall by the picture window.

"Don't try to be a hero," he warned Kimberly.

"His bleeding has got to be stopped!" she replied.

Amiina said, "There's a first aid kit in the bathroom. If we can get him in there, we can treat the wound."

"Go ahead," Islamov declared.

Amiina stepped around the breakfast bar and reached her arm around my waist. She was standing on my left side. Kimberly moved to my right side, where she also encircled my waist, clutching my leather belt with her fingers. The pain in my chest was excruciating. I took several steps forward, but then had to stop.

The neighbor blowing leaves turned off the blower and Islamov heard a noise from directly outside the front of the house. A car was pulling into the driveway. He hurried over to the front window to look outside.

In a surprisingly agile move, Amiina reached across the breakfast bar and grabbed a paring knife that had been resting near the sink. She handed it to Kimberly, who was still standing on my right with her back to Islamov. Kimberly pulled it close to her chest to hide it.

"Your American hubby is home," Islamov announced.

He backed away from the window and reentered the kitchen, where he readied his stance and aimed his pistol at the front door. It looked as if he intended to shoot Carlos as soon as the unsuspecting spouse stepped inside and shut the door behind him.

What happened next happened in nanoseconds, yet time seemed to slow as the actions unfolded in a slow-motion blur. Carlos breezed through the front doorway and froze, stunned, when he saw a stranger aiming a handgun at him. Amiina let go of me and bolted toward her husband. She was trying to put herself between Islamov and the man whom she loved. Islamov fired the Glock, but his aim was off because Amiina distracted him when she burst forward. The shot missed both of them. At that same instant, Kimberly turned loose of me and lurched forward. She plunged the paring knife into Islamov's shoulder. He turned and I saw a look of bewilderment flood his face. As he spun around, he backhanded Kimberly with his left hand. She was sent sprawling onto the linoleum floor. He swung his Glock around in his right hand and aimed it at her.

"No!" I screamed.

I started toward him, but Carlos tackled him first. They smashed into the kitchen table, which broke under their weight. As they fought for control of the semiautomatic pistol, Amiina grabbed the shotgun from the living room. She ran into the kitchen and handed it to me.

But I couldn't shoot Islamov without also hitting Carlos.

I turned and fired at the living room's picture window. The noise exploded through the small house as shards of glass and fabric were blown into the front yard. That had to get their neighbors' attention.

The shotgun blast startled the struggling men, but Islamov managed to use it to his advantage. He shoved the Glock against Carlos's chest and fired.

Amiina screamed.

Although injured, Carlos refused to release the Glock. But Islamov let go of the weapon, and with the paring knife still sticking out of his back, he scrambled to his feet and staggered out the back door.

Had I been able to lift my left arm, I could've pumped a new shotgun shell into the chamber, but because it dangled uselessly, I couldn't reload. Carlos, meanwhile, was fading fast.

As Kimberly and I watched, Islamov reached behind and yanked the small knife from his shoulder blade. He ran left across the yard.

The Viper had escaped, yet again.

54

Doctors were able to save Carlos Hanover after both of us were rushed to a Baltimore hospital, and the gunshot to my left breast proved not to be fatal.

This time.

The powers that be in Washington, D.C., decided it would be best if the world never learned about the KGB's layer-cake bomb and how it had nearly destroyed the city. The day after the explosion, the *Washington Post* reported on its front page how the FBI's Hostage Rescue Team had saved Russians being held captive in the old Soviet embassy by Chechen terrorists. Seven of the Chechens had been killed during the rescue, the newspaper noted, but their leader, Movladi Islamov, a.k.a., the Viper, had escaped. There was no mention in the story about how he'd tricked the FBI and slipped away from the embassy. Nor was there any story in the Baltimore newspaper about how he had shot Hanover and me during his failed attempt to seek vengeance against Amiina.

Barely noticeable in the *Washington Post*'s Metro section that same day was a brief article that said residents of Berryville, Round Hill, and Bluemont, Virginia, had been shaken by a series of violent tremors. The quakes were so strong they'd caused several older buildings to collapse. The newspaper said all three communities were near the federal government's top-secret underground bunker. But a FEMA spokesperson flatly denied that the Mount Weather Emergency Assistance Center (its official name) had anything to do with the disturbances. A National Weather Service official suggested they had been caused by an unexplained shifting in the earth's tectonic plates.

As soon as I was released from the hospital, Kimberly and I reported to the CIA director's office, where we were awarded commendations during a brief ceremony. Prescott Jones and Special Agent Rodney Ames were given medals posthumously. Of course, we were ordered to not tell anyone about our awards or explain why we'd been given them since the entire layer-cake bomb affair was being classified top secret.

During our "grip and grin" session with various senior officials in front of the CIA's in-house photographer, the director asked if there were anything he could do for me.

"I'd like to be returned to the U.S. Marshals Service."

Nearby, I saw CTC chief Henry Clarke's surprised face and heard an obvious sigh of relief.

"It's nothing against the CTC or the CIA," I explained. "With a name like Wyatt, being a deputy is sort of expected."

It's funny how in Washington, D.C., something as simpleminded as that logic was immediately accepted.

The CIA director spoke with the director of the U.S. Marshals Service, who also was at our awards ceremony, and by the time our photo-taking session was finished, the paperwork was almost done.

55

The man walked cautiously along a meandering path worn by cattle through the week-old snow. The morning sun fought unsuccessfully to cut through a film of gray December clouds. By the time he reached the summit he was perspiring, despite the cold weather, because of the heavy, waterproof white jacket he was wearing, the unfamiliar altitude, and the exertion required to climb a mountain, even though it was a small one. He scuffed his boot into the snow to clear it away from a slab of gray and green-speckled, rough granite, so he'd have enough room to lie down. Through binoculars covered with white tape, he peered down from his perch at a house more than a thousand yards away.

The timber was decoratively bolstered by stones creating a modern log home with a wraparound porch. Close by was a separate three-car garage with a four-wheel-drive Japanese pickup truck parked outside of it. A snow removal blade had been attached to its bumper. In this remote area, homeowners had only themselves to keep the roads clear.

Although the man knew almost nothing about Montana, the rural, undeveloped surroundings reminded him of his dacha. He longed for home. *Soon,* he thought. *Soon.*

There was no sign of activity inside the cabin. But the man knew his target was inside, sleeping, no doubt, oblivious to the wolf who had come calling.

Patience. Patience.

An hour. Another. But, finally, the prey appeared. First, he walked past a kitchen window. The man waiting on the cold granite precipice could see him through his lenses. The target was in a blue silk bathrobe. Seconds later, the rear door of the lodge flew open and he walked out onto the redwood decking where he fiddled with the controls on a hot tub before scurrying back inside, nearly slipping on the wet snow and slick planks as he crossed them in his bare feet.

The eyes on the mountaintop watched.

Wait. Wait.

Ten minutes later, steam was rising from the heated water, and five minutes after that the man reappeared. This time, he stepped gingerly across the decking with a coffee mug in one hand and a newspaper tucked under the same arm. At the Jacuzzi's edge, he carefully placed his mug on the rim and let the robe drop, revealing rolls of fat balancing atop spindly legs. As he braced himself to dip into the tub, his girth created near-tsunami waves causing the water to spill over and melt the snow.

Fully immersed, he flapped open an edition of the *New York Post*, already several days old, and began reading it from back to front. Sports.

There was no reason for either man to hurry. Neither had anything more important to do. The high-up hunter fixed on his quarry stewing in the hot bubbles while holding the tabloid up to keep it dry. Finally, the bather put the newspaper aside and reached for his half-finished cup of coffee. Just as he was lifting it to his pursed lips with his pudgy pinkie finger fully extended, causing its diamond ring to flash in the day's few rays, the hunter fired.

He'd taken aim at the bridge of the nose on the bather's face. It was an incredibly tiny target at this distance, especially when firing down a slope. But the bullet found its mark. It shattered the man's upper row of crooked yellow teeth and blew away the bottom part of his skull, sending a spray of blood, bones, and gray matter across the decking and white snow. Head shots are personal.

What was left of the man's face sank into the incarnadine water with the rest of his corpse, and then resurfaced to float and bob amid a spreading sanguinary froth.

The shooter retreated along the cowpath, moving casually, without the slightest hurry.

56

"What's this I hear about you blowing up an entire top-secret government installation?" William Jackson bellowed when I entered his cluttered office at U.S. Marshals Service headquarters. He extended his hand. "Welcome back."

A half hour later, I walked into my old office, where my secretary, Marcella Penbrook, greeted me with a hug. I disappeared into my cave to read a stack of memos and bulletins. A lot had happened while I was gone. Around five-thirty, Penbrook appeared carrying two FedEx packages.

"These just arrived," she said, "and I just received a telephone call from Kimberly Lodge's secretary reminding you of a meeting at five tonight. Ms. Lodge said, 'Don't be late.'"

"Isn't there a florist downstairs?" I asked, referring to the underground shopping mall in our complex.

Penbrook replied, "Yep, downstairs by the bookstore." Then she coyly added, "Interesting meeting." As she began to leave, she remembered the express deliveries and handed them to me.

One was from the Internet bookstore, Amazon.com. The sender of the other package was identified as Manuel Hernandez. He had a Mexico City address. I didn't recognize the name.

At exactly five p.m., I rang the bell at Kimberly's Crystal City condo, which conveniently happened to be only a few buildings away from our headquarters. I was carrying a box of a dozen long-stemmed roses and felt like a high school kid arriving for a senior-prom date.

"Who's there?" she asked, even though she had a security peephole, which I was sure she was using.

"Prince Charming," I replied. "Or the milkman. Take your choice."

She opened the door and was completely nude, which allowed me to check off one of the items on my Must Do list of fantasies. God, you had to love this woman!

"Roses?" she asked, although it was obvious. "For me?" That was obvious, too.

"Naked?" I replied. "For me?"

What can I say? When you're in those early stages of love, you act silly like this!

I stepped inside, kicked the door closed with my heel, and tossed the box of roses onto a corner chair. I kissed her and reflexively bent over to pick her up and remembered my arm. Instead, I asked: "Where's the bedroom?" Although Kimberly had visited me daily in the hospital, we'd not been alone together since our limo encounter.

"Too far!" she replied. She nodded toward the dining room table.

There went another fantasy check mark.

I've always enjoyed sex. What normal man doesn't? But there are different kinds of lovemaking. In my mind, there's none better than that combination of pure animal lust and blinding first love. It happens before you really know each other well. It's what my grandfather in Kansas once romantically described to me as the "you're so in love you don't even think her shit stinks" phase.

I did my best one-armed impression of Jack Nicholson clearing the table in *The Postman Always Rings Twice* and Kimberly spread her legs. It was everything it could be and then more.

After we finished, we both slipped on white terry-cloth robes, and Kimberly called for Chinese carryout. She rarely cooked. My cell phone rang while she was searching for something to put the roses in. When she heard the ring, she gave me an angry look, but I answered it anyway.

"Wyatt," Deputy Scott Breeden said, "I've got news. Igor Fedorov's been murdered. Most of his head was blown off."

"Let me take a wild guess. By a sniper."

Breeden gave me the basics. Fedorov had been moved out of Phoenix within minutes after I'd told Colonel Vladimir Khrenkov where the Marshals Service was hiding the Russian Mafia snitch. Deputies had flown Fedorov in a private plane to Los Angeles, where they'd immediately boarded another flight to Denver, Colorado. From there, they'd driven to Billings, Montana, a nine-hour trip that had taken them across the entire state of Wyoming. To further cover their tracks, they'd relocated Fedorov to an isolated log cabin nestled in a mountain range.

"How in the hell did he get found?" Breeden asked.

I had a hunch. Ending the call, I slipped on a pair of pants and a shirt and told Kimberly, "I've got to get something."

She gave me a disappointed look.

Fifteen minutes later, I returned, carrying the two Federal Express parcels from my office. I opened the delivery from Mexico City first. It contained a brightly wrapped carton that came with a hand-printed card:

"The enclosed El Presidente cigars have been made exclusively for you by Manuel Hernandez in Mexico City from the finest tobacco leaves in all of Cuba."

I dialed the number in the cigar carton for follow-up orders. Because there is a two-hour time difference between Washington and Mexico City, Mr. Hernandez was still at work. Luckily, he spoke English.

"Who sent me these fine cigars? There's no card," I explained, "and I'd like to thank him personally."

"I regret that I can't help you. He wired me the money through Western Union. All I know is that he had perhaps a Russian accent, and said he was a good friend of one of my other clients."

"By chance, is that client Major Igor Fedorov?"

"Why, yes, do you know him, too?"

"Actually, I do. But he moved recently and I don't know where he lives now."

"Yes, the other caller—the Russian who mailed you the cigars—he also asked me for Major Fedorov's new address. The major had been living in Phoenix but he'd moved recently to Montana. He loves my cigars so much that he always sends me his information as soon as he settles in to a new location."

I thanked him and hung up the phone.

I was opening the other FedEx package when Kimberly entered the living room.

"Colonel Khrenkov found out where Fedorov was hiding through his cigar orders," I explained. "Fedorov always kept his cigar vendor apprised of his whereabouts."

"Everyone says smoking is bad for your health," she deadpanned. She didn't seem surprised that Khrenkov had located and dispatched Fedorov. Actually, neither was I.

"What's that?" she asked, as I removed a thin volume from the Amazon.com delivery.

"It's from Khrenkov, too," I replied. "A book of Russian fairy tales."

"Why'd he send you that?"

Opening the cover, I found myself staring at a sketch of an ugly, skinny witch. Behind her was a huge gray wolf. The caption read: *Baba Yaga Kostianaya Noga watches you!*

I closed the storybook.

"Who knows?" But I did. I understood it perfectly.

"Slip off your shirt and pants and get back in that bathrobe," Kimberly demanded. "Let's eat on the balcony."

There was a slight December chill in the air, but the weather in Washington, D.C., had been mild. Neither of us minded. She'd set a small table there with paper plates and the plastic utensils provided by the Chinese takeout service.

"Impressive," I said.

"I've been too busy at work to get domesticated. The truth is, I don't even own china."

She gave me a plastic cup filled with white wine.

"A toast to us," she said.

We tapped our throwaway glasses together and gazed across the Potomac River at Washington. The evening lights were beginning to come on.

"What do you think happened to Moe Islamov?" she asked.

"He's probably back in Chechnya. But we'll know soon enough when he decides to resurface—hopefully far away from the United States and us."

"And Colonel Khrenkov?"

"I'd guess he's on his way to Moscow right now."

I watched her face in the dimming twilight.

"This view is magnificent," she said. "Washington takes my breath away. London, Moscow, Paris, New York. You can have them. I love this town. It's not just the cherry blossoms in the spring, the summer tourists who cause traffic jams, the self-important journalists, and bloated politicians. It's what this city stands for—democracy, a society where people can be free. It really is an incredible place."

"Hey, I thought you preferred to live overseas because of all the prejudices you face here."

"I've always thought that I did, but, I feel differently now. I guess what they say is true: You only really appreciate something when you are at risk of losing it. What we went through made me look at my life and this country in a completely new way."

"Yes, it's hard to imagine that all of this was almost destroyed," I said. "Human beings must really be the most intelligent life on our planet. After all, we've found a way to destroy ourselves!"

I was trying to be clever, but she either didn't get it, or did, and was mercifully choosing to ignore it.

"Washington looks so formidable," she said. "The statues, the marble buildings, the Greek architecture. It's all so historical and yet nothing really is permanent, is it? Everything in our lives is fragile."

She was standing next to the balcony's iron guardrail. I stepped behind her and wrapped my arms about her waist. She pressed her head back against my right shoulder.

"Tomorrow morning," she said, "I'm going to go out and buy some dinner plates, and real knives, spoons, and forks."

I realized that she was talking about more than buying housewares. She was talking about changing her life, taking more time off from work, shifting her priorities. What she was saying about our lives is true. Everything can change in the blink of an eye.

I lowered my mouth and playfully nuzzled her neck. And then I said something I never thought I would ever, ever say to a woman.

"I'd like to go shopping with you. I've been meaning to buy some plates and spoons, and all those other damn domestic things, too."

She replied softly, "Maybe we can save a few bucks if we share. You buy the flatware and I'll purchase the plates."

"Yes," I answered. "That sounds like a good idea."

ACKNOWLEDGMENTS

I would like to thank Ed Goodwin for his insights into the world of snipers and tactical hostage rescue teams. My friend, Petr Poliakov, helped me with information about Russia. Georgiana Atkins Havill ran her red pen through this manuscript and made dozens of corrections and helpful suggestions. All three made this book much better because of their generous contributions.

Several longtime friends encouraged me to write this book. They include Nelson DeMille, Walt and Keran Harrington, Marie Heffelfinger, Don and Sue Infeld, Richard and Joan Miles, Jay and Barbara Myerson, Mike Sager, Kendall and Lynne Starkweather, and Lynn and LouAnn Smith.

In addition, I wish to thank my literary agent, Robert Gottlieb of Trident Media Group, and my editor, Robert Gleason, at Tor/Forge Books, and my copy editor, Donald J. Davidson.

I would like to publicly express my gratitude to my family. They include Elmer and Jean Earley, George and Linda Earley, Gloria Brown, James Brown, Ruey and Ellen Brown, Phillip and Joanne Corn, Donnie and Dana Davis, Elsie and Jay Strine, and my children, Stephen, Michelle, Kevin, Tony, Kathy, Kyle, Evan, and Traci. As always, my biggest thank-you goes to Patti Brown Luzi-Earley, my wife, partner, and best friend, whose love makes each day even more satisfying and exciting than the last.

Finally, I wish to thank you readers for making it to the end of this novel! Please let me know what you think of the story by signing my guest book at www.peteearley.com. I may not be able to respond to each comment, but I will read every one of them.